DISCARD

Also by Lynda La Plante

Above Suspicion

The Red Dahlia

Clean Cut

Deadly Intent

Silent Scream

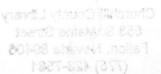

BLIND FURY

Lynda La Plante

A TOUCHSTONE BOOK
Published by Simon & Schuster
New York   London   Toronto   Sydney

Touchstone
A Division of Simon & Schuster, Inc.
1230 Avenue of the Americas
New York, NY 10020

Originally published in Great Britain in 2010 by Simon & Schuster UK Ltd

First Touchstone trade paperback edition July 2011

For information about special discounts for bulk purchases, please contact
Simon & Schuster Special Sales at 1-866-506-1949 or
business@simonandschuster.com.

The Simon & Schuster Speakers Bureau can bring authors to your live event.
For more information or to book an event contact the Simon & Schuster
Speakers Bureau at 1-866-248-3049 or visit our website at
www.simonspeakers.com.

Manufactured in the United States of America

10 9 8 7 6 5 4 3 2 1

Library of Congress Cataloging-in-Publication Data is available.

ISBN 978-1-4391-3931-8
ISBN 978-1-4391-3930-1 (pbk)
ISBN 978-1-4391-5774-9 (ebook)

For the Brothers—Robert, Lol, and John

Acknowledgments

My gratitude to all those who gave their valuable time to help me with research on *Blind Fury*.

Special thanks go to all my team at La Plante Productions: Liz Thorburn, Richard Dobbs-Grove, Noel Farragher, Sara Johnson, Hannah Gatward, and especially Cass Sutherland and Nicole Muldowney for their committed and valuable advice and support while working on this book. Many thanks also to Stephen Ross and Andrew Bennet-Smith.

To the constant encouragement from my literary agent, Gill Coleridge, and all at Rogers, Coleridge & White. To Susan Opie and my publishers, Simon & Schuster, especially Ian Chapman and Suzanne Baboneau. I am very happy to be working with such a terrific team.

To my fantastic editor at Simon & Schuster US, Trish Todd and her wonderful team: Allegra Ben-Amotz, Stacy Lasner, and Stacy Creamer. My thanks for all your support.

Prologue

Eva walked between the few parked cars at the London Gateway service station off the M1 motorway. Although the car park was not badly lit, she was nervous in such an alien, silent place. In total contrast were the blazing lights from all the various cafés, paper shops, and games machines. Yet at this hour of the night everywhere was empty, and no matter how well lit it was, she felt uneasy being alone as she passed through.

The ladies' toilets were white, vast, and cold, and the strip lighting gave the empty cubicles sinister shadows. There was an orange cone with a sign warning customers of the wet floors, but she didn't see anyone cleaning.

Eva waited patiently for the solitary man serving at the coffee bar to acknowledge her. When he eventually glanced toward her, she asked for a hot chocolate. He stared at her as he used the hot-milk machine, and the only words he spoke were to inquire whether or not she wanted chocolate sprinkled on top of the froth.

Eva carried her drink to a table close to a window overlooking the car park. She was the only customer. Her boyfriend, Marcus, had instructed her to wait for him there, saying he would join her as soon as the AA came and the car was fixed.

Eva and Marcus were on their way to Manchester to

meet his parents after announcing their engagement. He had borrowed a friend's car to use for the journey. It had started to backfire as soon as they drove onto the M1, and by the time they turned in to the service station, it was obvious that something was very wrong. It was one o'clock in the morning and freezing cold, so Marcus had insisted that Eva go inside and keep warm. The only reason the couple were traveling so late was that they both worked in a restaurant and had to wait until it closed for the night before they could start off.

Taking out her mobile phone, Eva placed it on the Formica-topped table by her hot chocolate. From the window she watched a car draw up with a family inside—a couple with two small children, one crying and one asleep. She saw the woman carry the sleeping child toward the ladies' toilets as the man carried the by now screaming child into the café. He ordered from the same truculent attendant. Eva watched him put the child down as he selected cakes and drinks, packets of crisps, and Coca-Cola. The family sat at a table at the far side of the café, away from the window.

Eva sipped her hot chocolate, taking another look at her watch. She fingered her mobile, wondering if she should call Marcus to see if the AA had turned up yet, but then decided against it.

Staring from the window, she noticed a woman walking across the car park smoking a cigarette; as she came closer, she tossed the butt aside. Eva did not see if she had come from a car, but watched her enter the station and head toward the toilets. It was quite a while before the same woman walked out. She had done something to her hair, and even though it was very cold outside, she carried her coat. She was wearing a tight-fitting T-shirt, a miniskirt, and high-heeled shoes. Eva watched her zigzag across the car park, then stop and light another cigarette before disappearing toward the petrol station.

She must be freezing, the girl thought.

Now, looking over at the family, she watched as they opened up the crisps and whispered to each other as one child still remained sleeping, cradled in the woman's arms. It was almost one-fifteen, and there was still no sign of Marcus. Opening her bag, Eva began checking through the pockets for something to do. She took out a glossy lipliner and traced her lips. She checked receipts and the contents of her purse, then glanced down at the small overnight bag she'd placed beside her.

Just then Eva's attention was caught by a man entering the café. She turned immediately, hoping it would be Marcus, but it wasn't. She heard him order a sandwich and a cup of tea. Tall and well built, he was wearing some kind of donkey jacket and dark trousers. She quickly looked away as he surveyed the café dining area, and she was still gazing out of the window when she heard the chair scrape at the table directly beside hers.

She could hear him unwrapping the cellophane from his sandwiches, and then she jumped as he said, "Cold, isn't it?"

She half turned toward him and gave a small nod.

"You driving?" he asked.

She didn't want to be drawn into conversation and just nodded again.

"Where you going to?"

She kept her eyes on her empty hot-chocolate beaker. "Manchester," she said quietly.

"Manchester," he repeated.

Eva picked up her phone and turned completely away from him, hoping he would leave her alone.

"You from there?"

"No."

"I'm sorry, I don't mean to intrude—was just wondering what a pretty girl like you is doing here all on her own at this time of night."

She made no reply, thinking that if she did, it would simply draw him into making more conversation, but her lack of response didn't stop him.

"If you need a lift, I'm going to Manchester. I drove down to London this morning."

Still she made no reply. Then she heard the scrape of his chair again and hoped he was leaving. She physically jumped when he leaned on her table.

"I'm going to have another cup of tea," he said. "Can I get you something? What were you drinking—coffee?"

"No, thank you."

She didn't turn to watch him head back to the counter, just continued to stare out of the window, willing Marcus to appear. She heard the stranger laughing and asking how long the muffins had been on display. She didn't, however, hear him heading back to the table and was startled when he placed a hot chocolate beside her.

"He said this is what you ordered. I've got sugar if you need it."

"No, thank you, I don't want—"

Before she could finish, he drew out a chair to sit opposite her, putting down a tray containing two muffins and his tea.

"Have one of these. He said they were fresh—I doubt it, though. In fact, I wouldn't be surprised if they were the same muffins I saw laid out when I was last here." He chortled.

"I don't want another hot chocolate or a muffin, thank you."

She bent down as if to pick up her overnight bag and could see his thick rubber-soled shoes, the reason she hadn't heard him approach the table.

"Don't make me eat both of them—go on."

"No, thank you."

She felt uneasy, but he was completely relaxed, taking a large bite of his muffin and wiping the corners of his mouth with his forefinger.

"Where are you from? I detected a bit of an accent," he said.

"I'm from the Ukraine."

"Really? I've never been there. What work do you do?"

"I work in a restaurant, but I am studying English."

"Good for you. Must be hard coming to a different country and finding a job when there's not a lot of work around. Mind you, you're a very pretty girl, so I doubt if you'd have any trouble."

She looked away from him as he continued eating his muffin. She picked up her mobile. "Excuse me, I have to call my boyfriend."

Eva scrolled through to Marcus's mobile number, but the screen registered no signal.

"Not getting through?"

"No."

"What make of phone is that?"

"Nokia."

"Is your battery fully charged?"

"I'm not sure."

He sipped his tea as she tried again to contact Marcus. She could feel the man watching her.

"I've got a Nokia," he said. "If you like, you can recharge it from my van."

She looked at him and shook her head. Again she made as if to pick up her overnight bag.

"You see that woman coming across the car park?"

Eva turned to see the same woman she had noticed earlier, smoking another cigarette and tossing it aside as she headed once more for the ladies' room.

"Hard to believe, isn't it, but she's a tart. Works the trucker stop, goes into the ladies' to wash up, then she's back out again chatting up the drivers. It's disgusting. The security around here is pitiful. I know the police move them on, but they're like homing pigeons, and I've seen her around here for years."

Eva picked up her overnight bag and rested it on her knees.

"I look out for young girls like you. Gimme your phone and let me make sure I've got the right extension to recharge it for you."

"No, really." She half-rose from her chair.

"What's the matter with you? I'm only being helpful, and my van is just across the car park." He leaned toward her, and she smelled his smoky breath. "You're not scared of me, are you? Listen, love, on a night like this, freezing cold out there, I'm only trying to be helpful."

"My boyfriend is coming any minute."

The man rocked back in his chair, shaking his head. "What kind of boyfriend is it that leaves such a lovely looking girl all on her own at this time of night? Come on, I'm just being friendly."

"No. You have been very kind, and I appreciate it."

Eva stood up, incredibly relieved as she saw Marcus pulling up directly outside in the car park. For the first time she smiled, picking up her mobile and slipping it into her handbag. She left the hot chocolate and the muffin untouched as she hurried out of the café.

The man watched her as she ran over to the beat-up Ford Escort, the young handsome boyfriend climbing out and opening the passenger door for her to get inside. He saw her reach up to kiss him, and then she turned to give a small wave toward him as Marcus got in beside her. Their headlights caught the man staring at them, but the car had driven off before either could see the look of blind fury pass over his face. He clenched his fists.

It was a while before he had finished eating the second muffin, but he didn't touch the hot chocolate. Instead, he placed it on the tray with his empty tea beaker and tipped the waste into the bin provided. He stashed the tray and walked out, turning up the collar of his black donkey jacket, almost hiding his face that still had such anger etched across it.

He had been certain about the girl. Seeing her lit up in the service station's café window, she had excited him; she was enticing him—she was no better than the cheap whore washing herself in the ladies' toilet.

She would have been exactly what he was looking for.

Chapter One

Detective Inspector Anna Travis held up her ID to a uniformed officer who directed her along the narrow muddy lane. Parking up on a gritty area alongside numerous other police vehicles, she stepped out of her Mini and swore as her foot was immediately submerged in a deep puddle. Opening the trunk, she took out a pair of Wellingtons and, balancing with one hand resting on the roof, she removed her shoes and put on the boots.

"Talk about off the beaten track," she muttered.

Despite the heavy traffic thundering by on the M1, the field had been hard to reach, even though it was not far from London Gateway Services. Anna could see the group of men at the far side of the field, and she recognized Detective Chief Inspector Mike Lewis; standing beside him was the rotund figure of Detective Sergeant Paul Barolli. Both men turned to watch her plodding toward them.

"What's the shout?" she asked as her feet squelched beneath her.

Mike gave her a brief rundown: the victim was a white female, discovered by a van driver called Brian Collingwood who had parked on the hard shoulder to relieve himself up against the hedge. Collingwood told the police that he was just turning to go back to his vehicle when he spotted the body lying in the adjacent field. At first he thought there had been an accident, so he climbed through the hedge and crossed over the ditch. It quickly became obvious that the girl was dead, so he did not approach but immediately rang the police on his mobile phone, then went back to wait beside his van until the traffic police reported the discovery.

"Is that him?" Anna nodded toward the man being questioned. He was making a lot of gestures, pointing back at the motorway.

"Yeah. By the time we got here, he was pretty agitated. He knew he was illegally parked on the hard shoulder but continued to explain that he had been busting for a piss. He's been unable to give any further details, having seen no other vehicle or witnessed anything suspicious. He also said repeatedly that he had not gone right up to the body but had remained about four feet away from her. When he's finished giving all the details, I'm going to let him finish his journey to Birmingham."

"You think this is one for us, then?"

Mike nodded. "We're waiting for the forensic team to arrive. We've made only a cursory check of the victim, as I think the less contamination of the area, the better."

Barolli rubbed his hands together. It was icy cold out here. "You are going to freeze," he said to Anna. "Didn't you bring a coat with you?"

"If I'd known we'd be in the back of beyond, I would have. Luckily, my wellies were in the boot."

"Here you go." Barolli took off his fleece-lined jacket and hung it round her shoulders. Anna was wearing a black suit and white collared shirt. Her wardrobe was full of similar suits, almost like her own uniform.

"Oh, thanks." She hugged it around herself as Barolli turned to the lane.

"We've had Traffic cordon off one motorway lane to allow the police vehicles access . . . Here come the lads now."

A forensic van drew up, followed by an ambulance.

"So what are you not telling me?" Anna wanted to know, and smiled as she said it. Having worked together on previous cases, the three of them were very relaxed with one another, and she knew there had to be an agenda.

Mike said the reason they had answered the shout was because on two of his previous, unsolved cases, it appeared to be virtually the same MO. The two earlier victims, discovered a year apart, had both been dumped beside the motorway. Their first victim had been hard to identify due to decomposition, but they had checked her prints and found she had a police record as a prostitute; the second girl remained unidentified.

"Is she on the game?" Anna asked, looking over at the corpse.

"No idea. She's young, though—I'd say late teens."

Anna watched the forensic team suit up and bring out their equipment. "Can I take a closer look?" she asked.

"Yeah, go ahead. We've put some stepping plates out, so keep to them. It's a flipping mud bath."

Anna headed toward the victim, carefully moving from plate to plate as if using stepping stones. There were two flags positioned where the van driver had stood, a few feet from the body, and the closer Anna got, she could see that from his position on the motorway's hard shoulder, he would not have been able to see the body.

The dead girl lay on her right side, half in and half out of the ditch, one arm outstretched as if she were trying to claw her way free. Her left leg was crooked over her right, again appearing as if she had tried to climb out of the ditch.

She was, as Mike had suggested, very young; her long red hair, worn in a braid, was similar in color to Anna's. The girl was wearing a pink T-shirt, a denim miniskirt, and a denim bomber jacket with a bright pink lining and an unusual embroidered motif of silver flowers on the front pocket. She wore one white sandal. There was no handbag and, from their initial search, nothing that could identify her.

Anna returned to Mike, who by now had a cup of coffee in his hand.

"You say you've had two previous cases?" she asked quietly.

"Not me personally. I had the most recent, but the first was a couple of years ago. So then we also took on the first discovery as a possible linked double murder. If this has the same MO, that'll make three."

"Were the first two girls killed in the same way?"

"Yes. They were strangled, raped, no DNA, no weapon, no witness—and like I said, my girl remains unidentified."

"Both found beside motorways?"

"Yep."

"And the first victim was a prostitute?"

"Yes. She worked the service stations, picking up lorry drivers, doing the business in their cabs, and then often getting dropped off at the next service station along the M1 to find new clients before heading back to the first."

Anna stood watching while photographs were being taken of the victim and the area, before a tent was erected around the dead girl.

It was two hours later before they arrived at the incident room. This had been set up at the police station closest to the crime scene, in a new building in Hendon, North London, with an entire floor given over to the murder team.

Already a group of technicians were setting up the desks and computers. Anna was pleased to see she'd be joined by DCs Barbara Maddox and Joan Falkland. Mike Lewis and Paul Barolli had also worked with the women on previous cases, and it promised to be a friendly atmosphere.

"Nice to see you again," Barbara said to Anna as she prepared the incident-room board.

"Long time. I've been on three other cases," Anna told her.

"Joan and I have sort of stuck with Mike and Paul." Barbara nodded over to Joan.

"Were you on the other murders Mike told me about?" Anna asked.

"Yes, both of us were. I'm going to get the board set up with all the previous case details, as apparently, this one looks like it's got the same MO."

Anna shrugged, since until they had the postmortem report, they wouldn't know for sure.

"Mike said she was very young," Barbara commented.

Anna nodded. She was taking her time arranging her own desk, relieved to have such new equipment at hand.

"They've got a terrific canteen," Joan informed her as she wheeled in a trolley stacked with the old case files.

Anna had time to sample the canteen at lunch, and it was not until early afternoon that she began to select files to catch up on the two earlier cases. By now the board was filling up with photographs and details. Anna still felt they might be presuming too much without confirmation. Although the victim had been removed to the local mortuary for a postmortem, Anna was told they would have to wait twenty-four hours before they would get any further details.

Meanwhile, Mike Lewis had set up his office, and Barolli had installed himself at the desk opposite Anna. "How's life been treating you?" Barolli asked affably.

"Okay—I've worked a few other cases. How about you?"

"Well, we've been on the other two for about a year, and then I went on to something else over at Lambeth."

"So to all intents and purposes, the cases were shelved?"

"Yeah. Without getting one of the victims identified, it was tough. The first one"—Barolli turned to gesture to a photograph—"was Margaret—or Maggie—Potts, aged thirty-nine, string of previous arrests for prostitution, drug addict, and known to work the service stations. We had no handbag, no witness, but got her ID'd from fingerprints. She was raped and strangled."

Anna looked at the mug shot posted up. Maggie Potts had been a dark-eyed, sullen-faced woman, her bleached-blond hair with an inch of black regrowth.

When she sifted through the crime-scene photographs, she could see the similar pattern. Potts's body had been dumped in a field not far from the M1 motorway. She had been wearing fishnet stockings, which were torn, and her shoes were found beside her body. She had on a short red jacket and a black skirt that was drawn up to her waist, and her knickers had been ripped apart. The satin blouse was stained with mud and wrenched open to reveal a black brassiere.

Anna glanced at the thick files representing the hundreds of interviews with people questioned about the last sightings of Maggie Potts. The team had interviewed call girls, service-station employees—from the catering staff to the petrol-station attendants—lorry drivers, and others in an endless round of inquiries and statements.

"This is the one we never identified," Barolli said, tapping the second victim's photograph. "We tried, but whatever we put out came back with fuck-all. We had her picture on the TV crime programs, in missing-persons magazines—you name it, we tried it to find out who she was—but with no luck. She was a pretty little thing, too."

Anna turned her gaze on the Jane Doe, and as Barolli had said, she was exceedingly pretty, with long dark hair down to her shoulders, bangs, a pale face with wide-apart blue eyes, and full lips. She didn't look jaded or hard; on the contrary, she looked innocent.

"How old was she?"

Barolli said they couldn't be certain but had her aged between twenty to thirty.

"Looks younger, doesn't she?"

"Yeah, that's what made it so tough to deal with, that no one came forward, no one recalled seeing her at any of the service stations. According to the postmortem, her body was very bruised, and there were signs of sexual activity suggesting she was raped. She was also strangled. She had nothing on her—no bag, no papers, nothing. If you think we made extensive inquiries on that old slag Potts, with this girl we tried every which way to find out who she was—Interpol, colleges, universities, but after six months we flatlined."

Anna looked over the details of the young woman's clothes. They were good labels, stylish but not new, and she had been wearing black ballet-type shoes; she had tiny feet, a size three.

"I hope to Christ we get this new girl identified," Barolli said quietly.

"You reckon the same killer did both previous cases?"

He shrugged. "Same MO, but who knows without any

DNA? Only thing we got was a few carpet fibers, but where she came from, who she was, how she came to be murdered are still unknown."

"Did you check out the Jane Doe's clothes?"

"What do *you* think?" Barolli glared. "Of course we did, but it didn't help. We actually traced where the shoes came from, but they sold thousands."

"Yeah, they were quite fashionable a year or so ago; now it's all stacked heels."

Anna continued to read the files all afternoon, but when it got to five-thirty and there still had been no word from the mortuary, she went home. It was quite a drive from the station to her flat over at Tower Bridge, and although it had not been a particularly tough day's work, she felt tired. She meant to read up on more details about the previous cases but instead watched some TV before going to bed. There was nothing on the news about their victim. Anna sincerely hoped she would not turn out to be another murdered girl who would remain unidentified.

The following morning the postmortem details still had not come through. Anna did not get asked to join Mike Lewis and Barolli when they went over to the mortuary, so she spent the entire morning examining the extensive files, reading the thousands of statements culminating in no arrests. She constantly looked up at the incident board, where the two dead women's faces had been joined by their new victim's crime-scene pictures.

It was after lunch when Mike Lewis called a briefing. Their victim had died from strangulation, he announced. She had been raped and had extensive bruising to her vagina and abdomen. There were no signs of drug use. Her last meal had been a hamburger and chips and Coca-Cola.

She was in good health. A fingerprint search had proved negative, but it was hoped that dental work would bring a result, as she had very good teeth, with two caps that appeared to have been done recently. These were her two front teeth, so she could have been in an accident; that again might narrow the field. Her hair was in good condition, and she had no broken nails or defense wounds.

The dead female's T-shirt was from Miss Selfridge, and her skirt from Asda. Her white sandals, the second of which had been found under the body, were hardly worn and still had the price tag on the left sole. Again, this would mean they might get a clue to her identity. Mike Lewis said that her age was between sixteen to twenty-five, and they would be going to the press to try and get a result.

By late afternoon the press office had sent out cleaned-up photographs of the victim and requests for anyone with information to come forward. The details were also passed on to the television news, while officers armed with the victim's photograph were still questioning everyone at the nearest service station. They had given out a direct line for anyone with any information to call. Usually, after such press coverage, they would be inundated with callers, but though they had a small number, none gave a clue as to who the young woman was. Many were time-wasters, but the team nevertheless had to take the personal details and information of every single one.

Two days later, and with continued requests for anyone able to identify the victim to get in touch, the team still had no clue. It was unbelievable to think that, like the second case, the third girl appeared to have no one reporting her missing, no one seeing her at the service station or perhaps thumbing a lift. As the team continued to question drivers and service-station personnel in an attempt to identify her, they felt deeply disappointed that they were getting no result.

On the fourth day, Anna received a letter. Barbara placed it on her desk, raising her eyebrows as she did so. "Fan mail?" the DC asked.

Anna turned over the envelope; stamped on the back was the address of Barfield Prison. She looked up at Barbara and joked, "It's probably from someone I helped get locked up."

Anna slit open the envelope and took out a blue-lined thin sheet of writing paper. Typed in the right-hand corner was the prison's address and the name CAMERON WELSH, Prisoner 6678905 Top–Security Wing.

She knew who it was immediately: Cameron Welsh was an exceptionally evil sadistic killer given two life sentences—with no possibility of being released—for the murder of two teenage girls five years previously.

Anna had been on the case with the then-DCI James Langton. The latter was now detective chief superintendent, and as usual, whenever his name cropped up, she felt a surge of emotion. Having been in love with him, lived for a short time with him, helped him recover from a terrible wounding, and then split up with him, she had been through a lot of hurt and painful self-analysis. His intensely strong hold on her had been almost impossible to get over for a long time—in fact, up until the last case they had worked on; however, they had at last reached a more amicable relationship, one born out of her admiration for him, even though at times the situation was still tough for her to handle. It was only during the last year that she had truthfully been able to put their past relationship behind her and to treat Jimmy Langton as a confidant. And he had, as he had promised, been supportive at all times during her recent cases.

Barbara rocked back in her chair. "Who's it from?" she asked.

Anna wafted the letter in the air, saying, "As I suspected, from a real shit bag. I've not read what he wants yet."

She opened the single folded page. Written in felt-tip pen, the writing was looped and florid. It read:

Dear Detective Travis, Anna,

I don't know if you remember me, but I recall you were very attractive when you were part of the murder team that arrested me. I have written to you before but you have never replied, though I do not hold that against you. I am not sure if you are attached to the present hunt for the killer of the girl found close to the M1 motorway. If you are, then I think I can be of assistance to you. I have been following the murder inquiry and I have made copious notes, as I am certain the same killer has two previous victims. I believe it would be very beneficial for you to have a meeting with me.

Yours faithfully,
Cameron Welsh

Anna's blood ran cold. Welsh had made her skin crawl when she had been present at interviews with him. He was extremely well educated, and she knew he had gained a degree in child psychology while in prison. She also knew he had been held in solitary, as he had refused to be placed on a wing. He had been moved into the prison within a prison at Barfield due to his constant antagonism of other inmates. While in prison, he had also had many altercations with officers, and even in the small secure unit, he still managed to be a loner. Anna knew because she had received three previous letters from Welsh and had even called the prison to gain further details about him. But there had been no contact for at least a year—until this letter.

She was about to toss it into the rubbish bin beside her desk but then stopped herself. She stared at the blue-lined paper and the looped felt-tipped writing, flattening the crease out with her hand. Could this creature really have something that might be, as he said, beneficial? She doubted it. In the end, Anna decided that she would discuss the letter with Mike Lewis. On previous cases, she'd been warned by Langton that she hadn't acted like a team player—and she had no intention of making that mistake again.

Mike Lewis was not in his office, so Anna returned to her desk just as Barbara came past, wheeling the tea trolley with some donuts and buns.

"You want a coffee?" the DC asked. "It's fresh."

"Yeah, thanks, and I'll have one of those," Anna said, pointing to a bun.

"I've lost four pounds," Barbara said, turning to indicate her flat stomach. She was still a little overweight, with a round, pretty face, and she had lightened her blond hair and had it cut short.

"You look good."

"Thanks. It's been hard. I've got my old man working out with me as well. He's lost half a stone, but he doesn't have the canteen goodies where he works. It's the donuts that do me in."

Anna helped herself to the pink-iced bun and placed it on a napkin on her desk as Barbara poured her coffee and passed it over.

"What did the letter-writer want?"

"It was, as I suspected, from someone I played a small part in putting away for the rest of his life."

"Gets me, you know, how they are allowed to write letters. In the old days they'd never let a prisoner have a stamp, never mind bloody phone cards. Was it something unpleasant?"

"Thinks he can help with our inquiry. Cheeky sod wants me to visit." Anna bit into her iced bun.

"I wouldn't go anywhere near him. Go on, chuck his stupid letter in the bin." Barbara started to move off.

Anna stopped her. "There was a lot of press about the two previous victims, wasn't there?"

Barbara nodded. "All we could get, to try and find out the second woman's identity—but nothing. Beggars belief, doesn't it, that not one person has come forward. I think she was maybe an au pair or foreign, you know, over here on some kind of work . . . Still, didn't make sense that no one recognized her, and she was lovely looking. Not the kind you'd forget."

Barbara went off to give Joan her morning coffee as Anna finished her iced bun and sipped her drink. Unlike a lot of the stations she'd worked in, the canteen here was well-organized, with a good breakfast and lunch menu. While it didn't solve cases, it certainly helped with morale.

It was over lunch with Barbara and Joan that Anna told them more about Cameron Welsh and his imprisonment at Barfield.

"That place is all new and streamlined, isn't it?" Joan asked.

Barbara shook her head, saying in disgust, "It's bloody better equipped than my son's secondary school. They've got computer courses, exercise classes, gymnasiums, and it was at Barfield that one of the feckin' prisoners almost caused a riot because he said that being forced to wear the colored shoulder band that shows who's a prisoner and who's a visitor was an invasion of his privacy. The world's gone bloody mad."

"Cameron has gained a degree in child psychology," Anna said thoughtfully.

"See what I mean? Don't tell me he murdered kids?"

"No, they were two teenagers."

"Boys?"

"No, girls—and apparently, he's held in the secure unit inside the main prison, refused to ever go on the wing, and keeps himself to himself."

"So what can he tell you if he's shut away in that unit?" Joan queried. "I mean, what can *he* know about the cases? If I were you, I'd contact the prison governor and say that no more letters from Welsh are to be forwarded to you. Sick buggers, all of them."

Anna nodded, still undecided whether she should try to bring it up with Mike Lewis.

"What was he like, this Welsh?" Barbara asked curiously, then gave a laugh. "Apart from being a scumbag, that is."

Anna tried to recall what Cameron looked like physically. "I remember he was very tall, sort of gaunt almost, and his face was very pale. Well, he'd been hiding out for some time, so whether that was why he was so thin, I'm not sure. All I can really remember clearly about him was that he had very penetrating dark eyes. I hated the way he looked at me. He was well spoken, though, and he held his own throughout the interviews. I never heard him raise his voice—he had this cool manner, as if we were almost beneath him. That was until DCI Langton came on board." Anna sighed. "Langton was heading the inquiry, and he had a really hard time cracking him. In fact, I don't even recall that he did, but we had enough evidence against the bloke—DNA, clothes fibers, and eventually even a witness—to go to trial, and although he still maintained he was innocent, thankfully the jury found him guilty."

"How did he react to the sentence?"

"He smirked and shook his head, Joan. That was about all the reaction he gave."

Joan pulled a face. "I'd stay well clear of him," she advised. "Remember what's-her-name from Hannibal Lecter, the way he tormented her?"

Anna laughed. "Cameron isn't exactly in the same category," but then she thought again and added, "Well, perhaps not far off. He tortured his two victims but used them for sex slaves rather than his dinner menu. When he tired of one, he went and found another. But I couldn't compare him with Hannibal or myself with Jodie Foster, and anyway, after what we've just discussed there is no way I would agree to seeing him."

By the time they returned to the incident room, Mike Lewis was in his office, so Anna decided to see what he thought.

Mike had only recently gained promotion, and Anna knew he was playing it strictly by the book. His office was very sparsely furnished, with a number of photographs of his twin boys and one of his wife in a leather folding frame. A row of sharpened pencils and a large notepad sat beside his computer and telephone. She often didn't notice that Mike was in actual fact rather good-looking, with thick, close-cropped blond hair. If she had to describe his looks, she would use the words *nice* and *ordinary*, because he was both. He had also been a strong right-hand man for DCS

Langton. Mike was quiet and methodical and a calming influence. Anna knew he was a dedicated officer, if not an exceptional one.

She watched him reading the letter without much enthusiasm. As he handed it back to her, he asked, "How long has he been inside?"

"Five years, almost six."

"Mmmm. Well, I can't see what he would know about our case, unless he talked to another prisoner and got some information via him, but I doubt it. You say he's in solitary?"

"No, he's in the secure unit at Barfield. That's the prison within a prison; usually, they are only placed in there if they have been trouble or they're terrorists. I think they also place heavy drug dealers in there, but there are only about six cells."

"Yeah, yeah, I know, but like I said, I doubt he has anything to offer us. He's probably just after getting a visit from you."

Anna agreed and folded the letter. "So I ignore it?" she said.

Mike sighed. "It's really up to you, Anna."

"I'd prefer not to see him."

"Okay, just make a note of it, file the letter, and thanks for bringing it to my attention."

Anna returned to her desk and put the letter in her briefcase. Barolli caught her eye. "The postmortem's in on our Jane Doe."

Anna went over to the incident board to read up on the details as Barolli joined her.

"Doesn't give us much, does it? Just that she was dead about twelve or so hours before the body was discovered."

"Still no ID?"

"Nope, but we're getting a lot of coverage on the case, and we're looking into dental records. Mispers have also been contacted, but no female of her description has been reported missing. You'd think with that red hair, someone would recognize her, wouldn't you?"

Anna stared at the victim's pictures and bit her lip. "Unbelievable. Someone somewhere has to know who she is."

"Right, but we held out hopes on that last case, the brunette, and we got zilch back. We're covering the nearest motorway service stations to see if anyone remembers her, see if she was hitchhiking, exactly as we did before, but it's bloody time-consuming."

"She doesn't look the type to me," Anna murmured.

"Type of what?"

"Girl who'd hitchhike or hang out, like Margaret Potts. I don't think she was on the game."

"Well, we didn't think our brunette was a tart, but nowadays you never know."

"How about Interpol?"

"On to it, but so far nothing's come in."

Barolli sucked in his breath. Both of them could see the truth from the notes on the board, the arrows joining each victim's injuries. They knew they had a serial rapist killer. But what they couldn't ascertain until the last two girls were identified was if there was a connection apart from their murders. If the victims had known each other, it would help the police to focus their inquiries. All they had were three dead women, all tossed aside like garbage close to the M1, and yet no witnesses.

"What about Margaret Potts?" Anna gestured to the first victim. "I see the team interviewed a number of known associates. Did they give any indication of a usual night's work?"

Barolli gave a shrug. "Yeah, but nothing that helped us. She worked between two motorway service stations. She'd either do the business in the guys' lorries or hitch a ride, especially if there were two drivers, and she'd do the pair of them en route to their next stop, then get out and turn the same tricks on the other side. Been at it for years."

"Can I talk to this girl?" Anna tapped the board where the name *Emerald Turk* was written up as helping inquiries. "Who is she?"

"Emerald—yeah, she shared a flat with Potts."

"Is that her real name?"

"I doubt it." Barolli gave a short laugh. "We had four different aliases for her, and she was a real bitch; didn't give us much—just how Potts earned her money."

"So she was doing the same circuit?" Anna persisted.

"No, she had a pimp and said the motorways were not her style."

"I'd still like to talk to her."

"Why?"

"To try to get a handle on who Margaret Potts was. On the whole service-station game. I'm not trying to tread on anyone's toes here, Paul, but you're all sort of ahead of me."

"Help yourself." He shrugged. "I doubt you'll get anything more than we did, though. She's a right tough cow, and tracking her down was a headache."

Barolli's tracing of Emerald Turk's whereabouts had been a problem because she changed flats or rooms constantly, but eventually, he'd got a contact address through Social Services and her phone number via Strathmore Housing Association. Emerald had two children, so he was able to gain more information, as the children had been fostered out twice. Now that she had a council flat, the kids had been returned to her, and for the past two years, Social Services had seen no signs of neglect on their home visits.

Anna did not make an appointment with Emerald but decided to call on her unannounced and see if she would agree to talk. She drove to Hackney and found the address on a high-rise council estate. Emerald lived on the third floor. The lift was not working, so Anna walked up. From the amount of garbage strewn in the corridors and urine stinking out the stairs, she didn't think that by any standards this was a well-appointed flat, as Social Services had claimed.

Emerald lived in number 34. Anna rang the bell, waited, and then rang it three more times before the door was finally inched open.

"Emerald Turk?" Anna asked.

"Yeah."

Anna showed her ID. "Can I come in and talk to you?"

"What about?"

"There's no problem, Emerald. I'm simply attached to a team investigating the murder of Margaret Potts."

The chain was still on the door as the woman looked at Anna and grumbled, "Listen, I already told the cops everythin' I knew. I got nothin' more to say, so piss off."

"Please, Emerald, I just want to talk. We've not been able to move the investigation forward, for lack of evidence. I'm new to the inquiry and just wanted to—"

"Like I said, I got nothin' to tell you."

"Just give me a few minutes, please. You knew Margaret, didn't you?"

"Yeah, and I told 'em everything, so fuck off."

Anna couldn't even see what Emerald looked like, as the door was almost closed. She wedged her shoe inside the door frame. "She was murdered, Emerald. All I want to do is just try and find out who she really was. You knew her, so you can help me with this. Please let me in. I don't want to have to come back."

There was a short silence. Anna would have given up, but then the chain was unlinked and the door opened wider.

"All right, you'd better come in, then. If this place smells cops, they'll get nasty, and I don't want no trouble from me neighbors."

Emerald stood back to allow Anna to enter. She was tall and skinny with a pale, narrow face, and she was wearing an expensive-looking gray velvet tracksuit with large fluffy rabbit slippers. "You'll have to come through to the kitchen," she said. "I'm ironing."

Anna followed her along a toy-strewn hallway and into a modern, well-equipped kitchen. It was bright and clean, with long white blinds at the window. Dishes were stacked tidily on the draining board. Emerald picked up the iron and nodded for Anna to take a stool by a breakfast counter. There was a basket of clean clothes beside the ironing board.

"This is very nice," Anna said, looking around.

"Yeah, all new mod cons, and I'm doin' me best to keep the place spic-and-span. Those nosy cows from Social Services drop in whenever they feel like it, and I ain't gonna give them any reasons for takin' me kids off me again."

"Are they at school?"

"Yeah, little local primary. They're there, thank Christ, until three in the afternoon."

Anna looked at the fridge, which was covered with bright-colored plastic magnetic numbers and letters. There were also numerous children's watercolor paintings stuck on a wall with Blu-Tack. One had big orange splashes of paint, and "Mummy" was painted as a stick figure with big feet.

Anna shifted her weight. The high stool was uncomfortable, and her tight skirt kept riding up her thighs. Stashed beneath the breakfast bar was a big red plastic bucket full of dirty nappies, and it smelled, as the lid was left off. Emerald caught Anna looking at it and gestured for her to put the lid on. She explained that her youngest child was still a bed wetter and that these were nighttime Pull-Ups that had to be put out with her recycled items. From the smell of urine that wafted in Anna's face, they hadn't been put out for a while. She secured the lid and inched it farther away from her stool.

The iron hissed steam as Emerald pressed pillowcases. She was fast, far more adept than Anna. "I got a babysitter helping me out of an evenin'." The woman continued ironing while she lit a cigarette from a packet taken out of her tracksuit pocket. "And I don't smoke in front of the kids."

Anna smiled, "I'm not with Social Services. As I said, I am on the inquiry relating to Margaret Potts's murder."

"I've not read anythin' more about her," Emerald commented. "Shame, 'cause she was a real nice woman. In fact, this is her tracksuit. She left a suitcase full of her gear with me, you see. Well, she wouldn't know I'm wearin' her things, would she, but I think of her often."

"I know what she did for a living," Anna said quietly.

"In which case you probably know what I do. I got a bloke that takes good care of me, not like Maggie. She had it rough due to her age, but she was a good person and didn't deserve to end up the way she did."

Emerald smoked and continued ironing as Anna asked if she could explain how Margaret worked.

"She'd sort of got her own patch out at the London Gateway Services. She'd travel there by bus or sometimes thumb a lift, then she'd chat to her regulars—truckers, mostly—but sometimes she'd pick up a punter in a car."

"Did she do her business in the car parks?"

"She had to be careful, you know—the security blokes could give her a real hard time. I think she'd bung them cash to lay off her, and then she'd just either do it in the lorries' cabs or travel up to the next service station—the one at Toddington, 'cause that has a bridge over the north- and southbound services, then she'd do the same thing there, coming back on the opposite side."

"Always at night?"

"Not always. Sometimes she worked a day shift, but she didn't like it. Well, you know—it was a bit obvious what she was doin', and they'd move her on or call out the cops."

"Did she ever talk about any of her clients?"

At this, Emerald laughed. "Nah. I doubt that'd be a popular topic of conversation. She was always knackered and slept late. One time we shared a place, but she got behind in the rent, so I left. She'd turn up sometimes wherever I was and kip down, but to be honest, I never really liked it, and these housing associations think you're renting out a room if you got anyone stayin'."

"But you liked her?"

"Yeah, I liked her—but I used to find it depressing, like I was lookin' at what could happen to me all the time, know what I mean? And then I had a spot of trouble—the bloke I was with at the time was doin' drugs and they took me kids off me, but I never done crack or brown. Maybe smoked the odd spliff—who doesn't?—but I left the hard stuff alone."

"What about Margaret?"

"Yeah, she'd take whatever she could lay her hands on—coke, mostly—and she'd drink. Can't blame her, really, having to drag her arse out to the friggin' M1 most nights, and sometimes it was freezing cold. She got knocked 'round a couple of times as well." Emerald sighed and dug into her laundry basket.

"Did she ever report it?"

"Nah. She was on the game—you get used to it, but you know, some of them wouldn't want to pay. Some bastard chucked her out of his cab once."

"Did she tell you about it, like who had done it?"

"No, just waited until her black eyes healed up." Emerald sighed more loudly. "I said all this before, you know. I'm just repeatin' myself."

"Did she have a pimp? Someone looking out for her, maybe?"

"No, she was a loner. Like I said, she wasn't young and knew all the tricks, so why shell out her hard-earned cash?"

"But you do."

Emerald's face tightened. "I'm in a different league 'cause of me responsibilities. I work out of a massage parlor, I'm not touting for business on the effing motorway, and my man takes good care of me."

"So she worked solo . . . What about other friends?"

"I never knew them. Listen, Maggie was a tough old boiler. She knew the risks, and she'd got the number of the blokes that had knocked her around, and like I said, she didn't always go with the truckers. Sometimes she was flush from a few punters she'd had in posh cars. She looked out for herself, and she even took down the license numbers." Emerald gave a strange laugh. "Said she couldn't remember their faces, but she'd remember their reg numbers—had 'em all written down."

"What, in a diary or notebook?"

"Yeah. Reckoned if they got nasty, she could tip off friends to beat them up."

"You mean other working girls?"

"Nah, strong-armed blokes. We all know a few. A couple are ex-coppers workin' for bailiffs who can run a trace on license plates so they can get their addresses."

Anna could hardly contain herself. "You wouldn't know where this notebook was kept, would you?"

"No idea, but it could have been in her stuff, I suppose. Did they find her handbag? It'd be in that, I expect."

"No. There was nothing to identify her—we ID'd her from her fingerprints."

"Oh, right. She'd done a few stretches."

"Would it be among the things you said she'd left with you?"

"No, I never saw it. There was just clothes and bits and pieces."

"Did you mention that you had some of her belongings when you were previously questioned?"

"Yes. The police looked through it all back then. To be honest, at the time I'd forgotten I had the suitcase. Well, I moved around a lot before I got this place. I even had gear stashed all over London, but when the Social Services found this flat for me, I collected it all. A few times she turned up, but like I said, I didn't like her bein' here when it had all been done up nice."

"Could I see the case?"

Emerald lit another cigarette. "I don't have it no more," she said, and shrugged. "It wasn't worth keeping."

"But you said it had good clothes in it, like that track-suit?"

Emerald unplugged the iron, mumbling, "I gotta go and do some shoppin'."

"You just threw it out?"

The young woman turned on Anna angrily. "Yeah. Like I said, it wasn't worth keeping, and your lot didn't want it, so I chucked it out onto a skip. There were just some blouses and skirts and shoes and this tracksuit, all right? There was nuffink of value."

Anna could feel Emerald's growing animosity from the way she banged the ironing board closed. It showed she was getting her temper up.

"I'm sorry if you think I am accusing you of anything, because I'm not. It's just that if we could find Margaret's notebook, it would be of great value, as we would be able to question the men she picked up. I'm not interested in anything else that was in her suitcase."

"Well, there was nuffink else. Now I gotta go out."

Anna stood up and placed the stool under the breakfast shelf. "I really appreciate you giving me your time, Emerald. By the way, is that your real name?"

"I wasn't christened with it, but me great-grandmother worked as a cleanin' lady for a high-society woman called Emerald. She'd given her some nice things, and it's me favorite color. Turk is the name of my father, but it was never on me birth certificate because he pissed off before I was born." Emerald stood with her hands on her hips. "Anything else you want to know?"

"No. Thank you for seeing me."

Heading back along the rubbish-filled corridor, Anna suspected that Emerald was lying about the contents of the suitcase, but there was little she could do about it now, as the original investigating team had already looked through it and found nothing of importance. She had a feeling, if she was correct and Emerald did still have the suitcase, that it would be thrown out as soon as she left. There was nothing for it but to return to the car and set off back to the station.

The moment she'd checked that the policewoman's car had gone, Emerald was on her hands and knees beside her wardrobe, dragging out boots and shoes as she reached for the suitcase. It was a cheap make, and the zipper had already been broken when she had used a pair of pliers to unlock the small padlock holding it shut. Margaret's name was printed on a travel label attached to the handle.

Opening it up on her bed, Emerald started to remove the few items she'd left inside. Tossing them out of the way, she felt along the lining, digging inside the side pocket, and took out a small red notebook. She didn't even look at it, but put it into her tracksuit pocket. Next, she stuffed the suitcase into a black plastic binliner, tying it at the top. To begin with, Margaret's suitcase had also contained two thousand pounds in ten- and twenty-pound notes, and a red velvet jewel case. Inside this there had been two small diamond rings, a gold moonstone pendant, looped gold earrings, and a thick gold bangle. Emerald had kept the gold bangle but got five hundred and ten pounds for the jewelry from a guy she knew in Berwick Street Market. She'd put the money to good use, buying the fridge-freezer, the kitchen stools, and the steam iron. She had intended getting the zipper on the suitcase fixed, but now she just wanted rid of it.

An hour or so later, Emerald carried the bag out of the flat. She had not far to walk before she saw a half-filled skip near a building site and threw the bag into it with some relief. She then hurried off to the local Tesco to pick up some groceries for the kids' tea. By the time she'd fed and bathed her two children, it was time for her to get changed and ready for work. Her babysitter arrived, and Emerald went off to the massage parlor, where she could forget all about the events of the afternoon.

The notebook was left in the pocket of the tracksuit. Emerald didn't want any repercussions. Even though Anna had explained the importance of the contents to their investigation, she could think only of the trouble she might get into for having sold the jewelry. She certainly didn't want anyone showing up claiming the money. It had all been spent anyway.

Chapter Two

Days later and the team had still not been able to identify their latest victim. It was immensely frustrating. Even with the extensive press coverage and television broadcasts, no one had come forward. Interpol had also been unable to assist, and neither had Mispers. It was beginning to look as if, along with their brunette victim, the police had another Jane Doe.

Mike held a briefing, but it was disappointing news: officers at the service station and viewing CCTV had so far come up with nothing. It seemed no one had seen the girl, and even though they were still making inquiries, it was looking as if they had reached a dead end. They also gained nothing from the clothing of either of the young women except for a few seat-cover fibers, but they were of a common variety used in a number of vehicles. The disturbing element was the consensus that all three victims had been killed by the same person, due to the MOs being virtually identical.

Mike concluded the briefing by saying that they had distributed appeals for information and warning leaflets at the service stations.

Anna wrote up the report of her visit to Emerald, detailing the fact that Margaret Potts had kept a notebook of the license plates of men who picked her up. But as Emerald had said she no longer had the suitcase or knew where the notebook could be, it was not much use.

Barolli went over to Anna's desk. "The bitch is lying," he said. "She never told me she had Potts's suitcase."

"I think she was scared it might get her into trouble. She was wearing the dead woman's tracksuit."

"You don't think she's still got the case, do you?"

"I might have, but she got quite agitated when I asked to see it, and said she'd thrown it out."

"You think it'd be worth getting a warrant to search her place?"

"From the way she reacted, I'd say as soon as I left, she would have got rid of it, if she still had it."

"Shit."

Anna declined to add that he had missed the opportunity when he first interviewed Emerald. She was annoyed that the woman had lied to her, claiming that the suitcase had been checked over when she had been interviewed previously.

"We never found Potts's handbag, and we didn't even have a description of it." Barolli grunted. "Maybe this notebook would have been in it."

"Probably. She must have kept it on her if she was jotting down reg plates. Strange that she would—" Anna broke off as a new thought occurred to her.

"Would what?"

"Well, Emerald said she was a wily old girl, tough, very streetwise, and yet she gets into a car or a truck with the killer. So, he's got to be someone she trusted enough or maybe had been with before."

"Fuck! If only we had the bloody notebook," Barolli said angrily.

"Well, we don't, but there's something else," Anna said,

then hesitated. "Again, this came from Emerald. She said that Margaret had contact with some heavy guys—ex-cops, she said—and they looked out for her."

"I don't understand."

"Well, when she was roughed up, she never reported it to the police, but would use the heavy guys to get the addresses from the plates and leave it to them to deal out their own rough justice."

Barolli pulled at his tie. "We'd better go back to Emerald Turk, search her place again, and see if she can give us some names."

Anna agreed and suggested the men might work for bailiff companies if Emerald couldn't or refused to help. Privately, she doubted that the woman would cooperate, but without much else to work on, they had to do something.

Barolli turned. Passing through the incident room was Detective Chief Superintendent James Langton. He waved at them both before entering Mike Lewis's office.

"I wondered when he would show up," Barolli murmured. "He won't like this. Word is he's up for the commander's position, heading up Murder and Serious Crime."

Anna said nothing, but for the first time in as long as she could remember, she hadn't felt disturbed at seeing Langton.

"You didn't get your promotion," Barolli said suddenly.

"That's a bit obvious."

"Well, I'm in the same boat. I've been before the powers that be twice, and I just don't seem able to crack it. It's all the fucking diversity stuff that gets me."

"Got me, too," she said, smiling. This wasn't actually the truth, since it had been Langton who had vetoed her promotion, but she no longer harbored any ill feelings toward him. On the contrary, she now realized he had been right, and she was not yet ready for promotion to detective chief inspector. But she fully intended to prove herself when the time came around again.

"This case isn't going to do any of us any favors," Barolli grumbled.

Anna wished he'd move off, but instead, he perched on the edge of her desk, his heel kicking against it.

"You going to see about getting a search warrant and interviewing Emerald Turk again?" she asked.

He sighed and then, thankfully, moved back to his own desk. "I'll run it by Mike," he said.

Anna turned as Barbara joined her, signaling to her that she was wanted in Mike's office.

"You don't think these Jane Does are maybe illegal immigrants, do you?" Barbara asked with concern. "If that's the case, we'll never get them identified. Maybe we should check around the embassies and clubs—churches, even."

Anna picked up her notebook, saying, "I think that's already in hand, Barbara. Did Mike say what he wanted?"

"No. I'd have put it through to your desk, but you were having a confab with Barolli."

Anna sat beside Langton, who gave her a warm smile and asked how she was. He seemed relaxed, while Mike was edgy, flicking a Biro pen. Then there was a pause.

"I'm very well, thanks," Anna replied, thankful that this was true and that Langton's sudden appearance had not affected her.

"You want me to tell her?" Mike began.

"No. It's this letter, Anna, from the prisoner Cameron Welsh. I had a look over it. I'm not that impressed because it could just be a load of bull, but considering the case is flatlining all round, we shouldn't just dismiss it, in case he does have information for us or you."

"I really doubt that he has," Anna said, somewhat surprised.

Langton nodded. "Yeah, I hear you, but he's been banged up for some considerable time and would have had a lot of opportunity to talk to any number of inmates—so you never know. I suggest you pay the bastard a visit, see what he's got or hasn't. I can't really recall if you had much interaction with him when we arrested him."

"I met him, obviously, and was in on a couple of interviews, but that was it."

"Well, you obviously made a big impression on him."

Anna made no reply as Langton continued: "From what I've read up on the case files, Welsh doesn't fit the profile of this sicko we're looking for, but then as I recall, he didn't fit the profile we worked on while hunting for him. Both his victims were held captive."

"He's gained a child psychology degree while he's been in prison," Anna said.

"Yes, I know, and he's also been in a pack of trouble while he's been at Barfield. Anyways, go and see him and take Barolli with you. Might as well see if he's bullshitting, but maybe he'll surprise us."

Anna stood up as Mike told her to talk to the prison governor to arrange the meeting. Privately far from happy, she left his office and returned to inform Barolli about Langton's suggestion.

"Shit, that's a schlepp and a half up there, isn't it? It's around Leeds—right?"

"Correct." Anna wasn't sure if the distance made it better or not. "I'll contact the governor and type up a letter of introduction."

It took three calls before she was able to speak to Jeremy Hardwick, the governor of Barfield. Hardwick was pleasant and listened as she explained, then he agreed that she should be allowed into the secure unit to talk to Welsh. So she made an appointment for the following afternoon and asked Barbara to work out how long the trip would take. Langton passed by her desk as he was leaving and paused.

"I've made contact with the prison," Anna told him.

"Good. Make them keep him in his cage, get what you can, and report back. I think it'll be a wasted journey, but right now we've nothing else."

She watched him look over the incident board and have a talk with Barolli before he left. But she felt nothing.

Before long, Barbara came over to Anna with a route map and the details she would need.

"Are you driving, or should I get a train timetable?" Barbara asked.

"No, this is fine. I'll drive, and Paul's with me."

"Remember, you'll need the fax from the prison and an introduction letter; plus, do keep your petrol receipts."

"Thank you, Barbara." At least she would be well prepared, Anna thought.

"So tell me about this geezer Welsh," Barolli said, slurping his coffee as he settled himself in Anna's passenger seat. She had picked him up from his flat in Notting Hill, and they were heading for the M1.

"Highly intelligent;" just got a degree in child psychology. He was well educated, went to public school and I can't remember which university, but he was reading law and dropped out. Anyway, he represented himself at his trial," Anna told Barolli, wishing he wouldn't slurp so loudly.

"So did Ted Bundy."

"What?"

"That American serial killer, killed Christ knows how many women."

"Yes, yes, I know who he is."

"Well, he represented himself at his trial. The judge apparently said what a waste it was that such a brilliant mind should be so deviant, as he could have been a successful man."

"Maybe Welsh could have been, but he just gave me the shivers," said Anna, remembering.

"Why?"

"Because of his manner—everything about it. He was so well spoken and so arrogant, treating us as if we were beneath him. He never showed any emotion whatsoever, even when it was obvious we had enough evidence to arrest him, not even when he was charged. During his trial, he used to doodle on a notepad all the time and was constantly interrupting the prosecution. Judge Oldfield laid into him after one session, and he was quite unapologetic, simply drawling that as he was the man on trial for his life, he had every right to question the prosecution's long-winded summing-up."

"How long did he get?"

"Oldfield gave him two life sentences without bail, so thankfully, he will die in prison. The judge said he was one of the most despicable men he had ever encountered, that his crimes were sadistic and violent, and that he had never at any time shown a fragment of compassion for his victims."

"How did he kill them?" Barolli seemed grimly intrigued.

"Held them captive, tortured and raped them over a

period of four or five months. The first girl was only seventeen, and the second girl was snatched eight months after he disposed of victim one's body. He buried her in the garden of his basement flat. It was a hideous place. Part of it was still like a cellar, with chains and bare brick walls, but the section he lived in was luxurious, and he owned the large walled garden. The area of the basement he occupied had every piece of high-tech equipment conceivable, with plasma TV, stereo, and an amazing kitchen extension with culinary devices a professional chef would die for. He actually owned the whole house but leased off the other flats."

"What work did he do?"

"He ran a very successful IT company with offices in Canary Wharf, and he employed four people, or he used to. By the time we got on to him, he'd closed it down. I think he was ready to move abroad."

Barolli tapped her arm and pointed as they headed toward the roundabout that led to the start of the M1. He asked if she ever used the big Brent Cross shopping center, as he had been there a few times. She shook her head, and he began telling her how much he had saved on the sale price of some fitted wardrobes for his mother. As they approached the motorway, there were numerous young guys holding up cardboard notices with various locations on them, from Manchester to Liverpool.

"London Gateway service station is the first up, isn't it?" Barolli asked.

"Yes," Anna replied.

"Used to be called Scratchwood Services," he said as he slurped more coffee. After a long pause, he returned to their previous conversation. "Doesn't make sense, does it?"

"What doesn't?"

"That he was so successful and yet still committed

murder. I mean, was he a freaky-looking bloke?" Barolli wanted to know, finishing the dregs of his coffee.

"No. On the contrary, he was very handsome—tall, well dressed."

"Fuck. I dunno. Hannibal Lecter—right? I mean, don't tell me in his fab kitchen he cooked his victims?"

"No, but he entertained lots of women. He honestly didn't fit any profile we had ever come across, and it took months of surveillance and more months compiling the evidence against him. Langton headed up the inquiry, and he was like a dog with a bone: he wouldn't back off him."

"He's something else."

Anna hesitated and asked if he meant Langton. Barolli nodded.

"Yeah. I wish I'd started my career under his wing, like you. I could have learned a lot from him. Now he basically just swings in, passes out orders, and swings out again, but I'd have really liked the opportunity of working alongside him in his earlier days."

Anna agreed, which led them to discuss how many cases Barolli and Langton had subsequently worked on together, from the serial-killer movie star to the Red Dahlia case. Where Barolli had not been as fortunate as Anna was in the many cases between.

"He sort of specializes in serial murders, doesn't he?"

Anna nodded and then recalled the horrendous case when Langton had almost been killed. She didn't want to think about the details even now.

"You had a scene with him, didn't you?" Barolli asked, and Anna gripped the steering wheel.

"Yes, but it was over a long time ago, and I don't really want to talk about it."

"Okay," said Barolli, unperturbed. "So let's go back to

this animal Cameron Welsh. You said that Langton was on to him—dog with a bone, you said, right?"

"Yes. We got the lead from an ex-girlfriend of Welsh's," Anna recalled. "We'd been on the investigation for about two months when she walked in, wanting to speak to whoever was in charge of the inquiry. She was very attractive and had worked for him in the city, but he had recently fired everyone, and at first we thought it was maybe a case of sour grapes. There had been a lot of press about the discovery of the second victim, but at that stage, we didn't even know he'd killed before."

Anna recounted how, after a lengthy talk to Langton, the girl had said she was certain the victim had been a temp in Welsh's office a year or so previously. Langton had checked back and discovered that their victim had indeed been working for Welsh and had been sent to him by an agency. They then brought Welsh in for an interview. He was, Anna explained, polished and cool, and had an answer for everything. All they had was the girl's statement. Welsh had dismissed the accusations as ridiculous and maintained that, as he had recently closed his company, she was simply trying to implicate him in a crime with which he had absolutely no connection.

"So old Langton reckoned he was going to jump the country?"

"Yes and no. It wasn't that—he kept on saying that it was a gut reaction and we now had to delve into Welsh's life for clues."

"What did the girl say he'd done, apart from fire her?" Barolli stuffed the coffee cup down beside his seat.

"She said he had come on to her and she had been smitten with him. He had invited her to a couple of dinner parties, and she was really a bit overawed by him, but when he asked her to stay over after one of these dinners, she refused. Her reason was that she'd had a lot of wine. He was polite, saying he would drive her home, which he did. Then, for a long time afterward, he was cool toward her. She said he hardly acknowledged her at work, and it was very distressing."

They were driving in the middle lane, Anna not going over the speed limit. Barolli complained about the speeding vehicles passing them, and then he patted the dashboard, asking how long she had owned the Mini, how much she'd paid for it, and did she find the automatic easier than the gearshift. He had an annoying habit of asking her a question and then answering it himself. He felt that with a car that could go over a hundred, it was better to have a shift gear than automatic, and if he was given the choice, he would go for a shift, but then he wouldn't consider buying a Mini, as he liked something more substantial.

"Did you choose this color?"

"Yes."

"What color would you call it?"

"Navy blue, Paul, and the upholstery is leather."

"I like two-tone cars, white and black." He waved his hand at the signpost indicating the mileage to the service station and suggested that she pull into the London Gateway Services so he could get her a coffee. Anna said she didn't want one but agreed to drive in and wait when Barolli said he needed to use the toilet. She parked and watched him entering the service station, irritated as she saw him pause to buy a newspaper and a chocolate bar.

Over on the far side was the large lorry parking section. Strange to think that this was where Margaret Potts came night after night to pick up johns, Anna thought. Eventually, Barolli returned with a packet of crisps as well as the chocolate bar. As they drove past the garage forecourt and headed onto the slip road back to the motorway, Anna exclaimed, "Look! Can you believe it?"

Standing hitching a ride was a teenage girl. She wore boots, a miniskirt, and a fur-hooded anorak. Anna drew up beside her and lowered the passenger window, leaning across Barolli to say, "You shouldn't be doing this. Haven't you seen the warning posters?"

The girl gave her the finger and moved away as Anna inched the car forward. Barolli glared at the girl, who glared back at him as he shouted, "You know, two girls have been found murdered not far from here. You're taking a big risk, love."

"I'm waitin' for me dad."

Barolli muttered under his breath, then said, "Just you be careful."

The girl stalked away, and there was nothing they could do. They both remained silent as they headed onto the motorway. Barolli opened his bag of crisps. He shook the bag toward Anna, seeing if she wanted one, but she didn't. It made her grit her teeth as he crunched one crisp after another, letting crumbs fly everywhere. She was amazed at how much noise he could make eating as he delved into the pack. At the same time, he was looking over the newspaper he had on his knee.

A short time later, they spotted the flapping yellow scene of crime ribbons.

"You know the van driver? This is only a short distance from the service station, so why didn't he take a piss there?" Barolli wondered as Anna saw a fragment of crisp fly out of his mouth and land on the dashboard.

"Maybe we should bring him in again," she suggested.

Barolli, leaning back on the headrest, closed his eyes.

"Maybe." He yawned. "Right, carry on about this Cameron Welsh guy."

But Anna remained silent as she concentrated on driving, hoping he would fall asleep.

"What else did the girl tell Langton about him?" Barolli prompted her.

"Just that he had been cool toward her and it got to her. I think she also claimed that she was infatuated, and because he was totally ignoring her, she said she sort of became a bit obsessed by him. She admitted it all, and according to Langton, since she was honest about herself, she didn't come across as someone determined to cause trouble for Cameron Welsh."

Barolli yawned again. "So what was it?"

Anna described that at the lengthy interview, the girl said that one evening a few weeks after the cooling-off incident, she was waiting for a bus after work and Cameron drew up to offer her a lift. She got into his car. He asked if she'd like a drink, and feeling euphoric, she went with him to a wine bar. When they left, she asked if he could drive her home, and he suddenly became angry and told her to get out and find her own way. The next minute, he was slapping her around the face, hurting her, and then he banged her head against the dashboard and her nose started to bleed. She began screaming, and a passerby stopped and rapped on the driver's side window. Apparently, Cameron got out and told the man that it was all a misunderstanding and it was over. The passerby looked toward her and asked if she was all right; she had a handkerchief pressed to her bleeding nose. At the same time Cameron was apologizing to her, saying over and over that he hadn't meant to slap her and he was very sorry.

They drove off, and Cameron was like a different person,

very apologetic, and when they drew up outside her flat, he opened her door for her and helped her get out of his car. He kept on saying that he didn't know what had come over him, and that he had never hit a girl before, and asked if she could forgive him. He also said she could take a few days off work. And then he drove off.

Anna suddenly remembered the girl's name: Hannah Lyle. Hannah had gone on to tell them that she had taken a couple of days off work, and when she returned, there was extra money in her paycheck. Cameron was not in the office, and Hannah had taken the opportunity to ask one of the other girls what she knew about him. It was then that she learned about a couple of other young women who had worked for him, and it was known that he had slapped them around, too. That was probably the reason why the new young temp had never returned, the girl said, although she'd been working there only a couple of weeks. The pair had discussed the temp; although Hannah had not known her well, she had liked her, and had wondered why she left so suddenly. Hannah subsequently left the company, and almost a year later, she'd been watching a television program requesting information about a murder victim when she became certain it was the girl she remembered from the office.

"What happened then—Langton brought him in?"

"Yes, and at first let him go—but you know him. He had this gut feeling we'd found the right guy, but we had nothing to go on apart from the statement from Hannah Lyle. He started to dig around, finding out as much as possible about Cameron Welsh's background."

Barolli leaned forward with eyes closed to lower the air-conditioning, which annoyed Anna, as it was a perfect temperature for her.

"Go on," he prompted.

Anna continued, relating that there were no police records of Welsh and not so much as an outstanding parking ticket. The man was a model citizen who paid his taxes, and his company was in good shape, as were his personal accounts, in which there was over a quarter of a million pounds. They went on searching his background details but found nothing incriminating. Without any evidence to back up his hunch, Langton decided to interview anyone who could give them an insight into Cameron's character. Anna took a deep breath, remembering how frustrating it had felt.

"To be honest, the team began to feel they were wasting valuable time, but then some of the interviews started to add up, especially from—"

Barolli interrupted her. "His family?"

"No. Both parents were deceased. It was a couple of fellow students and employers from before he opened his own company. One man in particular said he had never liked him and felt that Cameron was complicated and a compulsive liar, with a disturbing attitude toward women. This was also implied by everyone questioned. Apparently, he was brought up in South Africa, and his father was violent toward their servants. He was ex-military and strict with Cameron. His mother, however, was a beautiful ex-debutante type who married beneath her; we got all this from a student Cameron had been at university with. The other guy said he had liked Cameron at first but then got put off him as, when drinking, Cameron would become belligerent and often morose. From their conversations, it sounded as if Cameron's mother had protected him from his father's abuse, but when he was twelve, she ran off with a close friend of her husband, and this had a traumatic effect on the boy."

"Some friend," Barolli commented.

"Which one?"

"His university pal. Why did he do that to Cameron? Just dump him because he had problems."

"Oh, right. In fact, it was nothing to do with that. They fell out due to Cameron making a pass at his girlfriend. She had become afraid of him, so the two boys argued about it—and Cameron ignored him from that time on."

Anna recalled the interview when she had watched in amazement as Langton used the information he had gleaned about the mother-son relationship, embroidering on the facts, implying that the relationship had been an incestuous one. The suggestion had enraged Cameron, who, up until that point, had been controlled. For a moment he had looked as if he would explode, but then he had fought to control his anger. He did swear at Langton, insisting that the detective had no right to bring up his mother in connection with why he was being questioned. His face had distorted with rage, but yet again he managed to retain control, although his hands had been clenched the whole time. He maintained that he had no relationship whatsoever with his mother, and that he had not had any contact with her, even when she had begged to see him; nor had he gone to her funeral.

"It was a real lesson, watching Langton open Cameron up, because he switched from asking about his relationship with his mother to implying that he had subsequently become close to his father . . . which released more vitriol. He seemed unable to stop spewing out how much he had detested him, how he'd spent his formative years living in fear of him, in a country he hated, and it wasn't until he had watched him dying of cancer that he felt free of his father's domination, returning to live in England with his mother's parents."

However, although the grandparents had taken him in, Cameron's trials were not over, for they showed him little or no affection. His grandmother had always been against her daughter's marriage, and being forced into caring for the grandson she had never previously met had created difficulties.

During the interview, as Cameron went into lengthy detail about his background, he required hardly any prodding from Langton. What emerged was the supremely overconfident, egotistical side of the man's character; he claimed that he had learned to hide his feelings and to portray himself as whatever his grandparents needed to form an attachment to him. They were never aware that he hated them as much as he hated his parents. When they died, Cameron had inherited a considerable amount of money, investments, and properties, and so careless was he in boasting about his wealth that it led to Langton gaining search warrants for two properties that, until Cameron had mentioned them, they had not been privy to his owning. As a result, they discovered the crucial evidence to eventually charge him with the murders.

Barolli was fast asleep, and Anna drove on in silence through the changing landscape, waking him only when they approached the Barfield prison boundary. They had to show their warrant cards and the fax from the prison to the officers at the gates and were instructed to park in the staff section of the car park.

Barfield was one of the few privately owned prisons. A modern build, it was a massive, sprawling place. They were met by an officer and led to the administration section and then through to the governor, who was waiting in his office to offer them tea or coffee. Both Anna and Barolli refused, saying they were eager to meet with Welsh as soon as possible. The governor, Jeremy Hardwick, turned out to be a tall, balding man with disconcertingly large ears, which he was overly fond of pulling at the lobes. He also had a fresh feel to him, as if he were athletic, rising to his feet and shaking their hands vigorously.

He read Anna's letter of introduction and asked for more details, as to meet with Prisoner 6678905 would entail them crossing out of the main prison into the high-security smaller prison.

Anna outlined the reason why they were there, even though she had already given the details over the phone. However, it gave her the opportunity to ask about Cameron and his present behavior. The governor was not exactly evasive, but before saying anything, he suggested that Cameron remain in his cell throughout the interview and that they talk to him through the bars, as the cells in the secure unit did not have the usual cell doors.

"It's just a precaution," he added.

"Do you think he could be dangerous if the cell remained open?" Anna asked.

"I doubt it, but it is necessary we take every precaution. And as you are a very attractive woman, I want you protected." Hardwick gave her a kindly smile.

"So you think he is dangerous?" Anna wanted to be clear about this.

"No. It is, as I said, just a precaution—and I will also have to request that the other inmates in the secure unit are locked in their cells. Usually, they have free access to their open spaces, and we do have some problematic inmates in there. There are four officers on duty at all times, and the security level is tight."

"But you don't think Mr. Welsh could be physically dangerous?" Anna repeated.

The governor hesitated and then shrugged. "To be honest, I wouldn't put anything past him, and as he has written to you personally, Detective Travis, he may have some kind of ulterior motive in requesting you to be here in person. I sincerely doubt that he could have any information regarding your inquiry, and I feel this could simply be a ploy to have you meet with him. You have to understand the lengths inmates go to to relieve the day-to-day boredom."

He tugged at his right earlobe. "It's rather like working with children at school, but the prisoners have no lessons, just twenty-four hours of every day to think up schemes and ways to create problems of every possible kind to aggravate the officers, themselves, and other inmates."

"Because they have nothing else to do?" Barolli asked.

"That is partly the reason, or one could call it bloody-mindedness. We try at Barfield to lessen that aggravation in any way we can, because obviously, these are not children, and their 'games' can have severe repercussions. The prisoners held in the inner secure prison are specifically the ones we have found difficult to control, or who refuse to take any of the many productive courses we have on offer."

"Does Welsh have any other visitors?" Barolli asked.

"No, he has never requested a visitor's order."

"In five years?" Anna asked, surprised.

"He has had no visitors," the governor said quietly.

"What about other prison agencies? I know many people working in that capacity often become friendly with an inmate."

"No, there is no one. He has made no friends with any-one from Social Services, male or female. He has obviously had the opportunity but has always refused to join in any of the interactive out-of-cell activities, even in the secure unit, which is a controlled environment."

Anna asked if they could be given a list of inmates with whom Cameron Welsh had been locked up or had shared a cell.

"He has never shared a cell. He refused to ever be placed with another inmate, and he created major problems when placed on the sex offenders' wing."

"I know he's earned a degree while he's been here. Did he have a tutor or work within the educational department?"

"No. He earned his degree with the Open University."

"But surely he would have had to be interviewed?"

"Apparently not."

"So during his sentence, he has never been close to any other prisoner?" Anna needed a precise answer.

"He worked out in the gym, so he could have made contact with another prisoner, but that would have been some time ago. They do have a small gym in the secure unit that he uses daily."

"What about the other inmates in the secure unit?"

"Well, obviously, he has to be in contact with them, and I can give you their names—they are a drug dealer, a Mafia-connected prisoner, and a terrorist. Although we have facilities in there for eight inmates, we currently have only four, which will enable you to interview him with the cells on either side unoccupied."

Barolli asked for the other inmates' records to ascertain if any of them could have contacts involving their case. It took some time before both he and Anna were able to de-termine that all three had been held at Barfield before the women in question were murdered. This meant that what-ever "information" Welsh claimed he had could not have been passed to him recently.

"How do the prison officers get along with him?" Anna asked next.

"Their job is to basically monitor rather than befriend, so they keep their distance, but at the same time they are trained to have awareness of their inmates. It is much harder in such close proximity, as you will see in the secure unit, which is small in comparison with all the amenities we have in the main prison compound. The officers se-lected have already proved to be dedicated and have spent time on the main prison wings beforehand."

Hardwick stood up abruptly and gestured to the door, saying, "Right. As I have a busy schedule, I have arranged for two officers to walk you over to the secure unit. So you will see for yourselves how Mr. Welsh is today."

Anna and Barolli were led into the main prison yard, pass-ing the high-wired fences surrounding the exercise yard. There were numerous prisoners playing handball, while others smoked and chatted in groups, but all of them stopped what they were doing as the newcomers passed. There were a lot of wolf whistles and catcalls, especially at Anna, referring to her red hair.

"'Ere, Red, show us a smile!"

There were more abusive sexual shouts, but Anna kept facing front, not for a moment acknowledging the catcalls. Eventually, they approached a barred-gated walkway some distance from the exercise yard. The security cameras were positioned high up on the fence corridor as they came to a second barred gate, and after that was unlocked, they ar-rived at the prison within a prison.

The secure unit was a large square building with cameras trained on the main entrance. The two officers gave their names and the names of Anna and Barolli before it clicked open. One officer walked in front of them, the other behind as he relocked the gate. They strode along a narrow windowless corridor before they entered the main area. This was surprisingly light, with large glass doors opening onto a small walled exercise yard. There was a room with high windows almost at ceiling level, and they were told that this was the inmates' workroom. The open space contained a Ping-Pong table and a snooker table. Here the four guards sat around a small table reading the morning papers with mugs of tea, while a large television set attached to the wall was turned to Sky Sports. All stood to be introduced. Anna noticed that they were young, fit, and all about six feet tall.

The two accompanying officers left Anna and Barolli with the four guards, with instructions that as soon as the visitors were ready to go, they should contact the main gate. A fresh-faced blond officer who introduced himself as Ken Hudson offered tea or coffee and gestured toward a small, well-equipped kitchen. It amused Anna that he directed his conversation toward Barolli rather than to her, as he had confused the rank and was unaware that she was actually Paul's superior.

"That's where they can cook their meals if they want," he was telling Barolli.

"If you don't mind, we'd just like to talk with Cameron Welsh and not take up any more of your time than necessary," Anna interrupted. She was keen to get started.

Hudson realized he had misjudged the situation and blushed. He told them that all the inmates were in their cells. "They're not happy about it, but we felt it better that you have no interruptions. They're all nosy sods and would have pestered the pair of you. Especially *you*." He smiled at Anna, and it was her turn to blush.

"So the sooner we get through, the better," she said stiffly.

"Okay—follow me. We have two aisles with the cells off them, and Cameron's off the first one. We were instructed to keep the cells on either side empty, so there's no other prisoner in aisle one." The young man was protective of her, explaining that she would have no cause for concern, as he would be watching from the monitors.

"Thank you." Anna smiled and then paused. "Can I just ask you about Welsh for a moment?"

"Sure."

"How do you find him?"

Hudson shrugged. "He's no trouble if he's left alone; he doesn't mix with the other blokes, and we hardly ever get a word out of him unless he's complaining about something or other. He's a fussy eater, and due to having cash sent in by his solicitor, he's allowed to order his own food from the prison shop; mostly, it's vegetarian. He even gets that sushi sent in, and he likes a lot of fruit drinks, but we have to always make sure the kitchen is clear, as he won't cook in there unless it's empty. The other blokes didn't like it. To begin with, you know, they tried to start up conversations with him, play cards, whatever, but he wasn't having any of it. He even works out in the yard alone; anyone else goes out there, he walks back in. If it's sunny, he gets a chair and places it with his back to us and sits sunbathing for hours."

"Does he watch television?"

"Yeah. Not in the main area, though; he's got his own portable one, and he's also got his computer, and gets sent in books every month. His cell is wall-to-wall books, but he won't let any other guys read them, none of us, either. They're mostly hardbacks. He's got quite a selection."

"What does he do all day—when he's not sunbathing, that is?" Barolli asked, and Anna wished he didn't sound so sarcastic.

"Reads or writes. He's also particular about his laundry. They're allowed to use their own sheets and bedlinen in here, and his are pristine Egyptian cotton. He also never uses the barber, but we sit and watch him cut his own hair; he's particular about that, and it takes him forever. We also have his cell searched frequently. That includes checking his computer hard drive and making sure he's not abusing the fact that he's allowed to use one."

"Does he get a lot of letters?" Anna asked.

"Yes. There's lots of mail for him, mostly to do with his writing. He's doing various courses and Open University stuff, as he's intelligent, but . . ."

"But?" Anna prompted.

"He's a weirdo—you know, his obsession with everything being perfect. I think he's got that obsessive-compulsive thing, as everything has to be lined up exactly to his liking in his cell, and he's fussy about hygiene. He'd be in the showers five times a day if we allowed him, washing his hands all the time, scrubbing his nails, washing his hair twice a week, and he's got God knows how many expensive shampoos and creams. If any of the inmates or us get a cold, he's paranoid about coming anywhere near and has this face mask and uses Vicks up his nose to ward off catching germs."

Hudson stopped at that point and asked them to wait. Again he directed his gaze to Anna and hesitated, his cheeks rosy with embarrassment. He bent down to speak softly. "I'd button your blouse to the neck, if I were you," he advised her. "If he's got some perverted reason for wanting you to visit, don't allow him a second of satisfaction."

She put her hand up to her blouse immediately. It wasn't unbuttoned to reveal any hint of cleavage, but it was nevertheless showing off her slender neck. "Thank you," she said.

"Let me go and tell him you're here."

Anna and Barolli were midway along aisle one. She quickly buttoned her blouse to the neck. Hudson walked past an empty cell and then stopped.

"Cameron, you've got two visitors."

They heard a murmur but could not detect what was said.

"No, two. Detective Sergeant Paul Barolli and a Detective Inspector Anna Travis are here."

Again they heard a murmur, and Hudson looked back at them and then back at the cell.

"Well, you've got two. If you refuse to see them, then you'd better tell me now, as I'll have to take them back to the main prison."

Hudson listened for a moment, then came to rejoin Anna and Barolli. "He said he only agreed to talk to Detective Travis, and he doesn't want to meet you." He nodded to Barolli.

"Tell him we're leaving, then," Barolli said. Hudson nodded and made to return to the cell, when they saw a hand with a small round mirror positioned outside the cell bars.

"He's checking you out," Hudson said quietly.

"Please tell him we don't have time for games. We're leaving."

Hudson walked back to Cameron but said nothing as the hand was withdrawn. Again there was a low murmur.

Hudson walked into the cell beside Cameron's, took out a chair, then went into the cell on the other side and took out a second chair. He placed them both in front of Cameron's bars and gestured for Anna and Barolli to join him, saying he wanted Anna to sit on the right and Barolli on the left.

Anna kept her eyes down as she took her seat and Barolli sat in his.

"Okay, Cameron? You've got Detective Sergeant Barolli and . . ."

"Anna. Anna Travis," she said, taking charge. "Good morning."

Hudson left them, and Anna looked up and into the cell. Cameron was sitting on a similar chair facing forward, his legs crossed casually. She was shocked to see him, because he looked so refreshed and pristine. His dark hair was silky and cut to just above his shoulders, with a part in the middle. His face was tanned, and he looked to her even younger than when she had last seen him. His blue prison-issue shirt was pressed and his trousers creased, and he was wearing leather open-toed sandals.

"Good morning, Mr. Welsh," Barolli said coldly.

Cameron pointedly ignored him as he stared at Anna, saying, "Well, well, you have grown up—and you are wearing your hair in a different style. It's very flattering."

She found it difficult to meet his eyes, but looking at a spot above his head, she began: "You said you had information—"

"Please, one moment, let me first offer you a drink. I have still or sparkling water: which would you prefer?"

"Neither, thank you."

He didn't address Barolli, turning his own chair a fraction so that he wouldn't even have to see him. His cell, although small, was immaculate. The cot was made up in military fashion, the sheet folded over the blanket and his two pillows stacked. One wall of the cell had bookcases from floor to ceiling, mostly hardbacks, arranged by size. The opposite side of his cell contained a small computer desk with a laptop and printer; there were packs of A4 paper, notebooks, and envelopes all stacked in a neat order. Beneath the desk was a crate of bottled water and a box of biscuits, and a shelf high up on the wall contained pristine white towels. Lined up were various shampoos and creams, a brush and a comb, and shaving equipment.

The barred section had an interlocking mechanism that would move the gate sideways, leaving the cell open. It was a strange feeling sitting opposite him and looking into the immaculate cell, but Cameron appeared to be totally re-laxed, leaning back in his chair.

"You wrote to me—" Anna began again, and again, he interrupted her.

"I did, and I have on three other occasions written to you, but I have never received a reply."

"I am here now."

"Indeed you are. May I call you Anna?"

"No. My name is Detective Travis. Mr. Welsh, this is not a social visit, and I am here to discover if in fact you do have information regarding the murder inquiry. Please don't waste either my time or Sergeant Barolli's."

"Time," Cameron repeated softly, and then he smiled. "I want you to know, Detective Travis, that I have no grudge against you whatsoever. You did what you had to do, and I think you did it rather well. So . . ." He turned and ges-tured at his cell. "I certainly have the time, and obviously, I have spent many hours pondering my own situation, my own case. What interests me, and I am sure will interest you, too, is trying to understand what drove me to com-mit murder. I have retraced my life in detail, never allowing

myself to feel self-pity, but more fascinated by what moment—was it madness or desire—that drove me to kill.
This self-contemplation has opened up many areas about
which I truthfully had been in denial; I now believe that I
have two personalities, and only when committing murder
are they joined."

"Mr. Welsh, we are not here to discuss your case," Barolli
said curtly.

Cameron didn't glance at Barolli but continued as if
there had been no interruption. "This self-contemplation
and self-analysis proved to be unsatisfying, since I have
only myself as a template, so I subsequently broadened my
research to delve into other killers' minds. The outcome is
the reason why I wished to see you, Detective Travis. My
attempt to understand why I committed murder has en-
abled me to get inside the general mind of a killer, because
I have been inside my own."

Barolli sighed with impatience, and again Cameron gave
no reaction to his presence.

"Have you brought in documents pertaining to your inquiry?" Welsh went on.

"No."

"Well, that is a waste of time, isn't it? For me to help you,
I will need the postmortem photographs and reports and
the forensic details. Without access to these, I doubt if I will
be able to assist you in capturing the killer."

"That won't be possible, Mr. Welsh," Anna said.

"Then you should *make* it possible," he snapped, "because if you give me access to this material, I will be able to
guide you toward your killer."

Barolli banged back his chair and stood up, and Cameron for the first time turned his attention toward him.

"This is a waste of time," Barolli growled.

Cameron stood up, and Barolli got to see for the first time how tall he was—well over six feet. He was also exceptionally fit, his body lean and muscular.

"Is that what you think, Sergeant Barolli—that I am wasting your time? I guarantee that I will not have any further meetings with you. Impatient little man, aren't you?"

Barolli glared at Anna to get out of her seat to return to the main area.

Cameron moved closer to the bars and addressed Anna. "Let me get into his mind. I will *become* the man you want and give you an insight into who he is."

Anna stood up, still refusing to look at Cameron directly as he continued. "You have three dead girls—one prostitute and two unidentified victims. You have no suspect and no witness, no DNA—you have nothing! But I guarantee I will be able to help your inquiry. Trust me. However, I need to have access to all your files to date on all three cases, the pathology and forensic details and statements and . . ."

Anna at last plucked up the courage to look at him directly.

Their eyes locked for a moment, then she turned away, picking up her chair to walk back down the aisle following Barolli. All the hair on her body was standing up, as if she had stepped into an ice-cold room. Cameron Welsh was the last person she would trust, and she swore that she would not subject herself to another visit. Due to the prison security they had to wait for the guards to take them back into the main prison. She could sense that Cameron Welsh was looking at her via the small hand mirror.

Chapter Three

Anna was writing up her report on the incident board and couldn't help overhearing Barolli chatting with Mike Lewis.

"Bloody drove all the way to Leeds to sit and listen to this egotistical bastard telling us that he could help crack our case. He only wanted all the forensic and postmortem reports and the photographs . . . sick fucker."

"If we want an insight, we could always bring on board a profiler," Mike said.

Anna joined them. "But not one of them is a killer," she pointed out.

Barolli was surprised, asking if she was having second thoughts.

"No. I think he just wanted us—or me—there for his own kudos in the prison system. He will brag how he was able to get Met officers to come to him."

"You should have seen his cell," Barolli fulminated, "lined with hardback books like a library; he even offered Anna still or sparkling water! I dunno about it being a prison within a prison. It's more like a ruddy holiday camp, and he was as tanned as if he'd been to the South of France."

Mike looked at Anna and grinned. "Must be out of a bottle, as it's not exactly sunbathing weather. So, wasted journey?"

She was about to agree when Detective Chief Superintendent James Langton walked in. They all turned, and he gave them a brief nod of acknowledgment, then came over to survey the incident board. He read Anna's note about the prison visit and indicated for her to join him, tapping the mug shot of Cameron Welsh.

"How did you find him?"

"As arrogant as ever. In fact, he looked even younger than his mug shot."

"Shows what three meals a day and no stress can do. You want to take me through the meeting?"

"It's all there. He didn't have anything, and we think it was a ploy to entertain himself."

"So he wrote to you."

"Yes. That's a copy of the letter he wrote—you've already seen it." Anna pointed to the board.

"Taken a fancy to you, has he?"

"I would say he's too in love with himself to fancy anyone else. He makes my skin crawl."

Langton looked at her and smiled. "What if he could get inside our killer's head?" he said.

"I truthfully think his own head is stuck so far up his arse that he'd be incapable. He just wants to pull our strings. All this is a sick game, and I don't want to see him again."

"Got under your skin, did he?"

"Yes—and Barolli's. Ask him what he was like."

"I will. Okay, thanks."

Anna returned to her desk as Langton went into Mike's office. They were there for quite a while. Meanwhile, the incident room was quiet, as the officers had no new evidence and still no identification on their victim. Both Jean and Barbara had been working through all the Mispers on file but had no result.

Emerald Turk's address had been searched while Anna was at Barfield, but no suitcase had been found. Barolli had also started looking for any ex–police officers who might have known Margaret Potts, but his inquiries fell on stony ground. It was depressing; the case was grinding to a halt.

Barolli came up to Anna's desk and pulled at his tie. "I've been on to bailiff companies, but so far I've had no luck in tracing anyone who knew Potts or anyone who was an ex-copper. I dunno how far back I need to go in checking out retired Flying Squad guys, because they're usually the ones that take up security or bailiff work. Maybe we need to talk to Emerald Turk again."

Anna shrugged. They were grasping at straws, but to date, Emerald had been the most informative person with regard to the first victim.

"I don't know if she can be any more help, but I don't mind doing it," Anna said. She wished they at least had the victim's suitcase, and even better, her notebook with the license numbers.

Barolli ran a hand through his hair. It was hard to believe that they had no ID on two young beautiful girls and were still concentrating on Margaret Potts because they had little else to go on. Joan had been working on the possibility that they could identify their girl from dental records, but even though they were able to show on *Crimewatch* the two un-usual front-teeth implants, they had not received a single call.

Mike came out of his office and signaled to Anna for her to join him and Langton.

Langton was sitting behind Mike's desk, flicking through

reports. He looked up and smiled at Anna as she came in. She was slightly thrown, although he had promised that their relationship would be more relaxed. She sat down and waited for him to finish glancing through the reports. Eventually, he let out a long sigh. "Not good, is it?" he said.

She knew he was referring to their inquiry, and she nodded.

"We have nothing, which is worrying," he went on. "Pity the team didn't get Potts's suitcase—even better, the bloody notebook with the license-plate numbers. That'd have been really helpful." He smiled at her again, and she started to find it unnerving. "Shame you didn't question Emerald Turk first time round and not that impatient bugger Barolli. Knowing you, I doubt you'd have let it slip past you."

She was even more puzzled and glanced at Mike Lewis, who was leaning against the wall, his hands stuffed into his pockets.

"Maybe not," she said.

Langton stretched back in his chair and puffed out his breath. "I've got a lot of cases I'm overseeing, but this one causes me the most concern. Three dead women estimated to have all been killed by the same perpetrator—and from the MOs, it's maybe more than estimated—but nevertheless, we have no leads connecting each victim. Hard to, when two remain unidentified. All we know for sure is that Potts was earning her keep shagging punters from the service stations, but whether or not the other two girls were also on the game . . ." He shrugged. "Then we have this creep Cameron Welsh. Now, if he is tugging our strings out of a misguided ego trip and he just wants to prove something to himself, do we dismiss him out of hand? What if he does have information? What if he could, as he said, get into the mind of our killer?"

"I very much doubt that," Anna said, but she sensed what was coming and wouldn't look at Langton.

"We have to go back," Langton said, "and this time I will allow him to look at the postmortem report and—"

"You may be right, but I hope you don't want *me* to go and see him again."

"Sorry, but I do. He wants to interact with you. In Barolli's report, he said Cameron turned his chair away from him so he wouldn't have to look at him, and directed his entire conversation to you."

"Well, yes, he did, but I'm female, and I think he just wants to get his rocks off having me there."

"Fancies you, does he?"

She was getting angry. "I wouldn't know what that sick twisted creep felt about me, but I would prefer it if someone else went to talk to him."

Langton stood up. "I'll tell you what we'll do: you go and visit him again and see what he comes up with. If you are unable to deal with it, then we'll arrange for one of the others to be with him."

"It's not a question of me being unable to deal with it. I just feel uncomfortable and would prefer not to be the one to interview him again."

"You won't be alone; Barolli will accompany you. I've already arranged it with the governor."

Anna stood up. "So I don't have an option?"

"Afraid not. Drive up there first thing in the morning. That's all. Thank you."

Anna wanted to slam the door of the office, but instead, she walked out with her hands clenched, trying to control her temper. In the incident room, she told Barolli they were on another scheduled visit to Cameron Welsh, and he swore.

"It's a bloody waste of time, didn't you tell Langton that?"

"Why don't *you* tell him?" Anna snapped, then added that perhaps he shouldn't, as Langton didn't like the fact that he hadn't found the suitcase belonging to Margaret Potts.

Barolli was still bad-tempered when Anna collected him the following morning. He remained silent for a long time, obviously furious at having to take the long journey again and the fact that he had let himself and the team down by not interviewing Emerald Turk well enough. The team still had no result in tracing the ex–police officers who were used by Margaret Potts to get back at the men who had beaten her up. The consensus was that even if they did trace them, they doubted it would progress their case. Langton, however, had insisted they continue in case one of the men picked up by Potts was their killer.

Anna and Barolli arrived at the prison and went through the same lengthy procedure. This time they did not meet with the governor, as he was unavailable. There were four different officers working inside the secure unit, and they were concerned that the three other men held there didn't like being locked up in their cells to allow Cameron to speak to his visitors.

Welsh was sitting in the same position behind the bars in his cell, with his hair tied back in a ponytail. He was as immaculate as ever and again offered them still or sparkling water. Both refused, keen to get on with it and to leave as soon as possible. Welsh seemed to detect that Anna did not wish to speak to him. She sat, lips pursed, as Barolli passed through the bars a copy of the first file from the pathologist. This contained on-site photographs of the victims and detailed reports from the postmortems.

This time Welsh acknowledged Barolli, smiling and thanking him for the file. He edged his chair around to his desk and sat looking intently at each photograph. He made copious notes, and Anna became impatient, glancing at Barolli, who lifted his eyes to the ceiling. On this occasion, they heard the odd catcall from the other inmates, jeering and shouting abusive remarks about Welsh being a squeeler, but Welsh ignored them, as did Anna and Barolli.

Barolli glanced at his watch. Without looking up, Welsh said quietly that he was sorry for keeping them waiting, but he wished to make a thorough investigation if he was to assist them. He placed to one side the first file and requested the forensic reports. Yet again he spent ages on every page and made many notes. Anna forced herself to calm down and use the time to observe Cameron from her position outside his cell.

First she looked over the hundreds of books, noting that they were all in alphabetical order as well as arranged by size. There were many psychology, forensic, and medical manuals, and numerous volumes of true-life crime, legal textbooks, and court trials. She could see no modern novels, but two shelves contained classics, and these were alongside well-known playwrights—Ibsen, Chekhov, Shakespeare—and some of the book covers appeared to be old, perhaps secondhand, bought online or possibly from specialist journals. She paid attention to the shampoos and lotions, expensive ones, the conditioners and facial creams and suncreams and fake tanning lotions. His toothpaste was a whitener with bleach, and he had an old-fashioned boracic-powder tin. His battery toothbrushes were lined up like soldiers, as were his battery shavers and various aftershave lotions.

Barolli yawned loudly, and Welsh looked up, then returned to his notebook. He picked up a battery sharpener and started sharpening his pencils.

"Your killer is obviously working on long-haul drives for some kind of trucking company. The times of the murders are important. He is a night driver, as it is unlikely that any victim was killed in daylight."

"We are already covering that line of inquiry," Anna said sharply.

"Good. I thought you would be. Are you focusing on the tarts who hang out at the motorway service stations?"

"Of course."

"I hope you've put up warning notices. These girls are like wasps—swat them away, but back they come, and I think . . ." He tapped his whitened teeth with the eraser on the end of his pencil. "I think he's killed more than these three girls. Oh yes. This man has been busy for a long time."

"Please pass the files back," Barolli said.

Cameron reluctantly collected up all the papers and photographs. "I'd like to keep them," he said.

"I'm afraid that won't be possible," Anna told him.

"Pity. I need more time with them." Welsh handed the files to Barolli, ignoring Anna. "Can't you get permission from DCS Langton?"

"No."

"You can go, then. What I will begin working on until your next visit is the routes, and I will have more details for you after that."

Anna had her hand resting on the bars, waiting as Barolli

replaced the files in his briefcase. It was only a fleeting touch as Cameron trailed his fingers across hers, but it sent shock waves through her.

"Sorry," he said, smiling.

Anna wanted to tell him in no uncertain terms that no way would she be returning to see him! She was even more sure it was a waste of time, since he had told them nothing new or added anything of any value to their case. All it had done was give him the sick pleasure of gloating over the pictures of the victims.

Driving back, Anna and Barolli got into a heated argument, as he felt they had gained useful information.

"Like what?" Anna demanded.

"For one, that there could be other victims, so we check back into cold cases; and second, he was right on the button for checking out long-distance lorry drivers; and third, that they would be working nights."

Anna angrily retorted that they were, in case he hadn't noticed, already doing exactly that, and Welsh had given them nothing new whatsoever.

"Okay, but you tell me how he knitted it all together—from what? Newspaper coverage? He may have even watched *Crimewatch,* but he was, to my mind, quite informative."

Anna decided not to get into any further arguments with Barolli, who had started to annoy her. She was glad that he slept for the rest of the return journey.

Anna had just finished writing up the report of the meeting when Barbara tapped her on the shoulder to say there was a call for her from Cameron Welsh.

"Let Barolli take it—say I am not available," she said crossly, but Barbara explained that Cameron had insisted he speak to her directly.

"Tough. Just who does he think he is? Please, Barbara, tell him I am not available, and if he has anything to say, let him talk to Barolli. I refuse to speak to him."

Anna waited, watching as Barolli took the call. He said little, making notes and recording their conversation. When he replaced the phone, he turned to Anna. "Listen to this."

"I'm all ears," she said tetchily.

Cameron Welsh didn't like the fact that Anna had not taken his call, since, as he had said to Barolli, he was attempting to fast-track her career. Barolli had laughed and joked that perhaps Cameron could fast-track *his,* and it appeared to amuse the man, because he went on to discuss his theories at length. He suggested that the murder team should focus their inquiries on companies that delivered into, not out of, London. This was due to the fact that the victims were discovered near motorway service stations that had a drive-over or bridge from one side of the M1 to the other. So their killer, he estimated, would pick up his target from the services *before* the one nearest to where the victim was discovered, not the one closest, which he believed the police were currently focusing on.

Anna was tapping her foot with impatience.

"He said he'd have more details when he'd finished working on his profile of the killer," Barolli went on, "and would require us to visit again."

"This is preposterous! As if we haven't considered that possibility, even more so as we know that Margaret Potts picked up her clients and then returned via—"

Barolli interrupted her. "Yeah, yeah, I know, but we've not considered that he picked them up on his way *into* London."

"Because we've concentrated on where the bodies were found, not on the other side of the motorway heading into London."

"But what if he was delivering into London and picked up the girls then? He could hold them in his vehicle, then dump them when he was leaving. Bodies could have been held by him for days."

Anna sighed, still not in any way impressed. "Fine, go along with it, and rope in more officers to make further inquiries, but I sincerely believe he is bullshitting us."

Barolli didn't, and he went in to talk to Mike Lewis about the phone call. Mike listened and was almost as doubtful as Anna, but Barolli was insistent that, given time, Welsh could bring them something. He informed Lewis that Welsh had requested another opportunity to look over their files.

"Tell you what, Paul, bring up the old files on Cameron Welsh and look at Travis's connection to him, and then we'll talk to Langton and see what he thinks we should do."

Mike Lewis and Barolli went over the arrest and inter-rogation of Cameron Welsh.

"Jesus, he was a sadistic bastard. No wonder Travis doesn't like having to confront him. Maybe she's right. This could all be a ploy done to give him some perverse satisfaction." Mike sighed.

"I don't agree. I think he has given us some informative material, and you have to understand that he's not kept the files—so what if he does know a lot more and is stringing us along?"

Mike was still uncertain but eventually agreed to in-stigate further inquiries focusing on trucking companies delivering into London on a regular basis.

Due to the massive stack of information that resulted, the team was inundated. Mike had a meeting with Langton, who was as dismissive of Cameron's input as Anna, until the thought occurred to him that Cameron's psychobabble about getting into the mind of the killer might also be a cover-up.

"Could Welsh have had an interaction with another prisoner, one who was released and fitted the time frame?" Langton wondered.

"Well, we got a list of prisoners, but according to the governor, Welsh is a real loner and never shared his cell," Mike pointed out.

"Maybe, but what about when he was held before his trial? It would mean a lot of digging back, but as we've still got no identification on two victims, we're gonna have to get out the spades."

Anna had not spoken to Langton, but she knew he had been discussing the latest visit to Barfield with Mike Lewis, and when they had the next briefing, she was certain he was going along with the idea that Welsh had information. She sat at her desk listening as Mike told them he wanted a check on all the inmates and prisoners held with Welsh before his trial who could possibly have had a conversation with him.

"We're grasping at straws here, but we have to look at the possibility that someone may have admitted to Welsh that he was the killer and that he got away with it. This prisoner would have had to be released for the time frame of the murders, so it does at least cut down a lengthy elimination process."

With the paperwork piling up from the new lines of

inquiry, the team was kept busy, and they had yet to identify the two victims. Knowing that Anna was not happy about the focus on Cameron Welsh, Mike asked her to come into his office.

"Listen, I know how you feel about this, Anna, but stay with it. We have to work together."

"Fine, but do you mind if I focus on Margaret Potts?" Anna didn't want to be uncooperative, but she could barely contain her exasperation. "I don't think we have covered the only identified victim's background. I want to go back to Emerald Turk, and I still think we should continue trying to trace the guys she used to help her out when she was knocked around."

"Okay by me, and we'll keep our heads down trying to come up with a possible connection from inside the prison," said Mike, knowing that he had to keep working on all the possibilities.

Anna sifted through the previous records of Margaret Potts. On file they had three arrests for prostitution, and backtracking through the court appearances, Anna saw that one of the fines had been paid by a Stanley Potts. They knew she had been married, and that she had two children taken into foster care, but they had never interviewed anyone save Emerald Turk. Anna went over the list of prostitutes who had been arrested alongside Potts and could know more about her, and she checked to see if any of them had ever worked service stations. It was painstaking work, and she knew it could well prove to be not worth the effort.

To track down Stanley Potts took almost the entire afternoon. He had been in Parkhurst Prison when Margaret's body was discovered and had refused to be interviewed. He had subsequently stayed in numerous hostels and halfway houses, moving around almost as much as Emerald Turk. But at last Anna got a recent address from a probation officer who, although no longer in contact with Stanley, recalled him moving into shared accommodation with two other ex-prisoners.

It was late in the afternoon by the time Anna left the station.

The shared accommodation was a run-down semi-detached in Camden Town. The three-story house had been divided into four flats, and Stanley Potts was listed on the bell at the front door in flat 2. There were other names scribbled beneath his, and it looked as if numerous people had lived or were living in flat 2. When Anna rang the bell, it took a fair while before she heard footsteps. Finally, the door opened a few inches.

"Good afternoon. I am Detective Travis, and I am looking for a Stanley Potts—I believe he lives here?"

"Yes."

"Is he here now?"

"Yes, it's me."

Anna showed him her ID. "I would really appreciate you talking to me, as I am on the team investigating Margaret Potts's murder."

"Can't help you, love. I was in prison and hadn't seen her for years before that."

"Yes, I know. This would be just for me to get an insight into her background. You were married?"

"I just told you, I got nothin' to say. I'd not set eyes on her for years."

"Could we just talk? I won't take up much of your time.

It's just that there are a few things you might be able to help me with," Anna persisted.

"Like what?"

"Well, her friends . . ."

"I don't know any of them."

"Please, Mr. Potts, could we do this now, because I don't want to have to ask you to come into the station."

The door opened a fraction more, and Anna could get a look at him. The man before her didn't resemble the mug shot from the files. He was square-faced and unshaven, with thick, gray-flecked curly hair, and it looked as if he had speckles of paint in it, with even more specks over his dirty shirt.

Stanley was about five-eight, solid with a beer belly, and his trousers were held up by a broad leather belt. He had on old worn carpet slippers with no socks, and there were more signs of paint splashes on his dirty trousers.

Anna followed Stanley down a dimly lit hall with bicycles chained up along the wall, alongside an old-fashioned Hoover.

"In 'ere," he said as he reached a door.

The room was dark, with an old horsehair sofa and chair and a threadbare carpet. On a coffee table were the racing papers, cans of beer, and overflowing ashtrays; stacks of newspapers lay on every available surface. The room smelled of beer, stale tobacco, and curry.

"You want to sit down?" He gestured to the armchair and sat in the center of the sofa. "Not found who done it, then?" he added.

"Sadly, no, we haven't."

He lit a cigarette, his fat fingers nicotine-stained and with black nails.

"You were married to Margaret?"

He nodded.

"Can you recall anyone who might be able to help me get to know her?"

"No. The prison governor told me she'd been bumped off. I read about it in the papers as well." He didn't sound particularly sad.

"During your time together, surely you must have met some of her friends, or someone she was close to and would have remained friendly with after you separated?" Anna suggested.

"No. What she did was her own business. She was useless. My kids were always filthy, and she never cooked, gave 'em Kentucky Fried Chicken morning, noon, and night. They was out of control—that's why I kicked her out, then my kids got taken away. Best thing for 'em, 'cause she was no bloody good with them, and I was workin', so I never knew they weren't going to school."

"Did you know Emerald Turk?"

"No."

"Anyone you can think of that might be able to help me?"

"Nope."

"Do you still keep in touch with your children?"

"No."

"What about men your wife might have known?"

"She knew a lot, but I wouldn't call 'em friends. She was a tart," said Stanley matter-of-factly.

"I am especially interested in men she might have used to help her get her own back on a punter who didn't pay. A couple of times she was beaten up, so she needed some help—you know, to pay them back."

Stanley shook his head. The ash from his cigarette drooped to over an inch long. "Listen, love, me and Maggie parted ways and not on friendly terms. I was glad to see the back of her."

"But you had feelings for her once. You paid a fine when she was in court for prostitution."

He frowned and sucked in a lungful of smoke, then flicked off the ash onto the carpet. "Maybe I did—don't remember. That'd be some time ago, and it could've been me brother. He might have helped her out, but not me."

"Your brother?" asked Anna with interest.

"Yeah. He used to have a thing with her."

"Would he have given your name to the court? It was a five-hundred-pound fine."

"She probably paid him in kind, if you know what I mean."

"Do you have his address?"

"No. We don't get on—it's obvious why. He's a bastard, and he never helped me out. I've not seen him for more than five or six years."

"What work does he do?"

"Works for a bailiff company, or he did. Like I said, I've not seen him. He was shagging her, though, like every man that come into the house."

"What's his name?"

"Eric."

Anna stood up, eager to get away from the cigarette smoke and the stench of the flat. Stanley looked up at her and then jerked a thumb at a sideboard. It was hard to see anything for old newspapers and used food cartons. He shuffled over to it, throwing papers aside, opening drawers.

"Hang on a minute . . . I was wonderin', was there anythin' of value found after she was murdered?"

"Value—like what?"

"She had some nice jewelry. She got me mother's

diamond engagement ring, and by rights I should have it back, unless she sold it. Knowing her, she'd take the pennies off a dead man's eyes, but it was a nice stone worth a bob or two, and I gave her a gold bracelet that cost me a few quid."

"There was nothing. She didn't have her own place when she was killed, but I think she left a suitcase with some contents, so I'll make inquiries for you."

Stanley opened a drawer and rooted through it, bringing out a dog-eared brown envelope. "You can have this—I got no use for it. It's her birth certificate and crap."

He passed Anna the envelope, but she didn't open it.

"Thank you for seeing me, Mr. Potts," she said as sincerely as she could.

In reply, he plonked himself back down on the sofa, not bothering to show her out.

In her car, Anna opened the envelope. There was, as he had said, a tattered birth certificate, along with a few old photographs. Some were stained and creased. There were pictures of Margaret aged about seventeen, others of her holding two small toddlers. There was also a Valentine's card. Anna was surprised by the scrawled writing and the flowery verse that said how deep their love was. It was signed, *Loving you with all my heart, Stan.*

Later that evening, Anna sat eating her supper at her kitchen table, looking at the contents of the envelope, the faded photographs especially. Her kitchen was compact, with a small breakfast bar and a more comfortable high stool than the one she had sat on at Emerald's. She used her microwave oven more than her new gas one, and her fridge was small, fitted with a freezer compartment on the top. She'd made an omelette with salad and had stuck a list of groceries to the fridge door with a magnet. Her fitted cupboards had mostly tins of tomato soup inside. She was out of milk so had her coffee black.

She finished eating and placed her dirty dishes in the sink, washing them up before returning to look over the photographs. It was hard not to feel saddened by the knowledge of what had happened to these people. In one photograph, a young Stanley Potts stood with his hand resting on his wife's shoulder. Her face had been scribbled over, perhaps by one of her children. Anna replaced everything in the envelope to take into the incident room the following morning. She was eager to get the team tracing Eric Potts; it was too much of a coincidence that he worked for a bailiff company. Perhaps this was the man to whom Margaret had turned when she needed help. He might also have contact with the ex–police officers. It could be the lead they so badly needed, at last.

After taking a shower, she checked her laundry basket, adding to the note on the fridge door that she had to remember to take in her laundry and collect the fresh sheets in the morning.

Anna had not been living in her flat that long, yet long enough to have made some kind of effort to make it less austere, but it never seemed to be a priority. There was the photograph of her beloved father by her bedside, and her dressing table contained a neat row of cosmetics and perfumes, but Anna even put her hairbrushes and combs in a drawer. In some ways the neatness was a comfort; it wasn't obsessive, because when a case occupied her day and night, the laundry basket overflowed and she did leave clothes on the back of her dressing-table chair and the floor. Her lack of interest in any culinary attempts made her slack on her food shopping. The stations' canteens were good enough.

The one luxury she always made an effort with was pristine laundered cotton sheets and white duvet covers, with a matching white pillow; she also had numerous white cotton nightdresses. She delighted in slipping between the chilled, sweet-smelling sheets, and on this night, having felt she had made some breakthrough in the case, she fell into a deep sleep almost as soon as her head hit the pillow.

First thing in the morning, Anna set the wheels in motion at the station to trace Eric Potts, before she headed out to visit Emerald Turk again. It was a gray day; dark clouds were gathering, and heavy rain had been forecast. As she parked a short distance from the high-rise block, she saw Emerald herself carrying two carrier bags filled with groceries, heading straight toward her.

"Morning."

Emerald stopped and stared at her, then continued walking toward the entrance. Anna followed, making her way up the filthy stairs and along the corridor to Emerald's front door.

"What you doin' here?" the woman said aggressively.

"Hoping to see you."

"Well, now you have." Emerald opened her front door and tried to shut it again at once.

"Please don't," Anna said. "I just want to talk to you. I can do it here or down at the station—it's up to you."

"What do you want now, for chrissakes! This is fuckin' harassment."

"Let me in, please."

In total contrast to the previous visit, the kitchen was a mess. Dirty crockery was stacked in the sink, and there were numerous empty wine bottles lined up on the floor, with more dirty glasses on the draining board. Emerald took off her raincoat and chucked it aside. Beneath it, she was wearing jeans and a T-shirt with flip-flops.

"Have a party last night, did you?" Anna asked.

"What's it to you? It was me bloke's birthday, if you must know. And I've got a fucking terrible hangover."

"Do you know Eric Potts?"

"Who?" Emerald massaged her brow.

"Eric Potts. He's Margaret's brother-in-law."

"No. Never heard of him, but if he's anything like that fat slob of a husband of hers, I wouldn't go near him with a bargepole."

"So you knew Stanley?" Anna asked, recognizing the description.

"No, I never knew him, but he used to beat the shit out of Maggie. She told me what he'd done to her for years, and she got the hell out because she reckoned that one day he would kill her. She said he used to take all her money, spend it down the bookies, and she had to hide her hand-bag, as he'd nick her purse and take every penny so she couldn't feed her kids."

"She never mentioned Eric?"

"No."

"He was a good friend—paid her fine once."

"Well, maybe that was before I knew her."

"Did you know her children were taken into care?"

"Yeah, I knew that. She used to cry about them but reckoned that they were better off without bein' around her husband. When he was drunk, he'd knock them about as well as her."

Emerald walked out of the kitchen. She snapped that if it wasn't a problem, she was going to the toilet. Anna cleared a space around the breakfast bar, moving a stack of dirty children's clothes and dropping them onto the overflowing laundry basket. She waited, heard the toilet flushing, and then Emerald returned.

"This suitcase—" Anna began.

"For chrissakes, your mob came looking for it yesterday! I told you I've not got it, is that why you're back here? Didn't you believe me? I've not got Maggie's fucking suitcase."

"Her husband reckons that it might have had some jewelry in it, specifically a diamond ring."

"There was nuffink in it but shit, I told you. I never found no diamond rings, and if he's saying they was in the suitcase, he's a lying bastard. Christ, she didn't even have a room of her own; she had fuck-all, and if it wasn't for me, she'd have been sleeping rough on the street."

"Who else used to put her up besides you?"

"I dunno. She used to just turn up and ask to doss down wiv me. I've told you all this, I told you last time you was here."

"The last time I was here, you brought up the fact that Margaret used to keep a record of the men she'd picked up," Anna reminded her.

"Yeah, I told you that she'd get the numbers off their vehicles."

"You said that she had friends, ex-coppers who could trace the addresses of those who ripped her off or hurt her."

"Yeah, but who they were, I dunno. I got no interest in hirin' heavies to look after me, 'cause I got a bloke, and I don't do service stations, all right?"

"You never heard her talk of her brother-in-law, Eric Potts?"

"No, and I never met her prick of a husband, either. All I know is what she told me about him."

"This notebook—are you sure you didn't find it?" Anna pressed her.

"Fuck me, I told you I've not seen it! For chrissakes, why would I lie about somefink like that? It don't make sense."

"You didn't find any jewelry in Margaret's suitcase?"

"No, I fucking didn't!"

Emerald was getting so angry her face was red, and she kept waving her hands around. Anna decided not to push it any further. Emerald hurled items out of the laundry basket until she found the tracksuit jacket, snatching it up and almost shoving it into Anna's face.

"I got this, this T-shirt I'm wearin', and some other gear, and that was all. And I don't like you accusin' me of lying, so why don't you get the fuck out of here. Go on—GET OUT!"

Anna apologized as she headed down the hallway. "Thank you for seeing me. I wasn't implying that you had done anything illegal."

The front door was slammed after her, and she heard the chain link being put into place.

Alone, Emerald felt as if she was having a panic attack. She couldn't get her breath. As she went into the kitchen to pour herself a glass of water, she had to sit on one of her stools to calm down. She was still holding on to the tracksuit top and was about to toss it aside when she felt for the book. It had been left inside the pocket since Anna had last been there, and she took it out, swearing to herself. It could have easily dropped to the floor during the interview, but then if it had, she'd have made up some excuse that she hadn't even known it was there. Yet she did know, and she was scared that she'd lied. But it still didn't make her want to do the honorable thing. Instead, she threw it into the bin.

"Fucking coppers. Bastards."

Anna had just reached her car when she got a call from Barbara in the incident room. They had traced an Eric Potts. He worked for a bailiff's company with offices in Hendon. Whether or not it was Margaret's brother-in-law, they were unable to confirm, as he was out on a job and wouldn't be back in the office until lunchtime. Anna had been pondering whether to return to the station but now decided she'd have an early lunch and make her way over to meet with Eric.

Back at the station, the team continued slogging through the list of ex-prisoners, placing to one side possible suspects who might have had information for Cameron Welsh. The officers questioning everyone at the service stations were having no luck, with no one able to recall their redheaded victim. Barbara received yet another call from Cameron Welsh. He said he wished to speak to DI Travis, but when told she was not in the station, he said he would speak with Paul.

"Paul, your friend Cameron's on the line!"

Barolli took the call, but this time Cameron was distinctly unfriendly and quite cold about DI Travis not taking his calls.

"She's out working, Mr. Welsh, so if you have anything to say, please go ahead. I'm all ears."

"I have more details I wish to discuss with you and Anna, but I find the cell door being closed very constricting. I want you to get permission for us to sit outside in the recreational area."

"That may not be possible."

"Then I won't see you. Pass on my message to Anna." The phone went down, and Barolli tutted.

"He's really pushing himself, cheeky bastard." He turned to see Langton standing by the incident-room board, which unnerved him slightly.

"What did he have to say for himself?" Langton asked, turning to face Barolli.

"Claims to have more information but wants us to talk without the bars."

"Ignore him. Let's see how long it'll be before he calls again."

"He was peeved that Travis wasn't here to talk to him."

"Really. Well, if this is all down to him having the hots for her, he can go and stuff himself. Where is she?" Langton demanded.

Barbara signaled to him. "She may have got a trace on a relative of our first victim, Margaret Potts. He works for a bailiff company and could be the person Maggie Potts used to track down punters who knocked her around."

"Where did Anna get him from?"

"She traced Potts's husband—it came via him."

Langton threw a cool look at Barolli, who squirmed in his seat.

"Got to hand it to her," the detective said sheepishly. "Always busy, busy . . ."

When Langton moved off to Mike's office, Barolli turned to Barbara and asked in a different voice, "When did all this go down?"

"About an hour ago. She'll be on her way to interview this brother-in-law. You never know, he might have some information we could use. Nothing else is happening, is it?"

Barolli pursed his lips. Yet again Anna had trampled over

him, and he knew that if she was able to get this information now, he should have been able to find it months ago.

The office was above a fish-and-chip shop. The name of the company appeared to be Debt Collectors, with no other sign—just a small arrow in red felt-tipped pen on the card stuck to the door. Anna climbed up a narrow staircase, where the pungent smell of fried food hung in the air. From outward appearances, at least, the business didn't look as if it were exactly flourishing.

At the top of the second staircase, a makeshift partition with a frosted-glass door had been built across the landing. Anna rang the bell, and the door was opened by a thin-faced woman in her late fifties with iron-gray hair and a matching suit.

"Yes?"

Anna showed her ID, and the woman stepped back.

"Come in."

The small reception area was cramped. A desk and two chairs and a large old-fashioned filing cabinet were all that could fit into the small space. Two doors led off from the reception, and Anna was politely asked to sit, and the woman introduced herself as Mrs. Kelly.

"I am a sort of general dogsbody. We have two offices, and my husband owns the company. We're unusually busy right now, with a lot of people wanting their debts sorted. It's strange, isn't it? Bad times for some and good for others."

"Is Mr. Potts in?"

"Not yet, but he's due any moment. He's training two new employees, and they were out early, but I told someone who called wanting to get particulars from him . . ."

"That would have been from my station." Anna passed her card to Mrs. Kelly.

"Yes. I said he was expected back at lunchtime, but sometimes there may be a problem that needs sorting. My husband is in his office, if you'd like to talk to him."

"I would, yes, but can you tell me a little about Mr. Potts first?"

"Ask my husband. I'll just tell him you are here." The woman glanced at the card Anna had passed to her and crossed a few paces to knock on one of the office doors. She gave a small smile. "One moment."

Mrs. Kelly was fast, darting into the office before Anna could say anything. She came out almost as quickly and held the door ajar. "Ron will see you, Detective Travis."

Ron Kelly was a short, squat man with a pair of wide red braces and checked trousers. The thick leather belt around his waist looked as if it held his girth in too tightly. His desk was filled with files and trays overflowing with papers. A computer took up most of the rest of the space on his desk. In here, the smell from the fish-and-chip shop was overpowering.

"Sit down, love, I'm Ronald Kelly." He was pompous, and when he stood to shake Anna's hand, he seemed no taller than when he was sitting behind his desk.

"Let me just say that Eric's one of my most trusted employees," he went on immediately. "He's been with me for nearly eight years, so you won't hear me say a word against him. Lovely bloke, he is—do anything for you, *and* he's good at his job."

"I actually wanted to talk to him about his sister-in-law, Margaret Potts."

Kelly looked confused.

"Margaret Potts was murdered, and I am investigating her death," Anna explained. "I would just like to ask Mr. Potts some questions about whether he knew her well and could perhaps help me trace some of her friends. I was given Eric's name by his brother, Stanley."

"I don't know anything about the poor woman, but I know of the brother. I've not actually met him, but he's a bad lot, by all accounts. I'm certain Eric has nothing to do with him. In fact, I've not heard him mention his name for a long time. He was in prison, wasn't he?"

"Yes, he was."

"So this poor woman was his wife?"

"Yes."

"Eric's not said anything to me about her, but then, he's a private sort. We don't mix socially, and he's not in the office that much. Most of his work is out on the road, see."

"What work did he do before he came to your company?"

"Army. He'd done twenty years' service. I've been looking for his CV, but to be honest, after so many years working here, I couldn't tell you where it is. I'll get the wife to try and dig it out; she handles most of the paperwork."

"Thank you, but I doubt it will be necessary. Do you employ a lot of ex–army officers?"

"Yes and no. Got a couple on the books along with ex-coppers, but not all of them are regulars like Eric. I bring them in when I'm overloaded. Funnily enough, right now we've got a shedload of work on. Eric's out with two guys this morning, showing them the ropes. There's a lot of outstanding debts at the moment, with nonpayment of rent a big problem."

At that moment, Mrs. Kelly tapped on the door and popped her head round to say that Eric had returned and was in his office.

Anna stood up. There was nothing more she could gain from Mr. Kelly, but as she walked to the door, she paused.

"The ex–police officers you employ—I'd appreciate you giving me their details before I leave. Thank you."

Eric Potts bore no resemblance to his brother, Stanley. He was six feet tall and muscular, with sloping shoulders, a man who obviously did weight training. He was wearing a charcoal-gray suit and a white shirt and a smart tie, and his handshake was strong. He offered Anna a cup of coffee, which she declined. He had a flask in front of him and a mug, along with a sandwich. Unlike his boss's desk his desk was devoid of anything else, and the office was much smaller. The window behind him had a broken blind and looked as if it had not been washed for years. The other odd thing about his office was that it smelled of room spray—or it could have been his cologne; whatever, it was strong and obliterated the smell wafting up from the fish-and-chip shop.

"Your boss speaks highly of you," Anna said pleasantly, taking a seat in front of him.

"Well, so he should," Potts replied. "I've worked for him for eight years, and I don't think he's lifted his butt off his office chair once in all that time." He grinned to reveal very white teeth; he was really quite a handsome man. His hands were large, and the knuckles looked like those of a boxer's. In fact, a slightly crooked nose gave him the look of one.

"I met your brother," Anna said quietly.

"Stanley," he said as softly. He sighed, shaking his head. "One of life's losers, I'm afraid. Never held a job, and if he did any work, it'd be down the betting shop. He was addicted to gambling and drinking—and he and I fell out years ago."

"You knew his wife."

"Margaret. Yes, I did. I know what happened to her, but the sad thing was, no matter how many times you'd try and tell her to stop what she was doing, she just wouldn't listen."

"You knew she was a prostitute?"

"Yes."

"So you kept in touch with her after she left your brother?"

"Yes. Not on a regular basis, though. Years could pass and I'd not hear from her, then she'd turn up."

"At your home?" asked Anna.

"Yes. Usually when she was broke or needing a place to stay for a while. It caused problems with my wife, as they didn't get along; plus, I've got two kids, and often she'd be the worse for wear on drink or drugs, so eventually, I had to put a stop to her coming round."

"Did you still see her?"

"A couple of times she'd call me and I'd meet her in a café, but I hadn't seen her for almost a year before I read about her being murdered." Unlike his brother, Eric appeared genuinely upset talking about it.

"No one ever approached you to ask about her?"

"No. Why should they? Like I said, I hadn't seen top nor tail of her for more than a year. Last time we met, I gave her some money. I said to her it'd be the last and that I couldn't go on shelling out to her, as I had my own commitments, and I warned her again that she could end up in a bad way doing what she was doing."

"What exactly did you think she was doing?"

"Come on, love." Eric gave Anna a weary look. "She was a tart and getting on in years—not that she didn't try and keep herself looking good. She did, and when she was young, she was a real looker. How she got involved with my brother was always beyond me. You know about him, do you?"

"I know he spent time in prison."

"Not that. The way he knocked her around and he mistreated their kids. He was a useless husband and father. When she left him, her kids were taken into care, thank Christ, but she herself had taken enough."

"Did she run to you?"

"Me? No way! I was married, remember? She took off with some other tosser who put her on the streets." Eric wiped a hand across his face. "You couldn't say anything to her about him or about what he was making her do. She was, to my mind, caught in a vicious circle, beaten up by her husband and then knocked about by this creep. Got what he deserved in the end, though—died of a drug overdose."

"Stanley implied that you and Margaret were lovers. In fact, he blamed you for breaking up his marriage."

Eric changed color. Opening one of his desk drawers, he took out a small bottle of brandy, removed the top, and poured two measures from the lid into his mug. He gave a rueful smile and replaced the bottle. "That idiot accused everyone of screwing her—me, his neighbors, Uncle Tom Cobleigh. But she was a decent girl, and whether or not we had a bit of thing is neither here nor there. I cared about her, I always did, and that's why she felt she could come to me when she was in trouble."

"Did you know she was working the service stations?"

He nodded.

"And do you know how she would travel to them? I presume she didn't have a car."

He shrugged. "I think she'd catch a lift, maybe, but I couldn't say for sure, 'cause by the time she was ducking and diving with the bloody truckers, I'd given up trying to help her. All I know is she'd pull in the blokes at the service stations, do whatever to earn a few quid, then come back by morning."

"But you did help her, didn't you?"

"I said I gave her a few quid now and then, yeah."

"No other ways? I know Margaret kept a logbook of her punters' car and lorry registrations, and if they didn't pay her or knocked her around, she'd get help in tracing them."

"I don't want to get into this." He put his big hands up.

"Mr. Potts, Margaret's body was found dumped in a field beside the M1 motorway. She'd been raped and strangled. There was no handbag, nothing to identify her but her fingerprints from police records. We have no suspect and no witnesses—but what if one of the men she was able to get revenge on killed her? If you know anything about any of the men she picked up, it won't get you into any trouble, but we would like to question them as possible suspects."

He leaned back in his chair. "Look, a couple of mates— ex-coppers—helped out, and yeah, we did pay the blokes a visit, but not for a long time. Like I said to you, I'd not been in contact with Maggie for a year or more before she was murdered."

"Do you still have the information?"

"No. Got rid of it as soon as it was done."

"What about friends of Margaret's? Do you know any- one I could talk to that she knew well?" Anna wasn't going to give up.

"No. Listen, I might sound like a right dickhead, but you can only go so far with someone, know what I mean? She had her head kicked in, and the bloke threw her out of his cab. I got his company address from my pals, and I called on him. I gave him the same medicine he gave to Maggie, and he handed over fifty quid. I was having problems with the wife not wanting her staying on our couch, but she was a right mess—black eyes and a broken nose. I said to her that this time that was it: I wasn't gonna do it again, and she had to straighten out her life—go into a hostel, anything but stop living the way she was."

"She didn't want to report it?"

"No way, not with her record."

"So when she wasn't staying with you, where did she live?"

"Rough. There's a place she used in the West End—you know, book in for the night, or she crashed out with one or other of the other women she knew, but I didn't know where, and I never met any of her so-called friends. I say *so-called* because they were always nicking her things. Not that she had much, just bits of jewelry from my mother."

"Did you ever meet a woman called Emerald Turk?"

"No."

"Margaret had a suitcase. Did she bring it round to your place when she stayed?"

"Suitcase? Yeah, I think she had one, although she'd use the lockers at one or another station for most of her belongings. She never had much. Not that she didn't try and keep herself clean. When she stayed at my place, she was always in the bath and washing and ironing, another reason the wife didn't want her around."

It was totally unexpected: Eric suddenly put his hands over his face and wept. He then took out a handkerchief and wiped his eyes and blew his nose. "Fucking tragic life," he said shakily. "And don't think I haven't felt like shit sometimes, 'cause she didn't deserve to end up the way she did."

He opened the same drawer and rifled through it for a

moment. He brought out a small, cheap folding frame with two photographs inside it. He opened it and passed it to Anna. "That was Maggie when I first knew her."

The photograph was of such a pretty woman, smiling at the camera, wearing a white cotton dress and sitting on a park bench. In the opposite frame, facing her, was a picture of a young Eric in army uniform. "I loved her once," he said softly.

Anna returned to the incident room. With her she had the name of the company and driver that Eric had "seen to," and two names of ex–police officers who worked sporadically for Ronald Kelly. She doubted they would gain any vital information regarding Margaret Potts's killer, but what they might succeed in was getting a clear indication of exactly how she worked her stretch.

They still had two victims unidentified, so until they knew who the girls were, the team was concentrating on Margaret's murder for clues. They did not know if either of the young victims was a prostitute; all they had was that they were killed in the same way and possibly from thumbing a lift at a service station.

Writing up her report of the day's interviews, Anna was furious to be told by Mike Lewis that Langton had given the go-ahead for yet another prison visit to Cameron Welsh. She would have to drive all that way again with Barolli first thing in the morning, and the governor had agreed to allow them to interview Welsh out of his cell in the open section of the secure unit.

Anna passed to Joan and Barbara the ex–police officers' names and contact numbers, plus that of the lorry driver who had mistreated Margaret Potts. She suggested that one of the team get on it straightaway, adding sarcastically that it might just give them the lead they needed, rather than wasting time with Welsh.

It was after ten that evening when Langton rang Anna at home. He said he'd read her report and that her diligence, as always, had paid off. It would be an even better result if the ex-cops were able to give them the names of more punters Margaret Potts had been seeing; they could haul them in for questioning.

"The more insight we get into how she worked and from which service stations, the better, so I'll handle the talks with the cops. I'll be able to put the pressure on them . . ." He paused. "Are you listening?"

"Yes. I actually would have liked to talk to the lorry driver myself, but as I'll be schlepping all the way to Barfield Prison again . . ." Anna was tired and didn't bother hiding how she felt.

"Eh, eh, don't get uptight with me. I know you don't like it, but it's you he wants to talk to. I think if he has anything worth our while, you'll be the one to get it. That's the reason I want you back at the prison."

"You are more optimistic than I am. I personally think this is just feeding his grotesque ego."

"Maybe, but let's see how this visit pans out."

"Okay," she said flatly.

"Everything else all right with you?"

"Yes. Thank you for asking."

"Good night, then. Oh, I'm having another go at asking the public to help identify our Jane Does. We're running a slot on *Crimewatch* again."

"That's good. 'Night."

"'Night."

Anna replaced the receiver and got into bed, conscious

that the case was presently going nowhere, even with her added information. It would, she knew, open up if they could just identify their victims. As it was, the entire focus was on Margaret Potts's murder, a case that was virtually cold before she even came on board.

As she had felt on previous murder inquiries, the more she delved into a victim's past life, the more the character became visible, almost alive. Margaret Pott's life had been miserable. The thought of this woman with no place to live, carrying her worldly possessions around in a suitcase and sleeping in hostels and wherever she could get a bed for the day to make ready for the next night's hideous work, was unbearably depressing. The poor woman had lost her children and, Anna felt, was so worn out by abuse that even though she had been warned over and over again of the dangers, she continued risking the only real possession she had: her own life.

Chapter Four

The drive felt even longer, and Barolli yet again slept most of the way. They went through the same security searches, and this time the governor was present and had asked to see them in his office. He said he wasn't too happy about allowing them to interview Welsh in the communal area of the secure unit, and that the other prisoners held there were not to be locked in their cells. He explained that the other three had made vociferous complaints about being locked up to enable one prisoner to talk to the visitors, and it was a problem for him to show Welsh too many privileges.

"Do it for one, and everyone wants the same treatment. Right now the secure unit is running smoothly, and I don't want it disrupted. You have to understand that the men held there are not necessarily the worst offenders, but offenders we think are a risk if placed on a main wing of the prison. They have too much money, for one thing. A drug dealer inside is always a kingpin because of what he can arrange to be brought in; you would be amazed at what lengths they can go to in order to supply drugs inside the prison."

Barolli was surprised, asking if they were allowed money in the unit or even in the main prison.

"No. It's what contacts they have on the outside. Money

can buy deals, big bribes to pay for visitors to bring in their drugs, which are then passed on to whomever. The Mafia-connected prisoner has been with us for seven years, and he also has access to big money: we're concerned that he could engineer and fund escapes. It's not the cash they have inside that matters—it's what they have access to *outside.*"

"Cameron Welsh's cell is well equipped," Anna observed.

"He's another one. We do allow them to have their own computers, but these are monitored, and he insists on certain foods. To be honest, it's easier for us to let him order them in through the prison shop rather than have the extra people needed to cook for him. All deliveries are obviously carefully checked, and we have regular cell sweeps, more so in the secure unit, as the inmates there all have various electronic gadgets, from stereos to TVs, but again, everything is carefully monitored. Likewise the guards. We have a big turnaround so that no officer can get too close to an inmate or vice versa. And as I said, the prisoners in there have access to money, so we keep a watchful eye on the teams working alongside them."

Anna glanced at her watch. The governor seemed to wish to keep them in his office, while she just wanted to get the visit over with and drive back to London. Barolli, however, was listening intently and asking so many questions that Anna could have kicked him. Now they'd got on to a famous vicious serial killer and how much fan mail he received every month, let alone gifts and marriage proposals.

"I think we should see Mr. Welsh now," she interrupted as Barolli was asking about what kind of woman would want to be married to such a man.

"You'd be surprised," Hardwick told him, ignoring Anna's request, "but as I have said, we monitor everything that is sent in to them. There are children's toys sent into a pedophile, if you can believe it—sickens me, but they come in by the sackload. Teddy bears, little dolls." He shook his head. "We have a clearout every few months and pass them on to children's homes."

In the incident room, Langton, accompanied by Mike Lewis, had tracked down the ex–police officers. Mike was virtually silent throughout the interviews as he watched Langton work each man over, repeating that he wasn't there to get them into trouble with the law, even though he was aware they had broken it. All he wanted was the name of any person they had traced for Margaret Potts. They could either comply, or if not, he could get unpleasant, implying that as ex–police officers, they could go to prison for illegal use of classified information. He pointed out that it could have a chain reaction, as every person they had asked favors from, employed with the Met or working at DVLA, could lose their jobs.

By midmorning they had gained only four names and addresses, and these were not felt to be of much use, as they covered a period of six years. By midday the team had traced a lorry driver and a traveling salesman. Both had agreed to come in to the station to be questioned. The police were unsuccessful with the other two, as they no longer lived in England.

"I really think we should go to the secure unit," Anna interrupted Hardwick again, and this time she got her way. Two officers took them through the maze of corridors, out past the main prison exercise yard and into the secure unit. They went through security checks, as before, to reach the secure unit's recreational area. Four officers were present, reading newspapers, and they stood up to meet Anna and Barolli. They had arranged a table with one chair on one side and two on the other, near the exit into the unit's exercise area. They offered tea or coffee, but both declined, Anna eager to get on with the talk.

Anna sat beside Barolli, removing files, a notepad, and pencil from her briefcase. The guards did not return to reading their papers but stood at various points in the room.

"He obviously knows we're here," Anna said, irritated by the delay.

One of the guards positioned by the aisle leading to Cameron's cell announced that he was coming.

The prisoner strolled toward them.

"Good afternoon," Welsh said, smiling as if joining friends in a tearoom. He carried a notebook and loose foolscap pages. "I presume I sit here." He gestured to the vacant chair opposite Anna and Barolli.

Welsh was as perfectly groomed as before and this time wore his hair loose. It was thick and silky-looking, and he had a habit of tossing his head back and running his fingers through it to move it away from his face.

"Did you have a good trip up here?" he asked, sitting down and placing his notebook and papers in front of him, along with four sharpened pencils. These he laid out in a neat row. "There's not a lot in the papers about our case," he said, pointedly looking at Barolli and not at Anna. "All gone quiet, I suppose. Well, let's see what we can do about that. Have you any developments that I should know about?"

"We've been following your suggestions after our last visit," Barolli began.

Anna could barely stand it. Barolli appeared to be inflating Welsh's already enormous ego.

"Good. Now, what I've been doing is studying maps of the motorway and circuitous routes, specifically focusing on ones possibly used by your killer." Welsh laid out in front of him printed pages of maps, placing them side by side along the length of the table. "The red markings pinpoint the CCTV cameras."

"We are aware of these routes and their security cameras," Anna said coldly.

For the first time Welsh turned to look at her, but she held his gaze, and he turned back to pick up his notebook.

"It is imperative you discover how Margaret Potts traveled to the service stations. It's possible she knew her killer, had even *serviced* him before." He gave a soft laugh, amused by his wordplay, but as neither Barolli nor Anna reacted, he shrugged.

"Have you talked to any other women working the same way as your victim? They would certainly know her routine." He glanced up. "Well— have you Anna?"

"We have interviewed a number of girls, but none knew her well or could give us her usual routine."

Welsh's pleasant manner dropped, and he pointed at Anna. "You should stop being so protective of your precious position, Detective Travis, and start listening to me. I believe the killer knew Margaret Potts. She was not a young woman; she'd worked the service stations for years, correct? She wasn't a young druggie, wasn't stupid enough to go with any punter, she'd check them out first. You think about getting up into a trucker's cabin and giving him a blow job, even traveling with maybe more than one so she'd give it to both of them. They have beds or bunks for long haul, so she'd know which of the vehicles were a safe bet and not visible to the coppers or security guards. On the other hand, if it was just some punter in a car she'd clocked in the car park, she'd suss them out before plying her trade." Welsh sniggered. "Let's face it, the sort of punter that wants to do business with an old slag in a service station car park or on the hard shoulder of a motorway is more than likely to be a married man who isn't getting it at home. Who's to know what he's been up to? His family couldn't find out, as there'd be no trace on his credit cards; she was paid cash and not a lot, so they go on their way, and nobody is any the wiser."

"That could possibly fit the profile of Margaret Potts, but we have two other victims, both young."

"True enough," Welsh agreed, "but as you don't even have these two girls identified, you have no alternative but to concentrate on the first victim. I have another idea that you should look into because it's possible, as I have said, that Potts knew her killer. What if he was closer to home than you have contemplated?"

"She was almost living rough," Barolli said.

"She couldn't live rough all the time—she had to have some bolthole she'd go to, and if you go back and check for someone she knew, you may find a motive to kill her."

"What could be the motive?" Anna asked. She was reluctantly intrigued, as she was the only person who had met the ex-husband and his brother.

Welsh rocked back in his chair and closed his eyes. "Excitement, if it was someone who had a grudge against her, even hated her for what she was, a cheap whore. He knew how she earned her living, and he waited, tracking her moves, becoming more sexually aroused by what he was intending to do. Stalking her, watching her picking up clients, enjoying the risk it would be to surprise her. This excitement can last for months, and . . ."

He opened his eyes. His face was impassive, but his eyes were alert like an animal's. "I know this excitement," he said. "I've experienced it, and it is very, very pleasurable to keep your victim in sight, knowing what you intend to do to her: wrap your hands around her neck and strangle the life out of her, rape her. She will be yours to do what you want with, and that is also a sexual turn-on, to know what is coming."

Anna opened her briefcase, replacing her notebook. She'd heard enough. She suspected he had an erection beneath the table, as all he was describing was his own sickness, his own pleasure in committing the murders for which he was in prison.

"He watched her," Welsh went on, "and could even have offered her a lift to go to work. It seems no one saw her on the night of her death, correct? So this would be the night he planned to kill. He could have made some excuse that he needed to go up north on business. She might even have known that he wasn't living in London. So that could be another clue: did she know someone who traveled around a lot? It could even be someone close to her—a husband, a lover, someone from her past."

Anna felt the chills; could it have been one of the brothers? But she remained silent.

"You say she had no place to live, but if she was working the stations night after night, then she had to have earned quite a substantial amount. Did she pay it over to a pimp? Have you found any bank accounts, *post office* savings accounts? Did she have money? Was it worth killing her for?

Any jewelry? It's a motive that could link with the possibility that she knew her killer and they knew what she was worth."

Again, Anna recalled that Emerald had said Margaret worked alone and had no pimp but relied on her contacts, her brother-in-law, looking out for her. There was also the stylish tracksuit that Emerald was wearing, the suitcase full of clothes that she had said were not worth anything. What if there had been more, like the diamond ring her husband had said belonged to his mother. Could Margaret Potts have had more possessions than they had estimated? She had the sense that Cameron Welsh was able to read her mind, and he was touching on possible motives that no one else on the team had considered.

Barolli had started to act edgy, as they were constantly being monitored by the other inmates. They would come and stand a few feet away from them, staring at Welsh and then Anna. The officers would gesture for them to move away. None of them spoke, which was also unnerving. If anything, they appeared to be slightly afraid of Welsh, who would glance at them and toss his hair away from his face. None of the officers seemed to like the fact that the three of them at the table occupied a lot of the space in the recreation room. Twice, one or another prisoner had walked out into the exercise yard and stood gazing into the room, leering at Anna.

"Do you have anything further to discuss? We don't have much longer," Barolli said. Anna had kicked him under the table. She wanted to leave, but by this time so did he.

"I would appreciate it if you left me the files on the investigation to date, as I need more to work on," said Welsh. "So much of what I have said is pure conjecture, and I think I could be of further assistance."

"I'm afraid that will not be possible," Anna said, placing her briefcase on her knees, ready to go.

"Why not?"

"They are highly confidential, and I think we have given you more than enough time. The reality is that *you* have given us nothing that we are not already privy to and working on."

"I don't believe you," he said angrily.

Anna stood up. "Whether or not you believe it is immaterial, but thank you for your time."

Barolli rose to his feet. "We do appreciate the trouble you've taken, Mr. Welsh. You have done a considerable amount of work, and I feel sure, although the team is working along similar lines, we will be taking on board all your suggestions."

Barolli signaled for the unit guards to call the main prison so they could be led out. Welsh was furious. He swept all his papers onto the floor and yet remained sitting. "That's it, is it?" he demanded.

The officers moved closer, and one told him to pick up the papers. Instead of doing so, he got up and walked swiftly away, returning to his cell.

Driving back, Anna was unable to keep her anger in check.

"Whatever you may think, it was another waste of time. As if we haven't considered everything he told us."

Barolli glared at her. "I disagree. What about the possibility that she knew her killer and—"

"I have already questioned her husband and her brother-in-law. In the meantime, because I did trace them, Langton is checking in to the possibility. We'll get the information about who harassed our victim."

Barolli shook his head. "Well, thanks for telling me."

"He gives me the creeps, and you weren't the one subjected to the ogling by the other prisoners. Twice he touched my foot under the table, and if you can't see it, that's all he is doing—making himself out to be numero uno in the secure unit."

"I think he already is."

"Now we've given him even more kudos. Well, you did—talk about stroking his ego!"

"Maybe if you did, we'd get more out of him."

"He doesn't have anything," she snapped, hands gripping the steering wheel.

"You think what you like. I beg to differ."

Anna was completing her report when Mike Lewis came over to tell her they had a Tom McKinney in the interview room.

"He's a truck driver that Margaret Potts had dealings with. He still works for the same delivery company, which supplies watercoolers. His firm is based in Scotland and Manchester, but he does the long haul back and forth to London twice a week, delivering to Bayton grocery stores."

"Did he admit to getting beaten up by her contacts at the bailiffs?"

"I've not talked to him yet, and there's another bloke coming in later this evening—a salesman for a cosmetics company. Both of them had dealings with her, so we may be able to get a lead at least on how she worked her area of the service station. I want you in on the interview."

"Can you give me a few minutes while I finish up the report?" asked Anna, pleased that she would be working on a line of inquiry unconnected to Cameron Welsh.

"Sure. How did it go?"

"Well, Barolli and I have different takes on it. Welsh did

bring up the fact that maybe Potts knew her killer, could have been stalked by him. I might go and interview her brother-in-law and husband again, but to be honest, I didn't get a feeling from either of them that they would want to kill her."

"Okay. When you're ready, I'll see you down there—interview room one."

Anna was eating a sandwich and carrying a cup of coffee as she headed for the interview room. Mike was already there, explaining to Tom McKinney the reasons they had requested him to come in for questioning. The man was huge, very overweight, and his body odor was so pungent that the small room reeked. He was sweating profusely, with his big hands laid flat on the table, as Anna was introduced to him.

"You do understand that you are simply assisting our inquiry?" Mike said.

Tom nodded, then wiped his forehead with the back of his hand. "I thought at the start it was about me driving license. I had a bit of a prang a few days ago, not my fault, but that's why I came in."

"But you now know we are asking you about a woman called Margaret Potts."

Anna sipped her coffee. Tom looked from one to the other. "I don't know who she is."

Mike glanced at Anna. "She was a prostitute, and she was murdered."

Tom's mouth gaped. "You want to talk to me about *that*? I dunno her, I've never heard of her."

"But you did know her, Tom," Mike said quietly.

"No, no, I never even heard of her. I don't understand what this is all about. I mean, why? Why you got me in?"

"Because we know that you picked her up at a service station and—"

"Hang on, when was this? I've been off sick for months and only just got back to work, and then I had this problem with a bloke in a Transit van. He bloody gave me a false address and—"

Anna showed him the mug shot of Margaret Potts, laying it flat in front of him. "This is Margaret Potts."

He squinted at it and licked his lips, then shook his head, saying, "I don't know her. I swear on my life I never met this woman."

Mike explained patiently that they had a witness who had described contacting him for a specific reason: he had refused to pay Margaret Potts for her services and had been abusive toward her, and as a result, the witness had traced him via his license plate to his place of work and had a confrontation with him on behalf of Margaret.

"You paid him fifty pounds, didn't you?"

Mike paused as Tom puffed out his cheeks, sweating even more, but eventually, he admitted to meeting Margaret Potts. "She called herself Maggie. I didn't know her other name, but she didn't look like that photo; she was all made up and fancied herself. She was an old bitch and with a mouth on her, and I did shove her out of me cab because first she said it was a tenner, then she said it was twenty-five quid. My wallet was on the dashboard, and she grabbed it, so that's why I slapped her around and kicked her out. She wasn't hurt, 'cause she stood there screaming abuse at me."

"She has been murdered, Tom."

"Fuck me, you can't get me for nothin' more than what I just said. She was a dirty whore that was always hanging out at the London Gateway Services. I'd seen her there loads of times on my way back to Glasgow. I used to make my deliveries and then grab a bite to eat there before I drove up the motorway."

"How many times did you pick up Maggie?"

"Just that once. I swear before God it was just the once. I'm married, and if my wife knew I'd been with such a slag, she'd kill me. It was just that one time, and she set that bastard on to me."

It took another half hour before they got the exact details of how he had been contacted by a big bodybuilder type. McKinney never even knew his name, but the man had called his company, and when he was next delivering to London, the guy had found out his destination and was waiting there for him.

"He threatened to tell me bosses about that tart and said if I didn't cough up the cash, he'd make sure I'd never even be able to pick up a pack of fags. So I paid him, never heard nothing more."

From his description of the bodybuilder, Anna was certain it was Eric Potts who had threatened him.

McKinney was released without any charges, and they opened the window to get some fresh air into the room.

"What do you think?" Mike asked, wafting a file in front of his face like a fan.

"I think I need to talk to Eric Potts again."

"But that incident took place almost a year before she was murdered."

"Yes, I know."

Anna repeated to Mike her talk with Cameron Welsh and went into more detail about her meeting with Eric, who was now a possible, but doubtful, suspect.

"Would the brother-in-law have been stalking her? Doesn't sound likely to me."

Anna shrugged. "He did admit to caring for her. Maybe

it was more than that. Let me see what else I can get out of him."

Returning to the incident room, Mike gave a briefing and the update of the interview with McKinney. His description of exactly how Margaret Potts worked the service stations added nothing new to their inquiry. Margaret would usually be hanging around the lorry parking area and was a well-known fixture, as McKinney had admitted seeing her there on numerous occasions. Although he'd confessed to going with her only the one time, both Anna and Mike suspected that he might have lied.

Tom had explained that she would wait for the men to come out from one or other of the cafés and then approach them as they returned to their trucks to offer her "services." He had said he had seen her getting in and out of a number of vehicles over some considerable time. He also said that she would sometimes climb aboard and drive out with the driver to go to the next service station. She offered a blow job, a hand job, or full sex. It was all horribly seedy, and it would mean yet another round of officers interviewing truckers who were known to do regular stops.

McKinney was unable to tell them how far up the motorway she would travel as she was picking the guys up at the London Gateway. She was wary about being caught by any of the security cameras, but if a john wanted full sex, then they would drive somewhere out of the way and she would go into the back of their cabs. She would then, they presumed, either go back home or return to work.

During the briefing, DC Barbara Maddox listened, sighing inwardly at the awful way this woman had earned her living. She was certain that neither of the still unidentified girls would be working the same deal. Both were young, and the postmortem reports stated that they had been raped and strangled. The last victim's hymen had visible tear damage, so it was possible she had been a virgin before the attack.

Mike looked over the board and back to the team. "That's it," he told them. "Not much to go on, is it? Let's hope we get something back from the next TV appeal for information on our two Jane Does."

The following morning, Anna, accompanied by Barolli, went back to the debt collection agency. She was not anticipating gaining anything more from Eric Potts and told Barolli to give her some breathing space.

He bridled. "What do you mean?"

"Just don't get too heavy or interrupt too much. I want to take it slowly."

"Whatever." Barolli got out and slammed the car door shut. He looked toward the fish-and-chip shop, which was closed, as it was only nine-fifteen. The seedy office door was also closed. It appeared the building had previously been used by a minicab company. Their cards and a torn plaque were hammered into the brick wall.

"It's up on the second floor," Anna said.

Barolli grunted, pressing the bell. "Doesn't look as if they're open for business."

Anna stepped back to look up to the dirty windows. "Light's on. Ring again."

Barolli kept his finger on the bell for a few moments. There was a loud click, and the door opened automatically. Mrs. Kelly stood on the second landing, waiting for them to come up.

"I'm just going out for some fresh coffee. Do you want to see my husband? Because he's not coming in this morning."

Anna asked to see Eric Potts. Just as Mrs. Kelly began to say he was also not in the office, they heard heavy footsteps on the stairs behind them. It was Eric.

Anna introduced Barolli as Eric unlocked his office, asking Mrs. Kelly to bring him coffee and a toasted bacon sandwich. He seemed slightly edgy, pushing open the door to walk in ahead of them.

"I got a lot on today," he said, taking off his coat and hanging it up on a nail hammered into a wall.

"This shouldn't take too long. It's just I need to iron out a few things," Anna told him.

"I dunno what they could be, as I've already told you everything, and don't think I liked giving up the names of the blokes that work for us here. It's hard enough to earn a living right now, and I hope helping out Maggie isn't gonna get me or them into trouble."

He sat at his desk. Anna took the only other available seat, leaving Barolli to stand by the door.

"We traced the lorry driver, and I just wanted to clarify that it was you who talked to him and received money from him on behalf of Margaret."

"I admitted it, didn't I? It was the big bloke that delivered watercoolers, right?"

"Yes. He claimed that he only ever picked up Margaret that one time and, I would say, regretted it." She smiled.

Eric shrugged his massive shoulders.

"I need to ask you about any other incident you personally handled," Anna went on.

"I just did it that one time for her. I've got too much on my plate to run around after anyone else. Like I said, a couple of blokes here did a bit of collecting for her, but not recently. It was all a long time ago. She's been dead two years, for chrissakes."

"You cared for her, didn't you?"

"Yes, but that was also a long time ago, and apart from the odd call, I hadn't seen her. I also told you I didn't want to be bothered with her anymore, as my wife didn't want her at the house."

"These other times you saw her, where did you meet?"

He sighed, saying that he had already mentioned meeting her in a café. He then remembered a couple of calls from her to his office and said he had met her at the same café by King's Cross station.

"She just needed money, as always. I think she used the station ladies' room to wash up and sometimes left her belongings in the luggage lockers. It's got to be at least eighteen months before she was murdered, and I told her then that I'd had enough of being a cash cow for her."

"How did she take it?"

"Well, she looked pretty ragged, so much that I gave her more than I'd intended; plus, I told her not to come round to the house anymore."

"How did she react to that?"

He sighed again, becoming visibly irritated. "She didn't like it, because once we'd been intimate. She reckoned I'd always be an easy touch."

"Were you intimate with her during her marriage to your brother?"

"Yes," he snapped.

"But you claim that you did not continue to have a close relationship with her after she left her husband."

"I maybe saw her a couple more times and had sex with her, but then I met my wife, and by this time I knew Margaret was on the game. I told you how I warned her to take care of herself, but she would still turn up after I got married, and eventually, my wife told me to get rid of her."

"Get rid of her?" Anna asked sharply.

"Christ! By that she meant, tell her to stay away. We'd got a kid and another one on the way, so I was to tell her to stay out of our lives."

"Did Maggie ever make any threats?" Barolli leaned forward, resting his hands on the desk.

"Threats? Like what?"

"Well, if your wife didn't like her and didn't want her around, it seems to me that maybe she was jealous."

"She's fucking ten years younger than Margaret was, and if you mean did she make threats to me, it would be ridiculous! She could see that she was just a slag and was after money, and she didn't want me shelling out to her all the time."

"Did Margaret threaten to tell your wife that you'd been intimate?" Barolli was still leaning on the desk.

"Hang on . . . just hang on a minute here. I know what you're doing—you're trying to make out that I had some kind of motive to kill Maggie, right? That's what this is all about, isn't it?"

"Young wife, young family, and as you described her, a slag coming round hitting on you. I bet you didn't like it, did you, Eric?" Barolli leaned in closer.

"No, I fucking didn't. I made sure she didn't come to the house."

"So she did threaten to tell your wife?"

Eric stood up, towering above Barolli. "Listen, pal, are you looking for a smack in the face? I don't like what you are insinuating. I've been honest with you about Maggie, but if you think I'd be worried about any threat she made to screw up my marriage, then you have got it wrong."

"But she did threaten? Come on, you must have been really pissed off after what you'd done for her."

"Please sit down, Eric," Anna said quietly.

Eric sat down in his chair. There was a long pause, and gradually, he calmed himself down. "As I said, you have got it all wrong, mate. Despite all the shit life had thrown at her, Maggie was one of the nicest women I've ever met, and she got upset when I told her not to come to the house. Yeah, okay, she did say something about my wife not really knowing how close we'd been and that I wouldn't like her spilling the beans about us, but she promised that she wouldn't come over again. She said we could just meet on the odd times, like in the café I told you about."

"So this last time you saw her, did you part on amicable terms?"

Anna touched Barolli to warn him to move away from the desk.

Eric nodded.

"Didn't you feel guilty about walking away from her? You knew she was desperate, had nowhere to live, and was working the service stations."

"Yeah, I knew, but like I also told you, I had warned her over and again not to take risks and said that if she was in real need, of course I'd be there for her. I just didn't want her calling me at home or turning up whenever the fancy took her."

Again there was a lengthy pause, and then Eric addressed Anna. "I used to care about her, and all the bad times she'd been through with my arsehole of a brother, losing her kids, being knocked around, sometimes even hospitalized. Despite all that, I never saw her cry—she was a bloody punching bag, and yet she didn't cry—but that last time I saw her, I turned round as I walked out of the café and she was crying. So yeah, I felt bad, and you can imagine how I felt when I found out she'd been murdered."

Anna stood up and thanked him for talking to them. As she made to head out, Eric pushed back his chair.

"Instead of wasting time talking to me, you should be out there trying to find who killed her, because she didn't deserve that. No way did she deserve that."

As they reached Anna's Mini, Barolli received a call from the incident room. Anna sat waiting for him in the car. It had been, as she had anticipated, an unproductive inter-view, and they had not gained any new information apart from the fact that their victim had made some halfhearted threat—unless she had read Eric incorrectly and the threat was taken seriously by him, enough to make him want to get rid of Margaret permanently.

Barolli got into the car. "A woman called in after see-ing the TV requests for info. She reckons the last victim came into her charity shop and bought the jacket shown on the TV. It's a cancer-research shop over in New Malden. Maybe it won't be a wasted morning after all."

Chapter Five

Anna and Barolli parked up in a side road by the Waitrose car park, then walked along New Malden's High Street. There were numerous charity shops, and Barolli double-checked that it was a cancer charity, as there was a children-in-need shop and a heart-foundation shop all within a short distance.

"Lot of Chinese live around here," Barolli said as they passed a Japanese grocery shop. There were several sushi delis, and High Street was busy with the big department store called Tudor Williams. Every store appeared to be having a sale.

The cancer charity shop was well positioned, with a window display of women's clothes, china, and children's toys.

"Well, this looks affluent—must be all the Chinese," Barolli waffled. "Those boots in the window look very small, don't they?"

Anna didn't pay him much attention. It was a long way from Hendon and Ronald Kelly's business. In fact, it was a village atmosphere. She gave Barolli a nudge, as he was still peering into the window display. They entered the shop.

The assistant, Eileen Mayle, an elderly woman wearing a pink twinset with pearls, had eagerly written down all she could remember on a notepad while waiting. She could describe the redheaded victim, but as the police had shown her photograph on the TV program, they couldn't rely on this too much as a positive sighting. However, she also spoke of the victim as having a strong accent, possibly Polish, and explained that the reason she recalled this customer was because she had tried to buy the jacket, which was priced at six pounds, with a fifty-pound note. The shop assistants always paid close attention to anyone trying to use fifty-pound notes, because they had been caught out a number of times. In the past, customers had bought a couple of small items for a few pounds and then, having taken their change, left the shop. Later, the notes had been found to be forgeries, so the staff now refused to accept them. The girl was even more memorable because she returned a while later with the correct amount of money to buy the coat.

"Did you think it was a fake fifty-pound note?" Anna asked.

"I couldn't honestly say, and I didn't have the marker pen to test it, so I couldn't take it. She took a while to understand, as, like I said, she didn't speak good English, and the reason I think she might have been Polish is because I had a cleaner from there once and the accents were similar."

"Was she alone?"

"Yes, she seemed to be, and I'd never seen her before."

"Thank you very much, Eileen. You have been very helpful. If there is anything else you can remember, please call this number." Anna passed over her card.

"I've been trying to think of her name, because I wrote a note to keep the jacket for her, and in case I wasn't here, I put it on the bag under the counter. I've been racking my brains to remember, because I'd pinned it to the bag, but she took it with her."

This was almost too good to be true.

"And did you remember it?" Anna asked eagerly.

"Well, not her surname, but her Christian name was Estelle."

The next port of call was the Polish embassy in Portland Place. Anna and Barolli sat in her Mini as they checked some facts about immigration. Barolli scrolled through the information.

"They've got this Works Registration Scheme introduced in 2004 when the new countries joined the European Union. This allows the UK to monitor where citizens, say from Poland, are coming into our labor market. They've got to register under this scheme if they want to work for an employer."

"Well, let's hope we get some luck with Estelle."

Armed with the photograph of their victim, Anna asked if the embassy personnel could assist in identifying her. It was a tedious interview, with a number of the staff who at first were certain she had never been to the embassy, and it was not until Anna asked if the bar and kitchen workers could also be questioned that they got a result.

A waitress, whose English was poor, was brought to meet them as they waited in a small lounge. They used a barman to act as interpreter, as the girl became flustered when questioned. She was certain the victim was a girl called Estelle Dubcek who had worked as a relief waitress on two occasions. She did not know where she lived, and said that Estelle had not been at the embassy for several months, but she thought she was working as an au pair somewhere in Knightsbridge.

Returning to the station, Barolli kept on moaning about how people would not come forward. If their victim was

Estelle and she had worked in Knightsbridge, why hadn't the host family made contact after the extensive press coverage? Anna asked Barbara to start checking all the domestic employment agencies in the Knightsbridge area, and at the same time to contact Interpol and Passport Control. By six o'clock they had no further development; it was yet another frustrating day.

Just as Anna was getting ready to leave the station, Barbara received a call from a Mrs. Henderson who lived in Walton Street, close to Harrods. She said she had been contacted by the domestic agency she had used to hire an au pair for her two young children. The girl she had hired from the agency had lasted only a few months before she had to return to Poland for a family bereavement. Knowing she was leaving her boss without help, the au pair had suggested a friend whom she had met at the Polish embassy. The girl was no longer working for Mrs. Henderson and had not been for the past few months, but she had been called Estelle Dubcek.

Anna asked why the agency had made contact if the au pair did not come to her via them.

"Because I complained about the original girl they sent to me, and they would have replaced her, but when I said I had already hired Estelle, they got quite unpleasant."

Anna arranged to call on Mrs. Henderson that evening. The house was impressive, and Mrs. Henderson, an American, was an elegant and rather brittle woman who explained to Anna that she and her family would be leaving England in two months' time. The house was only leased, and the bank her husband worked for had recalled him to America.

"My children have already left with their nanny. I used the agency for the au pairs to help her out mostly on the weekend, as that is her time off. But as I mentioned to you, I was not that happy with them, and they cost a fortune."

Mrs. Henderson gestured for Anna to sit down. It was a well-decorated large room with long bay windows over-looking Walton Street. The sofas and chairs were covered in pale yellow damask and matched the draped curtains. A large ornate fireplace with a fake log fire had a long glass-topped table in front of it, stacked with *Vogue* and *Tatler* magazines.

"Can you tell me what you know about Estelle?"

"Well, not that much, really. She was pleasant enough, but her English was poor, and to be honest, it wasn't an ideal arrangement. And then when we got the news to pack up, I didn't bother replacing her."

Anna showed her the photograph taken of the victim, but only a head shot. Mrs. Henderson recognized her straightaway.

"Yes, that's Estelle, she had long red hair. Has something happened to her?"

"Yes, she was murdered."

"Oh dear God, that's dreadful."

"So I will need to know all you can tell me about her."

Mrs. Henderson shook her head. "There's not a lot I can add to what I have already said."

"Did she live in?" Anna prompted.

"For the first month she did, but it wasn't really work-ing out, as she wasn't used to looking after small children. She couldn't cook, and she spent most of the time reading. I honestly didn't see a lot of her; the only reason she was here was because the other girl had to go back to Poland."

"Where did she go after she moved out?"

"Back to wherever she was living before, I presume. She

would come in on a daily basis but stay over on the weekends when I really needed her."

"Do you have an address?"

"No, I'm sorry, I don't. I did have a mobile phone number for her."

"Do you still have it?"

"Yes, it will be in my phone—and I also have a bag belonging to her. When I told her she would no longer be
required, she was truculent about it, but I explained why,
that we were going back to the States, and she accepted it
and left."

"And this was when, exactly?"

Mrs. Henderson crossed to a desk and opened a drawer,
taking out a leather-bound diary. "Three months ago. I
paid her for the next month, expecting her to at least stay
over the following weekend, but she never returned."

Anna asked if Mrs. Henderson could show her the bag
Estelle had left. It was a cheap black haversack, containing a nightdress and underwear, a pair of socks, and three
English-language books. There was also a lined notebook
with jottings and spellings, obviously used by Estelle to
learn written English. They also could see that the spell-
ing of her name was Dubcek. There was nothing else—no
phone numbers or addresses. Anna thanked Mrs. Henderson and left, taking the haversack with her.

She would have liked to go straight home, as by now it
was after seven, but she persuaded herself to return to the
station to share what she had just learned.

At eight o'clock, Anna was still at her desk working on
her report. Making sure she had done everything by the
book, she passed the haversack to the property lockup. Mrs.
Henderson had also given her the contact number and

address in Poland for the previous au pair, whose name was Katia Rieika. With luck, they could track her down to ask for more details about Estelle. But first Anna rang Estelle's mobile phone number. To her surprise, it was answered straightaway.

The voice had a heavy accent and it took a moment for Anna to ask who she was speaking to.

"Katia. Who is this, please?"

Anna explained slowly that she was trying to trace Estelle and believed that this was her mobile phone number.

"No, this number is mine. Estelle not here."

It took considerable time to explain that it was very important for Anna to meet with Katia, as there was some concern about Estelle.

"She not here, she go away."

Eventually, Katia agreed to meet. Anna would have preferred to see her the following morning, but Katia said she worked in a breakfast café and had to be at work early. So Anna asked if she could come and talk to her now.

Anna had to drive to Earl's Court, and it was almost nine by the time she parked outside the address off Earl's Court Road. The house had been divided into numerous studio flats. Rows of bells and scribbled notes were taped to the door to indicate the various occupants. Katia Rieika lived on the second floor, and as soon as Anna rang number twenty, the heavy door buzzed open.

A girl was leaning over the banisters as Anna looked up the wide, old-fashioned staircase. The hall was dusty, and a large table bore mail stacked in rows for the tenants. Mounds of flyers were heaped beneath it, along with old free newspapers and circulars.

Katia turned out to be a very attractive dark-haired girl dressed in a black woolen skirt and sweater. She ushered

Anna into the studio room, which was spacious, containing two beds, a large wardrobe, and a small kitchen alcove. It was untidy, with clothes strewn around, and on a table were dirty mugs and food cartons.

Katia was impatient and had her mobile phone out, ready to show Anna.

"Did Estelle use your phone?"

"Yes. Only when she needed it, but it is my phone, I pay for it. I can prove it. I got the last bill two days ago. You want it?"

Anna said that she would like to see it. She then sat on an old floral-covered easy chair and opened her briefcase to show Katia the photograph of Estelle. The other girl recognized her and was distressed when told she had been murdered.

"I need to know everything you can tell me about her," Anna said.

Katia picked up a box of tissues and wiped her eyes, then sat by the table, getting over the shock. Estelle had been living with her for a while but couldn't find work until Katia told her about Mrs. Henderson.

"I tell Mrs. Henderson that I go back to Poland, but I just didn't want to work for her anymore. Pay was not good, and I did not like her, and she made me do cleaning and ironing as well as looking after the children. So I suggested Estelle work for her, as she needed money. She owed me rent and kept on borrowing from me. I work two jobs now, one in the café, and then I work nights in a club. I earn three times the money."

Bit by bit, Anna learned that Estelle had not registered to work in the UK and had come to England via France eighteen months ago. She had met Katia at the Polish embassy, and they became friends. At first she had slept on

Katia's floor, as there was another girl sharing the studio, but when she left, Estelle moved in. She had then taken over Katia's job with Mrs. Henderson.

"When she didn't come back here, didn't you feel concerned?"

"No, I think she live in with Mrs. Henderson, and my boyfriend was here, so it was okay."

"But she used your mobile phone?"

"Yes, sometimes, but I ask for it back because I need it."

"Did Estelle have a boyfriend?"

"No. I don't think she have one. She was doing house-cleaning for a while, but not much money."

"Did she have any friends that I could talk to?"

"No. She didn't know nobody, and I work early in mornings, so I didn't see much of her, and she lived in at Mrs. Henderson's."

"But that was only on weekends."

"Look, I tell you everything. I got someone else living with me now. I don't know nothing else about her."

"What about family?"

Katia shrugged and said that Estelle maybe had someone she knew in Manchester, but who it was, she didn't know. She got up and opened one of the wardrobes, taking out a large cheap canvas suitcase. "I got this, all her things inside, but she don't come back for it. I don't want it, I need the space."

Anna sighed and tried to think of a way of getting more information out of Katia, but the girl was becoming impatient to leave for work.

"Did you notice anything else missing?" Anna asked.

"No. There was a backpack—is that what you call it? A small thing, and an overnight bag. They not here; she maybe took them with her."

By the time Anna left Katia's studio with the suitcase, it was nine-thirty. She decided she would go home and check the suitcase in at the station the following morning.

Anna showered and made herself a sandwich before she opened the suitcase. She laid it on her bed, and as she removed each item, she noted it down: two pairs of shoes, two skirts, sweaters, and T-shirts with some underwear. There was nothing else, no passport or notebooks or makeup. The clothes were all worn but clean and well pressed. Anna knew about the haversack or backpack but not the overnight bag. Could that have meant Estelle was leaving London to visit the person Katia said she knew in Manchester?

She had hoped that the itemized bill for the mobile might be of use, especially if there had been one to Manchester. However, Katia had given her the names of all the calls, and these also included ones made by Estelle to her, and she said there were no other numbers listed for which she didn't know the recipient. Estelle had given the phone back to Katia a month ago. Frustrated and tired, Anna repacked the suitcase and went to bed.

The next morning, Anna dragged the case into the station, and there were plenty of jokes about her filling up the property locker, as every item she had brought in had to be recorded in the exhibits book and bagged. She made out her report of the meeting with Katia and added the notes to the incident board. Then she sat at her desk, listed the Polish embassy, the Walton Street address, and the Earl's Court studio. She was wondering why Estelle had bought from a charity shop in New Malden, a good distance from where she'd worked and lived. She had also tried to pay with a fifty-pound note, and this would have been after she left the employment of Mrs. Henderson. Anna tapped her teeth with her Biro, flicking through all her notes, sensing that something didn't add up. She put in a call to Katia. There was no reply for such a long time that Anna was about to give up when Katia answered, the clatter of crockery and the hiss of a coffee machine audible in the background.

"I'm so sorry to disturb you, Katia, it's DI Anna Travis. I just wanted to ask you if you knew anyone living in New Malden?"

"New Malden?" Katia repeated slowly.

"Yes. We know Estelle bought something from a charity shop there, and it's quite a way from Earl's Court."

"I have never been to this New Malden," Katia growled.

"Do you know anyone living there?"

"No. I do not know where it is."

"It's not far from Kingston, Wimbledon, Raynes Park—"

"No. I don't know any of these places."

Anna sighed and thanked Katia, who yawned as she hung up. It was catching; Anna yawned as she closed her notebook. She next rang Mrs. Henderson, apologizing for any inconvenience and saying she wondered if there had been any calls made by Estelle on her boss's landline. Mrs. Henderson said that she doubted it, as she made a point of asking anyone employed at the house not to use the private phone. She did agree, however, to check her phone bill.

"Could you keep a particular lookout for any calls to New Malden or Manchester?" Anna asked. She doubted that Mrs. Henderson would get back to her, but at least she felt she had covered everything possible in trying to ascertain Estelle's whereabouts before she was murdered.

She decided to go to the property locker to retrieve the

English books found in Estelle's rucksack, in the hope that they might reveal whether Estelle was going to any particular evening classes to study English. However, none of the books had any college listed. It was yet another dead end.

Shortly after lunch, Barbara took a call from a man by the name of Mikhail Petrovich. He asked to speak to Anna Travis.

"Did he say what it's about?" Anna asked.

"No. Just wanted to speak to you."

"Put him through, please." Anna picked up her desk phone. "Anna Travis speaking. How can I help you, Mr. Petrovich?"

"It's about Estelle. I knew her, and I've been told she's dead. I am very sorry and I want to help you."

Anna switched on the tape to record the call. The man did seem to be genuinely distressed. He said he was a waiter working at a small hotel on Kingston Hill in Surrey. Anna became tense listening to him as he explained that he knew Estelle because she lived with his girlfriend in Earl's Court.

"Your girlfriend is Katia Rieika?"

"Yes. Estelle used to live in her place, that is how I know her."

"Mr. Petrovich, I would really like to talk to you in person. Can I come and see you?"

Anna arranged to meet him at the hotel, but in the car park, as he didn't want the management to think he was in any kind of trouble.

Barolli looked over as Anna grabbed her briefcase. "Where you off to?" he asked.

"Kingston Hill. Got someone who says he knew Estelle."

"You want me to go with you?"

"No, it shouldn't take long."

• • •

Mikhail Petrovich was a handsome young man with slicked-back black hair. He was waiting in the small car park as Anna drew up in her Mini and wound down the window to announce herself. He got in to sit beside her.

"I thought you would maybe come in a police car," he said.

"No, this is my own vehicle."

"Very nice. I like this make of car, but I would have it convertible."

"Do you mind if I tape this conversation?"

"No, I don't mind, just so long as Katia doesn't know about me calling you, because she is very jealous. That's why she kicked out Estelle, because she knew I found her attractive. Like I said, I was quite fond of her."

Mikail told Anna that he had been with Katia when she received Anna's call that morning. He had not started his shift until noon, so he went into the café to help Katia open up. He said she didn't know Kingston or any of the other places, but he did, as he lived at the hotel he worked in. He stayed with Katia on his days off. Petrovich was an undermanager and very proud of it. He had worked in England for seven years and had been dating Katia for almost eighteen months. He had met Estelle when she began renting the studio, and he had felt sorry for her.

"She had no immediate family, except an uncle who she wanted to meet up with, as she had never known him. She had little money and hated working for Mrs. Henderson, as she was so rude to her."

"Did she contact this uncle?"

"I don't know, but in secret we met, and she was upset because she said she didn't have good clothes, so I took her to the charity shop in New Malden, also two more in

Wimbledon, to buy things. They have nice secondhand clothes, expensive things going real cheap. I wait for her outside, have a cigarette."

"Did you pay for the things?"

"Yes, I give her some money."

"Was it a fifty-pound note?"

"Yes. I got my wages and give her fifty quid. The lady not want that big note, so I bought cigarettes to get change. Estelle keep the rest."

Anna swiveled around to have a better look at him. "That's a lot of money, and yet you say she was just a friend?"

"Yes, I say that, and I mean that. We didn't do sex, she was not that type of girl—she was proper and innocent and I liked her. She was desperate, and all I wanted was to help her, but without Katia knowing, or she would go ballistic, very jealous. Nothing happened between me and Estelle, but I will be honest, I hoped when she came back, we would get to know each other better." Anna showed him the photograph, and he nodded. "Yes, that is Estelle."

He turned away to stare out the window before he brought himself to ask what had happened to her. Anna gave him only a few details, adding that perhaps Estelle was intending to go to Manchester. She also asked if Estelle was the type of girl who would thumb a lift.

"Maybe. You see, I couldn't give her any more cash, and Katia had kicked her out of the studio because she owed rent, so she had no money for a ticket."

"Would she have had sex for money?"

He sucked in his breath and his face tightened. "*No.* I tell you, she was a good girl, but with trouble—no job, no money, and that is why I tried to help her."

"She was here illegally, wasn't she?"

He hesitated, then admitted that she was not registered to work in the UK, but she wanted to make an application and hoped that her uncle would help her. He looked at his watch. "I have to go back to work."

Anna asked when was the last time he had seen Estelle, and he recalled that it was the same day she had bought the new jacket for her trip to Manchester.

"So she was definitely going to travel from London to Manchester?"

"Yes. Her uncle was the only person she believed could get her the correct papers. Did she get there? Was she killed in Manchester?"

"No, she never made it there."

He turned to look at Anna. His dark eyes were filled with tears, and he clenched his hands. "Money. I was saving for a car, so I did not give her any more when she needed it. Now she's dead, and I will have to live with that. I really liked her."

Anna watched him walking back to the hotel reception, his head bent. He took out a handkerchief, and she knew he was crying. She was about to drive away when Mrs. Henderson rang. She did have a call registered from her landline to Manchester, and four further ones to mobile numbers she did not recognize. At last the day was beginning to be a productive one. Anna fed the numbers back to the incident room and asked for the call to Manchester to be a priority. This would begin to pinpoint whether or not Estelle was heading there on the day she died—or was on her way back.

By the time Anna returned to the station, they had located Andre Dubcek. He was devastated to be told that his niece had been murdered, as he had expected her to contact him when she arrived in Manchester. He agreed to come down to London but couldn't do so for a couple of days, as he had a business to run. Barolli had spoken to him and didn't think they would gain much from interviewing him, as he had never met Estelle. He had asked a lot of questions about when it had happened and how she had been killed, and he appeared to be greatly shocked.

The fact that he had not contacted them after either the newspaper reports or the television crime shows was simply because he had no idea what she looked like; in fact, he said he had been surprised when she contacted him. Andre was married to a local girl from Chorlton, had three children, and ran a small bakery. He told them that Estelle was twenty-two years old.

It felt to everyone that they had made a breakthrough simply by being able to identify their victim. But it still left one more to go, and they were no closer to producing a suspect. Estelle's photograph now had her name beneath it, alongside the pictures of Margaret Potts and Jane Doe.

Anna left the station at seven, satisfied that she had had a productive day, if not one that helped solve the women's murders. She was in the car park when Langton drove in and did his usual erratic parking job. She waited by her Mini as he headed toward her.

"You've got some developments today?" he said.

Anna explained quickly how she had been able to identify Estelle and that they had contacted a relative.

"Good work, but we're still almost at square one. Bloody unbelievable, isn't it? She's Polish?"

"She was, yes. Seems to have been quite an innocent."

"Couldn't be that innocent. Comes over here, no job prospects and an uncle who's never met her. Do we know her age?"

"Twenty-two."

He sighed and then gave Anna a pat on her shoulder. "Good work, though, Travis. Let's hope tomorrow we go one better. This case is growing cold on us."

Anna's newfound relaxed interaction with Langton felt a little strained, as if he was going out of his way to be pleasant to her. Perhaps he was.

By the time she arrived home, she didn't know why she felt so depressed. There were a few eggs in the fridge and little else, as her grocery list was still stuck to the fridge door. There was a half bottle of red wine on the kitchen worktop, however. Anna poured herself a glass and couldn't be bothered to eat anything. She carried the glass into the sitting room and switched on the TV, propping her feet up on the coffee table.

She couldn't lift the depression; she knew she was really not looking after herself. She didn't exercise, she didn't cook decent meals, and she was eating mostly fry-ups in the station canteen. She had made no new friends, and her whole existence was focused on work. She was also drinking at least half a bottle of wine a night, despite trying to keep it to one and a half glasses. She sometimes drank more and sank into bed cushioned by the alcohol to help her sleep.

Now, unable to concentrate on the TV, she drained the glass and returned to the kitchen to get a refill and then headed into her bedroom. She took a shower and, wrapped in a bath towel, stared at herself in the long wardrobe mirror. Sipping the wine, she let the towel drop to really look at herself. She'd put on weight, and her hair needed a trim. In fact, her face looked pasty, and doing a slow turn, she could see that her waist was much wider than usual, as were her thighs. Flabby, she felt flabby: unfit and ugly. She took a few more sips of wine as she got into her nightdress. It had been bought for warmth and comfort, and that was exactly what it looked like.

She flopped down on the bed. Tomorrow she would join a gym, and she would also go on a diet, start to eat more healthy food, and cut out the wine. Sleepily, she drained the glass, but just as she was about to go and clean her teeth, her phone rang.

"Hello, Anna."

She knew who it was immediately and wanted to re-place the receiver at once.

"You still awake?"

She remained silent, furious that Cameron Welsh had obtained her private phone number.

"Anna?"

"Mr. Welsh, you have no right to call me at my home. I have nothing to say to you."

"Take the number out of the phone book, then."

"Good night, Mr. Welsh."

"Don't you want to hear why I've called you?"

"No, I don't. Please do not call me again."

"Isn't that rather a childish attitude to take, Anna?"

She was about to slam down the phone when he added, "I have more information."

"To date you have simply wasted our time, Mr. Welsh. You have given us nothing that we haven't already—"

"I have now," he interrupted her angrily.

She did not respond.

"I want you to come and see me again. It's connected to a friend of Margaret Potts. She knows—"

"That won't be possible." She replaced the receiver and pulled out the cord in case he tried to call her again.

Even though Anna took a sleeping pill, sleep didn't

come easily. She tossed and turned. Cameron Welsh's voice was playing over and over in her mind. She woke drenched in sweat from a nightmare, feeling his hands squeezing her throat. She sat up, taking deep breaths, trying to calm herself, but by calling her at home, he had invaded her privacy. It felt as if he were stalking her the way he had stalked his victims, and she was angry at herself for allowing him to have such power over her.

Not wanting to go back to sleep, she brought her briefcase into the bedroom and began to sift through all her notes pertaining to the previous interviews with Welsh. Although she refuted that he had given any conclusive information that moved the case forward, he had nevertheless underlined the importance of Margaret Potts's relatives, which had eventually been, in some ways, productive. They had traced the man Potts had been abused by, but it had not resulted in tracing their killer, although it more or less confirmed how the dead woman worked the service stations. However, that wasn't enough for Anna to believe Welsh truly had anything valuable to offer.

Anna arrived at the station early and went straight into Mike Lewis's office. She told him about the phone call and explained how much it had bothered her. Mike suggested she change her number straightaway to unlisted. He then said he would contact the governor at Barfield to make sure Welsh was not allowed any further late-night calls unless monitored, and if he had a mobile phone, it was to be removed.

"It beggars belief if he does own one, but you never know what they can get permission to use nowadays."

"That secure unit is like a holiday camp," she snapped.

"Did you check the number?"

Anna shook her head and repeated what Welsh had said to her about having further information.

"Well, if there is another visit, you won't be going. Either I or Barolli will go," Mike reassured her.

"It'll be a waste of time," Anna grumbled. "It's just supposition on his part, and I think he has a thing about me. It's me he wants there to gloat over, and he's started giving me nightmares. It's that slimy voice of his." She shuddered.

"What do you think he meant by this friend of the victim Margaret Potts?"

"Mike, we've interviewed her ex-husband, her brother-in-law, and Emerald Turk. She never had a regular place to live; she dossed down on their floors or in their spare rooms or used a hostel."

Mike nodded, but then his phone rang, so Anna had to return to the incident room. She was writing up on the board the late-night phone call when Barolli joined her.

"Boyfriend called you at home, did he?"

"Very funny. I'll be losing my sense of humor over Welsh. He sickens me."

"What's this about a friend of Margaret Potts?"

"He was trying it on, but if you want to act on it, go ahead. I am having nothing more to do with him. Besides, I want to work on finding out more about Estelle Dubcek."

Mike joined them and said he had spoken to the governor of Barfield, and they were doing a strip search of Welsh's cell. The prisoners were not allowed to make calls after nine-thirty, and Jeremy Hardwick was very certain Welsh would not have access to a mobile, as they were against prison regulations.

Barolli snorted, knowing full well that inside prison, a mobile phone went for a considerable amount of money, and far from being against regulations, they were passed around easily.

Relieved that she would no longer be forced into any meetings with Welsh, Anna threw herself into the next task. As they'd had such good feedback from the last television crime show, they were preparing to run again the requests for anyone able to identify the second victim. Barbara had compiled the list of the girl's clothes and acquired exact copies ready for showing on the TV appeal.

Chapter Six

Anna looked again at the information on Estelle Dubcek, the date she finished working for Mrs. Henderson, and the meeting with Mikhail Petrovich. Aware that Katia had told her she couldn't stay there, Anna wondered where Estelle had slept. Her body was discovered wearing the jacket bought from the charity shop. She had left clothes at Katia's and more belongings at Mrs. Henderson's. Knowing when she purchased the coat, they were able to pin down the date she was in London. Anna calculated that three days were unaccounted for before the body was found. Had she gone to Manchester and been returning to London when she was killed? Yet her uncle had said she never turned up. It left Anna wondering if she should question Petrovich again. He could have lied, but she doubted he was connected to the murder. Then there was Katia; was *she* lying?

Anna sighed and started to think about Welsh's phone call. Should she question Emerald Turk again? In many ways, she felt they had already covered her connection to Margaret Potts. She didn't think that either Margaret's husband or Eric Potts could give any further clues. It was obvious they needed a breakthrough, and it didn't seem to be coming, no matter what direction the team investigated.

She went into the incident room to mark up the timeline. It was quiet, unusually so for such a big investigation. They had three dead women with no connection bar the fact that they were murdered close to motorway service stations and were believed to have been killed by the same man.

As Anna underlined in red the three missing days, Barbara joined her, wondering if it was possible that their victim had been held captive by the killer.

"It's possible," Anna agreed. "From what I can gather, she didn't take much luggage, maybe just an overnight bag, and could have started out hitchhiking a lift to Manchester."

"Barolli's checking out a white van that was on the CCTV footage at the service station used by Margaret Potts. It's a Ford Transit van and—"

"When did this come in?" Anna looked over at Barolli, who was on the telephone at his desk.

"They got it on three different dates," Barbara explained as she pinned up the black-and-white photographs.

Barolli finished his call and hurried to join them. "Okay, things are moving. From the license plate, the Transit van belongs to a John Smiley—I've got an address for him in Kilburn. Joan's just checking it out and running him through the national computer to see if he's known to us."

Just as they felt they had a break, Joan discovered that the address was for a rented property, and the suspect had moved out five years previously. She could find no police record on file, but from local agency inquiries, they learned that John Smiley was married with two young children.

The neighbors and other residents at the address in Kilburn could give little information to Barolli. His last call was to the landlord, who lived in a house opposite. The man was able to tell them that Smiley was a good tenant, and when his lease was up, he moved out. The landlord had not met his wife but knew the children had been at a local school. He remembered the white van, as it was parked in the residents' bays, but couldn't give any details about what work Smiley did. Pressed by Barolli, who said that surely Smiley must have given some details about his work when he took over the lease for rental, the landlord said he had paid a substantial cash deposit.

The next interviews were at the local school, which provided little more than the information that the two Smiley children, Stefan and Marta, had attended the nursery section, and then the eldest moved up to the primary school. The headmistress, a precise woman in her late forties who was wearing thick brown stockings, was able to give a description of Mrs. Smiley as a pleasant and caring woman. She would always bring both children to school in person and was always present at any prize-giving, Nativity play, and so on. She had never met the children's father and was sad when she learned they would no longer be pupils. She couldn't recall if she had been told where the family was moving, and then she stopped and thought for a moment.

"I think Mrs. Smiley was Polish, so perhaps they moved back there. We have so many nationalities at our school that it's sometimes hard to remember."

"And you have no idea what Mr. Smiley's work entailed?" Barolli asked.

"No, I'm afraid not."

Afterward, Anna sat with Barolli in the patrol car. They were disappointed, especially Barolli, who really thought they'd got a breakthrough.

"Maybe we have, you know. It's a bit of a coincidence, isn't it, that our victim was Polish and so was Smiley's wife," Anna said.

"We don't know that for sure, but we can check with Births and Marriages."

Returning to the station, Anna left Barolli to mark up the new development. Joan was working on tracing any parking tickets or traffic violations that involved Smiley and the Transit van. It seemed impossible that in this day and age a family could uproot itself and disappear, and yet by the end of the day, they still had not discovered the whereabouts of John Smiley and his family. They were running checks through school registers in and around the Kilburn area, Social Services, employment agencies, the Polish embassy, voting registers. Anna was concentrating on vehicle license and taxation. John Smiley could have sold the Transit van, but it was still registered to him under his old address. If Smiley still owned the van, it would by now require its motor official tax, so that was another avenue to check out. It was tedious, frustrating work and occupied almost everyone on the murder team.

The following morning, there was still no news. Mike Lewis was getting a lot of pressure from Langton, but they were coming up with one dead end after another. During the briefing, which left them all depressed, they got a surge of energy when a call came in from the TV *Crimewatch* team. They had hoped to get a result, but they were stunned by just how good a result it was. A woman caller who refused to identify herself said she was certain the murdered girl was called Anika. She didn't know her surname but thought she'd worked in a Turkish restaurant in Earl's Court.

Mike Lewis and Barolli headed out, leaving Anna to continue trying to trace John Smiley. Midmorning, they still had no result, and she was glad to leave her office to interview Estelle's uncle, who had come down from Manchester by coach.

Andre Dubcek was a small man but overweight, bordering on obese. He was wearing a crumpled cheap navy suit, the buttons of his shirt straining over his stomach. He sat with a cup of coffee, and when Anna entered the interview room, he jumped to his feet to shake her hand vigorously.

As the station was not that old, the interview room walls were not the usual cold shade of light lavatory green, but were a warmer color, with deep cream and pinkish brown overtones on the ceiling. There was the obligatory bare table and two chairs side against one wall, close to the tape recorder. There were also—and not in use for this interview—the cameras positioned high up on the wall and focused on the seating area.

Anna drew out a chair and sat opposite Andre. He had a strong accent but a good grasp of English. He explained that he was Estelle's father's brother. Anna noticed his thick stubby fingers as he made a lot of wide-handed gestures.

"I am shocked, so shocked. I have brought some photographs that I have, but only from when Estelle was a child."

Anna looked through them and could see what a pretty girl Estelle had been. Andre pointed out who was who, and kept repeating it was sad that he had not had more contact with his niece. Estelle's father had died young of lung cancer, and her mother had remarried and, sadly, died in childbirth, when Estelle would have been twelve years old. She had subsequently been brought up by her grandparents, and then when they had passed on, she was virtually on her own.

"I never write, just maybe a card at Christmas. We were

so far away, and I have children and a business here, and times are very hard."

Anna let him talk on until she felt he was relaxed enough to talk about the telephone call from Estelle. He said his wife had answered, and she had been excited, passing the phone to him. He gave one of his flat-handed gestures.

"Maybe I was not as much. I thought Estelle would be asking for money for a ticket, but then she said she was in London. She wanted to visit, meet my wife and her cousins, and . . . well, yes, it was for money. She said she had no place to live and wanted to maybe find work here with me while she learned English."

Andre had agreed that she could stay with his family and, if possible, he would find her work in his bakery. He recalled the date she had rung: the day before she met with Petrovich. She had said she would call when she got to Manchester, as she wasn't sure if she could afford the train fare.

"I told her to get a coach, because it's much cheaper, and she said she would maybe do that . . . and I never heard from her again."

There was nothing more he could add. Anna could see he was distressed, as he kept pressing his hands flat on the table.

"I didn't have no place to call her, no number. She contact me."

"She rang you from a mobile?"

"I dunno, I never checked."

"We got your number from a Mrs. Henderson whom Estelle worked for. Did you only ever receive the one phone call?"

"Yes, she call just once."

• • •

Andre left the station shortly afterward to return to Manchester. It was yet another dead end. Anna made a note on the incident board regarding their interview, then returned to her desk to continue the search for Smiley. He might have gone abroad, but his van was obviously still in London, so they needed to discover if he had sold it. Anna made more calculations, comparing the dates from the CCTV footage of the parked van against the murders. Of the three different occasions, two matched the dates the last two victims were discovered, but there had been no signs of the van at the time of Margaret Potts's murder.

Anna called across to Joan to ask if she would scroll through previous cold cases with a date similar to when the sightings of the van had been recorded.

"Christ, we don't need any more bodies," Joan grumbled.

"Just start on it, Joan, and if you don't get anything from the service stations, search on."

Anna's desk phone rang; it was the headmistress from Smiley's children's school. Anna was surprised.

"The reason I am calling is because I was talking in the staff room after you had left, and one of our junior teachers, who'd been in the nursery section as a trainee, recalled Mrs. Smiley. She said she was Polish, and she also recalled her talking about some blinds—"

Anna interrupted. "I'm sorry, I am not quite following . . . Blinds?"

"Yes, you know—wooden slatted blinds. Mrs. Smiley apparently told her that her husband worked for a company that made them. They're rather expensive and trendy, and they come in different shades of wood and various sizes."

Anna clarified that they were window blinds, and she

was told that the company made them to measure and fitted them.

It was too much to hope that the teacher recalled the name of the company, and she didn't, but it meant they were another step forward.

Barbara wrinkled her nose at the news. "Blinds? Wooden blinds like in Switzerland at the skiing chalets?"

"No, for homes here, slatted blinds made to measure in wood. It's got to be quite a specialist company, as they deliver and fit them. So start checking all the companies."

Barbara and Joan worked together, literally going through every listed company in the Yellow Pages, on the Internet, and in the directory. While they were checking, Anna joined Mike and Barolli, who had returned from Earl's Court. Their remaining victim had been identified by two waiters and the manager of the small restaurant. Her name was Anika Waleska; she was a Polish student who had worked for cash in hand four nights a week and the odd weekend as a relief waitress. They had no details of where she had lived, just a phone number. One night she had simply not turned up for work and had not been seen in months. The phone number was a mobile no longer in use and had been bought from a telephone warehouse.

The police began to check back with the Polish embassy in the hope that they could give more details. The incident room was hopping, with every telephone in use as thorough checks were made via Interpol and the UK border agency. They now had a link between their two young victims, as both were Polish—but that excluded Margaret Potts.

Joan got the breakthrough, and everyone went quiet as she had finally traced their only suspect. John Smiley worked for a company called Swell Blinds. They had moved from their warehouse in Hounslow to Manchester five years ago, and John Smiley was still employed by them. She had a contact number for him, as well as the address and details. The company still delivered to London and in fact did business all over the country. The blinds were handmade in a factory in Salford, near Manchester.

"Did you explain why we want to contact him?" Mike asked, worried that Smiley might be tipped off and disappear.

"No, I didn't, because I know how important this could be, so I played it quite casual and just said it was a routine inquiry." Joan gave a raised eye to Barbara, who hid a smile. Sometimes in his new position as DCI, Mike got under their skin. They were both old hands and knew enough of police procedure to act accordingly.

They had made big steps forward. Mike contacted Langton to tell him that their third victim had been identified and the owner of the Transit van traced. Langton suggested they move on Smiley fast but keep it low-profile. No sooner had Mike replaced the phone than Joan was startled to receive a call from Smiley himself.

"Is he on the line now?" Mike asked.

"Yes."

"I'll take it in my office."

Everyone waited, and Mike eventually returned to the incident room.

"Well, Smiley by name and nature. Very helpful; said he's delivering in London tomorrow and he'll come in first thing."

"You believe him?" Barolli asked.

"Yes. He has no idea what we want to see him about, as I said it was connected to him not changing addresses on his van."

"I don't like it," Barolli muttered.

"You want to go all the way to Manchester? I don't, and if we need to confirm that he is in actual fact delivering tomorrow, we can contact his boss—all right?"

"I'd just like to know he's not about to do a runner."

"Listen, contact Manchester Murder Squad and ask them to keep an eye on him. He's got a mortgage, a wife, and two kids, so I don't think he's going to do a disappearing act."

"Yeah, they said that about Ronnie Biggs."

Anna could see the tension mounting between the two men, and to defuse it, she asked if the team could move on with tracking down anyone who had known Anika Waleska.

"It's coincidental that Smiley's wife is also Polish, and there may be some kind of connection there," Anna said.

Barolli was at it again, suggesting she read up on just how many Polish immigrants had been shipped back out of England. "We're bloody inundated with Poles," he said rudely.

Anna gestured to the board, snapping, "Not murdered, though, all right?"

The following day, Langton appeared, sat himself down at one of the desks, and impatiently demanded a briefing. He was playing with a small piece of string, tying and untying a knot as Mike gave him a runthrough of the new details. His foot twitched while he tied and untied the knot. As Mike finished, he stood up.

"You're out by three days—correct?—from the time Estelle was last seen to her murder? And you got the ID via a phone-in from *Crimewatch* on Anika, right?" He sighed and chewed at his lips. "They got this anonymity deal, but did you get any hint about who the caller could have been? Did she work in the same restaurant?"

Mike said there was no way the program would give them any assistance on tracing the caller; that was what it was all about, anonymity assured.

"Fuck that. Go back and ask if they'll run a request for the informant to come forward on their next show. Maybe she'll cough up."

Langton paced in front of the board and then stopped, noticing Anna's detail about her phone call from Welsh.

He glanced at Anna. "You got your number changed?"

"Not yet."

He returned to perch on the side of her desk. "Okay, I want to visit the prick. Now, I know you don't want to set eyes on him again, Travis, but let's put the bastard to bed or see if he's fucking us around once and for all, eh? So first thing in the morning, all right?"

Anna nodded, not liking it and also not wanting to spend the long journey with him, but she didn't have an option.

"Right, let's see how the meeting with this guy Smiley pans out."

"Shall I order a patrol car for tomorrow?"

"Nope, you can drive. You must know your way there blindfolded by now." He smiled. Then Langton tied and untied the knot and remained silent, looking over the board again. "I want a check on any previous cold cases that might have similar MOs to our three girls."

"Already doing that," Joan murmured, although she had not as yet begun the check.

"I don't like the missing three days. We need to go back

and question Katia and the boyfriend. The victim had to stay somewhere. You don't think he was shagging her?" he added, turning to Anna.

Anna shook her head. "Petrovich described Estelle as naive and not in any way sexually permissive."

"Yeah, well, he might say that, but if this Katia was jealous, he might have screwed her in his hotel. He lives in, right?"

"Yes, but on his days off, he stays with Katia."

"Go back and question him again, because we need to know if our killer picked up the poor girl and held her captive. Have you checked out the coach stations?"

Barolli said that they had, plus the train stations, armed with photographs, but no luck. Langton retied the knot, which was becoming annoying to everyone.

"Okay. Have another session with Eric Potts, see if he ever saw our white van. We don't have it on CCTV footage for the approximate time Potts was murdered, but we're not likely to, as it's two years ago now and the suspect has owned the van since living in Kilburn, right?"

Langton put away his piece of string, checked the time, and announced that he had to leave. As he passed Anna, he promised that he would get on to the governor of Barfield to make sure they did a sweep of Welsh's cell. He warned her not to pick up her landline until she had the new number.

As always, the whirlwind effect of Langton's periodic visits left everyone uneasy.

"What's with the string?" Barolli asked, and Mike smiled.

"He's given up smoking. It's something to do with every time you feel the need for a fag: you tie a knot, then untie it, and the urge subsides."

Anna hoped that the urge would not be present on the

drive up to Leeds, as it would get on her nerves even more than Barolli's antics.

Mike passed out Langton's orders, and Anna, along with Barolli, sorted out the next round of interviews. They called Eric, but he was not available. They decided not to contact Emerald Turk but to pay her another unscheduled visit to check if she had ever seen the white Transit van.

Emerald was as belligerent as she had been on the two previous visits. It helped that this time Anna was accompanied, and instead of interviewing her in the kitchen, they conducted it in the sitting room. Children's toys littered the entire room, stacked on the sofa and easy chairs. Emerald made no effort to remove anything but stood, hands on her hips, in the center of the room as Barolli and Anna remained by the door.

"Have you ever seen this van?" Barolli passed over the picture of the van.

Emerald glanced at it and then shrugged. "I dunno. It's a common sort of van, isn't it?"

"Might have been parked close by; maybe Margaret was driven here in it. Have another look."

Emerald sighed and snatched the photograph. "No. She's been dead two years or more, so why would I fucking remember this van?"

"We think the driver may be connected to her murder," Anna said quietly.

"Well, she wasn't run over, was she? So no, I've not seen it, and I dunno anyone drivin' one. Is that all you come for?"

"Thank you for your help," Barolli said, glancing at Anna.

"My pleasure," Emerald replied sarcastically, kicking a red tractor out of her way as she walked toward them.

"The suspect delivers blinds—wooden slatted ones," Anna said as Barolli turned halfway out of the door. "Did Margaret ever mention knowing someone who did that?"

Emerald shook her head at Anna. "No, she fucking didn't. She was usually half-cut when I saw her. If you ask me, you lot are like the blind following the blind." She snorted a laugh.

Eric was in his office when they called and he confirmed that he had never seen Margaret get in or out of a white Transit van, nor did she ever mention that she knew anyone selling blinds. They returned to the incident room just as Mike got the message that John Smiley was in reception asking if he could leave his van in their car park. Mike asked Anna to join him for the interview as Barolli was told to go down and show Mr. Smiley where he could park and to have a good look over his van.

John Smiley was tall and well built, with a slight combover. He was dressed in green overalls with a Swell Blinds logo embroidered on the pocket and printed on the back of his overalls. He was quite a good-looking man, with dark eyebrows and dark brown eyes, though his teeth were slightly stained with tobacco.

He came into the interview room smiling, confident. When he sat down, he apologized for not having informed the DVLA about his change of address.

"I kept on meaning to get it sent in, but at first we didn't have a permanent address in Manchester, and we rented a flat. Then we moved from that place to another before we found our house."

Mike opened a file and made a note. "Have you now registered the vehicle?" he asked.

"I'm going to do it first thing in the morning. I've got the form with me."

"So you own the van, Mr. Smiley?"

"Yes, I do. The firm supplied me with one when I first started working for them, then they traded it in for this one and I bought it from them. I got it for a good price. I was glad that I did, 'cause when the firm moved, a couple of guys who didn't have their own transport got made redundant."

"Have there been other drivers using your van?"

"No way, never. I keep it in very good condition—even the kids aren't allowed to mess it up. To be honest, I thought when the company moved from London to Manchester, they'd suggest trading it in for a new one, but they were economizing, cutting back on a lot of expenses."

"I am going to show you two photographs, and I'd be grateful if you could tell us if it is your van caught on the CCTV camera." Mike slid the pictures across the desk.

Smiley looked carefully at both of the photographs and then nodded. "Yes. You can even see my license plate, so it's definitely my van."

"Can you tell us why you were at the London Gateway service station on both these occasions?"

Smiley took out a small, well-thumbed diary and glanced at the photographs in front of him before flicking through the pages. "Yes, I'd been delivering to a Mrs. Freeman in Kensington. She wanted the blinds measured for a conservatory."

Mike made a note, then gestured to the second photograph. Again, Smiley looked through his diary after reading out the date on the photograph.

"Yes, that was delivering four sets of floor-to-ceiling

oak blinds to a Mr. Leatherhime, big house in Cobham. My firm will have all the receipts of payments and delivery dates. These are just for me personally." He closed his diary.

"So take me through how you stopped off at the London Gateway Services on both occasions." Mike leaned back in his chair.

"Well, it's a fair old way from Manchester to London, and I usually try to get there and back as fast as possible. I want to be with my kids and put them to bed, or at least say good night to them, if possible. My wife gives me a packed lunch, and I eat on the way, and then I stop off at the London Gateway on the way back and use their toilets, because to be honest, I don't like to ask customers if I can use theirs. So I have a bathroom break, usually order a coffee to take out, and keep going."

"Always at the London Gateway?" Mike asked, looking down at his notes.

"No, sometimes I don't need to, but as it's the first service station on the M1, when I need to go, it's usually about that time. I leave early, around four-thirty to five, and it's a four-hour drive, sometimes a lot longer if there's traffic or an accident. It can take me up to six hours, as the M6 is always slow and can put me back a couple of hours."

"So you stop off at the London Gateway and use their conveniences?"

"Yes, sir, but not on a regular basis. It'd depend on whether or not I needed to use them. Our orders have been on the slack side, so I've not had to do many trips for the past few months."

Mike removed the photograph of Margaret Potts, saying, "Have you ever seen this woman?"

Smiley seemed to give it a lot of attention before he shook his head.

Estelle Dubcek's picture came next. "How about this girl?"

"No, sorry. I don't think I've ever seen her."

"This girl?"

Smiley leaned forward to look at Anika Waleska's photograph. He hesitated and then shook his head again. "No."

"Do you ever give hitchhikers a ride?"

"Me? No, never, not worth it. It's too much of a risk, never have and never will."

"Tell me about your wife."

"My wife?"

"Yes."

Smiley puffed out his cheeks and eased around in his chair. "I dunno what you're asking me about her for. She can't drive, and she's never driven my van. You know, I'm getting to feel a bit uncomfortable. What's this really about? It's not just my vehicle license not being updated, is it?"

"No. You are just helping our inquiries, Mr. Smiley."

"What about?"

Mike gathered up the photographs. "These women were murdered."

Smiley opened and shut his mouth. "I don't understand."

"We are just eliminating people with a vehicle caught on the CCTV cameras in the areas where these women's bodies were discovered. You happened to be at the location on two of the occasions."

"My God. This is serious, isn't it?"

"Yes, Mr. Smiley, very serious, but I think you have explained your reasons for being at the London Gateway, so I just need to iron out a few more things. How long have you been married?"

"For twelve years. I've two children, aged eleven and eight—a boy and a girl. My wife is called Sonja. She and

I met when I came out of the army; she was working in Aldershot."

"Was she from there?"

"No. She's originally from Warsaw in Poland. She came over to England with her mother twenty years ago."

"Do you speak Polish?"

"No. Truth is, she hardly speaks it herself now, and we lost her mother four years ago. She was still living in Aldershot and went a bit senile. We were going to bring her to live with us in Manchester when we got settled, but then she got pneumonia, spent a few days in the hospital, and never came out. Seventy-two, fit as a fiddle before, but just a bit confused, know what I mean?"

"Did your wife ever come on these trips to London?"

"No, no way. She works as a dinner lady at the local school, and she's keen that the children always have someone at home. She's a wonderful mother, which is why I try to get back before their bedtime. Kiss them good night."

"Have you ever picked up a prostitute at the service stations?"

"*Me?*"

"Yes, Mr. Smiley. It's nothing to be ashamed of; we are asking everyone we interview."

"Never. For one, I wouldn't fancy it, I'm too fussy about personal hygiene, and for two, if my wife was ever to catch me doing anything so stupid, she'd castrate me." He laughed. "Just joking, but the truth is, I wouldn't jeopardize my relationship. I love my wife, in fact, I worship the ground she walks on, she's . . ."

He picked up his diary again and thumbed through it to take out a small Polaroid picture. He passed it across the table. "That's Sonja a few years back—she was a real looker, and to be honest I'd sown my wild oats before I met her. Twelve years in the Paras, and we were a wild bunch, fought in the Iraq invasion, got decorated, and I was even thinking about enlisting for another tour when I met Sonja. There was no more gallivanting around for me after that, and she's a good few years younger."

Smiley left the station half an hour later, assuring Mike Lewis that he would have his van registered by the following morning. Neither Anna nor Mike said a word as he replaced the photographs and notes in a file. Eventually, he stood up and stretched.

"What do you think?"

Anna had not made one note. "Bit too much information. Guy's got verbal dysentery, but we can check out his company's deliveries and—"

Barolli entered the interview room, interrupting her. "Transit van is clean enough to eat your dinner off. There's not a mark on it, and considering it's eight years old and with quite heavy mileage, it's in very good condition, new tires and everything. The two front seats look hardly used, and the two rear passenger seats have been removed, to make more room for storage, I suppose. There's no carpet, but rubber matting and shelving in the rear."

Barolli looked from one to the other, saying, "You suss him for this?"

"Not right now, Paul, but we'll need to check out all his details. He's an ex-Para, with commendations, and he's been with the same company ten years. No police record, just a slip up on his vehicle license being out of date."

"Yeah, yeah, yeah." Mike headed into the corridor.

"What do you think?" Barolli asked Anna.

"I don't know. He was affable and not thrown by any of the questions. Didn't break out in a sweat, answered everything we needed to know and more."

"Another dead end." Barolli sighed with frustration and followed Lewis out.

Anna shrugged. Was it? She had not picked up anything suspicious, and there was only one slight show of nerves when they asked him about his wife. He had not asked for a solicitor to be present, and she wondered if he lived up to his name, not that he had smiled, apart from when they said he could leave. She had no gut feelings about him, just that he had been overtalkative.

By the time Anna returned to the incident room, Mike had relayed the content of their interview to Langton by phone.

"Said he'll be at your place by seven-thirty tomorrow morning."

Mike walked off to his office, and Anna caught the raised eyebrow between him and Barolli.

"I've got one, Anna," Joan said, rocking back in her chair.

"One what, Joan?"

"Victim. Murdered four years ago, case went cold, victim never identified but found not far from Newport Pagnell service station."

But Anna was packing up her briefcase, ready to leave. "Let Paul handle it," she said. "I need to get off home, as I've got an early start. Good night."

As soon as Anna left the incident room, Barolli did a nasty mimic of her with his hands on his hips. "And we all know who's picking her up for that 'early start'! I'd put money on it he'll shag her before they leave for Barfield."

Chapter Seven

Anna was waiting in her car outside her garage at exactly seven-thirty. She didn't want Langton coming into her flat. But he surprised her by turning up carrying two Starbucks coffees and a bag of muffins.

"Morning. I reckoned you wouldn't have had breakfast, so I brought it along to eat on the drive."

Langton got into the passenger seat, propped the coffee on the tray between them, and slammed the door closed. He swore as he opened the bag because one of the muffins was chocolate.

"I asked for plain. Do you like chocolate? Because I can't stand it."

"Yes, thank you. Just not straightaway."

They drove off, Langton eating his muffin and swearing again, as the coffee was too hot. She couldn't help but smile, since he had sugar around his mouth, like a child. He quickly wiped it off with a napkin.

"You get anything from Smiley's interview?"

Anna repeated that she had felt he was overtalkative, but apart from that, he showed no sign of nerves.

"Ex-Para, so he's got a lot of training under his belt. Must be a tough sod. They checking out his explanations as to why he was at the service station?" Langton asked.

"I think so, and they'll also check the deliveries he says he made on the two days."

"Happily married, right?"

"He says so. Two children, mortgage on the property, and no police record, just the discrepancy over the vehicle's registration documents."

"Mmmm. We should keep him in the frame." Langton took out his length of string and began tying a knot.

"Is that working?" she asked.

"I dunno, but apparently, it takes twenty seconds for the urge to come and go, so tie a knot and untie it, and you shouldn't feel the need for a cigarette."

"How long have you been trying it out?"

"Few days. It's driving me nuts, but I've not had a cigarette for twenty-four hours. Slipped up yesterday because I couldn't find the string. I've not got a pack with me and no lighter, so maybe it's working. If it doesn't, I'm thinking about going to a hypnotist."

Anna smiled again. She was so unused to his chatty manner, and she almost laughed as he swore, unable to untie his last knot.

"I had a friend who went to a hypnotist," she said. "It took all of five minutes, and when he came out, he thought it was a total waste of fifty pounds, then he went up to a kiosk to buy a pack of cigarettes and instead asked for a packet of peanuts."

Langton looked at her. "Did it work after the peanuts?"

"Yes, apparently so, but he put on weight."

Langton laughed. "I doubt that would happen to me; I never put on weight." He rested his arm along the back of her seat. "You have, I notice."

"Me?"

"Yes, around your hips. Not been working out?"

She flushed and continued driving.

"So how's your love life?"

"Mind your own business."

He withdrew his arm and sipped his coffee. "Just making conversation. Don't get all arsey."

"I'm not."

"Yes, you are. You get these two pink spots on your cheeks, dead giveaway when you get rattled." He pressed his seat farther back, complained about the lack of legroom, and then fiddled with the radio. "Do you want the news?" he asked.

"Don't mind. There's some CDs if you want to listen to music, and there's *The Times* on the backseat."

Langton turned off the radio and reached for the newspaper. They drove mostly in silence as he read the paper, but he had an annoying habit of reading out bits of articles and nudging her every time he turned a page.

"I can't read in cars," she said.

"Thank you for that vital piece of information, Travis. To be honest, I never have the time to read the upmarket rags; it'd take hours. I think they're bought by commuters because sitting on a train every morning for a couple of hours, they've got nothing better to do. I do a crash zap through all the crap ones, keeps me updated . . ."

"Do you read books?"

"When do I have the time? It's mostly autobiographies, but I can't remember the last one I read. I've had Napoleon on my bedside table for six months. They've got his horse's skeleton in one of the war museums—Chelsea. It's surprisingly small. I think it was an Arab, but then he wasn't a big fella . . ."

Anna realized that in all the time she had known him, they had hardly ever had a normal conversation, one that wasn't connected to a case they were working on. She wondered when he would get around to discussing their investigation, but he continued reading out sections from the paper until they headed onto the M1. He tossed the paper into the backseat all crumpled up and with the pages muddled. She found that irritating, as she hadn't even had time to glance at it. It reminded her of her father getting angry when she had taken out the art section of a Sunday paper before he had finished it. She also recalled that, like Langton, her father never seemed to have the time to read the morning papers, but his Sundays were spent poring over all the weekend editions.

"Stop in at the London Gateway," Langton said suddenly.

"What?"

"When we get to the service station, drive in. I've not had a look around yet. Then go to where Estelle Dubcek's body was discovered. Pull onto the hard shoulder so I can get out and have a look."

Anna nodded. He was leaning over to pick up her files, which were stacked on the backseat with her briefcase. "You mind if I look over these?" He was already opening the file containing the photographs, so it was rather pointless even replying.

"Pretty girls. I don't believe there wasn't one person who didn't remember them, maybe gave them a lift. Picked up, strangled, and raped. Doesn't make sense. Both Polish, like Smiley's wife—it's a big coincidence."

Langton sifted through the files and then tossed them back onto the seat behind him. "No one identified them at train or coach stations, so how did these kids get to the service station? They had to get a lift from someone, or they

were snatched maybe trying for a ride. Not so with Margaret Potts, we know about her, but these two young girls . . ."

"We're here," Anna said, driving into the London Gateway.

Langton directed her to the car parking area. He got out
and stood for a long time looking around and then bent
down to her window. "I'm going to use the loo, do you
need to go?"

"No. I'll wait."

She watched him striding toward the conveniences, sipping her cold coffee, waiting. It seemed an age before she
saw him coming out from the restaurants, and then he disappeared again into the shopping area. It was ten minutes
before he headed back toward the Mini.

"Okay. Next drive into the truckers' area and point out
where the Transit van was parked," he said, and slammed
the passenger door so hard the Mini rocked. Anna did as
he suggested, and he was another fifteen minutes walking
around the parked vehicles, looking at the CCTV cameras,
and talking to one driver for a while before he returned.

"The van was parked almost under the surveillance camera," Anna pointed out, passing him the photograph.

Langton nodded and then asked her to head off to
where Estelle Dubcek's body had been discovered. They
drove toward the slip road passing the service station's petrol station, and Anna remarked that the last time she had
been there with Barolli, they had seen a young girl hitching
a ride. Langton said nothing as she headed back onto the
M1. He was checking his watch to calculate how long it
took to get to the area on the hard shoulder where Estelle's
body had been discovered.

Anna eventually parked and Langton got out, gesturing
for her to join him.

"Okay, so this is where the guy says he parked his van to take a leak, right?"

"Yes."

Langton looked around and then crossed to the hedge. He stood for a while, turning toward where the ragged crime-scene ribbons were still in place. "He pisses here, looks over there, and sees the body?"

"Yes."

Langton chewed at his lip, twisting his string around his fingers. He then pushed his way through the hedge and jumped over the ditch. "She was lying here, her head facing north, yes?" he shouted.

Anna nodded. The ground was still muddy, but he cautiously continued walking to where the body had been lying. He shouted to her again. "Anna, go back to the car, give me a toot on your horn when you see me."

She did as she was asked and stood by the side of the Mini, waiting. It was some while until his head appeared over the hedge. She pressed the horn.

"Now sit in the car and use the horn again when you can see me," he called out.

It was not easy to catch a glimpse of him until he was heading toward her from behind the hedge. She tooted the horn.

Langton got back into the car, and she switched on the ignition, but he put his hand over hers. "Wait a minute. Just let me think for a second."

He was silent, staring toward the hedge. Then he reached behind him and picked up the file of photographs and studied those taken of Estelle's body at the murder site, looking up at the hedge row.

"I want that guy Collingwood brought back in to check his statement; my gut feeling is that there's something he's leaving out." Langton whistled through his teeth. "Our killer knew he couldn't be seen from the hard shoulder, and the small dirt track that was used for all the forensic vehicles runs alongside almost up to the hedge, right?"

"Yes. It was very muddy and quite narrow."

Langton muttered to himself. "I want you to head off the motorway and backtrack to the lane the team used. I need to have a look at it." He took out a small black notebook and started jotting down something, but she couldn't tell what.

It took quite a while to drive to the next junction, and then find the nearest turn to take them back in the direction of the crime scene. It took even longer going down the back lanes until they came to the small opening for the track that led across the side of the field to the murder site. Anna could feel the wheels of her Mini dragging through the deep muddy ruts and pulled up. "I think I should stop here. We've had more rain, and the last thing we need is to get bogged down."

He nodded, getting out, and she watched him walk up the lane, skirting puddles and then crossing to where the body had been discovered. When he returned, his shoes were caked in mud, and her carpet on the passenger side was soon covered. She now had to reverse down the lane. When they reached the broken gate at the entrance, Langton asked her to drive back in the opposite direction.

"That part of the lane is very rough, and I don't think we could use it. All the police vehicles came the long way round," Anna pointed out.

"See how far you can get," he snapped.

Anna was loath to head along that route, as it was muddy, with deep tracks making ridges that she had to bounce over. Langton rolled down his window, telling her to stop as he looked up to the trees above. Then he told her to continue.

"We could get bogged down, you know," she said crossly.

"Yeah, yeah, keep going."

She did so at a snail's pace, the car jolting and bouncing while the mud splashed as high as the windows. She was growing increasingly annoyed, only too aware that the traffic officers had warned everyone to stay clear as the lane was such rough going; they had posted specific directions to use the way she had driven in. She was about to insist on turning back when the lane widened and a cinder track appeared. Although there were many potholes filled in with rocks and stones, it was a much easier surface to drive on.

"Keep going," Langton said again, jotting down the mileage in his book.

To Anna's surprise, the lane got wider, and after a sharp right turn, there were wooden boards that led onto a small tarmac lane, clearly used to lead to some outbuilding. Langton gestured for her to keep going, so she drove on for a couple of miles, passing a barn and more outbuildings, and then they were on a wider road again. On one side was a hedgerow. At one point there was a wide gap rutted with heavy tracks.

"Turn in there," Langton instructed.

They drove through and came out at the far side of the truckers' parking section at the service station.

Langton got out, and Anna could see him talking to a man sitting in his cab eating a hamburger. She saw him gesture toward the way they had come. After more conversation, he returned to the car.

"Okay, let's go back the way we came and join the motorway there," he said, and slammed the door shut. He sat with his notebook out and jotted down page after page before he whacked it against the dashboard. "The killer came that way. He drove from the truckers' area into that lane. He's someone who knows this area, knows he could get to that field to dump the body and not be seen from the road. The time code of the CCTV footage of Smiley's van meant he was parked in the truckers' stop, but the body was discovered hours after he had left. His van is not that big, so he could have easily driven the route we came. Some of the trees have branches broken, so if it wasn't him, it could have been someone with a fair-sized vehicle."

Langton continued to explain his theory as Anna headed back to the M1. He was certain the killer had the girls in his vehicle; perhaps they were already dead and he needed a place to dump their bodies. Langton now doubted that their victims were ever seen at the service station—they could have been trussed up in the back of the van.

"What about Margaret Potts? She was seen there and was a regular."

"Yes, I know, but that truck driver told me that some of the girls service their customers out in that lane—said he'd heard about a few men backing out into that dirt track so they could do the business—and I'd say Maggie Potts would have known that area."

Langton got on the phone to the incident room. He wanted all the outhouses and barns they'd seen across the fields searched, and anyone working there questioned regarding any vehicles driving down the back route. Anna mentioned that Smiley's van was in pristine condition when Barolli checked it out. If he had driven down that back lane, he would have gotten scratches from the overhanging trees.

Langton called the incident room again, this time asking them to check out the size of any truck that would get damaged and then to compare that to the dimensions of Smiley's van.

"Do you think the killer kidnapped the girls?" Anna asked.

"Yeah, possibly. I don't know."

"Margaret Potts is the odd one out, then, isn't she?"

Langton nodded, knotting his string impatiently. "She comes two years before Estelle is murdered, and then we have Anika Waleska between them."

When Anna mentioned that Joan had brought up a file of another unidentified victim found four years previously, Langton was immediately back on the phone, asking for details. He said little but listened for some considerable time, grunting and barking out instructions for the team to keep digging up more cases with the same MO. He snapped off his phone. "I think our killer's been at this for a long time, so we might get more. In fact, I am bloody sure of it. Joan's come up with a girl between twenty and thirty, never identified."

"Found at a service station?" Anna asked.

"Yeah, Newport Pagnell, naked and wrapped in a blue blanket."

"That's not the same MO as ours," Anna said.

Langton raised his hand, wagging his index finger. "Four years ago! Maybe the killer switched his style, and you know"—he chewed at his pencil—"what if Margaret Potts recognized him, maybe had shagged him before? We need to open up that early case."

"With no clothes, just a blue blanket, there's even less to go on than with Anika and Estelle."

"Yeah, yeah." He went back to his notebook, flicking the pages back and forth while his right foot twitched. "Smiley went to work in Manchester five years ago, so it's in the time frame. What we need to do is look around and see what we can dig up on him when he worked in London."

He was back on the mobile again to the incident room as he asked them to check out John Smiley's army record and to question any employees who had worked with him in London.

Barolli replaced the receiver.

"Langton again," he told the others. "We've got to arrange for a check on John Smiley's army record, dig out anyone we can find who knew him or knows him from when he worked in London."

Mike Lewis was busy orchestrating the search team to go to the farm that owned the outhouses and barns, and Joan and Barbara continued their trawl through records of dead cases that could be connected to the current investigation. Two officers were out talking to the Thames Valley detectives who had been on the four-year-old murder inquiry, requesting all of their files.

Barolli passed a cup of tea to Mike, saying, "Looks like he's placing John Smiley in the frame."

"Yeah, seems so. Can you do the check on his army pals and get over to their regimental HQ at Colchester?"

"I'll be gone all day," Barolli said reluctantly. "It's a fair old journey over there."

"Just do it. Meanwhile, I'll be going back to the landlord of his previous house, and we need to get from Smiley's employer anyone who knew him when he worked in London. If the company moved lock, stock, and barrel to Manchester, some employees might not have gone up there with them."

Barolli had left by the time Barbara had been able to

contact Arnold Rodgers, the boss at Swell Blinds. Barbara was diplomatic, first thanking the man for his assistance in giving details of John Smiley, then saying that they now required lists of any employees who had not moved to Manchester with the company. She had already checked with Companies House, she told him, but they had no record of how many staff were working for Swell Blinds. Arnold became agitated and admitted that some people were paid cash in hand. Basically, he was worried about not paying National Insurance and kept repeating himself.

Finally, Joan was able to get the names of three ex-employees, although Rodgers had no address or contact phone numbers for two of them. The first was a woman called Wendy Dunn, a part-time receptionist, who agreed to be interviewed. It turned out that she lived in Feltham, southwest London, not far from Barbara, so Mike gave her the go-ahead to leave the station early. He himself was feeling frazzled. The peremptory stream of orders issuing from Langton meant a lot of checking and organization, and he was loath to let anything slide, because he knew he would be grilled on his boss's return.

Langton had slept for the latter part of the journey. He woke up as soon as they drove through the prison compound and ran his fingers through his hair before straightening his tie. Anna warned him that the governor liked to talk but had so far been accommodating.

They went through the usual security details before being led into the staff building, where the governor was waiting with fresh coffee and biscuits. Langton accepted, and soon they were chatting like old friends. Anna was impressed by the way Langton appeared so at ease and in no particular hurry to interview Welsh. She herself was eager to get it over and done with, but Langton, to her annoyance, accepted a tour of the prison.

She felt very much the second-class citizen, trailing behind as the two men walked side by side, talking nonstop. They went to the gym, they went to various cell blocks and canteens and the huge visitors' section, stopping over and over again to talk to the prison officers. Langton constantly asked questions, showing genuine interest as Anna hovered after him.

The gates between each new section of the corridors had stringent security measures. On each occasion, the governor would speak to a surveillance camera, one of the locks on the gate would click open, and he would use his personal set of keys to open the second lock. They eventually reached what looked like something from a *Doctor Who* episode. It was a high-tech glass capsule that housed all the monitors for the prison's exterior, wards, and corridors. Altogether, the tour took over an hour. It was by now three o'clock, and Anna knew that after interviewing Welsh, the drive back would be a long one. She probably wouldn't get home until after ten.

Wendy Dunn was in her mid-seventies, older than Barbara had expected. She immediately offered her visitor tea and biscuits, and not until they had settled themselves in her living room in the neat and tidy council flat did she begin to talk. She had worked for Arnold Rodgers for twenty years on a proper, employed basis and had then retired. However, she had returned to work for him on a casual basis for three years before he packed up the company and moved to Manchester. She admitted that she was paid in cash so she did not have to pay tax; it was only a small amount, but under the counter. She had mostly taken the orders and sometimes made cold calls for the company when work was slack. She was sweet and, Barbara felt, an honest woman. She was a widow with four grandchildren, and after Swell Blinds moved, she had not done any other work.

Barbara eased the conversation around to John Smiley.

"Oh, he was a lovely man," Wendy said immediately. "Help anyone, he would, and he was a very good, hard worker. He had two young children."

Barbara asked about his wife, Sonja.

"Well, I only met her a few times, once at a Christmas party, and she was lovely looking, then I think I met her at Mr. Rodger's drinks party. The last time was when I went round to say goodbye to John. I'd got him a little something. He was a kind man, and when I needed some of my own blinds fixed, he did them for me—never would take a penny."

Wendy gestured at the wooden slatted blinds on her kitchen window as they walked through to put the tea tray down. "They're lovely, aren't they, and very light and easy to draw up and down."

Barbara agreed that they were stylish, and she tried drawing them closed and pulling them up again.

"Was he happily married?" she asked.

"Oh, yes. I think Sonja ruled the roost, though; she was houseproud and kept him on a tight rein. He was always short of money." She laughed.

"How do you mean?"

"Well, she'd pack up a lunch for him; he never went to the cafés with the others and said he was saving for a house of their own. The children were well behaved and always dressed well, and John worshipped her, was always talking about his Sonja."

Wendy would have chatted on for hours and was even able to give another employee's contact number. He was Portuguese, she said, and did a lot of the paint-spraying and was working at a factory. Barbara had heard enough. She thanked the older woman profusely, then went off home.

Mario Gespari lived in Hounslow, Mike Lewis learned when he gave him a call the next morning. Gespari was also able to give yet another name—Graham Gregory—as the two of them were both now employed in the same paint factory.

Mike looked over to Joan and grimaced. Here were two more to interview, and if they were as glowing about John Smiley as Wendy Dunn had been, it could all be a big waste of time.

Joan was sifting through dead files of cold-case murders. "How far back do you want me to keep going?" she asked.

"Keep it to five years, which is when Smiley left for Manchester."

"Well, I've done that. I found the one we're checking out, the body wrapped in the blue blanket."

"In that case, leave it for now."

"If you say so, but I don't want to get it from Langton if he thinks I've not done what he wanted."

"All right, all right, go back eight years, then."

"Go back eight years?"

"Yes! Just get on with it. Jesus!"

Joan pursed her lips and returned to her computer screen. "Somebody's not a happy bunny," she muttered to herself.

Anna had tried to signal to Langton that she was eager for them to get on with the Welsh interview by looking pointedly at her watch numerous times. However, he had ignored her, still deep in conversation with the governor. At long last, he said that perhaps it was time they went over to the secure unit.

Waiting to meet them was the nice young fair-haired officer Ken Hudson, whom Anna had met when she and Barolli had first visited.

Ken Hudson shook Langton's hand and smiled at Anna, then led them into the main recreational area.

"This is very pleasant," Langton observed, looking around.

Hudson introduced him to the three other officers, who shook hands, then asked if they wanted Welsh brought out, or did they prefer to talk to him in his cell.

"Whatever is convenient for you guys," Langton said.

"He's been playing up," Hudson commented.

Langton asked if by that he meant Welsh was violent, and Hudson shook his head.

"No. Just been bloody-minded and difficult, hogging the kitchen too much, making sarcastic remarks to the other inmates under his breath—you know, goading them to have a go at him. He's a smart bastard and he knows it, but he's been dressing himself up in readiness for the meeting with you." He nodded toward Anna.

Langton suggested they first talk to Welsh in his cell, but with the gate open.

"Okay. I'll just go and tell him you're here—not that he won't know. He expected you earlier."

"Did he?" Langton said with a smile.

As Hudson headed off down Welsh's aisle, Langton glanced at Anna and asked softly if she was okay. She lifted her eyes to the ceiling. "Fine. Just wondered if we were ever going to get started."

Hudson returned to get them. He'd already placed two chairs outside Welsh's cell. Welsh appeared at his open door, looking tense and angry.

"Mr. Welsh, go and sit down in your cell. Do it or we walk out," Langton said quietly.

Welsh gave a smirk. "Yes, *sir,* Detective Chief Superintendent Langton."

Welsh disappeared and was sitting with his legs crossed when they took their seats in front of him. He was in a pristine white shirt and jeans, with leather thongs. His cologne was strong, his hair shining and glossy, but his eyes were a giveaway to his pent-up anger.

"We meet again," he said, curtly nodding to Langton.

"So we do, Mr. Welsh."

"Must be important to get the big brass here in person. Afraid *she* can't handle it?"

"On the contrary, Mr. Welsh. I wanted to be here because you intrigue me."

"Do I now? Well, you are fortunate I agreed, because I wasn't going to give another minute of my time after that bitch got them to sweep my cell."

"If you can't be polite to Detective Travis, this meeting is over."

"I am so sorry, Detective Travis, if I sounded rude, but you know I paid a lot of money—"

Langton interrupted him. "We're not here to get into a discussion about your mobile phone. You had it against the regulations, and you know it. So if you are ready to talk, then let's get started. I am not prepared to listen to any bullshit from you, is that clear?"

"Yes, *sir.*" Welsh gave a cowering movement with his head, mocking, as if he were afraid.

"I also want it made clear to you that if you attempt to

contact Detective Travis on a personal level again, I will make sure you get your privileges removed. That's more than a sweep of your cell, that's the books, the laptop . . ."

"Yes, sir."

"Good. So now we can get started."

There was a pause. Welsh remained with his head bent low and then tossed back his hair. "Have you acted on my information to date?" he demanded.

"You have given us nothing that we were not already checking out. I am here simply because you said that you can, as a killer, get into the mind of the man we are hunting."

Welsh stared at Langton. "You are not even close to tracking him down, are you?" he said.

"We have some leads."

"Like what?"

"Listen to me, Mr. Welsh. I don't have the time to play any more games or arrange any further visits. You now have the opportunity to either assist our case or not."

"Tell me why you came after me. It was down to you, wasn't it?"

Langton shifted his weight in the chair. He took out the piece of string and began to tie a knot.

"Is that to stop you wanting to smoke?"

"Yes."

"You really want to smoke a cigarette now, don't you?"

"Yes."

"We are allowed to smoke outside in the exercise yard. I don't. It's a filthy habit."

Langton glanced at his watch and replaced the string in his pocket. "I asked you a question, Mr. Welsh, and you are trying my patience. You killed two young girls. I could try and understand why, with all your privileges, you wanted to destroy not just their lives but your own. You made the choice. I maybe won't ever understand someone with your intellect wanting to be empowered by the act of rape and murder, so why don't you—"

"Why were you so sure I was the killer?" Welsh interrupted.

"We had a witness, and you were our prime suspect. It was only a matter of time before we discovered the evidence. It wasn't as if you had covered your tracks. I am beginning to think that this is all a waste of time."

Langton made as if to stand, and Welsh leaned forward.

"If you had not had the witness, you never would have caught me. That was, I admit, my mistake—but you know, there is always a witness. I realize that now."

"Are you saying we have a witness?"

"Of course you do—Margaret Potts. I am surprised you haven't reached that conclusion. She knew the killer, and as I told little Anna here, you need to go back to her."

"That could be difficult, since she's dead."

"She holds the clues. She knew the killer; she wasn't the same as those two pretty young girls, she was old, used up—a dirty slag who had worked the service stations for years, correct?"

"We have no connection between Margaret and the two young victims."

"There isn't one. She didn't know them. I am saying she knew *the killer*—and that if you go further back, you'll find more cases, more victims."

"Why?"

"This man has been around for a long time; he's gotten away with it for a long time, he isn't suddenly having the urge to kill. Margaret Potts was murdered two years ago. I believe she's the link because he so nearly got caught. He had to get rid of her. This would mean he believed he'd got away with it, and spurred on with his success, his fury builds and he can't control it. Then he kills again, twice. He has honed his methods in the way he finds the girls. Do you understand what I am saying? He finds them, wants them young, wants them innocent, and they are trusting enough to go with him. They were not drugged, they were not beaten, they had no restraint marks on their wrists or ankles."

"They were raped."

"Yes, yes, I know that, but do they have marks on their bodies as if they were bound and tied? No! Were they drunk? Were they drugged? No! They went with this man of their own accord. They were willing to be with him, so he is a man who is trustworthy, just like myself. My victims wanted to be with me, they found me attractive, so that makes your killer also a very attractive male. Are you following what I am saying?"

Langton gave a dismissive shrug. It clearly annoyed Welsh, who clenched his fists.

"I know this man, understand me? I know how he thinks, how he works, how he can spot a victim and maybe even stalk them, but he has something that is an immediate connection. Maybe it's just because he's as good-looking as me. Who would consider me a dangerous predator? And that is what you are looking for, a predator." Welsh tossed back his silky hair, smiling.

"Go on," Langton said quietly.

"Well now, let me think. I would say he could even live a double life. He could have a wife, children, a nice home. It's when he's away from them that he becomes the animal, the hunter. You have to understand that it will be an

obsessive-compulsive need, probably because he is dominated by a woman—his wife or mother—but someone he
respects, maybe even loves. Her control of him is what sets
the seeds for him to want to strangle and rape, to dominate
his victims."

"How old do you think he is?"

"I'd say mid-forties. This has taken a long time to fester
inside him, but as soon as he is away from the comfort
zone, away from the suffocation of his respectable life, he
rises up; his cock is hard just thinking about what he in-
tends doing. Your killer will fantasize about his plans, and
for that he needs space, a job that will take him away from
that closeted environment."

"What work do you think he does?"

Welsh sighed. "I've said he's a driver. A trucker, maybe,
with long-distance hauls—anything that takes him out of
his perfect loving home. He commits his crimes far away
from anyone who knows him, and I would say he is very
well liked, respected, a good steady man, and his alter ego
won't ever manifest itself with anyone close to him; on the
contrary, he will be above suspicion." Welsh leaned back
and smiled. "You know, you may never catch him."

Anna had not said a word throughout the meeting, and in
fact, Welsh had hardly looked at her. When at last she and
Langton stood up to leave, he turned toward her.

"Maybe next time we can have a more private talk, just
you and me, because I haven't finished. There's more to
come from me, and I would like you to get the kudos for
nailing this killer. It would benefit your career."

Langton took her arm, smiling at Welsh and thanking him profusely. The officers appeared in the aisle as if

they'd been waiting for the signal. As they headed toward Ken Hudson, they could hear Welsh's cell gate close with a clang.

In the secure unit's recreational area, Anna and Langton sat and waited for their escorts to take them back through to the main prison. Langton accepted a coffee, but all Anna wanted was to get out. She had found it sickening listening to Welsh's gloating.

Langton spoke quietly to her. "I think while we're here, instead of returning to London, we should make an un-scheduled call on Smiley. It will save another long journey, and we're not that far from Manchester here."

Overhearing, Ken Hudson looked up. "My parents have a bed-and-breakfast. I could arrange for you to stay there, if you like. It's between here and Manchester."

Anna was loath to agree, but Langton was already saying, "We'd really appreciate the offer. Anna, we could pick up toothbrushes and toothpaste on the way."

"There's probably everything you'd need at the house," Hudson said, and explained that it was nothing special, but at least it was clean, and his mother cooked up a great breakfast.

"That's very kind of you, Ken, but I don't want to put your mother to any trouble," Anna protested.

"It won't be. She's got no one staying at the moment; in fact, times have been slack lately. She used to foster a lot of kids, but she's getting on a bit now, and my father's retired."

So that was that. Anna could see she'd have to go along with the idea.

Ken said that he would be off duty in half an hour and he could drive them there. Langton pointed out that Anna had her car, but they could do with directions. "Do you live at home?" he asked.

"No. I've got a resident officer's flat here, but I see my folks as often as I can. I can go over there with you, if you like."

"Really appreciate that, Ken, but it won't be necessary. Mind you, I'd love it if you could give us a tip on where to get a good curry."

Anna was becoming extremely tense. A curry and a night in some bed-and-breakfast with Langton was not something she wanted by any stretch of the imagination. She was even more infuriated when Langton insisted on going to have yet another conversation with the governor. Excusing herself, she said she would wait for him in the car park, claiming she needed some fresh air.

Anna was turning on the Mini's engine to recharge her mobile phone when Ken Hudson joined her, bending down to tap on her window. He was wearing motorbike leathers and carrying a crash helmet.

"I've contacted my mum, and she's looking forward to meeting you."

Anna got out as Ken gave her a detailed route map of how to get to his parents' and the names of a couple of Indian restaurants not far from the house.

"I was thinking I might ride over there. Maybe we could have a bite to eat together."

"I don't think so, but thank you," she said as politely as she could manage.

"How about another time? I go to London quite often, as I've got a sister living in Richmond."

Anna gave him a dismissive smile and looked around for Langton.

"Whereabouts do you live?" Ken asked.

"I have a flat near Tower Bridge."

"Oh, nice. Is it a loft conversion?"

She sighed, not wanting to get into any further conversation with him and by now anxious to leave, as it was getting dark. She took in the biker's gear.

"How could you have given us a lift?" she asked. "You look as if you're on a motorbike."

"Yeah, but my mate's got a car I could use. If you want to leave your car parked here, I could—"

"No, I really think we should go, but thanks all the same." She was relieved to see Langton heading toward them, smoking.

"Sorry to keep you waiting. You got directions, Anna?"

"Yes."

Ken smiled and said he had also given her contact numbers for a couple of good Indian restaurants.

"You going to join us, then?" Langton asked.

By now Anna's head was aching.

"Thanks, I'd like that," Ken said. "I can follow behind until I see you are on the right route; it's about an hour's drive."

Anna couldn't believe it. Next minute, Langton had walked over to Ken Hudson's motorbike. The two of them stood with their backs to her, obviously discussing the machine, and she wanted to scream. Ken eventually put on his helmet and sat astride the big motorbike, revving the engine. At last Langton returned to the car.

"That is some bike he's got there—a Harley-Davidson, immaculate condition, customized paint job on the tank."

"Can we go now?" Anna said impatiently.

"Ready when you are. I think he's taken quite a shine to you." Langton grinned.

"Oh, please."

Anna passed him the directions as they drove out.

Behind them, sounding like thunder, was Ken on his bike. He stayed well back until he roared past with a wave.

"Always wanted one of those," Langton said, looking after the bike and black-helmeted rider. "Nice young bloke, isn't he?"

Mrs. Brenda Hudson was a plump, friendly woman who was waiting at the open front door of her freshly painted semi-detached, with its paved front garden. Ken's bike was already parked, alongside a Metro.

Anna was shown into a small box room, which smelled of polish and clean linen. The single bed had a floral duvet and matching pillowcase. Mrs. Hudson hovered, asking if there was anything she could get to make her guest more comfortable, offering tea and placing down a bottle of water.

"Ken said you weren't expecting to stay over, so I've got some disposable toothbrushes and little toothpaste tubes. I collect them when we go to hotels; there's also shampoo and bath foam."

"This is very kind of you, thank you," said Anna. "If you could just show me where the bathroom is . . ."

"Of course, dear. It's at the end of the landing, and I'll bring you fresh towels."

Anna sat on the pink toilet seat that matched everything else in the communal bathroom: the pink bath, the pink tiles, and the pink shower curtain. She had rinsed some toilet paper under the cold tap and held it to her face, as she felt worn out and her head was thudding. She took deep breaths, trying to calm herself and pressing the tissue into her eyes.

By the time she had returned to her bedroom, the clean towels had been left on her bed, along with the toothbrush and toothpaste. Anna combed her hair and sat on the bed for a while: she could hear Langton laughing downstairs. She could have strangled him, but then she sat up and told herself to get it together. She took a few more deep breaths and stood up, determined to at least try and be pleasant.

In the cozy sitting room, which had a large sofa and matching chairs with a huge plasma screen TV and fake log fire, Langton was talking to Mr. Hudson. The man rose to his feet as Anna entered and shook her hand.

"Very pleased to meet you, dear. The wife is just bringing in a cup of tea for everyone, unless you want something else?"

"No, a cup of tea will be fine, and if you have any aspirin, I'd be most grateful, thank you."

Mr. Hudson was a well-built man, rather handsome, with the same fair good looks as his son, but his hair was receding. He left them to go and help his wife.

"Got a headache, have you?" Langton asked.

"Yes. It was a long drive and a long session."

"Useful though. You know, he virtually described John Smiley—and while I was with the governor, he let me make a few calls. Three ex-employees of Swell Blinds, according to the team, all said the same thing. Smiley was an exemplary worker, well liked, and none of them had a bad word to say about him. We're getting all the files about that victim wrapped in the blue blanket brought over—it's a possible new case. Mike Lewis said the officers making inquiries about the barns and outhouses knew that a lot of lorries did use that back road and—"

Just then Mrs. Hudson came in carrying a large tray of sandwiches and cakes. Langton jumped to his feet to take it from her and set it down on a coffee table. Mr. Hudson then brought in a big china teapot and some aspirin for

Anna. It was hard not to like them. They were a delightful couple and were obviously devoted.

As they had their tea, Mrs. Hudson pointed out all the photographs of children she had fostered over the years, telling them how many she still kept in touch with. She admitted she had never thought about fostering until her own children were in school. It had started with one child, and then the agency would call and ask if she could see her way to caring for another, then another. Next they were shown the albums of her own children: her daughter, Lizzie, in Richmond, who had two children of her own; her youngest son, Robin, living in Australia; and then Ken.

"He was more trouble than the other two put together," she said affectionately.

She laughed as her husband started recalling some of the teenage Ken's escapades, from his running off to join a circus to motorbike racing, proudly showing them a cup he'd won at sixteen as a dirt-track rider champion. It was at this point that Ken walked in. He had showered and changed and was wearing a light blue denim shirt and jeans.

"Oh, Christ, she's not going on about me, is she?" He hooked an arm around his mother and kissed her. The adoration on her face was touching.

Anna sat back, listening to Ken's stories of his attempts to join various circuses. He was funny, describing how his father, whom Ken called by his Christian name of Roy, would get someone to use a megaphone to call him home. At that point, Langton excused himself, explaining that he needed to make some calls.

Anna helped Mrs. Hudson take the tea things out to the kitchen and put them in the dishwasher. The kitchen was like the rest of the house, tidy and with every surface shining, and when she put the milk jug back in the fridge,

Anna could see it was stocked with plastic containers, all
labeled. From the rows of well-thumbed cookbooks, it was
obvious that Mrs. Hudson took great pride in her domestic
abilities.

When Ken came in to say that he had booked a table at
the local Indian restaurant, Anna noticed how at ease he
was with his mother. He towered above her as she started
to protest that she could cook dinner for them, and he insisted that it would not be necessary.

"But they'll want one of your full cooked breakfasts—
right, Anna?" he said.

Anna agreed. Now that her headache was receding, she
found herself liking him more and more. He suggested
that he would drive his father's car so that his guests could
enjoy a glass of wine.

Langton had shaved and was keen to go and eat. He sat
beside Ken in the front seat of the car, which was as spotless as the house.

"Don't you drink?" Anna asked.

"Not really, except maybe the odd pint after a game. I
play rugby every weekend. We've got quite a good team
made up from the officers and a few from the local clubs."

Their conversation was easygoing, and by the time
they'd ordered at the small restaurant and a bottle of red
wine had been opened, Anna was at last totally relaxed.

The food was not exceptional but was reasonable, and
Langton, like Anna, seemed to be enjoying himself. Not
until they had ordered coffee did the conversation turn to
the reason they had been to the prison. Langton asked Ken
what he thought of Cameron Welsh.

"He's a complex individual," the young man said. "I
don't like him; he's manipulative and doesn't mix with anyone. He spends most of his time studying."

"Child psychology, wasn't it?" Anna asked.

"Yes, and I think he's embarking on economics. He's very intelligent, but like I said, he's to my mind very warped. I can't stand his obsession with his clothes and food fads. He's got more shampoos and conditioners for his hair than my sister. He's also independently wealthy, so that makes it easy for him to order in all the books he needs. He's not allowed cash, obviously, but we can't stop him ordering from Amazon, and as it's for educational reasons, there's no real reason to."

Langton asked when Welsh had been inside the main prison. Ken said he hadn't had much to do with him; he just knew there had been trouble, as Welsh constantly antagonized the other inmates.

"Welsh was more intelligent and better educated than any of them, and he knew it and delighted in creating problems. They found out he'd been doing a Joe Orton in the library once, so that caused a stink."

"Orton? Who's he, an inmate?"

Anna was surprised that Langton didn't know. Ken explained that Orton was a brilliant writer who had been charged with cutting out and pasting obscenities in his local library books.

"He was murdered by his boyfriend a good few years back, but Welsh, like him, cut out pages and pasted stuff inside the books, so he got into trouble."

"You think he's homosexual?" Langton asked.

"No, no, I don't, although the way he fancies himself up, he could appear to be. He has a hatred of women, so who can tell what goes on in his head? All I know is he's never made any sexual approaches to any inmates that I am aware of."

"Why do you say he hates women?" Anna asked.

Ken explained that when Welsh was submitting his papers for the Open University, Ken had been asked to double-check them in case there were any attempts at communication concealed in the essays. Inmates with twenty-four-hour lockup spent their time finding ways of sending out messages or even trying to arrange an escape.

"Have you got a degree yourself?" Anna asked, impressed but not wanting to sound as if she was.

"Yes. I'm only working in the prison for a couple of years. I eventually want to work with underprivileged teenagers. I suppose it's from the years watching my mum handle all the kids she took on. She'd still be running herself ragged with them, but she had open-heart surgery two years ago. That's another reason I chose Barfield—it's close enough for me to keep an eye on her. If I didn't, I know she'd get roped into doing too much."

Langton yawned and poured himself another coffee. "Are you basing Welsh's hatred of women on his murders?" he asked.

"No, since his victims were not low-class women. You see, Welsh has a real, deep-seated hatred of sexually aware women, like prostitutes. It's obvious that he had a sick obsession. I think it stems from how he believed his mother rejected him. In his papers, he had to discuss child abuse and how to handle a badly affected youngster, and he wrote a long section about the need to understand how a child reacts to parental rejection. He focused on the loss of a mother and the abusive overcontrolling father. I don't think he was ever subjected to sexual abuse himself; it was more a mental thing. He talked about how a child will withdraw into his or her own world, and he elaborated on what I presumed were painful memories from his own life. It may have appeared cushioned by wealth, but he consistently underlined the importance of the damage that occurs when a child is excluded from the natural normal love from a parent."

"She ran off with a close family friend, didn't she?" Anna poured herself another coffee. Langton had remained silent, deep in his own thoughts, but Anna was enjoying the conversation.

"Apparently, but I think it was a woman she ran off with, not a man. I base this on something he came out with when there was a possibility of having a female prison visitor. I got a tirade against the fact that some women choose to become visitors of long-term prisoners. He said they were all lesbians and that he wouldn't have one clean his shoes. I remember he went on to describe the woman his mother had left him for as an evil bull dyke. Whether or not it was true, I don't know . . . but the fact remains that he was left at a young age to be brought up by his father."

"Do you mind if we call it quits for tonight?" Langton asked shortly afterward, and signaled for the bill.

Anna was disappointed. She would have liked to spend more time chatting with Ken, but it was late, and she presumed that Langton would want an early start the following morning. He was fast asleep as they drove back to the bed-and-breakfast.

Although Ken offered to make more coffee, they both refused and went up to their rooms. Anna used the bathroom first; she had a quick shower and washed her hair and, coming back to her room, found a small hair dryer on the bedside table. She could hear Langton banging around next door as she brushed out her hair. She could also hear him speaking on the telephone but couldn't make out who he was talking to. Eventually, she went to bed, and no sooner had she drowsily turned off the bedside light than

Langton was banging on her door, calling out that he was going down for breakfast.

Anna had slept better than she had in months. Dressing in a hurry, she opened the curtains and saw Ken outside, getting onto his motorbike. She couldn't believe it was already eight o'clock.

Breakfast was a substantial affair of sausages, fried eggs and tomato, and crispy bacon, with a pile of toast. Mrs. Hudson insisted on making a fresh pot of tea, so Langton and Anna were alone in the small dining room.

"You sleep all right?" he asked.

"Yes, out like a light. What about you?"

"Terrific. I've been with the incident room again, and judging from the new information regarding John Smiley, he is even more like the description from Cameron Welsh. Married, kids, good job, hard worker, with no one having a bad word to say against him."

"That could also be because he is just that, a decent guy. We've nothing on which to make an arrest. The only evidence against him is he was parked at the London Gateway Services; plus, we've checked out his delivery drops for that period, and they have been verified."

"I know. Aren't you going to eat that sausage?"

Anna passed it over and watched as he thudded the HP sauce over it and attacked the sausage as if he were ravenous. Anna had started to notice how much Langton ate, wolfing down the sandwiches at tea yesterday afternoon, then the curry in the evening, and now he was piling through his breakfast at breakneck speed, hardly pausing between mouthfuls.

Mrs. Hudson came in with the tea and more toast.

Langton was charming. "I'll make certain I come and stay here again," he said.

"Ken was sorry he had to leave, but he's on duty this morning," Mrs. Hudson explained.

They finished breakfast, and Langton insisted that he pay for himself and Anna, although Mrs. Hudson wouldn't hear of it. Langton tucked the money into her apron pocket anyway, and then, gesturing for Anna to hurry, he walked out munching a piece of toast covered in marmalade.

Mrs. Hudson began clearing the table.

"Is Ken married?" Anna asked, making sure Langton was well out of earshot.

"No. He's been close to it a few times, but he's such a ladies' man that I don't know when he'll ever settle down. You know my daughter lives in Richmond? She's got two children, and we go and stay as often as we can."

"Well, when you see him again, will you thank him for me? I really enjoyed last night, and the bed was so comfortable, I slept like a dream." Anna hesitated and then wrote down her mobile and new home phone number. "Next time you are in London, please give me a call, as I'd like to see you again." She meant she'd like to see Ken again, but before she could say anything else, Langton bellowed from the hall.

Anna was touched. Mr. Hudson had cleaned her Mini. All the mud from the previous day's rough riding down the muddy back lanes by the murder site was gone. Langton was smoking, and before Anna could thank Mr. Hudson properly, Langton told her to get moving, as he wanted to be back in London after lunch.

They drove off, Anna waving to Ken's parents as they stood watching them leave. "What a lovely couple," she said.

"Yes, they're sweethearts. They don't make 'em like those two anymore," Langton agreed as he studied the route for them to head onto the M6 and then on to Manchester.

"You've got marmalade on your tie," she said, watching him swear and rub it with his finger.

Swell Blinds's headquarters were in Salford, situated in an old warehouse complex with numerous other small firms. Anna and Langton didn't get there until after ten. The first thing they saw was a couple of Transit vans lined up outside in listed parking bays. They knew that Smiley was already at work, as they had his registration number. Langton had a quick glance over his van, and there was not a scratch or mark on it. It was, as Barolli had said, in pristine condition.

The reception was a small area cordoned off with glass panels. Mr. Rodgers was there with a rather elderly secretary behind an old desk with a computer and telephone. She had many filing cabinets to either side, and an in- and out-tray of receipts and orders in front of her. She left them to talk in private. Arnold Rodgers was edgy, and it took a while for Langton to put him at ease by assuring him that they were just making inquiries regarding an investigation in London. He made it clear that they were not on any account interested in Mr. Rogers's company.

"It's about some girl that was murdered, isn't it?" Rodgers said.

"That is correct, and we are here only because Mr. Smiley was parked at a service station near where she was found, and we are hoping he may be able to assist us. You know, if he saw anyone, any other suspicious vehicle."

Mr. Rodgers said he'd received a call from Wendy Dunn, and she had told him that she'd passed on the contact numbers of two other employees.

"She was very helpful, and we also really appreciate you giving us some time today," Langton said pleasantly.

"Do you want to look over the warehouse?"

"That would be good, yes, thank you. I believe Mr. Smiley is here, isn't he?"

"He's not, actually; he had a big delivery yesterday to Glasgow, so he's got the day off today. Do you want me to get him in?"

"No, that won't be necessary."

At that moment, the elderly secretary tapped and asked if Langton and his assistant would like a cup of coffee. They refused, with Anna less than happy at being referred to in such a way.

While Langton was talking to Mr. Rodgers, it gave Anna the opportunity to have a good look around the small office. It didn't appear that busy, and the phone had not rung once while they had been there. As the two men set off on a tour of the workshops, Anna asked them to wait.

"I'd be grateful if you didn't call Mr. Smiley and inform him that we are here," she said politely. "It's an informal meeting, Mr. Rodgers, and we'd like to keep it that way, okay?"

"Yes, of course."

"And we'd also like the details of Mr. Smiley's deliveries to Glasgow yesterday."

"Yes, of course," the flustered man repeated.

"Thank you."

The warehouse had two sections. One was for the cutting of the wooden blinds, which were stacked in rows of shelves in order of size. There was a separate area with coils of the cord used for threading them through. Three men were working on the long table with circular saws of various sizes.

The paint spraying took place in the second section, where one man was working in overalls with a face mask.

He was spraying and laminating wood, and there were many slats left to dry.

"This is it," Mr. Rodgers said.

"Does Smiley work in the warehouse when he's not making deliveries?"

"No, he's transport. He works alongside Rita in the office when he's not delivering. We have to have the exact measurements, and he also handles all that—sometimes goes out to measure a property before they submit the orders. We're very small, even smaller than we were, but we're managing to keep our heads above water. He's a trusted employee, you know," Rodgers went on. "A hard worker and respected by everyone in the company."

Anna and Langton left Swell Blinds shortly afterward, as there seemed little more useful information to be gleaned. Langton had collected a mass of leaflets and was checking out the prices. "Expensive," he observed.

"Thinking of ordering some, are you?"

Langton laughed and stuffed the leaflets into the glove compartment. "Wouldn't be my decision," he said.

Anna said nothing. She found it rather a sexist remark, implying that he left any home decor responsibilities to his wife. He never talked about her or his children, preferring to keep his personal life private. In fact, Anna wasn't even sure if he had remarried. She knew he had a stepdaughter called Kitty and a baby son, but it had been such a long time since he had mentioned the boy that she couldn't recall his name. It was strange, because although they had been virtually closeted together for almost two days, she felt more distant from him than ever. It was further confirmation to Anna that whatever had gone on between them was no longer an issue, and more and more, she was starting to see him in a different light. It wasn't that she didn't like or respect him; it was the age gap—something she had never considered. Beside Ken, he had appeared so much older, which he was, and she realized how little, apart from work, they had in common.

"Your son is called Tommy, isn't he?" she remembered.

Langton grunted in agreement but seemed disinclined to discuss it further. She tried again. "You must have little time to spare for the family."

"Time enough. Is this SatNav thing working?" He messed the screen.

"Yes, should be there in two minutes. It's 12 Buxton Avenue."

Smiley's house was only a few miles from the warehouse. The area was not that upmarket, with a lot of big council estates. They then branched off to a middle-class enclave of small semi-detached properties that looked almost identical but were better maintained.

Langton and Anna walked up the neat drive, noticing that the small square of grass looked freshly mow.

"We keep it very low-key," Langton murmured as he rang the doorbell. Smiley answered and looked taken aback to see them both.

"Just need to straighten out a few things, Mr. Smiley, as we were in the area. You mind if we come in?"

"No, come on through."

They followed him down a small narrow hallway, and he ushered them into his sitting room.

"Is your wife here?"

"She's in the kitchen."

Smiley gestured for them both to sit in the well-furnished room. The sofa was still covered in plastic.

"Sorry about that. It's to keep the kids' dirty feet off of it," he explained, and tried to remove it, but Langton said not to bother. He settled himself in an easy chair while Anna perched on the arm of the sofa. Langton asked a few questions about the deliveries, and then he opened his notebook.

"Tell me, John, do you ever use that back lane behind the truckers' stop at the London Gateway?"

"No, didn't even know there was one."

"I'd like to go over a few things about the two occasions we have your van on CCTV. Basically, if you can recall anything unusual, whether you noticed any of the trucks as being regulars . . . that kind of thing."

"I gave all the details that I could remember at the station. I only stopped off for such a short time, you see, and never really paid much attention to any of the other vehicles," Smiley repeated.

Langton took out Margaret Potts's photograph. "You were shown this before, John, but I just want you to take another look, to make sure . . . Ever see this woman, John?"

Smiley took the photograph and again said he did not recall ever seeing her, unless she was up by the back lane they had described. If she was, he wouldn't have taken much notice of her.

Too much information, Anna thought.

"Now, these two girls . . . The coincidence is they are both Polish, and I believe your wife is also Polish?"

"She is, yes, but I've never seen those two girls before. Like I said when I was at the station, if they were hitching a ride, I wouldn't have stopped. I've never given anyone thumbing a ride the time of day."

Anna watched John Smiley closely. Yet again he did not appear to be in any way distressed by their questions. He was wearing a white T-shirt and jeans with brown suede boots. He was, she thought, as she had before, quite a good-looking, fit man. The combover was offputting, but he was attractive in a macho way. He was also very clean, as was clear from the condition of his nails and his hands. The room had a similar feel to Ken Hudson's parents' but was not as cozy. For a man with two children, there were no toys or children's belongings anywhere.

"I'd like to meet your wife," Langton said.

For the first time, Smiley was ill at ease. "I've not mentioned anything about this to her," he said. "I don't want her getting upset. You know, with your coming here, it looks suspicious, and even though I've got no worries, I don't want her to think I've done anything wrong."

"It's just routine, and we'll make sure she's not worried. You've been very helpful, and I really appreciate your time."

Smiley left the room and Langton glanced at Anna. He nodded to the mantelpiece showing a few photographs of the couple's wedding and two rather stilted school photographs of their children.

Mrs. Smiley bore no resemblance to the pretty dark-haired girl in the wedding photograph, or the small picture Smiley carried of her in his wallet. She was about seventeen stone, with solid thick arms and legs like tree trunks. Her hair was cut short and worn in an unflattering style with a barrette on either side of a part. Her face was devoid of any makeup.

"This is Sonja," Smiley said as he hovered behind her. She was almost as tall as he was, and he sort of skirted around her to stand by the sofa.

Langton introduced himself and then Anna. Sonja gave them a curt nod. "What is this about?" She had little trace of an accent and cold blue eyes.

"We are just making inquiries, investigating a case that we believe your husband may have information about."

"What case?"

"A murder inquiry."

She turned to her husband and then back to Langton. "Why do you want to talk to John?"

Langton explained that his Transit van had been parked in a service station close to where the murders had been discovered.

"Not one, then, more than one?" she asked.

"Yes, that is correct," Langton said.

"Why do you think John can help you?"

"Because we are asking anyone we have on CCTV at the location to try and recall if they saw anything suspicious."

"I don't know anything about it, but my husband is a good man, and if he can, he will help you. Can you help them, John?"

"No, love. I only stopped off for a bathroom break, then, as usual, drove on. You know I like to get my deliveries over and done with as soon as possible so I can get home to say good night to the kids."

"You also fit blinds, don't you?" Anna asked him.

"Yes, it's all part of the delivery. I take the measurements sometimes before the orders, and then when I deliver, I put them up. We've found it's better if I get the exact size, as the blinds are made to measure. If they're out by so much as half an inch, we have to take them back to the workshop."

Langton showed him the photographs of Anika and Estelle once again. "Did you ever go to either of these girls' homes to measure for blinds?"

Mrs. Smiley looked at the photographs left on the coffee table and then back to her husband.

"No. I've never seen them," he replied.

"They were both Polish," Langton said quietly.

Mrs. Smiley picked up one photograph after another and then shrugged. "I never seen them; they look very young."

Langton then laid out Margaret Potts's photograph on top of the others. "This woman was also a victim."

"Why are you showing these pictures to my husband?"

"Well, we hope he might have seen them at the service station."

She pursed her lips and then looked at her husband. "Did you see these women?"

"No, love. I've already told them that."

Langton replaced the photographs in the envelope.

"Wait a minute." Mrs. Smiley pointed to Margaret Potts's picture. "This woman is older, different. Is she Polish?"

"No, she was from London."

"She was a prostitute who worked the service stations, picking up men, often truck drivers." Anna watched Mrs. Smiley as her mouth tightened into a hard line.

"I've seen her type in Aldershot, hanging round the soldiers on leave when they went to the pubs. Disgusting, they were. I worked in a bar for a while, and these women would drink themselves stupid."

"But you have never seen this woman?" Langton persisted.

Smiley shook his head, and then Sonja folded her arms. "Have you got what you come for, then? Only being it's John's day off, I need him to do some shopping for me before the children get home for their lunch."

"Do you have some of the blinds from the company?" Anna asked pleasantly.

"Yes, in the kitchen and bedrooms. We get them at cost price."

"Could I see them?"

Sonja hesitated and then shrugged her wide shoulders,

gesturing for Anna to follow her out of the room. The kitchen was orderly, with a pine table in the center and two place mats ready for the children's lunch. They had all the modern conveniences, dishwasher and washing machine, deep freeze and fridge, and in the windows was a set of pale wooden blinds.

"I'd have preferred white, but they only do them in different shades of wood," Sonja said.

The two women went up the stairs. There was a plastic runner all the way up and even on parts of the landing. Sonja was out of breath; she puffed and rattled as she gestured for Anna to go into the master bedroom.

"We got them in all the bedrooms. That's ours, and then our son, Stefan, has the box room and . . . this is my daughter Marta's bedroom."

The room had pink walls, pink bedcovers, a pink carpet, and dolls and a dollhouse were stacked neatly against a wall with a big pink chest. The blinds were a darker brown in this room.

"Very nice," Anna said. "She's very tidy."

"They both are. It's no good having nice toys if they break them, so they're taught to appreciate their things. My parents came to England with nothing. I never had such lovely things."

"Your mother died a few years ago, didn't she?"

Sonja glared at Anna. "How do you know?"

"Your husband told us when he came to the station."

"I don't understand. You've talked to him before, then, have you?"

"Yes, when he was in London."

"I see." She headed back to the stairs, grasping the banister rail, as she was so short of breath.

As they reached the hall, Langton was waiting. He

smiled. "We'll be on our way now. Thank you for your time, Mrs. Smiley."

"Goodbye." Sonja went straight to the kitchen, and John Smiley hovered to show them out.

"I'm sorry not to be of any help," he said, and promised that if he remembered anything at all, he would call them straightaway.

Anna looked back at the house as she put her key into the ignition. "I bet she's having a go at him. She didn't know he'd been to see us in London. God, she's an unpleasant woman, and that house is like a show home. Even the children's rooms are in military order."

"She'd scare the pants off me," Langton agreed.

"She's not very fit, either. Just moving up the stairs had her heaving for breath."

Anna adjusted the rearview mirror as they saw John Smiley exit from his house carrying an array of empty shopping bags. "I bet she's got him on a short rein. I didn't get anything new from talking to him, did you?"

Langton made no reply. They drove in silence for a while.

"Back to the station, sir?"

"What?"

"I said, do I drive straight back to the station?"

"Yes."

Anna wondered if he felt, as she did, that the whole trip had been a big waste of time, apart from enjoying Ken's family. She began to replay in her mind the previous evening, wondering if she would get to meet up with Ken again. It had been a while since she had felt physically attracted to someone, and the fact that he wasn't connected to the Met was a major bonus. None of the male officers she worked alongside interested her, apart from Langton.

She began to calculate how many years she had been emotionally tied to him, to the detriment of ever finding herself a partner.

"He ticks all the right boxes," Langton said quietly.

"Smiley?"

"Who the hell do you think I'm talking about?" he snapped.

"Unless we're wrong and the boxes you are referring to are from Cameron Welsh, as I wouldn't trust a word *he* says."

"It's not about trust; it's his take on our killer, and it's bloody close to John Smiley. That elephant-sized wife and that bloody sterile house, he must feel suffocated. He looked to me to be totally dominated by her. He must relish the trips away from home—I know I would."

"But that doesn't make him our killer."

"Too many coincidences. Caught on camera at the service station twice, the sumo wrestler of a wife who just happens to be Polish, like two of our victims. Again, going over what Welsh said, Margaret Potts is the odd one out, a hardened tart. If he's right, could she hold the clue? Could she be a witness? To what, I dunno."

Anna concentrated on driving, glancing at the SatNav screen to make sure they were on the right route.

"Too many coincidences," Langton repeated. "What about him saying there has to be a witness?"

"Doesn't mean that we have one with this case. I am sure if you did a ratio check on nondomestic murders, but serial killers—"

"He was right, Anna, there *is* always a witness, and we need to find ours. Now, if it was Margaret Potts, we are going to have start backtracking."

Anna sighed. They had already spent a long time

gathering information on Margaret Potts's background, and with a woman who had no permanent address, who had worked as a whore for so many years, it was going to be difficult to uncover anything that they had not already investigated.

"We have to find the link," Langton persisted.

"But I've interviewed her husband, her brother-in-law, and this Emerald Turk woman. Maggie didn't have friends, and she lived rough at hostels."

"Find out how long Swell Blinds were established in West London. We want to go back over their records from before they moved to Manchester. So John Smiley pays house calls to measure the blinds: did Margaret Potts meet him then? Did she recognize him at the service station? We've only got two dates caught on CCTV footage, but what if he was more of a regular, one of her clients?" Langton got out his piece of string and began twisting it around his fingers. "I agree with Welsh: this man has killed before those two Polish girls. We need to check out this new victim wrapped in the blanket. Dig around to see if we have any others, because I think we're going to find them. If he was picking up victims before the company moved to Manchester, the time frame fits with a possible break in his sickness. Then he starts it again."

Anna decided that rather than get into an argument with him, she'd stay quiet. The fact that Langton was judging everything by what Welsh had said to him surprised her. She had not picked up any gut feeling that John Smiley was their killer; he had at no time appeared to be lying. The only time she had felt a hint that anything was suspicious was when he had talked about the back lanes behind the London Gateway service station.

Langton then called various other teams on different

cases for an update. Just realizing that he was also overseeing numerous other inquiries and with the same intensity and hands-on control impressed Anna, even if she did think he was wrongfooting their investigation.

It was late afternoon when they arrived back at the station, and they could see at once that there had been a lot of new information added to the board in the incident room. Mike Lewis gave them an update, listing all the interviews and the fact that the back lanes were used on a regular basis by some of the other girls. The inquiries around the outhouses and barns had produced a lot of descriptions of various trucks and vans, along with the news that a farmer had moved on some travelers who had parked their wagons there. An old caravan had been searched, and blankets and sleeping bags had been brought in, along with hypodermic needles and condoms.

It was obvious that there had been a considerable amount of legwork done since they had been in Manchester, but Langton ignored it, instead asking to see the file on the blue-blanket victim.

The case was four years old, the victim never identified, her naked body wrapped in the soiled blanket, on which there was no laundry marking. She had been strangled and raped, and her body was badly bruised. Her age was between twenty to thirty, and there were no police records of her fingerprints. She was dark-haired. The one piece of evidence the original team had hoped would help identify her was a small tattoo of a lizard on her right hip. There had been no jewelry, no clothes, and although the Thames Valley Murder Squad had given extensive press and television coverage, no one had come forward.

Mike Lewis said that the victim was found by a farmer,

and her body, wrapped in the blanket, had been left in a field by a ditch. It was equidistant between two service stations, but closer to the M6 motorway than to the M1.

Langton stared at the dead girl's face. It was impossible to say whether or not she was a prostitute, but the postmortem had revealed that she was sexually active; also, the rape had been violent. The killer had left no DNA, and she had no restraint marks and no defense marks on her nails and hands, either. She had been strangled, possibly by her own tights, and there were three lines around her throat, as if her tights or a cord had been wound around it and drawn into a garotte. The killer had taken it away.

The victim's photographs were pinned up alongside those of Anika Waleska and Estelle Dubcek. Although the team had now identified both girls, they had no information about how they had come to be in the area where they were found. Three days were missing from when Estelle was last seen, and nobody recalled seeing Anika for weeks before her body was discovered.

"Could she be foreign? Polish, like the other two girls?" Langton asked.

Mike shrugged. "No idea. I mean, with the Anika girl, we've been trying to trace a dentist who fixed her front teeth, but we don't know if that was done in the UK, and we've not had any joy from the television network regarding their anonymous female caller who tipped us off on her identity. They put out a request for her to get in contact, but she hasn't, and we've been back to the Polish embassy for help but got no result."

Langton moved on to the photograph of Margaret Potts. He tapped her face. "If Potts died because she witnessed something, then she's our best bet. We're going to have to concentrate on her and go back and interview everyone who knew her again."

Mike glanced at Anna, but she gave no reaction. "Okay, we'll keep on going," Mike said.

It was Barolli who asked if John Smiley was still in the frame. Langton shoved his hands into his pockets. "Yeah. We'll have to get Mr. Rodgers, who owns Swell Blinds, to give us more details of Smiley's routes and visits for measuring up the blinds, and to go back to before the company moved to Manchester." He turned to look again at the board. "Hard to believe, isn't it? Three, maybe four victims, and we're nowhere. But I don't want to give up; we keep on going even if it feels like we're wading through treacle. Go back and keep at it until we get a result. We might have missed something."

"The van driver who discovered Estelle's body is coming back in. Is there a reason?" Mike asked.

"Yes, my gut instinct. I think he lied, and I want to question him in person. I don't believe he could have seen the body that easily, unless he already knew it was there. I want to find out why he lied."

The team was depressed after Langton left. Mike suggested they take a weekend off, recharge their batteries, and return on Monday to start refreshed. Anna remained behind, typing up her report of the prison visit to Welsh and the interview with Smiley. By the time she left the station, it was after ten, and she couldn't wait to get home and take a leisurely relaxing shower. It had been a very long day with a long drive, and her back ached.

Her home phone was ringing as she opened the front door. For a moment she was reluctant to answer, just in case the weekend leave had been canceled. But it was Ken. He asked at first if she'd had a good drive home, and when she said she had literally just walked in the door, he commiserated.

"I hope you don't mind me calling. Mum gave me your number."

"No, I'm glad, as I wanted to thank you. I really enjoyed meeting your parents."

"I'm thinking of riding down to see my sister. I've got the weekend off."

"So have I." She found herself smiling.

"You free for dinner tomorrow night?"

"Yes."

They agreed to meet in the early evening and then decide whether to take in a show or just eat out. She gave him her address and directions and found she was still smiling as she turned on the shower.

Langton might not have gotten a result from the trip up north, but she had, and it was the first time in longer than she could remember that she looked forward to spending time with someone who had no connection to work.

Chapter Eight

Anna spent the first part of Saturday cleaning her flat, going to the laundry, and buying more wine and groceries. She had a hair appointment in the afternoon and used the free time to check through cinema listings and a few stage plays she thought might be of interest.

Ken arrived at six, bearing a large bunch of flowers and a bottle of wine. He wasn't wearing his leathers and explained that he'd left his bike at his sister's so he could shower there before coming across town to see Anna. He was wearing a casual leather jacket, jeans and a T-shirt, and tough black leather boots. He made her laugh as she put the flowers in a vase, saying that he thought he'd been so well organized to arrange to visit his sister and get changed, but had forgotten to bring shoes.

He was impressed with her flat, admiring the stunning view as he stood on her small balcony overlooking the river. Anna smiled, appreciating what the now-familiar skyline must look like to someone seeing it for the first time. She came to stand beside him, and they discussed how they would both like to spend the evening. He had seen most of the latest films, as there was little else to do on his evenings off from the prison. They checked out the *Evening*

Standard's Friday theater listings, narrowing the choices down to *Hamlet* at the National Theatre or a new play that had rave reviews at the Royal Court. They decided on the latter, as Ken was keen to go to an Italian restaurant on the King's Road called La Famiglia, which served Tuscan food. He'd eaten there before and loved it.

"It's very popular." He grinned.

"In that case, we'd better book a table." She grinned back, adding, "I'd hate to come between you and your food."

As Anna drove west through the early-evening traffic, Ken remarked that his sister had also asked if Anna would like to have lunch with her family the next day. "I'm sorry if I sound like I'm crowding you, but I'll be staying over there tonight. I've got a friendly game on tomorrow morning over in Twickenham, which is partly why I came down this weekend."

Anna found a parking spot quickly, and yet again he made her laugh as he at first said she'd never get into the small space. He closed his eyes as she reversed in one, inched forward and it was done.

"That was impressive—not that I wasn't confident, of course! It would have taken me a few attempts, but the classic would have been to watch my mother—well, she'd never have even attempted it. My old man checks his bumpers every time she comes back from the grocery store."

They were in plenty of time for curtains up, and Ken wouldn't hear of her going dutch on the tickets.

"About tomorrow—you won't have to watch the game, but I'll need to call Lizzie, as she'll be cooking up a storm, roast chicken and all the trimmings."

They went into the theater and sat in their seats.

"I'd like to watch you play, and yes, I'd love to come for

lunch," Anna told him, filled with a mixture of excitement at being asked and trepidation at meeting his sister so soon.

Ken rang his sister on his mobile and then remembered to turn it off. Anna did the same.

"I was at the Royal Shakespeare Company, and in the middle of *Julius Caesar,* this bloke's phone starts pinging out Beethoven's Fifth," Ken told her. "I hate the things. It was so distracting not just for the audience but for the actors."

It was at this point that the loudspeakers asked for all mobile phones to be turned off, and they grinned at the shared joke before settling back as the play began.

Anna could not remember the last time she had been to the theater, and she found Ken's closeness to her comforting. He couldn't help but touch her shoulder, as he was so big, but she hoped that wasn't the only reason that his arm was pressed against hers.

During the intermission, they stood outside the theater rather than join the crush in the bar, enjoying the sight of the crowds around Sloane Square. He was gently protective of her, making sure she didn't get jostled by the other audience members as they made their way back to their seats for the second half.

After the final curtain fell, they walked down the King's Road, and she liked the way they stopped together, looking at many of the stores still open. She also liked the friendly atmosphere once they reached the restaurant. They were at ease with each other, discussing the pros and cons of the production. Ken was obviously a keen theatergoer and was surprised how few shows she had been to, living in London.

"I suppose it's down to work. There never seems to be much time off, and when I do have free nights, I am usually going over the case files," Anna said, beginning to wonder what she'd been missing out on.

The dinner was delicious, and once again, Ken refused to let her pay. As they strolled along the King's Road—and it was quite a walk back to her car—she felt completely natural when he caught her hand. They'd stopped to look into the big Harley-Davidson franchise, where Ken pointed out the model that was his, remarking that he often came by there to buy extra parts to customize his bike.

By the time they returned to her car, it was almost midnight. Ken suggested he catch the tube from Sloane Square to Richmond, but Anna insisted she drive him to his sister's.

It was actually a longer drive than Anna had thought, but she hardly noticed, she was having such a good time. She eventually drew up outside a small terraced house not far from Richmond High Street. They sat for a moment. Ken didn't ask her to come in but made sure she knew about the arrangement for the next day. If she wanted to see the game the following morning, his sister would be going, and Anna could meet up with her and her children at the house. He opened the passenger door and then looked back, smiling.

"I've really enjoyed tonight," Anna said.

He leaned across to kiss her. It was fleeting and not in any way sexual, and the next moment he was standing on the pavement watching her drive away. Anna realized she would have liked him to come back to her flat, but at the same time she was glad that she hadn't jumped into having sex with him, as she had done in a couple of previous relationships—if such they could be called. But this felt altogether different.

• • •

After a night of intermittent sleep, she was eager to see him the following morning. She drove back to Richmond, aware that she was falling for him, and the drive seemed to take forever. Eventually, she parked outside his sister's house.

Lizzie was a good few years older than Ken and had the same blond hair, worn in a loose knot. She was wearing a long skirt and boots with a fringed shawl, giving her a rather hippie look. Welcoming Anna, she explained that Ken had already gone to the rugby grounds. She then introduced her husband, Ian, who was sitting in the family kitchen surrounded by Sunday newspapers. He said he was on duty watching the chicken.

"He won't be coming with us," Lizzie said. "He's not a rugby fan—well, nor am I, but our boys play."

Anna then met her two sons. Ollie was dark-haired and angelic-looking, and the other, Oscar, looked like Ken, with thick blond hair and blue eyes. They were scruffy and loud, and no sooner had Anna been introduced than they piled into Lizzie's old Range Rover to get to the match.

Lizzie was an appalling driver, constantly turning around to tell the boys to behave. She was very funny, saying she had been up early to peel the potatoes and prepare the vegetables, but she knew when she got back, she'd still have to take over the cooking.

"Ken said you are a detective," she went on.

"Yes."

"The boys will be pestering you later for some grisly details. They are at the age when anything dead fascinates them."

"Do you work?"

"Good God, no, they take up all my time. I used to be a costume designer, mostly for TV commercials, and I might go back to it when they're a bit older, but right now I like to take them to school and pick them up—you know, be at home for them."

"What does your husband do?"

"Ian? He's got his own IT company, makes a fortune, and we just like to spend it for him." Lizzie laughed.

Anna had not spent a morning like this ever. She found she liked Lizzie, and she also liked the two boys who, although boisterous, were also well spoken. Their excitement was contagious. The game was rough, and Ken was cheered on by his nephews as they stood on the sidelines; even Anna joined in cheering and shouting encouragement to his team, although she was not sure of the rules.

By the time the game was over and they had returned to the house, the two women were chatting and laughing together like old friends.

Lunch was as Lizzie had expected, in need of her attention, as Ian had not put in the roast potatoes. Anna helped in the kitchen, setting the table, and, under instructions, made the big jug of gravy. By the time lunch was ready to be served, Ken had arrived, showered and sporting a bruise over one eye. He played around with the boys and then helped Ian carve and serve the big roast chicken.

They all ate in the kitchen. Anna said little, enjoying the robust fooling around and the meal, which was delicious. There was apple pie and ice cream to follow. Finally, when Ian asked who would have coffee, Ken said with regret that it was time he left, as he would have to return to the prison. This took a lot longer than he intended, as he had to give both his nephews a ride around the block on the back of his motorbike. It was obviously a regular event, as they produced their own helmets. The boys were tremendously excited; Anna could see that they adored their uncle.

She was unsure whether to leave at the same time as Ken, but he said that he would love a cup of coffee at her flat, if that was okay. Anna realized that apart from that once, at no time had Lizzie or Ian mentioned her work. It felt as if it all belonged to another world. Lizzie had asked how long she had known Ken, but before Anna had been able to answer, one of the boys had dropped a hot plate. She liked the way Lizzie said it was just an accident and not to worry, but she made him clean up the floor all the same.

Anna got back to her flat at the same time Ken arrived on his motorbike. She brewed up coffee as he perched on one of the stools in her kitchen. "So that's my sister," he said.

"I really liked her. In fact, your whole family is lovely."

"Wait till you meet my brother, Robin, the one in Australia. He's a real ladykiller and raking in the money selling properties. My mum says he's got all the best features from both of them, as my dad used to be a handsome man when he was young."

"What work did your father do?"

"He was a quantity surveyor, but he always hated it; it was a job to pay for our education and keep Mum happy. Now that he's retired, I think he's happier than he ever was. Loves just pottering around." Ken accepted a freshly ground cup of black coffee and asked about Anna's family. She told him and realized how empty it sounded: both parents dead, no close relatives, herself an only child.

The time flew past, and it was almost six when Ken said he really would have to be on his way. He put on a big studded leather jacket and carried his helmet and his rugby kit in a small leather holdall.

"Maybe we could do this again?" he suggested as she walked him to the front door.

"Yes, I would like that very much. I sometimes don't have the weekends off, though, it depends on the workload," Anna said, conscious that this had never bothered her before.

"Well, I'll call you. I doubt you'd want to come all the way back to Leeds. Do you think you'll be seeing Welsh again?"

"I sincerely hope not."

They looked at each other, slightly embarrassed, and then he tipped her chin up and kissed her lips. "I've wanted to do that all afternoon."

She couldn't think what to say, and the next moment he'd gone. She went outside to the balcony to watch his bike roaring off; all she could think was that she hoped he would call again soon. They had not discussed if either of them was involved with someone. In fact, it had been a totally relaxed weekend. And for her, it was almost unheard of not to have studied the case file or even spent a moment thinking about the investigation.

On Monday morning, back at the incident room, Mike asked Anna to work on the blue-blanket case files. Reading through the statements, pathology, and forensic reports, she could see there was little to go on, but she decided to focus on the small lizard tattoo. They had numerous pictures of it, and it didn't look to be professional; it was rather blurred and dark in color, almost navy blue. They had no details of where the victim had lived, so it could have been done at any one of thousands of tattoo parlors, that is, if it had been inked in the UK. Even though the photographs had been shown on television and in the newspapers, nobody had come forward to identify the tattoo.

Anna decided to pay a visit to the tattoo parlor nearest the station in Hounslow. She had to wait while the tattooist finished working on a customer before she was able to sit with him and ask if he could give her any indication whether the little lizard was a popular design.

Ron of Ron's Tattoos had so many studs in his nose, his lips, and his ears that it was hard for her to concentrate. His forearms and even his hands were covered in tattoos, and he had bitten fingernails, but he was very pleasant and brought numerous books to sift through to see if the design was one that had been printed up. They found a few that looked close to the photograph, but they were either larger or more snakelike.

"It's very dark ink." Ron pondered, looking at the photo.

"That's what I thought. Do customers usually ask for it to be a certain color?"

"Yes. I would have thought it'd be better more greenish, but that would be just my personal choice."

He turned the photograph this way and that; then he got an Anglepoise lamp out to have an even better and closer look. "It's not very good," he told Anna. "I wouldn't say it's exactly an amateur's work, but you wouldn't get a pro satisfied. It's also upside down."

Anna peered closer; she hadn't really thought about it, but when he pointed to one of the books with a lizard-type design, the animal had its feet down. On their victim's hip, it was facing up.

"Unless he fancied looking at it himself, or it was a dead one," Ron joked.

"It was actually on a woman, a murder victim."

"Bloody hell! Well, it's unusual for a woman, but then it takes all sorts. You wouldn't believe what I've been asked to ink on some women's bodies." He suddenly leaned back and wagged his finger. "You know what it could be? And I couldn't tell from the photographs, I'd have to see it on the skin to be sure, but . . . it could be something that was inked over another tattoo. To get them lasered off is quite painful, and we do quite a lot of covering up—you know, the guys get a girlfriend's name done, then they get ditched, so they want it changed."

"Could you tell, if you saw it on the body, whether it had been covering another tattoo?"

"Maybe, or you could ask someone with more experience. That might be a better way to check it out."

Anna thanked Ron, who handed her his card, saying that if she ever wanted a tat, he would give her a good price.

The victim had been held at a mortuary close to where the body had been discovered. When Anna returned to the incident room, she tried without success to speak to the previous murder team's DCI. Ron's suggestion had made her wonder if the team had gone to any lengths to ascertain whether this was ever tested. Just as she was leaving him a message, Barolli signaled to her. The van driver who had discovered Estelle Dubcek's body was in interview room two. As Langton wasn't at the station, Barolli was to conduct the interview.

Brian Collingwood was twitchy, picking at his awful acne spots. In front of him lay his statement. Barolli tapped it with his finger.

"The reason you have been called in, Mr. Collingwood, is because there seems to be some doubt over your original statement."

"I don't believe this! I should have just driven on," the man complained in a Birmingham accent. "I'm taking time out from my work again, you know."

"Well, let's make this as short as possible," Barolli said. "Mr. Collingwood, you stated that you parked on the hard shoulder, as you needed to relieve yourself." Anna didn't even look at him but concentrated on her notebook.

"Yeah, that's right."

"Can you tell us exactly what happened?"

Collingwood sighed. "I should have stopped at the service station, but I didn't, and then it was too late to go back, right? So I pulled over onto the hard shoulder and went to the hedge. I did what was needed, and as I was turning to walk back to me van, I saw the girl's legs."

"From the hedge?"

"Yeah, and I called the police. I was there for three hours, telling everyone what I just told you again."

"The problem is, Mr. Collingwood, the hedge is next to a wide ditch. It must have been difficult to see the body from there unless you already knew about it."

The young man went pale behind his blotches. "I am just telling you what I saw," he muttered. "I did my duty and called the police on my mobile phone."

"Why are you lying?" Barolli was relentless.

Anna looked up and could see that Collingwood was sweating.

"I am telling you the truth," he said obstinately.

"No, you are not. Now, you may have a totally innocent reason for not wishing to tell us the truth, but now is the opportunity to do so before this goes any further, do you understand? You could be charged for withholding evidence."

"I never did anything wrong! I swear, I never done anything wrong."

"But you admit you have lied?"

Collingwood chewed at his nails, looking down, and the sweat glistened on his forehead.

"As I said, I am sure you have a very good reason, and you are here just helping our inquiries. You are not under arrest. All we need from you is the truth about what exactly happened . . ."

Collingwood still wouldn't look up.

"Did you see something, anything suspicious—a vehicle, a car, a person? Come on, lad—let's have the truth now."

Collingwood took a deep breath. "All right, this is what happened. I did drive into the London Gateway Services. I was looking for someone I'd seen around there, but I'd not been that way for months, maybe even longer."

"Who were you looking for?"

"A—a friend."

Anna opened an envelope and took out Margaret Potts's photograph. "Is this your friend?" she asked gently.

Collingwood bit at what remained of his thumbnail. "Yeah, that's her. I'd met up with her a few times over the years."

Anna laid the photograph faceup on the table. Barolli shook his head. "Jesus Christ, Mr. Collingwood, you could be getting into real hot water here. Maybe we need to get you a solicitor."

"I never saw her, I don't need no solicitor, I've done nothing."

"This woman was murdered, Mr. Collingwood!"

"No, she wasn't the girl that was lying there."

"We know that. So if you also know that, then you had

to have got close to the victim in the field, a lot bloody closer than standing pissing behind a hedge."

Collingwood at last gave it up. He said that he just felt like seeing Maggie, that he had on various occasions paid her to give him oral sex, and on a few other occasions he had driven up the back lane and they had full sex. He knew she worked the service station and would often be behind in the lane waiting for customers, so he had driven there. When he had been unable to find her, he had reversed and driven back the way he had come, but he'd started becoming bogged down in the mud and grew concerned that if he kept on the back road, he'd be in trouble.

"So I was doin' a U-turn to head back to the London Gateway service station and drive in via the dirt-track road onto the M1 when I saw the girl. I could see her across the field. She was lying there, half in and half out of the ditch. At first I thought it was Maggie, you know, so I got out of me van and walked up the track. I got a few yards from her and could see it was this young girl. I didn't get any closer. It was the way she was lying, see? I knew she was a goner."

He went on to explain that he returned to the motorway but felt so bad about what he had seen that he parked up on the hard shoulder and called the police.

"I swear before God that's all I done. I got a seventeen-year-old daughter meself, and I kept on thinking about that poor kid dumped in the field, so I done my duty."

They went over his new statement time and time again, but Collingwood swore that he had not seen any other vehicle, nor had he seen anyone near the body or in the lane. He added that on other occasions there had been a bunch of travelers hanging out by the barns. He also admitted that when he had full sex with Margaret Potts, she had used an old caravan parked by the barns. She would often take her customers there. He didn't think it belonged to anyone, and it was never locked. He also said that he had not seen Margaret in a long time because he had been driving a different route.

"How long, Mr. Collingwood?"

"Two years, maybe even more. She mostly worked nights, that's what she told me, but I just chanced that she'd be working."

"How much did she charge you?" Anna asked.

Collingwood said that for a blow job, it was ten pounds, but if it was full sex, she charged twenty-five. Barolli glanced at Anna, unsure why she was so interested in the money.

"Have you any idea how many clients Margaret would have in a day or night's work?" Anna asked.

"Not really, but she had a lot of regulars. Well, she told me she had, but I wouldn't know."

"You ever see anyone else she went with?"

"No, and I wasn't what you'd call a regular. It was months in between times, and like I told you, I'd not seen her in years."

"Did she ever tell you she'd been beaten up?"

"No. She was well turned out, kept herself clean." Collingwood sighed. "She was a good sort."

"'She was a good sort,'" Barolli mimicked later, when the van driver had been allowed to go home. "Dear God, having that spotty twat crawl all over you—what a wretched way to make a living."

Anna sat at her desk working up the report of the

interview, tapping her teeth with a pencil. "You know, if she was working most nights, she had to have hoarded some cash. Otherwise, what did she do with it all? She didn't pay rent, she dossed down in hostels. We found no savings accounts in her name. I think I should have another meeting with Emerald Turk, only this time I want her brought in for questioning."

Barolli said he'd organize it.

"She had Margaret's suitcase," Anna reminded him, and he nodded.

"Probably be another waste of time, though. Same with that Collingwood; we gained nothing new, apart from Maggie sometimes worked the day shift as well, but she might have changed to only nights, who knows. I bet you won't get anything from the blue-blanket victim, either."

"True, there's nothing as yet, but I'm waiting for the DCI who led the inquiry to get back to me in connection with her tattoo."

Barolli laughed. "You got a big break on that previous case with the actress—the killer had her face tattooed on his back, right?"

"Yep, but this is different. I think the lizard tattoo may have been inked over a previous one. I'll just have to wait to find out."

"Be good if it was her name and address." Barolli sniggered.

"We should be so lucky."

Anna hoped that Ken would call her, but he didn't, and she spent the evening at home looking over all her notes from the previous Emerald Turk interviews. She was at her desk early the following morning.

When she got in, Mike Lewis was at Barbara's desk,

making a call to Mr. Rodgers, who was beginning to think he was being investigated for fraud. He had insisted that all his tax and VAT payments were in order, then contradicted this by saying that it would be difficult for him to go back five years to present them with all his receipts and orders. He was growing agitated, saying that when the firm moved from London to Manchester, he didn't have the space to retain all the old order files.

Mike Lewis tried to explain to him, as diplomatically as possible, that they were not investigating any taxation or VAT fraud, they were simply attempting to trace someone who might be of interest to their inquiry and who might have purchased some Swell Blinds.

Mike was trying to be patient but became alarmed when Mr. Rodgers asked if this was all connected to John Smiley.

"You know, he's a trusted employee. If you are trying to find out whether he has acted in any way that is detrimental to Swell Blinds, then I will have to let him go. Is that what this is all about?"

"Please, Mr. Rodgers, we have no intention of damaging Mr. Smiley's exemplary work record. All we are basically interested in is tracing a possible witness who may have ordered a set of blinds from your company during the few years you were based in London; this would be before you moved to Manchester."

It took a while longer before Mr. Rodgers promised to do what he could. After he hung up, Mike tapped the phone and said to the others, "I hope we don't get that poor bastard fired and then have nothing on him. Rodgers says they don't have that many records from London, as they don't have the storage space."

Barbara had a thought. "Mike, remember that old lady

called Wendy Dunn who worked for the company for many years? She ran the reception at the Hounslow office: she might be able to help."

"Well, get on it, then. We seem to be getting our thumbs right up our arses. If Langton keeps putting the pressure on me, I'll have to tell him to back off. We're going up one blind alley after another."

"Blind! Swish ones! Haw haw." Barolli ducked the empty coffee cup thrown by Mike.

DCI Vince Mathews, who had led the inquiry into the murder of the Jane Doe wrapped in the blue blanket, finally rang Anna back. He had a strong northern accent and spoke loudly.

"Her body was released after the second postmortem, and the coroner gave the go-ahead for burial. The local undertakers and our local council arranged a pauper's grave."

"Was her body embalmed?"

"No, love, cremated, and to be honest, after all this time, if we'd have embalmed her, the skin would be like leather, too shriveled for any light-source examination of the tattoo."

Disappointed, Anna thanked him and was about to hang up when he said, "Have you got all the photographs? We took the tattoo from every side and angle."

"I believe so," Anna said.

"Thing is, love, the human eye doesn't pick up anything that might be beneath the tattoo."

"Did anyone use the light-source tech units? Only I know they use infrared lighting."

"No, and we were discussing taking the tattoo—you know, cutting it out—but as we'd had no one come forward after the news coverage, we didn't think it would be worth it."

"Thank you for getting back to me."

Before he could say anything else or call her "love" again, Anna replaced the receiver. Frustrated but not giving up, she called Pete Jenkins at the forensic lab. He agreed to see her in the early evening and asked her to bring as many photographs as possible.

Anna grabbed a late lunch before the interview with Emerald Turk. Barolli warned her that the woman was a foul-mouthed bitch today, but Anna pointed out that was nothing new.

Emerald was sitting in the interview room swinging one leg over the other. She looked smart, as her hair had been styled and bleached very blond. She wore thick false eyelashes and had on oyster-pink lip gloss that matched her pink tracksuit top.

"You got a lot of nerve bringing me in. I presume it's down to you, right?" She jerked her head toward Anna as she sat down in front of Emerald at the interview table. "I told you everything—this is harassment. I had to get some-one to mind me kids and make their tea so I could get over here. If you keep on wasting my time, I'm gonna write to the newspapers."

"Thank you for agreeing to come in," Anna said quietly.

"I didn't. I was told that if I didn't get in the fucking pa-trol car, I'd be fucking arrested, and the two blokes wouldn't tell me what it was all about, just that I was wanted for questioning, and now, seeing you, I know it's bloody Mar-garet Potts again, isn't it? I wish to God I'd never met her."

Anna let the tirade go on until Emerald went quiet. "Would you like a glass of water?"

"No."

Barolli remained silent, sitting beside Anna, feeling rather queasy, as Emerald's perfume was very strong. He waited. Anna thumbed through her notebook, then checked her written report, in no hurry to question Emerald.

"Well—is it about the bloody suitcase?"

Anna didn't answer, so Emerald turned to Barolli. "I told her I tossed it out. It just had some old clothes in it, and the ones I didn't keep, I chucked with the case. You can't get me for doing that. She left it in my house." Emerald's foot swung up and down, and she picked at one of her false nails. "That fucking notebook, right?" She pointed at Anna. "Is that what this is about? Because I told you, I never saw it. I dunno where it is, and you said you didn't have no handbag from her, so I said it was probably in that, right? So what you want me here for? And sending a fucking patrol car . . . I got to live in that block of flats, you know."

"You look very pretty today," Anna said, smiling.

It took Emerald by surprise. Her lip-glossed mouth opened and closed like a fish's. "I wish I could say the same to you."

"Let's not get into silly slanging matches. You are here because I am not satisfied that you told me the truth."

"I fucking did."

Barolli leaned over and wagged his finger. "Just stop the swearing and show some respect."

"You show *me* some. I done everything I could—I told this one everything I knew about Maggie. I don't know any more, all right? The poor cow is dead, and you should be trying to find out who killed her, never mind bringing *me* in."

"I think you found more than clothes in Margaret Potts's suitcase, Emerald, because I know she was earning quite a lot of money."

"What's quite a lot to you? I know what she earned, and it was fucking rubbish. How much do you think she could make, givin' sex to down-and-out lorry drivers?"

"You maybe earn more from your massage parlor, but—"

"You mind your own business about what I earn."

"What else did you find in Margaret Potts's suitcase, Miss Turk?"

Emerald sighed, staring up at the ceiling. There was a long pause, her leg still swinging up and down.

Anna checked her notes. "You said there was a tracksuit, the one you were wearing when I first met you, a few other garments, and you brought up the notebook that Margaret kept with the car license numbers she recorded for her protection."

"Yeah, and I never had it, I also told you that."

"Her brother-in-law mentioned a family diamond ring, and her husband also mentioned some jewelry that he knew Margaret had. Added to these items of value was possibly her savings."

"Savings?"

"Yes, money."

"She never had any, and I never saw no jewelry. If you want to get another search warrant, you can rip my flat apart again."

The interview was going nowhere, and without firmed-up evidence, it was wasting time.

"Did you ever use a company called Swell Blinds?"

"What?"

"It's a company that makes wooden slatted window blinds to order."

"Did I know them? You must be joking. I never had no made-to-order blinds."

Anna closed her notebook and said, "Thank you, Miss Turk, and if you want, we can arrange for you to be taken home."

"That's very big of you, but I'll get a taxi."

Anna watched Emerald walking out of the station. Barbara joined her.

"Anything?" she asked.

"Nope. How about you?"

"Well, I've contacted my little lady Wendy Dunn. She lives on my way home and I'm going to drop in to see her again."

Anna shook her head. "I think this interviewing everyone over again is not only time-consuming but unproductive. It's not telling us anything that we didn't already know."

"Ah, but Mrs. Dunn says she's retained a lot of old files from Swell Blinds—not payment receipts but old orders from good customers in case they ever wanted new ones."

Anna gave Barbara a high five. "Let's hope she can give us a new lead, then. We sure as hell need one."

Pete Jenkins was his usual friendly self, asking if Anna wanted to look at the blue blanket brought to them from the earlier investigation. As she hadn't seen it, she agreed and drove over to the labs in Lambeth, South London. The blanket was pinned out on a long brown-paper-covered trestle table. It was filthy, covered with stains that had markings attached to them, ready for further DNA testing.

"It had long dog hairs all over it," Pete told Anna. "The original lab examination showed they could be from an Alsatian or similar breed; find the animal in question, and we can match them by DNA. There were also a few carpet fibers and what looks like vomit. The corner where you might have had a laundry mark has been hacked off."

"It looks like a big child's blanket to me. It's not a full-size one, is it?"

"No. It could be from a large single bed, we've not a lot to go on," Pete continued. "We're running further chemical tests on the color and hoping to run it by manufacturers. It is also worn in some places, almost bald."

They went over to his cleared desk, and Anna took out all the photographs of the tattoo. Some were in color and others black and white.

"Pity we don't have the actual body," he said. "We'd use infrared to illuminate the tattoo and then a filter to take out the blue, so we'd be able to see what colors are behind it. Different inks react to different wavelengths of infrared. So if the tattoo beneath the dark blue one had red or green or even a mixture, they would stand out. However, if there was blue in the original tattoo, it wouldn't."

"To be honest, Pete, it's just a thought. I don't know if it really does cover something else; it's just the dark color that's sort of odd, and also the lizard is upside down."

Pete laid out the photographs, placing the color ones to one side. "There is a process I am going to try. With these original digital photographs, I'm going to use Adobe Photoshop. What I'll be doing is taking the original image—we call it the RAW file—removing the blue channel and seeing if there are any colors beneath it or if an image shows up."

"How long will it take?"

"I'll work on it tonight for you and should get a result or not by morning."

"Thank you."

"Fancy a bite to eat? We've got a great Greek restaurant, just opened a two-minute walk away."

"Thanks, but no thanks. It's been a long day—I'll take a rain check."

"That's what you always say."

"You get a result, and *I'll* take *you* for dinner."

"Deal," he said, and shook her hand.

Chapter Nine

Anna was disappointed. There was still no call from Ken, and she was hesitant about calling him herself. She began to think that maybe she had read it all wrong, that he wasn't interested. She was making herself a salad when he rang. Since it took her a moment to wash her hands, it was already going on to voice mail when she reached it.

"Hi, it's Ken. Sorry not to have rung before and—"

She interrupted. "It's me, and I'm at home. Just didn't get to the phone in time."

"I'm sorry I haven't been in touch. I've had a bug, but I'm better now."

"Poor you. I was beginning to think you didn't want to meet up with me again," Anna said.

"I most certainly do."

Anna felt all girlish and giggled a lot as Ken chatted on about this and that. He said he could swing another weekend, as he'd agreed to switch to nights during the week, and she agreed to see him on Saturday. She hoped she would not be asked to work over the weekend but warned him that she might be called in.

"Are you playing rugby again?" she asked.

"Nope. I can get to you for lunchtime, is that convenient?"

"Yes, and it's okay to call me on the mobile. Leave me a message if I'm working, and I'll get back to you straight-away."

She gave him her mobile number, and he said that maybe they could take in another show.

"I'd like that."

"Good. Till Saturday, then."

She rang off with a huge smile, and then, just as she sat down to eat her salad, her mobile rang. It was Pete, and he had a result, although he wasn't sure it would be of much consequence.

"You were right, Anna, the lizard *was* inked over another tattoo."

She closed her eyes, hoping it would be the lead they needed.

"It's a date in red ink, a sort of scroll. I couldn't make out exactly what; it looked like a red ribbon and a red heart in the middle. There's something written on it: twenty-one *Lipiec* oh-two." Pete spelled out the word, then blew her away, as he told her that *Lipiec* was Polish for July.

Anna was late arriving for work next day, as she had been over to Pete's lab in Lambeth to collect the photographs and photo print of the tattoo's date. She burst into the in-cident room, eager to give the new details, but there was a lot of interest around Barbara's desk. The detective con-stable had two thick files with Swell Blinds orders going back four years *before* the company moved to Manchester. The amount of clerical work necessary to check with every customer would be a pain, but they would neverthe-less have to get it done. Beside each of the orders was the name and address of the customer, with appointment dates and sales contact. They needed to know if Smiley was the contact and whether any customers had links to the victims.

Joan asked if they were just to concentrate on the orders for the wooden slatted blinds, as they also had orders for the vertical variety.

"What are those?" Anna asked.

Joan pointed to the blinds along the incident-room windows—long strips of white canvas attached with thin chains and running vertically down the window.

"They let the light in or out, but they're used mostly in offices or for dividing sections. Swell Blinds had some big orders; they were contracted by a couple of major housing associations, big-time. Some of the new council estates use them, maybe because they're cheap."

Joan continued to sift through the orders, and Mike suggested she concentrate on house calls rather than the housing associations. He then turned to see Anna writing up beneath their blue-blanket victim the date and design from Pete Jenkins.

Anna explained what Pete had done. Although the picture was very blurred, they could make out the scroll and bows. Mike peered at it. "What is it?"

Barolli joined them. "I think it's maybe a wedding date," he said.

"Or a birthday, christening—could be anything."

"No, it has to be something the victim wanted covered—so if we go with a wedding date, it would make sense if it went wrong. That would be why she wouldn't want it as a reminder," Anna said.

"Okay, let's get cracking on it," Mike said. "Get on to the Polish embassy and see if they can direct us to whomever we need to contact regarding marriage licenses issued on that date."

"It's another link to our two Polish girls, Mike, and it could mean we do have a fourth victim," Anna said.

"Yeah, yeah, but let's keep it to this one. No more digging up any additional Jane Does; we've got enough cases."

Barolli stomped over to Anna's desk, his nose slightly out of joint. "Well, congratulations, Travis, you've done it again—but you know something? Cameron Welsh said there would be other victims, and if this one adds up, he's right on the ball."

"I am aware of that," she said tetchily.

"Maybe we need another visit."

Anna was about to say that if there was to be another trip to Barfield, she wouldn't be the one to go, but then it would mean she could get to see Ken.

"Yeah, maybe we do," she said, "but if you don't mind, right now I want to get on with trying to identify the blue-blanket victim."

The team, with extra clerical staff on board, began checking Swell Blinds's customers. By lunchtime it was clear that customer after customer was not only satisfied with the company but praised their workmanship *and* John Smiley.

The Polish embassy gave Anna a contact in Poland who informed her that there were many churches and civil courts, and without the exact location, it would take considerable time to produce the names of couples who had married on that specific date. Frustrated, Anna sent e-mails with pictures of the victim in the hope that it would help identify her, underlining that they were interested only in women aged twenty to thirty.

Meanwhile, Mr. Rodgers was sending down as many customer-service records as he could from Manchester—so there would be even more to sift through. Mike had mentioned to him that his ex-employee Wendy Dunn had been helping with their inquiry, and Mr. Rodgers angrily said that he was aware of it but felt that she should have contacted him for permission.

"He spent a long time explaining to me that I would be able to see that his company was doing good work. He's still nervous that we are doing some taxation investigation. Apparently, one of the reasons he downsized his company was that he lost one of his most lucrative orders, for Strathmore Housing Association, so I got a full account of how the housing associations were hand in glove with Social Services and that they weren't averse to underhand dealing." Mike flipped through his letter box.

"Like what?"

"According to Arnold Rodgers, these housing-association contracts are worth a lot of money. So you get builders, plumbers, everyone in the trade after the contracts. They need thousands of blinds or whatever made up for new estates or when they refurbish high-rise properties, and according to him, he lost the contract to a company that knew someone high up and were not professionals—you know, cutting corners." Mike rubbed his fingers together to make the point.

Anna was about to ask how much the contracts were worth when her e-mail began bleeping. Coming in were copies of marriage documents and lists of couples married on the date in question and from different locations all over Poland.

By late afternoon, the hours the team had put in had produced nothing that added to the investigation. Everyone was feeling the pressure, even more so when Langton made an appearance. Mike took him over all the new developments and how much work it had entailed, but the only piece of new information he was interested in was the discovery of the date beneath the lizard tattoo.

Anna had requested a Polish translator, whose first act was to look at the drawings of the tattoo scroll. The woman told them it was quite common in Poland for the families to give to the couples a scroll with a heart and ribbons in memory of their wedding day. They often would have it framed with a wedding photograph. She said that she had personally never known any girl to have it made into a tattoo.

Langton cornered Anna and said affably that he wasn't concerned that the translator didn't think a bride would have the tattoo; she was all of sixty so could be out of touch with what any young girl would or wouldn't do.

"Good work, though, and a slap in the face for that murder team. They could have taken it off her skin."

"We're getting a slew of couples from all over Poland who were married on that specific date."

"Good. Keep at it—we need a result on her."

Langton turned and signaled to Mike that he wanted a private word, and the two men disappeared into the office.

"I am going to have to halve the clerical staff, Mike."

"But we need all the help we can get! Especially now that it's official we're taking on a fourth victim."

"If that doesn't bring us a result, I will have to cut back the team as well. The budget's being swamped, and I can't justify holding on to so many people. You've had eighteen officers, Mike, plus your key team, and it can't go on."

"We're working flat out."

"That may be so, but you've not brought anything to

the table with regard to Anika Waleska or Estelle Dubcek, and the interviews with Margaret Potts's relatives gave you nothing new. Thank Christ for Travis; she's the only one so far who is using her initiative. That tattoo may open up this Polish connection."

"It could also open up another heap of inquiries."

Langton stood up. "If it does, that bloody Cameron Welsh was right: our killer could have been busy for years."

"We've not come up with anything on John Smiley."

"I know that," Langton snapped, and headed for the door. "I've pulled in a few favors from Manchester to keep an eye on Smiley, nothing obvious, but he's still, to my mind, a suspect, and as we've no one else even in the frame, we'd better go and visit Welsh again, so get that organized."

"Do you want to go and see him?"

"No, I bloody don't. I've given more than enough of my time, and I don't think Travis will agree to traipsing up to Leeds again, so get yourself or Barolli there."

"Yes, Gov, but you don't want us to delve into any more cold cases, do you?"

Langton hesitated and then shook his head. "You've got two more weeks, Mike, and then I'll have to review the whole inquiry. Get me a result or I'll have to pull it."

The following day, they still had nothing definite from the Polish marriage date, and the mound of receipts and con-tracts for Swell Blinds were still taking up hours of calls. Mike Lewis put the pressure on to try and get the team to bring in anyone who had known Anika and Estelle, return-ing to the restaurant and interviewing Katia and her boy-friend again. It seemed unbelievable that two young and attractive girls could just disappear and end up murdered without anyone knowing anything about them. Mike also put more pressure on to try and bring in the anonymous caller who had tipped off the *Crimewatch* program.

On Friday it felt as if the entire case had ground to a halt. Mike gave a briefing to warn the team about Langton's threat. They had by now lost four clerical workers, and Joan and Barbara were forced into handling the Swell Blinds contract inquiries on their own. The Polish translator was still at work, but she would also be withdrawn soon.

Anna had never known a case that seemed to drag down everyone involved. She just hoped they would not have to work on Saturday.

Mike asked for Barolli and two officers to continue overseeing the incident room during the weekend. Anna kept her gaze down, not wanting to make eye contact with Mike. When he came over to her desk, she thought he was going to ask her to be on duty.

"Langton wants another visit to Cameron Welsh," he said. "I know you won't want to go, so—"

"I don't mind as long as it's next week."

He looked surprised. "I'll get it organized, then. Thank you."

She watched him head back to his office; poor Mike looked really worn out. Yet even though she knew the pressure was on, she couldn't wait to leave. She had never in her entire career had something more important on her mind than her investigation. Previously, she would have happily volunteered to work over the weekend.

But now Anna did another evening of housework, put fresh sheets on her bed and flowers on the dining table, and finished all her ironing. She never gave a thought to work. On the contrary, she was up early on Saturday washing her hair, choosing what to wear, and checking out theater productions. Shortly after twelve, she heard Ken's motor-bike from her balcony, where she'd been looking out for him. She hurried down to open the garage so he could park his bike by her Mini. Ken was wearing his thick bike leathers, and Anna offered to carry his helmet.

"I was going to bring one for you in case we felt like a ride tomorrow," he said.

Anna paused on the stairs, noticing his overnight bag. "Are you staying at your sister's?"

He smiled and caught her hand. "I can, but I haven't arranged anything with her."

Her heart jumped; it had been racing from the moment she had seen him draw up on his bike.

Once in her flat, Anna helped him off with his jacket and took his overnight bag into the bedroom. "Would you like a tea or coffee?" she asked.

"I'm gasping for a glass of water. I didn't stop, came straight from my flat to here."

He sat at her breakfast table as she opened the fridge to show she had stocked it with anything she thought he might want. She couldn't keep still, and he reached out and caught her hand once more.

"Come here and let me look at you, Detective Travis."

She went into his arms and rested her head against his shoulder.

"I've been thinking of you," he murmured. "It was hard not to. I was really looking forward to seeing you."

"Me, too," she said, looking up at him, and they kissed passionately for the first time. They could hardly keep their hands off each other, and it was only a few moments before they went into her bedroom. She loved the feel of him, the smell of him, and their lovemaking was beyond anything she could have dreamed.

Eventually, they grew hungry. Anna wore a white cotton robe. Ken wore a towel wrapped around his waist as they went to make something to eat. They had a quick meal sitting side by side, constantly touching and kissing, and then couldn't resist returning to bed.

There was no theater, no attempt to leave her flat; they just made love over and over again. They slept wound around each other, and when they woke up they returned to the kitchen to make steak and salad. Anna opened a bottle of wine. They lay beside each other, and it wasn't until late at night that they talked about what they should do the following day. They thought about a movie, and Ken suggested they drive to Ham Park at Hampton Court Palace, where they could hire a motorboat to go up the Thames.

"I take my nephews there a lot when I'm down to see Lizzie. We can get all the way up the river, as far as Waterloo, or go the other way, Twickenham, Teddington . . ."

"I'd like that."

Sunday was beautiful, and when Anna drew back the curtains, the sun streamed into the bedroom. Ken lay on his stomach, still deeply asleep, as she went into the kitchen to brew up coffee. She had bought bagels and cream cheese with smoked salmon. As she prepared the tray, her mobile rang; she hesitated and then ignored it. She was not going to allow anything to interrupt her day.

Anna drove them to Ham and, as Ken had suggested, left the car at Hampton Court Palace. They walked hand in hand across the bridge and down to a small dock with motorboats for hire. They were not exactly high-powered; they more or less putt-putted along. Ken steered for a while until she took over. She was enjoying herself more than she could remember. He sat beside her with his arm loosely around her shoulders.

The round trip took over an hour and a half, and they then walked back across Hampton Court Bridge to have a hamburger and fries at Blubeckers restaurant. Ken had a beer, Anna had a glass of wine with her hamburger, and then she ordered a chocolate ice cream that they shared.

"How's your case going?" he asked.

"It isn't. We seem to be going nowhere, and I maybe have to pay another visit to Cameron Welsh. It's not as if I'd ever want to set eyes on him again, but it would mean that I could maybe stay over, see your flat, or even stay at your parents' again."

"That's terrific! And you'll stay with me—I'll make sure I'm off duty. Do you know what day?"

"Maybe midweek, but it's not been arranged yet."

"He's been up to his old tricks, by the way."

"Who—Welsh?"

"Yes, he's a real pain in the butt. He accused one of the other inmates of eating his lentil soup, then it was someone had taken his hair gel. He had a hissy fit about anything and everything, and he can get the other inmates to flare up by making nasty snide remarks under his breath, so we had a lot of tension to deal with."

"I wouldn't normally have agreed to see him again, but if it means having time with you, then I will have to deal with it."

"Has he been of any use at all, or is he just wanking around?"

She laughed and then thought about it. "Trouble is, my boss thinks he's said some very informative things that he reckons have helped our inquiry. I don't agree, but the fact is, he comes up with stuff that we are already checking out, so I suppose that shows he is on the ball."

"Like what?"

"The last time we were there, he said we should concentrate on a victim called Margaret Potts. He kept on and on about there being a witness."

"Witness to what?"

Anna explained briefly the situation with their case, concluding, "So, Margaret Potts is the odd one out, in that she had no Polish connection, unless . . ."

"Unless what?"

"Unless she saw the killer or knew him. The other girls were young and attractive, unlike her. She was a hardened prostitute."

"But why the interest in Welsh?"

"Because he has contacted the incident room, especially me, and keeps on implying that he has information."

"Could he have?"

"I doubt it. He's been in prison for the time the murders were committed. There was a possibility that he talked to another prisoner who may have been released, and that was why he kept on with saying that he knew something . . . but we've run checks as far as is possible and come up with nothing. Next, he says he can get into the mind of the killer, being one himself; it's all really tedious, because he's such a loathsome creature, but we have to deal with it just in case."

Ken ordered two cappuccinos and said that he would be glad when he'd done his time at the jail, as sometimes it felt as if he, too, were a prisoner.

"You know something I can never understand?" he added. "You have these animals like Fred West—how many young girls did he murder?—and yet they just disappeared without a trace, one after the other, even his own daughter."

"That's what is really difficult with our case. Fred West's victims were girls who wouldn't be missed—well, most of them. They went to his house of their own accord. It was as if he could pick out the ones no one would care about or report missing. We, by contrast, have two beautiful girls, and yet we can find no one who noticed their absence, no one who cared enough about them to report them missing. Even if they were, as we suspect, coming into the UK without the proper paperwork, it's hard to believe they could be picked up and murdered."

"You think they knew their killer?"

"We're trying to find some kind of link."

Ken signaled for the waitress to get the bill, and Anna leaned forward to touch his hand. "I'm sorry, we shouldn't have gotten into my work."

"Yes, we should. I'm going to have to if we see each other, just like I can have a good moan to you about my job. I didn't want to interrupt you talking, it's just that I'll have to ride back tonight, as I'm on early call tomorrow morning."

"What time will you have to leave?"

He leaned over to kiss her and grinned. "Got a couple more hours yet."

The flat felt horribly empty after Ken had left. Anna cuddled the pillow he had used, wishing he were still beside her, missing him badly already. It had been such an innocent, lovely day, and for once she fell into a deep long sleep. It wasn't until she was dressed and ready to leave for the station the next morning that she picked up her mobile. There were four calls from the incident room. She replayed them as she headed down to the garage. Two calls were from Barolli, asking her to contact him; the third call was from the Polish translator, asking Anna to call her; and the fourth was from Mike Lewis, and his message was terse.

"Call me back when you pick this up—urgent! I think we've got our bride."

Chapter Ten

"Where the fuck have you been all weekend?" Barolli greeted her angrily.

"I was with friends. I didn't expect to be needed, and if you ever speak to me like that again, as your superior officer, I will place you on a disciplinary report."

"I'm sorry. I thought you'd have your mobile with you. It came in late Saturday night."

"Have we an identity? Mike said something about you'd got the bride."

"He was being diplomatic, since you did all the tattoo business, but as no one could get hold of you and your landline is screwed . . ."

"I had to get a new number, unlisted. I'll give it to the office manager. So—have we got the girl identified?"

Barolli got out two sheets and said they had two girls who fit the description; both had been married on the same day, both were dark-haired and in their early twenties. "Mike is checking them out now. He's in with the interpreter, who, I've got to say, worked her shriveled butt off all weekend."

Anna took off her coat, wanting to hear more details, but Barbara signaled that there was a call for Barolli on line two.

"You look very refreshed," Barbara remarked to Anna.

"Thank you."

"Have a nice weekend?"

"Yes, I did, actually."

"Joan and me have square eyes, but we've finished the entire load of Swell Blinds contacts and—"

Barolli gave a yell as he placed down the receiver. "The anonymous caller just rang the TV station—she has agreed to come in to see us. Bloody marvelous! It's all happening this morning!"

He went off whistling as Anna checked her voice mail and opened up her computer. She jumped when Mike Lewis's office door banged open and he strode over to the incident board, prodded the picture of the victim from the blue-blanket case, and began to write: *Bibiana Nowak married Marek Ryszard in Krakow and number two is Dorota, who married Stanislav Pelagia in Warsaw. Both girls were aged twenty-two in 2002, both were dark-haired and around the same height, five feet five, again matching our victim, and neither has been seen for some time.*

Anna joined him and asked if both girls were still married. It was more likely their victim was either divorced or separated, since the wedding date on the tattoo had been covered up.

"We're just running checks, but because we've got blurred e-mail pictures, it could be either one of them."

Fifteen minutes later, they received information that they could delete Bibiana Ryszard. She had been traced so was still alive and still married.

Half an hour went by before they received the news that Dorota Pelagia had still not been traced, but they had tracked down her husband. He was in prison and had been for seven years, charged with armed robbery.

The officials in Poland were trying to locate Dorota's

family. Coming in via e-mail were two pictures of the young woman on her wedding day. She was wearing a short white dress and white shoes and stood holding a small bouquet. She looked shy and had a sweet soft smile. Her husband, Stanislav, towered above her, very broad-shouldered, with dark brooding looks. E-mails were criss-crossing back and forth as the team waited for further results.

"It's her," Anna said firmly. She picked up the photo of the victim taken at the mortuary, pinned it beside the wedding picture, and then did the same with the murder-site photographs. "They should get on to Customs, Passport Control, run the name to see if and when she might have entered the UK."

But Passport Control had no record of a Dorota Pelagia entering the UK, and they had gone as far back as 2003.

Further details were fed back to the incident room. Stanislav Pelagia had been arrested in March 2003, accused of domestic violence; he was released when his wife dropped the charges. Two further incidents had been recorded, and in each case no charges were brought.

"If Stanislav went to prison in 2003, we've got all the years since then in which she could have left him and arrived in England," Anna said to Barolli; she was standing by his desk.

"We're waiting to see if they can get any DNA for us to double-check that we've got the right girl. We can't go ahead and ask people to come forward with information if we're not one hundred percent sure she's our victim."

Barbara joined them. Now they had further details. Dorota had a sister living in Warsaw who claimed not to have seen her for between six or seven years. She knew Dorota had left her husband after his arrest. The family had been very much against the marriage, as Stanislav had a history of drug abuse, and they virtually cut off Dorota when she defied them and went ahead.

With the new evidence coming in, the team's low spirits lifted, but they would still have to wait for confirmation that their victim was Dorota Pelagia. Due to the assault charges brought against her husband, it was a strong possibility that she would have loathed the tattoo of their wedding day, even more so since he was held in prison.

They were disappointed to learn that no DNA samples were taken from Dorota when she had been attacked by her husband. By late afternoon there were still no known whereabouts, yet Anna was certain they had the right girl. It was pointless thinking about bringing over her sister to identify her, as they had no body, thanks to the cremation. They were dependent on matching photographs, so her sister had agreed to send over more.

At six-thirty the woman who had called the television program regarding Anika Waleska arrived in reception. She was accompanied by a lawyer who made it clear that his client wished to remain anonymous. Mike Lewis explained the importance of his client's telephone call, as it had led them to identify their victim, and he stressed that they needed further assistance. However, due to the severity of the case, and fully aware that she was assisting their inquiry and agreeing to be questioned, she would have to disclose her name.

So Anna and Mike Lewis were introduced to Olga but were given no surname. She was led into the interview room with her lawyer. It was hard to determine which of them carried the overpowering smell of mothballs. She was wearing a camel-hair coat, a silk head scarf tied beneath her chin, and large dark glasses. She was middle-aged and heavily built. Before they could ask anything, her lawyer again stated that it was imperative that nothing his client said would have legal repercussions. It was difficult to promise this, Mike said, because if Olga did have information that could implicate her in the murder, then they would have no option but to take action.

"I have nothing to do with hurting Anika." Her voice was a guttural rasp.

"How did you know her?" Anna asked softly.

"She work for me, not regular, but when I first meet with her."

Anna showed Anika's photograph, asking, "Is this Anika Waleska?"

"Yes."

"What work did she do for you?"

"I have a small company, housecleaning."

"How long did she work for you?"

"When I first meet with her, it was three years ago and she work full-time, but then she get other work, so it was not regular."

"How many girls do you employ?"

"I have maybe six or seven; it depends on what work I have coming in, and I send the girls out."

"Do your clients pay you directly?"

"Yes, then I pay the girls."

"Were you aware that Anika wasn't registered to work—had no National Insurance number?"

"I not ask questions."

"Can you tell us how she came to be working for you?"

"One of my girls bring her to me. They knew each other from Poland, and she was very nice girl."

Anna took out the picture of Estelle Dubcek. "Does this girl work for you?"

Olga looked at the photograph for quite a while and then nodded.

"Do you know this girl's name?"

"Yes. That is Estelle Dubcek, but she was trouble; only work for me six or seven months."

"When did you last see her?"

Olga shrugged. "Long time ago. As I said, she was not a good worker, not like Anika."

"Where did the girls stay when they worked for you?"

"I have a flat they use. I charge rent out of their earnings; they come and they go. Anika work for me and also restaurants at night."

"Did you know that Estelle wasn't registered to work, either?"

"I don't ask questions."

"Both these girls were working illegally."

"I say I not ask questions."

"But you must have known when they did not produce a National Insurance number."

"No."

"How did these girls know to contact you?"

"I have advertisements in Poland. Students, colleges, if they want work, they contact me or they introduce me to their friends."

"Olga, Estelle Dubcek was also murdered."

It was hard to see what the woman was thinking; her scarf covered most of her face, and the dark glasses made it impossible to see any reaction in her eyes.

"Two girls who worked for you have been murdered," Anna repeated.

"Listen to me, please. I call the television, I give them information that I knew Anika was working in a restaurant, but she was not living in my flat and not housecleaning. I wanted to help, but at the same time I did not want to become involved in any way. I have nothing to do with what the girls did after they leave me."

"Have you ever used a company called Swell Blinds?"

Olga looked confused. "No."

"Have you ever met someone called John Smiley?"

"No."

"Would you be prepared to give us the address of the people both Anika and Estelle worked for?"

"No, I don't want to do that. I have a very good reputation, I have built up clients over twenty years. They are good people, I have no people that are bad. My girls, I make sure are honest and well dressed and hardworking."

"And you take a big slice of their earnings, don't you?"

Olga gestured to her lawyer and then pushed back her chair. "I go now, that is enough. Thank you."

"And it's just housecleaning, is it?" Anna said, trying to keep control. She wanted to snatch the dark glasses away from the woman's face.

"I am honest woman, I have honest business."

"Two girls who worked for you are dead. You may be an honest woman, but you—"

She was interrupted as Olga stood up with her hands clenched at her sides and burst out: "I have pressure to come here, and I do so out of wanting to be a good citizen. You are trying to make things bad for me. I go now."

"Please sit down. We have not finished."

Olga's lawyer whispered to her, and she sat down again, taking a crumpled tissue from her coat pocket. "I answer everything and tell you all I know."

"Not quite. You see, it's possible that you are withholding

evidence. We will have no option but to continue questioning you. I would now like you to look at this third photograph."

Anna took out the photograph of the blue-blanket victim, who they were certain was Dorota Pelagia, and laid it down in front of Olga. She at last removed her dark glasses and stared at the photograph. Anna got out two more pictures, watching her closely. The woman had puffy bags beneath her eyes, and the rims of her glasses were imprinted on her cheeks.

"Oh my God, oh my God," she murmured.

Olga then turned to have a whispered conversation with her lawyer, holding the hand with the tissue across her chin so it was hard to determine what she was saying, apart from that she was speaking in English. Eventually, her lawyer requested a private conversation with Anna and Mike before he would agree to continue the interview.

Olga returned to the interview room half an hour later. She was wearing her dark glasses and was very subdued. Her lawyer had once more made it clear that for his client to continue, the police would have to agree that no charges could be brought with reference to her illegally employing the girls. In return, she would hand over a list of her clients that dated back five years, and allow them to visit the girls living in her flat. She would also submit tax and VAT receipts for her cleaning company and a list of girls she previously employed.

It was eleven-thirty by the time Olga left the station. Anna and Mike were privy to information that had opened up their case. Dorota Pelagia had worked for the cleaning company, so they had three victims linked together. All three girls had worked for Olga over the past five years.

None was full-time, and in all cases, they worked only short periods when they arrived in the UK. The work entailed housecleaning for not just private clients but hotels and offices. It would mean yet another extensive round of questioning and checking out all the names and addresses. So far, the police had uncovered no connection to Swell Blinds but hoped that they would discover a link.

The following morning, Barbara and Joan began cross-referencing all the data that they had from Swell Blinds to see if they had delivered to any of the new companies and private addresses Olga had listed. On the board were the details of the recruitment adverts placed in Poland. It appeared that the girls would answer, and Olga's contacts in Poland would subsequently arrange for them to come to England. They were given fake identity documents owned by a female Polish immigrant who was legally registered to reside and work in the UK. The same documents were sent back and forth, and the photographs were not even changed, since the girls were all about the same age, with dark hair or hair dyed to match the photograph as closely as possible.

The new arrivals were charged for this helping hand and were then moved into the flat owned by Olga to start working. She took 50 percent of their earnings, plus rent. It was obvious that the girls ignored the contract to work for Olga for a minimum of two years, since as soon as they had managed to save enough, they left. Olga said resentfully that it was always difficult to keep tabs on her workers; often the girls proved to be work-shy, belligerent, and to her mind, ungrateful.

Margaret Potts was the only one with no link. The time gaps between the murders were also of concern.

Had the killer been active during the years between? Dorota Pelagia was the first victim, her body found four years ago. Next was Margaret Potts, two years ago, and then Anika and Estelle, a year apart. It did, however, link more or less to the same time that John Smiley had left London to work in Manchester. Swell Blinds had moved five years ago.

Langton sat with Anna, drinking a cup of coffee, having been present for the morning briefing when the team learned of the latest developments. He was astonished that Olga had employed all three young girls and yet felt obliged to call the television company with regard only to Anika Waleska.

"I doubt she watches much TV." Anna snorted. "She's a horrible woman, and I'd really like to get her for tax evasion and her treatment of these girls. Just think how much she must be pocketing from all her scams. A lot of her so-called housecleaning is in cash payments; plus, she's got contracts for cleaning schools and hotels. Her full name is Olga Pavlova, but I can promise you there is nothing balletic about her."

"Eh?"

"It was sarcastic. There was a famous ballerina called . . . Oh, never mind."

"Yeah, she must be stashing it away. We can deal with her later, but right now we have to keep her sweet, as we need all the help we can get from her."

"She's got a flat in the Boltons in Chelsea, she drives a Mercedes, and she owns a big flat in Earl's Court that she rents out to her workers."

"Have you checked with Estelle's flatmate, Katia, and her boyfriend, Mikhail, to see if they were part of Olga's dirty business?"

"Barolli's on to that. I'll be going to talk to the present occupants of the flat."

Langton sighed and drained his coffee. "What about going to see Cameron Welsh again?" he asked.

"I've said I'll do it."

"That's very big of you." He gave her a quizzical look. "I didn't think you wanted to go again."

"I don't, but I think as I have been privy to all his previous interviews, I might be able to cut through the dross," Anna said, looking him in the eye.

"Fine, run the Polish connection by him."

"I think I might get the train, save that long drive. Maybe stay overnight and come back the following morning."

He stared at her for a moment and then shrugged. "Mrs. Hudson cooks up a good breakfast."

She gave a small laugh, agreeing, as he moved off. The conversation prompted her to confirm her travel arrangements. She'd leave early Wednesday morning and return on Thursday. She decided to call Ken at once to tell him. She was so eager to meet him again that it overshadowed any distaste at having to talk to Cameron Welsh, but if the prisoner acted up, she would just walk away.

Ken was thrilled and said he would meet her at the train station, drive her to his flat so she could leave her overnight bag there, and then take her to the prison. She would not be having his mother's cooked breakfast after all.

Anna stood on the wide steps of the house in Finborough Road, ringing the doorbell of flat three. Eventually, the big door with glass panels was buzzed open, and she entered a large hall with a mosaic tiled floor. These old houses around Earl's Court were all huge, four stories and with high ceilings, and at one time had been the family residences of wealthy people. Now most of them were subdivided and rented out.

Anna walked up the wide staircase; a pretty, dark-haired girl was waiting for her on the third floor. The flat was made up of one huge sitting room, two bedrooms, a kitchen, and a communal bathroom. There were four single beds in the main room, and the bedrooms held three beds each. It looked like a dormitory from an old-fashioned boarding school, with bags and suitcases littering every available surface.

Anna met with four girls and sat on one of the beds as they drank coffee from chipped mugs. Two could not speak any English, one was virtually acting as interpreter for the others, and the fourth girl had a terrible cold and was constantly sniffling and sneezing. Anna explained that she was not there for any immigration purpose but to ask them about three other girls. When shown the photographs, however, no one there recognized any of the victims. They had all been in London for six to nine months only, and it was obvious that they hated working for Olga. They complained about how mean she was and how they were putting in a sixty-hour week. No one could wait to leave, as it was not pleasant having to share such a crowded flat.

It took some time for them to explain how they had paid in advance for their paperwork, jobs, and accommodation in London, and how they were met at Gatwick airport by Olga's husband, who drove them to the flat. They said he was surly and rude to them and very much under Olga's domination. He helped in her company and organized the painting and decorating of other properties she owned and rented out.

Anna was quickly on to Olga's husband, asking them to describe him, as she wondered if he could be a suspect. He was Polish and, they said, much younger than she, but he had something wrong with him. He had asthma and was always coughing and wheezing so was more or less her full-time chauffeur.

"Does he drive a van for the painting and decorating?"

They were unsure, as he always drove them in Olga's Mercedes. If they had work a long way out of London, he would take them and collect them.

It seemed more and more obvious that Olga was coining it in, and by the time Anna left, she had called the incident room to get them to check out the husband.

It was disappointing, but by late afternoon, after lengthy interviews, they had no new information. Neither Barbara nor Joan, after cross-referencing Swell Blinds contracts, had found any match with any of the clients for whom Olga's cleaners worked. Depression was threatening once more.

Anna left early for an evening's grooming and to pack for the trip to Leeds. Only Barolli had looked at her with some suspicion, as he knew how much she hated Cameron Welsh.

Barolli had by this time interviewed Olga's husband, who, although unpleasant, was obviously a sick man, as he was gasping for breath during the entire interview. He did not own a white Transit van but drove a small ex–Royal Mail van carrying three workers used for decorating and all the various cleaning equipment and materials. His English was not too bad, but he constantly had to use a puffer to help his breathing. Barolli discounted him, doubting that he would have the strength to strangle or rape a young woman, let alone give his own wife a seeing-to.

• • •

As the train came into Leeds station, Anna was standing by the door, ready to jump out. Her heart was racing, and when she saw Ken waiting behind the barrier, she ran to him. She dropped her overnight bag as he scooped her up into his arms. She had never experienced such a strong feeling. It was like being a teenager, and she wanted nothing more than to stay close to him and not have to go to the secure unit.

Ken's flat was part of a complex used by officers working at the prison. A small building with ten modern flats, it had little to endear it, as it was like a square cinder block. His flat was spotless but sparse, with one bedroom, a lounge, a kitchen, and a bathroom. He had made no effort to personalize it, admitting that he intended to stay there only until he could afford to put a deposit down on his own place. He had, however, stocked the fridge with steaks and salad and smoked salmon. There was also a bottle of pinot grigio chilling for Anna, among the cartons of fruit drinks and health foods.

He brewed up fresh coffee, and they had some croissants with his mother's homemade jam, and then he led her into the bedroom. It, too, was devoid of anything personal. However, the bed was covered with a cheerful yellow duvet and matching pillowcases. There were no pictures, but Anna could see a stack of Harley-Davidson magazines, and in a small bookcase were his books on psychology and numerous autobiographies. The one thing he had spent money on was a large plasma-screen television; beneath it was a stack of DVDs.

Anna placed her toiletries in his white-tiled bathroom, where there was a pile of white bath towels and matching hand towels, a laundry basket, and a pair of rope sandals with a big white terry-cloth dressing gown. She liked putting her toothbrush in the holder beside his. Out of curiosity, she opened the small glass-fronted bathroom cabinet. It contained some aftershave, an electric shaver, and two fresh tubes of toothpaste. Anna didn't know the name of the aftershave she liked on Ken; she picked up an orange glass bottle with a wide silver top and couldn't help smiling: it was Clinique Happy for men.

When she came out of the bathroom, Ken was lying on top of the duvet, waiting for her.

"I'm on duty at two," he said, "off again at five. You can use the car I collected you in to come back here when you are through with Welsh, and I'll walk—it's not that far."

Anna flopped down beside him, and he immediately hooked his arm around her, drawing her close. "I don't know if I can get the next weekend off, so this is a bonus," he said.

They kissed, and she didn't want to move out of his arms. "I missed you," she said softly.

He rolled away from her and then leaned up on his elbow, looking down into her face. "I don't know whether it is the right time to tell you this . . ."

She felt her heart thud. What was he going to tell her? That he was with someone else, engaged, had a girlfriend— that this was just a passing thing and not to get too serious?

"I've never felt like this about anyone," he said instead. "It's probably too soon, and I'm no good at this kind of stuff, but you are suddenly the most important thing in my life."

She wanted to burst into tears; it was the most perfect thing anyone had ever said to her. She cupped his face in her hands, telling him, "I feel the same way. I can't stop smiling, and I chose not to drive so I'd have more time to spend with you."

They kissed passionately and then made love, and they would have gone on loving each other, but Anna knew she had to get to the secure unit in the time allocated. They showered together, and he would have taken her again, but she yelled that she had wet her hair and had to get it dried before she left.

She had never felt so unself-conscious and free. He plugged in his hair dryer for her and watched as she attempted to coax her hair into some semblance of a style, but she'd forgotten to bring her big roller brush. He sat on the edge of the bath as she reapplied her makeup.

"You look even more beautiful," he said as she dropped the bath towel, ready to get dressed. He couldn't resist taking her in his arms and smothering her with kisses.

By the time they had driven into the prison compound and Anna had passed over her ID, he had to hurry to the secure unit, while she went to pay a cordial visit to the prison governor. She was so happy that she didn't mind sitting in his office and even accepted coffee and biscuits.

Hardwick was as long-winded as ever, and she was surprised only when he brought up Langton's name, saying that he felt Langton would make an excellent commander, as his interest in prison reform was on a par with his own. She nodded her agreement, suddenly understanding why Langton had spent so much time with the governor. As with everything in his life, there was a hidden agenda. Then she recalled Barolli's comment that Langton was in the running for deputy commissioner.

Anna had requested that Welsh remain in his cell with the door closed as she felt safer that way.

Entering the unit, Anna glanced over at Ken, who gave her a small formal nod and a secret wink as the other officers went down the aisle to tell Cameron that his visitor was ready to see him. Anna waited, aware of Ken and aware of the other inmates walking around the unit. Two went out into the exercise yard, but they kept their eyes on Anna. She was relieved when she was told that she could proceed down the aisle to Cameron's cell. A chair had been placed outside. Cameron was sitting, as usual, facing out. He was wearing his hair drawn back in a ponytail, a white collarless shirt, and jeans.

"Good afternoon, Detective Travis," he said with a smile that didn't reach his brooding eyes.

"Good afternoon, Mr. Welsh. Thank you for agreeing to see me again."

"I've been looking forward to it. I think about you all the time. You occupy my dreams, my every waking hour."

"I thought I might give you an update on our case and see if you have any insights that may assist our inquiry."

"How very kind of you. What have you done to your hair?"

Anna touched her hair, a little unnerved. "I just washed it."

"How could you have done that if you drove here?"

"I came on the train."

"So when did you wash your hair?"

She pursed her lips. "Can we discuss the reason I am here rather than anything personal, please?"

"Are you staying at a hotel?"

"No. I am returning to London."

"You seem different."

"Mr. Welsh, I will walk away in one minute."

"Very well, Detective Travis, you may begin."

Anna took a deep breath and outlined the Polish connection; she informed him that they now knew all their victim's identities, which included the new case of the girl found wrapped in a blue blanket. He listened intently and without interruption, as she said that although they had paid close attention to his suggestions, they still had no connection between the three Polish victims and Margaret Potts, and that they had interviewed everyone who knew her again, but without any result. She also explained that the Polish girls were working for a domestic cleaning agency but at different times. It was possible that they might have known each other, but the main problem for the police was that they could not discover where the girls had moved on to, so they couldn't question anyone who would have information.

Welsh nodded and then turned to his computer table and picked up a notebook. "This woman who hired them brought them into England. Did she also use them as whores?"

"No. They might have gone on to earn money that way, but we have no details. The only prostitute was Margaret Potts."

"Did this woman have contacts anywhere else in England—you know, to pass the girls on to work for them?"

"No, she did not."

"So you have three girls who were here, all about the same age, not sexually permissive, but were murdered by the same man? It doesn't make sense. Your killer had to have access to them; if he didn't know them, then it is too much of a coincidence that all three went with him of their own free will. He had to know them or know about their situation. So take me through what you know about each girl."

Anna did so, finding this interview far easier to deal with, as Welsh appeared to be paying close attention to every word she said without any snide references or sexual undercurrent.

"The gaps in between the dead girls—have you reviewed any further cases that might be connected?"

"To be honest, we haven't. The four cases we have are taking up a great deal of time, not to mention financial resources. If we continue to look for other unsolved cases, it would make it difficult to continue holding on to the entire team allocated to the cases we already have, since we're under pressure to get a result."

"There will be more, but I understand that everything in this world today has a price. Justice doesn't have the finances—very sad, isn't it? Now, the girl in the blue blanket: tell me how you got to identify her."

Anna went into detail about the tattoo and what they knew about Dorota's life. She skirted giving any surnames or naming Olga at all, trying to keep her account as informative as possible without revealing too many undisclosed facts. Welsh jotted down notes and sometimes asked pertinent questions, but always, when he interrupted her, he did it politely.

"The girl who was joining her uncle in Manchester to work in his bakery: did she know either of the other victims?"

"We don't know. Why do you ask?"

"If these girls were trying to find work apart from turning into whores, maybe that was the reason they were heading for Manchester. But no! I would rule out the possibility that they were all going to Manchester or up north for any reason. They were picked up in London. Whoever picked them up was, as I have said numerous times, someone they trusted. Now, what if they didn't know him personally? What if he was a police officer or someone wearing a uniform? He would be seen as trustworthy. What if you go back to what I have suggested—that Margaret Potts knew him?"

"We have considered that, but we cannot find the connection to the girls."

"She didn't know them, she knew *him*. Your victim in the blue blanket, her body was found closer to the M6 than the M1. Go back over the press releases at the time of her murder and find out how many photographs were in the papers. I know you said the tattoo was described as a dark blue lizard, but there was one beneath it, correct?"

"I think we are going around in circles. We have considered the possibility of the killer wearing a police uniform that would not make his victims wary of getting into the van or truck he drives. So if they were thumbing a lift or—"

"He kills them in his vehicle, he has his fun with them, and then he dumps the bodies—but only your blue-blanket girl was naked. Why? Was she his first? What did he do with her clothes?"

By the way he was moving his body, shifting his weight, Anna suspected he was becoming aroused as soon as he started talking about the killer, and she was tempted to call the interview off. "She was his first."

"You have Margaret Potts as his second two years later. I think she picked him up at the service station, she recognized him, and so he had to kill her. The blue blanket was number one, and he got away with it. Next he's threatened by this disgusting piece of humanity, and he has to kill her. This would have started the excitement building because he's gotten away with it again."

He leaned back, and she could see that he had an erection beneath his jeans.

"You have no idea what it does to your sex drive," he told Anna. "You can't think straight, you can't eat, you are permanently in a semi-orgasmic state. Just recalling what you have done, thinking about your victims mewing and pleading with you not to hurt them as you squeeze the living breath out of them, and you come into them with the greatest orgasm imaginable; your own howls as the rush spreads over your body and screams inside your head." He swallowed. "No, this killer didn't pick them up and screw them in a field; he spent hours with them, wrapping the cord tighter and tighter—"

"I think that's enough now, Mr. Welsh."

"What?"

"My time is up, and I don't want to miss my train back. You have been very informative, thank you."

"You can't leave now—I haven't finished."

"Well, *I* have. Thank you, Mr. Welsh."

Anna almost knocked the chair to the ground in her haste as she stood up and walked past the cell gate.

"You will have to come back. Do you hear me? You will have to come back!"

She didn't reply. Hearing Welsh shouting, Ken appeared at the end of the aisle. "You all right?"

"Yes, but I'd like to leave now, Officer Hudson."

Welsh used his mirror to try and catch a glimpse of Anna as she walked away. He saw Hudson saying something to her; he also caught his hand touching Anna's back in an overfamiliar way; and he caught the look she gave him. It was so obvious that Hudson was fucking her—he knew it, he could smell it. That was why she'd come to Leeds alone. It wasn't to see him, it was to see that blond beefcake of a thickheaded officer, and he fought to keep his rage under control.

• • •

Anna was desperate for some fresh air, so she walked back to Ken's flat. She debated calling the incident room but decided against it. Opening the fridge, she took out the steaks and prepared a salad, making up some dressing, and then opened the bottle of pinot grigio and poured herself a glass. Welsh still made her feel violated: she loathed him, and knowing that he was sexually aroused while he was talking to her, sickened her.

She lay down on the bed and closed her eyes. The team had obviously discussed the possibility that the killer could pick up the girls wearing a police uniform, but they had no witness; nor did they have any idea where he had picked them up. Going over everything that had been said today, she knew there had been nothing new. Welsh had thought she would never come back.

She lay there thinking about Margaret Potts and whether she had recognized the killer, but as they knew so little about her daily routines, apart from at the service station, they had no idea how she could have known or recognized him—unless she had, as Welsh had implied, deduced something from the newspaper reports.

Anna sat up and sipped some more wine. It was not five yet, so she drained the glass and snuggled under the duvet to have a nap. She woke with a start an hour later when Ken closed the front door. She was sitting on the edge of the bed when he walked in.

"I've been fast asleep," she said guiltily. "I meant to get the steaks marinated and . . ."

He came over and kissed her, drawing her to her feet. "I need a shower, then we'll cook dinner together. How did it go with Welsh?"

She told him it had not been of much use, and while

Ken showered, she went into the kitchen to finish tossing the salad and start work on the steaks. She used a wooden spatula to whack and soften the meat. She found some microwave french fries and then set the table.

"How do you like your steak?" she shouted to the bathroom.

"Medium, and there are some chips in the freezer."

"Already got them. How long will you be?"

"Five minutes."

Anna set the horrible Formica table in the kitchen and then found plates and napkins. By the time Ken came into the kitchen wearing the dressing gown, the steaks were frying.

He leaned forward to kiss her neck, and she sniffed and murmured, "Mmmm—you smell nice. Let me guess, is it Clinique Happy for men?"

He stepped back and flushed.

"I saw it in your bathroom," Anna explained. "What—did you think I'm an expert on men's aftershave because I have sex with so many?"

"It was given to me by my sister," Ken said. "She'd probably bought it for her old man but gave it to me."

"I like it."

"Well, that's okay, then. I'll splash it all over my body."

They didn't waste time clearing away the debris of dinner but went straight to bed. Around midnight, Anna woke up and spent a long time looking at Ken's sleeping face, leaning up on her elbow. It had all happened so fast, and it was hard to believe that she was so besotted. He slowly opened his eyes as if he had felt her looking at him. She hadn't touched him because she didn't want to wake him.

"What?" he murmured.

"I love you," she said shyly.

He reached out and drew her close to him. "What are we going to do about that?"

She laughed as he slowly moved to lie on top of her.

Anna was still sleeping when Ken's alarm went off. It was seven-thirty, but he was not beside her. She got up and wrapped his dressing gown around her. There was coffee in the kitchen, but he wasn't in the shower, so she went into the lounge. He was doing push-ups on a blanket, wearing only a pair of boxer shorts.

"I didn't want to wake you," he panted. "Coffee is nearly ready, and there are bagels and smoked salmon, as I know you like them. I've got twenty minutes before I have to leave. I'm on early duty."

By the time she had drunk her coffee, he was dressed and ready to go to work.

"I've left a number by the phone of a local taxi firm. Sorry I can't take you to the station myself, but I have to be on duty due to having strong-armed the other lads to get off early last night. I don't know if I can swing it for the weekend, but if I can't, would you be prepared to come here again?"

"Yes, but not to see Welsh!"

Grabbing a quick swig of coffee, he kissed her neck and started to leave. Then he paused and turned toward her, saying, "Last night, did you mean what you said?"

She blushed and pretended not to understand. He came to her and cupped her face in his hands. "I love you, too, Anna Travis."

Then he was gone and she wanted to cry. She wanted to run after him and wrap her arms around him. Instead, she finished her coffee and ate too much, but because he'd bought the bagels and salmon especially for her, she felt that she should.

She did all the washing up and cleaned the kitchen, took a shower and washed her hair again, then packed. Taxi arranged, she went into the lounge, finding it strange being in his flat alone. He had left a set of dumbbells and the blanket he'd been using on the bricked wood floor. She bent down as if to pick it up, fold it, and put it away when she froze. It was a blue blanket—newer, cleaner, and with a prison laundry mark in the right-hand corner, but she was certain it was identical to the blue blanket found wrapped around the victim Dorota Pelagia.

Chapter Eleven

Anna had a terrible few moments of panic. Her mind went completely blank in a hideous mental block. She took deep breaths, refusing to allow herself to even contemplate the connection between Ken, the blanket, and the killer. She knew she would have to discuss it with him, and immediately, but the fear that he could be involved made her throw up in the toilet.

Afterward, she splashed cold water over her face and then called the prison to ask to be put through to the secure unit, as it was of the utmost importance. She was told that it was against regulations for the officers in the unit to take personal calls. Fighting to keep control of her voice, she explained who she was and said it was imperative she speak to Officer Hudson.

It was a while before Ken came to the phone; the first thing he asked was if she was all right. He was afraid there had been some kind of accident.

"I'm fine, Ken, but just before I left your flat, I noticed that you'd been exercising on a blanket. It's prison issue—a blue one—and I need to know why you have it."

"You're joking?"

"No, I'm not. It's very important. Ken, can you tell me about the blanket?"

"It was in the flat when I moved in. They give them out,

or they did, to the officers in the flats. Most of them bring in their own bedding, obviously. I don't think they are part of the prison issue anymore, but there must be hundreds still used in cells . . . What's so important?"

"Can I take it with me back to the station?"

"Whatever for? Are you having me on?"

"No. I wish I were, because I can't really discuss it with you, but can you call me later when you are off duty and I'll explain?"

"Explain it now, Anna. I was almost having a heart attack in case you'd been hurt."

Anna felt her body breaking out in a cold sweat. "All right," she said, and swallowed. "One of our victims was found wrapped in an identical blanket—the same color, but with no laundry mark. We'll need to find out if they were also issued to other prisons."

There was a pause, and then Ken asked if she wanted him to check it out for her.

"No, station will get on to it."

"Okay, but you be honest now, did you think I had something to do with it? You didn't, did you, Anna?"

"Of course I didn't," she lied, "but I just needed to check it all out with you. Look, I've got to go, the taxi is here to take me to the station."

She felt terrible that she had, for a moment, had a hideous suspicion that he could in some way be involved. During the taxi ride, she rang the incident room and gave them the blanket discovery, making no mention that she had found it in Ken Hudson's flat, but insisting that the team needed to find out how many prisons used the blue blankets for their inmates. She also spoke to Mike Lewis about the Cameron Welsh interview, repeating that he was adamant regarding the Margaret Potts connection and that he had even suggested the killer could use a police officer's uniform to entice the victims to trust him.

"Or it could even be a prison officer's uniform," she added, and felt her body break into a sweat again.

The journey to King's Cross seemed to take forever, as there were faults on the line and delays, so she didn't get back to the incident room until late afternoon. She immediately passed the blanket over to be sent to the forensic lab.

The team had discovered that the blankets were imported by a company in Wembley and made for them in China. The company had ordered a massive consignment, delivered over four years to five prisons, but had recently lost contracts, as the inmates didn't like them and preferred duvets. These blankets were also used at police stations in Manchester for prisoners held overnight in the cells. The remainder, since the prisons had stopped ordering, had been delivered to hostels around London. They were looking at hundreds of thousands of these blue blankets, and it promised another lengthy, tedious line of inquiry.

That night Anna had a call from Ken. He suggested that it was possible their killer had worked as a prison officer. Anna agreed but said it was a long shot.

"Do you know if officers keep their uniforms when they leave?"

"Yeah, some do. We get our uniforms, but many officers buy more comfortable black trousers. I doubt if they'd bother retaining the shirts with the epaulettes, although it's possible."

Anna didn't want it to happen, but the discovery had somehow damaged the innocent warm glow she felt toward him, and he picked it up fast.

"Listen, I think you and I had better spend some more time together and soon, because even though you are telling me you didn't feel any suspicions, I can tell by the way you are talking to me that it upset you. I'll pull what strings I can to get off this weekend, okay?"

"Yes, I'd like that."

"Good night. Love you."

She didn't say she loved him and felt guilty, so she rang him back straightaway, but his phone went to voice mail. She didn't leave a message but hung up.

The possibility that their suspect might have worked as a prison officer was a step forward, and yet it meant they were in an even worse position, because not only did it entail another round of inquiries, it also meant that John Smiley was less likely to be their prime suspect. And they had no one else.

The following morning, Pete Jenkins confirmed that the blanket did match the one they held at the lab. It was made from the same fabric, with the same stitching, but the old one had been worn, probably washed numerous times.

Anna had spoken again to Pete when she went home the previous evening and explained in more detail the importance of the blanket being prison issue, though it was virtually impossible to trace the actual batch and discover where it might have been sent. However, what it could mean was that whoever killed Dorota Pelagia four years ago might have had access to one and had perhaps even worked for the prison service.

Ken had ridden down to London on his Harley late Friday, and all the anxiety Anna had felt had disappeared. They talked about the case, about Dorota Pelagia, and the fact that Langton had threatened to pull half the team. Langton had admitted that they did have new developments, but ones that he felt had scant hope of a conclusion. It had been a depressed group when Anna had left, even more so as they all had weekend leave, bar the skeleton night-duty officers. It appeared they were heading toward a scaling-down of the entire investigation.

"Our prime suspect no longer fits the new stuff that came in. We have his CV from when he left the army and joined this company called Swell Blinds." Anna was lying in bed beside Ken, and when there was no reply, she realized he had fallen asleep. Easing herself out of the bed, she crept into the kitchen to make a cup of tea. Sitting on a breakfast bar stool cupping the mug between her hands, she didn't feel at all sleepy. More than ever, she was aware what it felt like to have someone to be with, despite the fact that Ken had fallen asleep when she was talking about the case. Never, in her entire career to date, had she worked on a case that looked as if it could go so totally cold. At worst, there would always be an ongoing investigation and even a couple of officers assigned to monitoring any new evidence. On all her other cases, she had learned something about the victims, but with this one, they still knew little about the Polish women. Only Margaret Potts's past life had they been able to piece together.

Anna sipped her tea, questioning herself. Had she over-looked something? Even though she had uncovered key facts, such as the lizard tattoo and the date of Dorota's marriage, it had not brought in a hoped-for result. They were still no closer to finding the killer.

Anna finished her tea and thought about returning to bed. As she passed her bedroom, she looked in at the sleeping figure of Ken. It was a good feeling to have him part of her life, and instead of going to look over her notes and case files, as she would have done alone, she slipped in beside him. Loving the feel of his back as she pressed herself against him, she fell asleep.

Their entire weekend was taken up with preparing a picnic, and as Ken had brought another helmet, Anna had the first-time experience of riding behind him. They rode out to Greenwich Park and had a long walk, getting to know more and more about each other. She never brought up the case; it was out of her thoughts, even more so when they came back and changed to go to the theater. They had dim sum for dinner in a place on Tooley Street and didn't return to her flat until late. The following morning they stayed in bed reading the Sunday papers before riding over to have lunch with Lizzie and her family. Anna helped cook and wash up, and Ken played out in the garden with the two boys. Lizzie looked out at them having fun and then turned to her guest. "Are you keen to have children, Anna?" she asked.

Anna was taken aback. It was something she had never really thought about, but the scene outside brought the truth home to her. Finally, she said that she was.

"That's good, because I sort of thought you were a career girl. Ken loves kids, and he's really a very special person, the way he looks out for Mum and Dad."

"They're lovely people."

"Yes. I always think they have more heart than anyone I've ever known, especially my mum. Strange, you know she had a big scare, open-heart surgery, and we thought we might lose her."

"Yes. Ken mentioned it to me, but she seems well now." Anna glanced out the window, watching as Ken held Oscar upside down, while Ollie screamed that it was his turn.

"He'll make a terrific dad," Lizzie said fondly.

Anna was so startled by the remark that she flushed. Before she could say anything, Ken burst in and suggested that they all go for a walk in Richmond Park.

In the end, Anna and Ken took the boys to the park, leaving their parents to enjoy a quiet couple of hours with the Sunday papers. By five o'clock, when they had returned to Lizzie's house and had tea and sandwiches, it was time for Ken to take Anna home and get back to Leeds. She tried to persuade him to stay another night and leave the next morning, but he refused, saying that he had to be at work early because he'd had the weekend off.

"When will I see you again?" she asked.

"I'm working next weekend, so it'll be up to you whether you want to drive up. It's also my parents' wedding anniversary."

Anna hugged him, saying that she'd be there if she got the weekend off. Then he was gone and the flat felt empty. She couldn't believe how much she already missed him. He had drawn her into his world, his family, and the warmth of their affection for one another spilled over to her. Having no parents and no relatives, Anna had been solitary and until now had not questioned how much of her time was spent alone or at work.

She kept on thinking about what Lizzie had asked—whether she wanted children—and the thought of carrying Ken's child made her well up inside. She had to admonish herself. He had not implied that their relationship would go that far, and she didn't know if he would want a long-term commitment, but it didn't stop her from daydreaming about getting married. This again was something she had never contemplated or even allowed herself to think about, especially during her long affair with Langton. Even though they had lived together, she had intuitively known it would never go further than that. She didn't even know if she had wanted it to, but one thing she did know: she had never contemplated having a child with him, and she was certain that it had never been something he had thought about or desired.

Anna tossed and turned, one moment thinking about what kind of bridal gown she would choose, whom she would invite to the reception, and the next warning herself to stop thinking about it. She decided that she would go to see Ken in Leeds the next weekend and, having made the decision, fell fast asleep.

Monday morning, Anna arrived at the station and could feel the lack of energy in the incident room. Barbara and Joan were gossiping over their mugs of tea, and Barolli was standing in front of the incident board with his hands stuffed in his pockets. Anna joined him.

"Nothing came in over the weekend?"

"Nope. I had bloody sleepless nights. I've never been on a case that had so much work done and so little to show for it—bar the amount of stuff written up here. I tried thinking if there was anything we've overlooked, but Christ Almighty, Anna, look at how many interviews we've done, how much work the clerical staff has had to wade through, and having that John Smiley as our only suspect looks like a complete waste of time. So all that crap we've had to delve into about Swell Blinds has also been pointless."

Anna looked at the photographs of the victims, the red arrows linking the girls, the Polish connection, the tattoo.

"I was thinking over the weekend, too," she said. "In every case I've worked on, I've uncovered details about the victims' lives, but with these girls, we've got blanks; we don't know where they went after stopping work for the domestic agency—all we know is that Anika worked in a restaurant, but we don't know where she lived. With Estelle, we have her working as an au pair, staying with a friend, and buying clothes from a charity shop, but we still don't have a clue where she went for the three days before her murder. As for Dorota Pelagia, we have no information about where she worked or lived, nor do we know of anyone who knew her apart from the hideous Olga—so where was *she* four years ago?"

"Tell me something I haven't thought about," Barolli muttered.

"I think we should do one big press conference with all the victims' profiles."

"Listen, they've had them on the crime shows, they've done the news coverage over and over again, and what has it brought? Fuck-all," Barolli grumbled.

Anna shrugged and went over to her desk.

"What did Cameron Welsh have to say for himself?" Barolli asked, curious despite his bad mood.

Anna gestured at the board but gave Barolli the gist of it, adding, "He also had a hard-on when he was telling me all this, so I suspect he was just wanking around."

"Did he keep on about Margaret Potts?"

"Yes. He has a hatred of prostitutes and always refers back to her as holding the clue. He says she must have known her killer."

"So what do we do? Go back yet again over all the information we have on her?"

"Well, we've been pretty thorough, and we've not found any connection."

Barbara joined them, asking if they should return the

boxes of receipts and contracts to Swell Blinds. Her desk was stacked high with them, as was Joan's.

"The only stuff we didn't check out were the orders for vertical blinds, as John Smiley didn't fit that sort, and the company's no longer got the contracts. Ones like that, not the wooden slatted ones." Barbara turned and gestured to the incident room's windows. "According to all these hundreds of calls, and there have been God knows how many interviews, every one of these orders that had John Smiley down as delivering or measuring have been checked out. We were told not to focus on the factory orders for hotels and other businesses that use vertical blinds. That includes the contracts they had for housing associations, schools, gymnasiums—"

"Go through them, Barbara," Anna said suddenly.

"All of them?"

"Yes. Sorry. If John Smiley fitted them . . ."

"But he was only on the wooden slatted ones, wasn't he?"

"I don't know, Barbara, but just cover yourselves to make sure we've not missed anything."

Mike Lewis then called Anna into his office, eating a sandwich as he gestured for her to sit. "Langton's gonna pull out half my team, leaving me with just a handful, as he can't get the finances to continue. We've had twenty-eight officers doing a lot of the legwork, and he needs them for other cases. Clerical staff have already been pulled, and he was going nuts about how much that bloody Polish interpreter cost."

Anna said nothing, as she had expected it would happen.

"Do you know how many blue blankets were issued over the past eight years?" Mike demanded.

"No, I don't."

"Five hundred and fifty thousand!"

"So where does that leave us?"

"With as much chance of tracking down where the blanket came from as winning the sodding lottery. They're in prisons, hostels, charity shops . . . it's fucking impossible, and for her, that's all we've got."

"Any chance of her relatives coming over?"

"No. Besides, she's been cremated."

"Wouldn't they want to take her ashes back to Poland?"

"We've not traced any family members apart from her sister. Besides, we'd have to pay, and with the budget out of control, I don't have the finances."

"But we might get something about Dorota's background if we keep trying. We know so little about the victims, apart from Margaret Potts."

"You talk to Langton. He's bitten my head off once too often. Have you any idea how much this case has cost to date?"

"If they weren't Polish, would—"

"Don't even go there," he snapped.

Anna decided to go up to the canteen for a coffee and bacon roll. Facing her was a window with vertical blinds. She stared at them as she finished her late breakfast.

Barbara was removing her cardigan as Anna got back to her desk. "I'm going to need my eyes tested again." The DC sighed. "If I'm not glued to the computer all day, it's sifting through this lot."

"Did Swell Blinds have any contracts for vertical blinds with police stations?"

"I've not come across one yet, but there's got to be hundreds of firms that make them. They're very popular because they're cheap."

Anna frowned. Something was niggling at the back of

her brain; she just couldn't bring it out. Opening her brief-case, she took out the three notebooks she'd filled during the investigation and began to skim through each one. She wasn't sure what she was looking for but hoped that some-thing would jog her memory.

"You look different," Joan said.

"Pardon?"

"I just said you look different. Dunno what it is, but you look . . ."

"Different. Yes, so you said."

"I'm going to the canteen—you want anything?"

"No, thank you, Joan." When DC Falkland had gone, Anna opened her handbag to take out a mirror and looked at herself. Yes, she *was* different; she felt different because she was in love.

"Nothing better to do?" Barolli said as he passed her desk, also on his way to the canteen.

Anna put her mirror away, then hurried across to Bar-bara. "The contract for the Swell Blinds company . . ."

"Which one? Take your pick."

"No, you said something about a housing associa-tion . . ."

"Yeah, they had a whopper of a contract but lost it, part of the reason Swell Blinds uprooted to Manchester." The DC began to search through a stack covered in yellow stickers. "Arnold Rodgers said something about losing the contract because there were so many companies after it who had contacts within the housing association. In other words, it was possible that money changed hands." Barbara continued sifting, asking, "You thinking of ordering some for your flat?"

Anna made no reply, waiting impatiently until Barbara handed over a thick set of documents stapled together.

Anna took them back to her desk, her heart jumping as she thumbed through the orders. Next she flicked through her notebook to her first interview with Emerald Turk. To trace her, she had gone through Social Services, and they had put her in touch with the Strathmore Housing Association, which had rehoused Emerald in a newly refurbished apartment in a high-rise block. Anna picked up the phone, trying to keep herself calm, but felt certain she was on the right track. She recalled looking toward the window in Emerald's kitchen and was positive that the woman had vertical blinds.

Anna tapped on Mike Lewis's office door and went straight in before he could answer. "I think I've got something," she said.

"Dear God, not another tattoo or blue blanket?" he joked tiredly.

"No, it's a connection between Swell Blinds and the possibility that Margaret Potts might have met John Smiley."

Mike leaned back in his chair, waiting.

"Emerald Turk was rehoused in Hackney by the Strathmore Housing Association. They had Swell Blinds under contract—this would have been shortly before they lost that contract and moved to Manchester. On their receipts, they don't have John Smiley as the man fitting the blinds, but I want to go and talk to them anyway."

Mike leaned forward, saying, "I don't quite see the connection."

"Margaret Potts stayed on occasion with Emerald Turk, even left her suitcase. She could have been in the flat when John Smiley fitted the blinds."

"Christ, it's a bloody long shot, Anna."

"But it is one, and I would also like to get another search warrant for Emerald Turk's flat."

"Leave it with me, but please get some kind of verification first that it was Swell Blinds."

Anna drove over to the Strathmore Housing Association in Hackney. As she was asking about a contract from at least five years ago, they were doubtful they would still have the information. Anna mentioned Emerald Turk's name, and that got a reaction. Half an hour later, Anna had learned that when Emerald Turk was given the flat, the housing association was still using Swell Blinds. Anna could sense there was some kind of a problem because the woman being interviewed explained how they had, from what she recalled, some trouble with the blinds; in some cases, there were complaints about them falling apart almost immediately.

"So we used another company, and we have been very satisfied."

"Did the housing association fit the vertical blinds in these properties, or did the company put them up?"

"Oh, we would have used their fitters. You have to understand that we are preparing properties for tenants all year round and can have anything up to a hundred or more that would require redecoration, furnishing, renewing the electrical appliances, replacing bathrooms. Some of our tenants are not only short of money but have lived in squalor or on the streets, and damage to our properties is not unknown."

"Would you have the name of the person who fitted the vertical blinds in Emerald Turk's flat?"

"No, we wouldn't retain that, as it was totally up to the

company doing the work. All the flats in Miss Turk's building would have had the same refurbishing, same kitchen
and bathroom fittings. We have major contracts out to ten-
ure every year."

"But you didn't renew the Swell Blinds contract five
years ago, is that correct?"

"I don't have the exact details in front of me, but we
have been satisfied with our present contractors. It's always
down to costs. We have to keep them at a bare minimum."

"Would you have any kind of record if Miss Turk had
had any problem with these vertical blinds?"

"I don't understand."

"If they were not satisfactory, who would handle the
complaint?"

"If she did have any problems, we would, of course—but
you are asking about a situation from five years ago, so I
doubt we would retain any record of it."

"Could you please check for me?"

It turned out that Emerald *had* made various complaints—about her hot-water system and central heating—
but they had no note of any problem with the blinds. Anna
then asked if the blinds would be in place and all refurbish-
ments completed before the tenant took residence, and she
was informed frostily that every attempt was made by the
association to ensure that the tenants moved into a totally
refurbished flat, but on occasion, due to the workload,
there might be minor faults that required attention.

Anna could see the look of expectation on the team's faces
when she returned. She put her hands up.

"It's possible. Right time frame. Swell Blinds *did* fit vertical blinds in Emerald Turk's flat, so this means there is a

possibility they were fitted by John Smiley. It is also a possibility that Margaret Potts was there, as she often stayed with Emerald."

Barbara said that of all the vertical blinds they had been able to check that morning, none had been fitted by anyone employed by Swell Blinds. So far they had no record of John Smiley doing work at schools or factories or on large orders.

"But he might have been sent to measure?" Anna asked.

Barbara shook her head. "Not according to Arnold Rodgers. He used the two men we interviewed via Wendy Dunn. These blinds are apparently easy to erect, not like the wooden ones, so he didn't use John Smiley because he's too experienced."

When Anna nodded, Barbara continued, "You see, with the wooden slatted blinds, you've got to also fit a top frame—you know, like a pelmet. You need to have precise measurements."

"Thank you, Barbara."

"I'm only just repeating what Mr. Rodgers said."

Anna glanced at Barolli. "Search warrant set up, is it?"

He nodded, and Anna checked the time; it was now after six. She said to Barolli, "We go first thing in the morning. She has to get her kids off to school, so we call at nine. Pick you up outside Tower Hill tube station at eight, all right?"

"Why not go there now?"

"She works nights, Paul. We go tomorrow morning." And with that, Anna picked up her briefcase and walked out.

Barbara whispered to Joan, "I think she's met someone. She's Miss Confident all of a sudden. Anybody know who it is?"

Overhearing, Barolli laughed. "We know Cameron Welsh

can't get out of his cell, but she did go up to see him on her own after swearing that wild dogs wouldn't get her to visit him again."

"You are kidding me?" Barbara said, and Barolli rolled his eyes.

"Yes, Barbara, I'm joking."

He turned to the incident board and moved closer to read the reports of the interviews with Cameron Welsh. "You know something? That bastard might have been right all along. He's said from day one that Margaret Potts holds the key, and here we are, how many bloody weeks later, finding out that maybe she does."

Chapter Twelve

As soon as Emerald opened her front door on Tuesday morning and saw Anna and Barolli, she shrieked, "I don't fucking believe this! You have got to be joking."

Anna showed the search warrant, but Emerald had already swung the door open wide.

"Bloody harassment, this is. Come in, make yourselves at home, why don't you? Do what the hell you fucking like!"

"Can we go into the kitchen, please, and with you present."

Emerald threw her arms up in exasperation, leading them into the kitchen.

Anna gestured at the vertical blinds. "I need to ask you a few questions about your blinds."

Emerald's jaw dropped. She looked at Anna and back at the blinds. "Eh? What you on about?"

"Can we sit down?"

"You can do tango dancin' for all I care. What do you want to know about the blinds for? They don't work. The kids pulled the cord and they've fallen down a few times, and the rod's come away from the wall. Is this about damage or somethin?"

Anna perched on a stool while Barolli remained standing

in the doorway. "I need to know exactly how long you have been living here."

"Five-odd years."

"When you moved in, were the blinds already in place?"

"They was, everythin' was here, but the ones in the kitchen soon got broken, and then the ones in the box room fell down. I never even bloody touched them. I had a lot of aggravations with me central heatin' and me gas cooker. I was gonna complain about the blinds as well, 'cause if they'd fallen on my kids, they could have cracked their heads open. Look, I'm not being made to pay nuffink, as it's been bloody five years."

"When you complained, did someone come round to fix them?"

Emerald shrugged, saying sullenly, "I never told them nuffink. It was me central heatin' I was worried about, but I might have told the bloke they sent to look at the boiler . . . and he might have passed it on to the people at Strathmore. Yeah, they did send someone. Yeah, that's right. I remember now."

Anna stared at Emerald, willing her to help them. "It's very important," she said. "Can you recall who came to repair them?"

"Why?"

"It's possible we are interested in talking to this person."

"Well, I dunno, it's a long time ago. He came twice or maybe three times, but you see, the kids were just small then."

"Emerald, I'm not here for any other reason than wanting to know about the person who came to fix these blinds."

The young woman took out a packet of Silk Cut and lit one, then she sat on one of the stools. "Jesus, let me think . . . I remember a bloke did come, but he said I'd need a new cord or something, or maybe the little chains had busted. They're all linked with these chains, and he was here for ages." She gestured at the kitchen window blinds.

"Can you describe him?"

She puffed out the cigarette smoke, thinking. "He wasn't English, good-lookin', I think . . . no, wait a minute. He took the ones from in 'ere away, and they was brought back by another geezer."

"Did you talk to this second man?"

"Yeah. He done them up in here, and . . ." She frowned, inhaled, and blew out a cloud of smoke. "He also got us some new ones for the spare bedroom—not like these ones, different wooden ones. Said he had some the right size in the van."

"Wooden slatted blinds?"

"Yeah, that's right, but they fell down a couple of years ago, and I haven't bothered to replace them. It's just used as the box room now—the kids have it as a playroom."

"Can you describe this man?"

"Not really. He was sort of tallish, dark-haired, and I had to go out, so I left him with . . ." She hesitated.

"Was someone else staying with you?"

"Oh, I'm with you," Emerald sneered. "Those bloody Social Services—it was fucking years ago! They trying to prove I rent out a room, are they? Well, it's not fucking true! I don't, and I never have done."

"Who was in the box room, Emerald?"

"Maggie, she was here—one of her drop-in and passing-out nights. She was here, so I left her to sort him out."

"Margaret Potts was here in the flat when this man fixed the blinds?"

"I just said so, didn't I? She was gone when I come

home, and the blind was up. I paid him some cash before I left."

Anna stood up and asked if she could see the box room. Emerald stubbed out her half-smoked cigarette and put the butt in the pocket of a bathrobe she was wearing. She hugged the gown closer, saying she was going to get dressed. "I took the kids to school and then come back for a shower, that's why I'm in me dressing gown."

"Just show us the box room, please."

The room was packed mostly with what looked like broken toys. A small single bed had a box of LEGOs sitting on top of a stained child's duvet. The only remaining part of the blind was a brown wooden pelmet; the rest lay in pieces on the floor.

"When did you see Margaret again?"

Emerald sighed and said she'd been over this time and time again, but she didn't see her for ages after that. Folding her arms, she said that she had also told Margaret that she couldn't stay. "I just didn't like her turning up, usually stoned out of her head or drunk, and so I never saw her for ages. Next thing, she gets murdered. I told all this to you."

"Do you remember the name of the company that fixed up your blinds?"

"No. Social Services and the housing association arranged it. They done the place up, all I did was pay this bloke a bit extra 'cause he said he could get a blind for this room on the cheap, and I didn't want to involve the housing association again. I dunno who he worked for. I only met him the once, and that was for only a short while, 'cause I had to go out."

"Did you see what vehicle he used to bring the blinds into the house?"

"No. I'm on the third floor."

"Did Margaret ever mention talking to the man?"

"No. She'd gone when I got back—I just told you."

Barolli asked if he could look around the rest of the flat, and Emerald told him he could do what he liked, then led the way back to the kitchen. Anna asked if Emerald would be prepared to come in to the station, where they would get a number of men on video. If she would agree, perhaps she could identify the man who was at her flat.

"Christ, this just goes on and on, doesn't it? It was a long time ago, and like I said, I hardly spoke two words to him."

"It's possible that this man could have been involved in Margaret's murder."

Emerald relit the butt of her cigarette. "You know, I wouldn't put it past Maggie to wake up and give the bloke a blow job if he paid her a few quid. She was like that."

Anna next asked if Emerald could recall the exact date she last saw Margaret Potts—this would be after the time she had stayed in the box room—but Emerald was very vague. "Does it matter?" she asked.

"Yes, it does. Where did you see her?"

"Listen, I feel a bit bad about this, but I never actually saw her again. I remember she rang me up once, a long time after, and wanted to come over and collect her stuff, and I told her that I wouldn't be in. I honestly didn't like her coming here, and that was the last time I ever spoke to her. Poor cow was dead not long after that . . ."

"Did she say anything to you that concerned you, anything unusual?"

"I think she was drunk."

"What time of day did she call you?"

Emerald wrinkled her nose and said that it would have been around nine in the evening.

"So was she calling you from the service station?"

"Might have been, I dunno. It was a pay phone—I remember that. This was all such a long time ago, it's hard to remember. All I know is, I said she couldn't come over."

Anna nodded and made a few notes in her notebook. "I really need you to think about the date that Margaret stayed, when you left her here with this man fixing your blinds. It's very, very important."

Emerald leaned forward, tapping Anna's knee. "I've remembered what she said when she got in touch. She said, 'Have you got the *Evening Standard*?' She sounded right pissed. Oh yeah, I remember now—that was the first call. It was earlier than what I said because I had to go out to work, but she did ring me again when I wasn't at home. She left a message with the babysitter, saying again that she wanted to come over and pick up her suitcase. I never heard from her again."

Anna made a note and underlined the word *suitcase*.

"I remembered that, but I'll never work out what friggin' date we had the blinds done."

"Best to think back . . . how long had you been living here? Was it shortly after you moved in or a few months later?"

Emerald got up and opened a drawer in one of the kitchen cabinets. She rooted around in it, taking out a lot of leaflets from electrical appliances and insurance coverage of washing machines and TV sets. "Well, it wouldn't be that long after I moved in, 'cause everythin' was supposed to be finished, right?"

Barolli returned to hover in the kitchen doorway. Emerald sat down, placing all the leaflets on the table; many were still in their envelopes.

"I moved in here April 2005 . . . that's right, isn't it? Been here five years now and . . ."

Anna was growing impatient as Emerald sifted through the guarantee forms and then shoved them aside. She returned to another drawer and took out a TV license then sat down again.

"Right: we'd not got a TV in, so this was after. It's got to be that winter, but dunno which day. All I remember is, I didn't have a TV then."

"So when you moved in, the blinds were working. Think about how much time it had been after you said they were faulty and then got them taken away and brought back."

"Bloody hell, I'm trying. Lemme get another fag."

Back at the station, the team was buzzing when Anna, using a thick red marker, wrote down the date that Emerald's blinds were repaired, that Margaret Potts was staying in her flat at the time, close to Christmas 2005, and that after she had left and a good time later, the following summer, Maggie had called her again.

"The date is near enough, and it took a long time working it out, but first Emerald had the kitchen blinds removed in November 2005, and then a different man returned the repaired blinds in early December. She didn't recall much about him but said he was tall and dark-haired. She was yet again unclear how long it was until some months later, she received a phone call from Maggie Potts in which she mentioned something about the *Evening Standard*. Dorota's murder was discovered in June 2006, so maybe Maggie had read the story and wanted to talk to Emerald about it."

Anna gestured at the dead girl's photograph and then moved on to Maggie Potts's photographs. "Margaret Potts's body was discovered in March 2008. This leaves quite a time gap between the phone call and her body being discovered."

Anna looked over at Barbara, as she'd asked her to check the *Evening Standard* news coverage around the same time. Next she underlined the month when Swell Blinds moved to Manchester.

She turned to the team while replacing the cap on the marker, saying, "We need to get a video ID set up and bring in Emerald and John Smiley, because he is now back in the frame."

Barbara had brought up the *Evening Standard* newspaper coverage and was scrolling through the lead stories. They all turned their attention toward her as she read that on June 15, 2006, the paper had issued a request for information connected to the body of a young woman found wrapped in a blue blanket.

The buzz was on, and Anna had to settle everyone down as they discussed the latest development. Dorota Pelagia's body had been discovered four years ago. When Margaret referred to the newspaper article in her call to Emerald, did it mean she knew something about the killer? Did she meet John Smiley at Emerald's? Had she seen him again at the service station? Was she perhaps in contact with him?

Mike Lewis had sat listening, and he now took over from Anna. "We are presuming a hell of a lot. If this is going to pan out and we can prove that John Smiley did meet Margaret Potts, then why wait so long before she got herself murdered—or, more to the point, why did *he* wait?"

There was a murmur around the incident room, suggestions flying from one person to another. Joan suggested that it was perhaps due to the fact that he had moved from London to Manchester, but she was ignored. Anna eventually quieted everyone.

"If we can prove that John Smiley *did* meet Margaret

Potts, it shows he was lying about never seeing her—and why would he do that? Let's get him back in and see what he has to say."

Anna was just stepping out of the shower when her phone rang. It was Langton, and he was calling to congratulate her. She thanked him and said that she felt sure Emerald was still lying about the last time she had actually seen Margaret. She thought the lie might be connected to the contents of Maggie's suitcase, since she was certain there had been money hidden inside, as well as a few pieces of quite valuable jewelry.

"She lied to me when I first interviewed her, because I think Margaret was more of a regular visitor than she likes to admit, but at least we've got this new connection, and maybe to John Smiley. If she can identify him, he moves back into prime suspect position . . ."

"We've never really had anyone else," Langton said, yawning.

"But not until now do we have a possible connection to a victim."

"Right. And yet again Travis uncovers it." He sounded as if he had been drinking.

"I hope if we do move forward, we'll have the finances and can keep the full team," Anna said.

"Don't tell me how to run the inquiry," he snapped.

"I'm not, but you know we have a terrific team, and they have been working full-time for weeks."

"Thank you for that information. Apart from that, how are you?"

"I'm fine, thank you."

She just wanted to get off the phone, but he continued

asking about the new possibilities that might be opening up the case. Finally, he went quiet. Anna was at a loss as to what he expected from her.

"Okay, that's it," he said.

"Thank you for calling."

"You know, you sound different. Want to tell me something?"

"No."

"Okay. Good night." He hung up.

She went to bed wondering what all that had been about, but she wasn't prepared to divulge anything about Ken to him. She *was* different, she was more confident in herself because of her relationship, and she was determined to keep it private. She had always hated the gossipmongering that went on about her previous relationship with Langton, and the realization that she had at last moved on from his hold over her emotions felt good. She didn't feel in any way that Ken had the same stranglehold; their love was somehow cleaner and gentler by far. She was loved, and it was special because she felt as if she could have another life apart from the Met.

As she got into bed, Ken called, and they spent over an hour chatting, neither wanting to end the call, wishing they were wrapped in each other's arms.

"I'm looking forward to the weekend," he eventually said.

It wasn't until then that she told him about the new developments, hoping it wouldn't mean she had to work instead.

"Whatever, let's just try and see each other as soon as possible," he told her. "I never stop thinking about you, missing you."

"I miss you, too. I love you."

"Take good care of yourself, Anna. Kiss you good night."

"Good night."

He laughed and told her to hang up because he couldn't. She did and then curled up in bed thinking about him, wanting to be close to him, the call from Langton forgotten.

It took two days to organize and film enough John Smiley look-alikes in order to be able to hold the identity parade. Mike then rang Smiley, requesting him to come down to London to assist inquiries. If he'd refused, they would have been forced to arrest him and bring him to the station, but he agreed. Mike asked if he wished to have a lawyer present. Smiley hesitated, asking how long it would take, as he would have to get time off work. Barolli was listening in to the call on the speaker. Smiley didn't sound scared, more confused than anything.

"Is this still about my van and me being seen at the ser vice station?"

"Yes. We need to eliminate everyone seen in a vehicle there on that day."

When Mike Lewis replaced the receiver, Barolli sucked in his breath. "He could do a runner, you know."

Mike shook his head, reminding Barolli that with two kids and an apparently oversize wife, it was unlikely; also, he knew that Langton was still using favors with the guys in Manchester, so if anything suspicious happened, they would make contact.

"To be honest, he seemed more worried about taking time off work."

"Yeah, I heard, and I'd say it has to be uncomfortable there with his boss. We've certainly been busy around him."

"Well, if we can prove he lied . . . Travis seems to think Emerald can identify him, but she's such a hard-nosed slag, I wouldn't bet on it."

"It's all we've got."

"I hear you." Mike's desk phone lit up; it was Barbara tipping him off that Langton had arrived in the incident room.

Langton was standing in front of the incident board, lecturing the team. "Do you know that a quarter of London's population, over one and half million people, were born abroad? The biggest groups are Indians and Afro-Caribbeans, but the rest are Poles arriving in large numbers and seeking work, like our three girls."

"I didn't know we had that many," said Mike.

"Well, we do, and I'm getting a lot of stick from the assistant commissioner that we are slacking in our inquiry. The last thing the Met wants is to be accused of sweeping this case under the carpet, never mind the pressure about going over budget. So, on one hand, it's cut the costs, and on the other, get a friggin' result."

"Well, we might." Mike took the chance to update Langton on the day's latest news.

"Yeah, we'll see how it pans out with the ID and if Smiley is still in the frame, but we need more," Langton insisted. "Even if he did previously know Margaret Potts, we've got no fucking evidence he was our killer."

"It proves he lied."

"Not enough. Citizens Prosecution Service wouldn't give us the nod to charge him on that."

Mike sighed, unsure where all this was going, concerned Langton was hinting at replacing him.

"Get ready for a big press conference, Mike, and even if Smiley gets off the hook, we can say the inquiry is questioning a suspect. I don't like being pushed by the top brass, so set it up."

"Yes, Gov."

"When Smiley comes in, I'll handle the interview, along with Travis."

"Whatever you say."

Langton moved farther down the incident board. "Barolli interviewed Emerald Turk first, right?"

"Yes, Gov."

"So we should have reached this conclusion about Smiley's connection two years ago. Thank Christ for Travis. She came up with the tattoo to identify Dorota Pelagia, and if we'd had that woman Olga in earlier, we'd have had them all bloody identified."

"We couldn't put pressure on the television programmers. It works because the callers can remain anonymous, and it took a lot of stroking for them to keep asking for her to come forward. Three programs' worth."

"Yeah, yeah, and I'm not letting her walk away from running an illegal fucking domestic agency," Langton said angrily. "Did her husband check out?"

"Yes."

"What about other employees?"

"Her agency runs with just him and three other guys who decorate and do the heavy cleaning."

"They checked out?"

"Yes."

"So we're back to John Smiley, whom we've had since Christ knows when as a possible suspect."

"Yes."

"YES! Well, pull your finger out, Mike, and either get the bastard sewn up or bloody move on. That prisoner Cameron Welsh has been bleating on about a witness. Seems the guy from behind bars can do more than any of you *or* your team. If need be, go back and talk to him again."

Langton stormed off, leaving Mike standing like a spare part. He was about to return to his office when something caught his eye on one of the postmortem reports. He moved from one report to another, reminding himself how the description of the strangulation of each victim was similar; the women had been killed by stockings or tights wound tightly around the throat. Only with one victim, Estelle Dubcek, did the forensics suggest it may have been some kind of cord or thin chain, due to the indentations left around the jugular. The fact that they'd never found whatever the killer had used, plus the removal of all personal items such as the victims' handbags, had not so far been an issue, but now Mike believed there was a lot more to it. He hurried over to Barbara's desk.

"I want you to call Swell Blinds and ask them to send samples of the cord used on the wooden slatted blinds, plus the small link chains used on the vertical ones."

Barbara pointed to the vertical blinds hanging in the incident room. "You mean those link chains between each strip?"

"Yes, that's exactly what I want, and I want them here as soon as possible. Bike them up, whatever is fastest."

Mike went over to the window and checked the manufacturer's name. These blinds were not made by Swell Blinds, but he didn't think they would be all that different. He unhooked the chain from the lower section, leaving four strips turned flat against the window. He then put in a call to Pete Jenkins at the forensic lab and told him to expect a delivery, explaining that the chains might not have the same indentation, but a similar one could have been used to strangle Estelle Dubcek.

"Similar isn't good enough, you know, Mike."

"Yes, I hear you. You'll be getting the real thing sent over later."

"Okay, I'll get on to it."

"Thanks, Pete, and I'll appreciate this is a priority."

"Always is. Bye now."

Smiley arrived in the early afternoon and was taken straight to the video recording room. He was wearing a suit with a white shirt and dark tie; he had also shaved, and his hair was combed back. Barolli reported that he was compliant, agreed to the video ID and did as directed, only talking about his concerns about how long he would be required, as he had to get back to Manchester.

At three o'clock, Emerald Turk was driven in to the station car park in an unmarked patrol car. She was taken into the video suite, and the two ID officers explained to her that she was required to look at all the men on the video. Each would hold a number. If she recognized the man who had fitted her blinds, she was to state his number. The team waited.

Emerald appeared to be enjoying all the attention, and as none of the team was allowed to speak to her, the two ID officers made a point of being patient and thanking her for her assistance. She watched the videos twice, and unlike most people in her position, she didn't say a word. She was asked if she would like to view the entire tape a third time, but she said she didn't need to see it again, as she was certain that number three was the man. Number three was John Smiley.

By four-thirty Smiley was sitting in an interview room. They had given him coffee and a sandwich, and he had

hung his suit jacket over the back of his chair. Langton and
Travis entered, and Langton asked if he would like to have
a lawyer present.

Smiley shrugged. "Do I need one?"

"That is up to you, Mr. Smiley. You are here to answer
questions and assist the inquiry. If at any time you feel you
would like representation, then you may ask for a lawyer to
be present."

Smiley cleared his throat and then said that he had nothing to hide. All he wanted was to answer whatever questions
they put to him and go home. "I shall have to make this time
up at the weekend," he fretted, "as my boss is starting to get
uptight about everything. He called me in last week to say
that he respected all the years I'd put in with the company,
and I told him, I said to him, that this was all about me being
parked in the wrong place at the wrong time."

Langton let him talk on as he gave the sign to Anna to
prepare the file of victims' photographs.

"Yes, that is one of the reasons we've asked you to come
in to talk to us, Mr. Smiley, and thank you for agreeing to
do the identification video."

"I was told I didn't really have any option, and then I
thought if I refused, it would look as if I was hiding something."

"You were," Langton said quietly.

Smiley looked confused.

Anna took out the mug shot of Margaret Potts and the
pictures given to them by Eric Potts. "You denied that you
had ever met this woman."

"Right. Yes, that's true."

"No, it isn't." Langton leaned back in his chair. "Mr.
Smiley, we have a witness. You apparently hung some vertical blinds and some wooden slatted blinds in her flat."

"No. I don't handle the vertical blinds."

"But you do measure and hang the slatted wooden blinds."

"Yes—that's my job. I measure first, then the blinds get made, then I go and put them up. I've told you all this."

"We know what you do, Mr. Smiley, but we also know that you were in a flat in Hackney and were paid in cash to—"

"Hackney? When was this?"

"Five years ago."

"Five years? No way. We'd already moved the business to Manchester by then, and I don't recall ever doing work in Hackney—definitely not in a cash deal. I don't handle the money side. Arnold Rodgers, my boss, sends out the invoices, and customers pay him directly."

"We have a witness, Mr. Smiley, and this woman"—Langton tapped Margaret Potts's photograph—"Margaret Potts was inside the flat, so you have lied, and you did meet her, didn't you?"

"No, I swear on my life, I never met this woman, just like I said when I was last here. I never met her, and I know what type of woman she is, and I wouldn't give her the time of day."

"What happened, John? You were there doing your job, and she was sleeping, woke up, maybe she was wearing a sexy nightdress and you got talking . . ."

"I never met that woman."

"It's pointless to lie. We know she was in that flat, we know you were there, and we have a witness who says not only did she see you there, but she also handed you cash. Why are you lying?"

"I'm not."

"I'll tell you why. You are ashamed of what went on

between you. Did she come on to you? Offer you sex, offer to give you a blow job, strip for you? Come on, John, we know you met her, it's useless to lie about it. Did you fuck her, John?"

"No, I did not! I never met that woman, and whoever it is saying that I did is the liar, not me. I'm married, I've got two kids, and I wouldn't want to go with a slag like that. And I wouldn't do any cash deals—it's more than my job's worth, 'cause I've worked for Mr. Rodgers for ten years, and I wouldn't jeopardize that."

"You couldn't resist her, could you?"

"I never touched her."

Langton sighed, picking up the photographs. He then gestured to Anna to lay down the photographs of the Polish victims. "Maybe you wouldn't want to admit screwing someone like Margaret Potts, but these girls, look at them, they're young and they're beautiful. What about them, eh?"

Smiley was sweating but holding firm. "No. I never knew any of them, and that's the honest truth. Now, you can keep asking me over and over, but you can't get me to admit nothing, 'cause I am telling you the truth."

Langton swung back in his chair, smiling. "No, you are not. We have a witness, John. We know you were in her flat in Hackney, and we know she paid you cash. I think you then paid that cash to screw Margaret Potts."

"No, I did not."

"So you admit you were in this flat in Hackney?"

"No."

"John, let me help you out here. I can understand why a man like you doesn't want to admit to having sex with a prostitute. You have a wife, and from what I saw of her, she's the kind of woman who wouldn't understand why you'd get your dick out for such a tart. She looked the type that would give you hell if she found out, so I can understand why you are lying. But you see, John, because we have a witness, it's possibly going to turn into something more serious than you just taking your trousers off."

Langton clicked his fingers for Anna to show Margaret Potts's photograph again. "This woman was murdered, John, strangled and raped, and these three young girls"—he slapped the table with the flat of his hand—"were also murdered—so you see how serious it is if you are lying about just getting screwed?"

Smiley had sweat beads over his forehead and upper lip.

"If you just admit it and say to me, 'All right, yeah, that's what happened. I paid her twenty quid and she went down on me. I finished the work and then I left,' that will be the end of the story. But because you lie and say you've never even met her, you have to see that from my side, it looks suspicious, doesn't it? It looks to me like you might have another reason for lying—and that reason could be that *you killed her.*"

Langton leaned on his elbows. Smiley had his head bowed.

"You could also be lying about not knowing these young girls, and because of that simple lie, you've gone and got yourself into a shedload of trouble. The reason for that one little lie is because you also knew every one of these girls."

"I don't like this," Smiley said, with his head still bowed.

"I don't like it, either, John."

Smiley eventually looked up. "I want a lawyer, because you are not asking me about why I was at that service station; you tricked me, and this isn't about that at all. You're trying to make out that I've done something terrible."

Langton began to restack the photographs.

"You never said who this witness was," Smiley went on. "Who is she? What's her name? I've got a right to know who's saying these things about me."

Langton stood up. "'She,' Mr. Smiley? Very well, we'll get you a lawyer. Might be a bit of a wait. Would you like another coffee?"

"*No.*"

Langton nodded to Anna, and she stood up.

"See you later, Mr. Smiley," Langton said briskly.

They left him sitting mopping his head with a handkerchief.

Walking along the corridor, Langton turned to Anna. "What do you think, Travis?"

"Not sure."

"I am." Langton paused and gave her a sidelong look. "Because we've got that lady Emerald Turk, we can keep him here for further interviews. I want him to stew, because it's all we've really got to hold him on."

"I'll get a lawyer sorted out."

"Wait a second. He's lying—right? You telling me you don't think he's the killer?"

"I'm not saying anything. The man is terrified of what his wife will say if he's going to be held in custody. But even if we get him to admit that he did know Margaret Potts, we have no evidence that he killed her or the three Polish girls."

"You ever think that maybe he's wily enough to know that if he admits to knowing Margaret Potts, he had to have also seen or known about her working the service station?"

They continued down the corridor, and this time it was Anna who stopped.

"All along we've kept on saying that Margaret is the odd one out—that she's older, tougher, and more worldly than the other three victims."

"Yes—and?"

"We would need to prove that Smiley didn't just see her once but that he kept on meeting up with her at the service station or elsewhere, because she wasn't murdered until two years later. Emerald Turk puts him in her flat bloody years ago, near Christmas 2005, so even if he admits that he did meet with her that one time, we have a very long gap in between."

They continued to walk along the corridor, and Langton put his arm around her shoulders as he listened.

"If we can find out that Smiley was a regular client of Maggie's, we have a phone call from her to Emerald in which she says something about the *Evening Standard* newspaper, but she also sounds drunk, so I'm not sure where I'm going with this."

"Try me," Langton said briefly.

"Okay. We've checked back to a possible day or night when the call was made from a pay phone, maybe at the service station. Margaret said she wanted to come over to Hackney to stay, but Emerald apparently refused. Anyway, the *Standard* ran a front page on the blue-blanket victim we now know to be Dorota Pelagia . . ." Anna stopped. "I haven't got this sorted in my brain because of the odd time frame, but what if Margaret Potts read about the blue-blanket murder and worked out that it was connected to John Smiley?"

"Tried to blackmail him, something like that?"

"Maybe . . . so she had to be got rid of—which is why she is the odd victim out, so to speak."

Langton had left his arm around her shoulder, and she found it a bit uncomfortable, but she wasn't able to simply shrug him away.

"It's possible," Langton agreed. "I mean, she might not

have known where Smiley worked, and had no means of contacting him until she saw him at the services, or alternatively, she was often in contact with him . . ."

Anna stepped away so he dropped his arm. "I think I need to go back and question everyone who knew her again, and that includes Emerald Turk. Again, this is something that's just sort of clicked and . . ." She came to a halt.

"Yes? Share it."

"Well, Emerald Turk was wearing an outfit she said had been left in Margaret Potts's suitcase. It was a very expensive velvet-type tracksuit, and she also said there had been some other clothes."

"Where's this going?"

"Money. Everyone tells me that Margaret Potts never had anything and was always desperate for cash, but if she was blackmailing someone—John Smiley—she might have had cash, and she wasn't seen around the service station a few weeks before her murder." Anna sighed. "I really need to sit down with all my notes and work out the time frame for all this."

Langton cupped her face in his hands, saying, "You take as much time as you need, sweetheart."

It was as if he were about to kiss her. Quickly, she pulled back, and just in time, as Barbara appeared in the corridor, heading for the ladies' toilets.

A lawyer was arranged for John Smiley, but it took over two hours for him to arrive. James Gregson was young and deliberated over virtually everything they told him. He expressed concern about the legality of holding Smiley in custody without formal charges, and Langton, taking the bit between his teeth, said they had direct witness evidence that Smiley knew and had met Margaret Potts. Gregson went off to speak with his client as Mike brought Langton up to speed about the possibility of the chain or cord from Swell Blinds being used to strangle the victims.

"Jesus Christ, when did you come up with this?"

"Looking over the postmortem reports. I've sent the link chain from the vertical blinds up in the incident room over to forensics, and we're waiting on a delivery of the actual cord and chains used by Swell Blinds. They're being brought down from Manchester."

"Get them from Emerald Turk's flat as well. She's got both, hasn't she?"

Mike hadn't thought of that, and he flushed, but Langton dug him in the ribs.

"Now you're cooking."

Smiley was with Gregson for two hours, and it was now after seven-thirty. At eight o'clock Langton and Lewis informed them both that Smiley's further detention for questioning had been authorized and they would continue the interview until the morning. Smiley was allowed to call his wife to let her know that he was to remain in custody overnight.

Langton made no mention to Gregson that they were waiting on a result from the cord and chains from forensics. It had been disappointing when Pete had called to say that the chain from the incident room was thicker than the indentations left on the victim's neck; although it was similar, the small raised links were wider apart. As the items from Swell Blinds had now been delivered from Manchester, he would hopefully have a new and possibly different result by morning.

Chapter Thirteen

Anna spent most of Thursday evening trying to mark up the exact time frame between Emerald Turk's statements and the discovery of the bodies. When Ken rang at ten o'clock, she was ready to call it quits for the night. He commented that she sounded tired, and she gave him a brief rundown of the long day. She doubted that she would get the weekend off, but even if it was just Sunday, she said she might drive up to see him.

"Well, it might be a waste of time." Ken groaned. "We've had a few problems, and with me skipping off for more free time than I'm allowed, it looks as if I'll be working."

"Sunday as well?"

"Yep."

"What's been happening?"

"It's Cameron Welsh—he's being a real pain in the arse. You wouldn't believe what he looks like."

"How do you mean?"

"He's not washed since around the last time you saw him. His hair is lank and dirty, he stinks, he's not shaved or eaten, and he's making trouble with all the other inmates in the unit."

"Do you know why?"

"We don't have to have a reason; sometimes it's just down to stir craziness, but we'll have to get a doctor in to see him if he carries on. It's often a prelude to something going to blow. He shat all over his bedlinen, and no matter how many privileges we've removed from him, he remains a belligerent nasty sod. Plus, he's been stealing from the other inmates, which creates havoc."

"Is he violent?"

"No. He has a thing against me, though—spat in my face this morning. Tomorrow we've asked him to be checked over, get something to calm him down, but we've had him screaming and shouting all night long. If you ask me, he's gone a bit gaga."

"When will you know if you have to work?"

"It depends. I have more experience than a couple of the other officers; it gets quite hairy in here. Secure unit is a small place and very claustrophobic. We have to turn around duty so we don't get as nuts as the prisoners."

"Well, let's hope we can meet up. I really miss you."

"I tell you, if it's not this weekend, I'm riding down the first opportunity I can get, and I'm sorry if I've sounded like a moaning twat. It's just I've had my fill today—in fact, I've got to go back in. I'm over in the main prison getting a bite to eat."

"Take care. I love you."

"Do you have a photograph you can send me?"

She laughed and said she'd dig one out, but they were mostly from her childhood. She asked him to send her one of him in return.

"Kiss good night, then."

Anna went straight to her desk and rummaged through the drawers, bringing out old photo albums. She thumbed through all the pictures of herself with her parents and then found one of herself at age eleven, doing a cartwheel. She took it out of the album and drew a heart on the back. *You make my heart somersault*, she wrote beneath it, then tucked it into an envelope, ready to send it off in the morning.

The next morning was busy. Langton had the press conference at Scotland Yard, and most of the team was there, so the incident room was quiet. Smiley would be brought up from the cells as soon as they all returned. Anna thought back to her first meeting with Emerald Turk. She wished she'd asked to see the other items of clothing that had been left in the suitcase, as somehow the tracksuit didn't fit all the depressing descriptions she'd been given of Margaret.

"Do you know what time the press conference is due to end?" she asked.

Barbara looked over and shrugged. "I know the boss had a lot of journalists interested, so if there's a Q and A session, it could go on for an hour or even more."

Anna decided that would give her enough time to drive over to talk to Eric Potts.

She was just parking her car outside the debt collection agency's offices when Eric appeared, carrying a coffee. She hurried toward him. "Mr. Potts, it's DI Anna Travis."

He glanced at her and gave an odd smile. "I know who you are. You got some news for me? It's been a while."

"Sorry, I don't, but we do have a few developments."

"I should hope so. I reckoned as I'd not heard anything and there was nothing in the press, it was all buried."

"No, not by any means. Can I have a few words with you?"

"Got to be a few, as I'm on my way to a job. Café owes rent, and if I leave it any longer, I'll be carrying out the goods while they're still serving the customers."

"It's in reference to the last time you saw Margaret. You said you met her in a café over by King's Cross station?"

"Yeah."

"How did she look?"

"What?"

"You've told me that sometimes she looked really ragged and was always asking you for money."

"That's right."

"This last time, did she want money?"

He sighed. "Look, I made it clear to her that I couldn't go on shelling out cash to her whenever she called me, and I also said that the wife didn't want her around. I told you this."

"Yes, I know—but can you think back? Did she ask you for money?"

"She always did."

"I shall ask you again: how did she look?"

Eric opened the lid of his coffee and took a sip. "She was cleaner than usual, but she'd aged. She was worn out, and she looked it."

"Did she say she needed money?"

"Maggie didn't have to say it. She was living at some other tart's place, I think, or a hostel—I don't honestly re-member. I walked away from her, you know, gave her a few quid, like, and walked off. Oh, Christ, I told you all of this before. When I looked back, she was crying, and I never saw her cry no matter what was done to her."

"Did she say anything to you before you left her?"

"No, not that I can remember." He sounded irritated now. "She could lie, you know; things were always going to be different. She said to me that she wasn't gonna be working the service stations, that she didn't need to do it anymore, but it was a lie, because they found her body near one, right?" Eric straightened, turning away from Anna as he remembered something. "Hang on—she had new shoes."

"What?"

"It's odd. See, I didn't want to look at her when I told her to stay away from me and the kids, so I kept me eyes down. That was when I noticed she had new shoes on, with high heels. She normally wore scuffed old things that were flat."

"Do you think her other clothes were new?"

He suddenly lost patience, snapping, "I don't fucking know! It was a long time ago, all right? Now I've got to go to work."

Langton was in no hurry to start the proceedings with Smiley, but was having coffee and sandwiches in the incident room. It had been a big turnout for his press conference, and the assistant commissioner had also been present. Langton looked smart in a dark suit, immaculate crisp white shirt, and sober tie. He was holding forth about the number of television crews interviewing him.

Barolli sidled up to Anna's desk and said quietly that George Clooney had handled the press like a pro.

"He loves it, doesn't he?" he said, looking toward Langton. "You know, rumor is he's gonna be the next murder and serious crime commander. The current one was at the conference, and they were very friendly. Langton's certainly hands-on when there're photographers around. I hear that those hands were all over you as well."

"I beg your pardon?"

"Barbara said she saw you and the gov in the corridor."

Anna was furious. "She should mind her own business, and you should keep that yapping mouth shut. Maybe if you'd done more of a thorough interview with Emerald Turk in the first place, we'd have been a lot further and faster than we have been!"

Barolli stepped back as if she'd slapped him. "That was a low blow."

"A true one, though—and don't think DCS Langton isn't aware of it."

She was angry at herself for rising to the bait so quickly. It would only create more gossip.

Langton started to come over, but before he could say anything, Anna stood up, afraid he would sit on the edge of her desk. She didn't want anyone putting two and two together and coming up with any more gossip, so she launched straight in with her latest news.

"Margaret Potts had new shoes on the last time she saw her ex-brother-in-law. She looked smarter than usual, and she might have had money, but she still took some off of him."

"That's not much to go on, but we do have a big development from Pete Jenkins. Mike sent over a cord and chain from Swell Blinds, and though Pete is not prepared to give it one hundred percent—"

"I'm not following you. One hundred percent about what?"

"The chain might have matched the indentations on Estelle Dubcek's neck—it's got those small raised dots. She's the only victim with them, but on Anika Waleska, he thinks the cord might be one of the type used to strangle her."

"Wow, that's some development! On the other hand how many products are there, not only from Swell Blinds but from every other company that uses them? It's a coincidence, though."

"Coincidence . . . remember my code? Never believe in 'em." He smiled, obviously pleased with the way things were progressing. "We had a good press conference, and there will be a lot of coverage, so I'd say Cameron Welsh will be gloating—so much of what he's said has made us think. It might be worth another visit."

"Apparently not. He's gone gaga."

"What?"

"He's refusing to wash or eat and is causing problems with the rest of the inmates in the secure unit."

"Really?"

"Yes. He's probably had his few moments of fame—dragging us all there to visit him has turned his head."

"How do you know all this?"

She flushed and could have kicked herself. "Just keeping tabs on him in case I have to go and see him again."

"You speak to the governor?"

"No."

"Who did you talk to?"

"Officer Hudson."

"Ken?"

"Yes, Ken Hudson."

Langton kept his eyes on her until she looked away, embarrassed.

"Okay, we go to interview room one in fifteen minutes. See you in there."

"Yes, sir."

Langton headed off, and now Mike Lewis came up to her desk. "The clock is ticking with Smiley. We've had him here since last night—what's Langton waiting for?"

"Could be evidence?" she said, getting up and pointing at the board.

"You know as well as anyone here does, we don't have enough to charge Smiley, and if that young lawyer's worth his salt, he'll know it as well." Mike puffed out his cheeks. "Come on, what about the possibility that it was the same type of cord and chain, for chrissakes."

"Same type won't hold up. It's got to fit exactly," Anna said.

"But Emerald Turk picked Smiley out of the video lineup."

"Whose word would you trust, someone like her or a man with a decent job and a family?" Anna sounded impatient.

"But she identified him."

Anna sighed. "Doesn't mean diddly squat. She could be wrong. It was nearly five years ago; plus, she admits to only seeing him fleetingly, and if the lawyer gets hold of all that, it's a no-go. The only chance we might get to keep him here will be if Smiley admits he lied about knowing Margaret Potts, but I don't think he's going to fall down like the pack of proverbial cards. He didn't even after Langton really hammered at him last night."

Anna went to prepare for the next round of questioning, leaving Mike Lewis feeling irritated. He knew he should have been the one interviewing Smiley with Langton. It hadn't helped that Barolli, with his usual spoon out, had told him that Langton and Travis were obviously still an item. Mike wandered to the board and noticed that Travis had written "new shoes" beneath the data on Margaret Potts; she'd also underlined it, and he had no notion what it meant.

"Barbara, what's this 'new shoes' that's been added?"

"No idea. Maybe she's gonna buy herself a pair."

Mike went back to his office and sat stewing. Barolli tapped and entered. "You want a coffee?" he asked.

"No. Did Emerald Turk hesitate over identifying John Smiley?"

"Apparently not. She watched the videos twice and then

picked him out. Maybe we'll get more from him after this session."

"And maybe we won't."

"Something's got to give, Mike; we've got front-page coverage in the *Evening Standard*." Barolli dropped the paper on Mike's desk.

"They moved fast," Mike said, cheered, then: "Yeah, I'll have a black coffee, after all."

"Good work on that Swell Blinds stuff," Barolli said. "Been slap in front of our faces for weeks."

As Barolli shut the door, Mike looked at the *Evening Standard*. The dead women's faces were lined up like a picture gallery, and on the next page was a photograph of Margaret Potts with information that the police were holding a suspect in custody after a lengthy investigation. He knew without reading it all that Langton was acting like a spin doctor. If Smiley was to be released, they would be virtually back to square one, but the Met could not be accused of dragging their feet.

Time was certainly dragging in the interview room, where James Gregson was proving to be tiresome. He claimed that his client was being held unlawfully, and if they had further evidence that he knew Margaret Potts other than a weak video ID, they should produce it or release Smiley immediately. He by now had the details of Emerald Turk, who she was and so on, and that Margaret Potts, a prostitute, had stayed in her flat. Smiley had also denied ever fitting any blinds for Miss Turk or being paid cash to install them. He denied that he'd ever had any interaction with Ms. Potts or met her at the service station.

Time and time again, Gregson asked for evidence that

implicated his client in anything more than being parked at the service station. Smiley had also denied ever meeting or having any kind of knowledge of the three Polish victims. Once more Gregson asked for any evidence that could implicate his client.

"My client, I believe, was unfortunately in the wrong place at the wrong time . . ."

Langton had listened as Gregson pompously suggested that they had no alternative but to release his client. "I would also like to add that I think this is bordering on harassment. Mr. Smiley has driven himself to the station to be interviewed, turned up of his own volition. At no time has he denied that he was parked at the London Gateway service station. I am also told that you have interviewed his wife, his employer, and a number of previous employees of the same company. Mr. Smiley has an exemplary employment record, he has no police record, and if this continues, he could lose his job."

Langton let him go on without interruption. Anna sat silently beside him, watching Smiley closely. He did not react to anything his lawyer said but sat impassively with his head tilted down.

"You must know, Detective Chief Superintendent, that Mr. Smiley should have had a lawyer present during his last interview *and* during the video identification process . . ."

Gregson was either waiting for Langton to interrupt him or query what he was saying, but he remained silent. Eventually, Gregson closed his thick leather-bound notebook and tapped it with his well-manicured fingernails. There was a long pause.

"I hear what you are saying, Mr. Gregson," Langton said finally.

"Well, I'm pleased that you—"

"Shut up. Shut up and listen to me. I have given you the best part of half an hour without interruption, and now it's your turn to listen to me."

"I resent the way you have just spoken to me."

"You can resent it as much as you like. It would be simple, Mr. Gregson, if your client would admit here and now that he did meet Margaret Potts, that he did know her, because we have a witness—"

"I'm sorry, but I have to interrupt you. This witness you maintain met with my client—"

"This same witness picked Mr. Smiley out as the man in her flat who came to repair a blind and offered to put in place another one at a lower price. She left Mr. Smiley alone with the victim, Margaret Potts. He can deny it, he can swear on his children's lives that he was never there, but he was."

Langton had found John Smiley one of the hardest nuts to crack. Because he had shown no emotion, it was difficult to know if they had gained any ground with him. The DCS was becoming so frustrated that Anna was afraid he would lose his temper for real, so she intervened, her voice softer and quieter, in an attempt to draw a response and calm the atmosphere.

"Mr. Smiley, we don't want in any way to jeopardize your work, and I know it is difficult for you taking so much time off."

Smiley leaned forward, his tone bitter. "If I get the sack, I will sue the police for harassment. I did not know that woman Potts, and this so-called witness is lying. God help me, I don't know why anyone would do such a thing, but—"

"Her friend was murdered; she was raped and strangled. If you are afraid that by admitting you knew Margaret—"

"I DIDN'T KNOW HER. HOW MANY MORE TIMES DO YOU WANT ME TO SAY IT? *I DIDN'T KNOW HER!*"

Gregson quickly placed his hand on Smiley's arm to quiet him. This was the first time he had lost control. Langton stepped in again.

"Fine. You must then know of someone else working at Swell Blinds who did the work for this witness, someone with access to the wooden slatted blinds, someone who could arrange to put up a pair on the cheap and fix the vertical blinds that needed to be repaired."

Smiley was back in control. He shrugged and said that as far as he knew, there were a number of employees who used to work only on the vertical blinds but might also have access to the slatted ones.

"We used to get a few in that weren't the right size—you know, if I hadn't done the measurements properly, so we'd have a stack of them that were useless; anyone could have picked them up from the warehouse. I would say that was what this woman was paying cash for. We've sold off some at one time or another."

"Then give us the names of employees you think might have sold them to our witness."

"You ask Mr. Rodgers—he's the one who knows who was employed and who wasn't. Some of them were cash in hand, especially the ones doing up the vertical blinds for the housing association contracts. They would have twenty or thirty flats to work on. I'm the professional one, because I only did the top clients."

Langton jotted down a note, passing it to Anna; she glanced at it and then folded it over. "I'd like you to look at this photograph, please, Mr. Smiley. Specifically, look at the markings to the victim's neck."

Smiley glanced down and then peered closer.

"Can you see the small indentations that have cut into her neck, where something was wound round three times and then drawn tightly?"

Smiley nodded, staring down at the photograph.

"On this victim, you can see the strangulation marks, but made by something different, something without links," Anna continued.

Again Smiley really gave his attention to the photograph.

Langton tapped Anna's knee beneath the table to keep going.

"These marks were made by a link chain and a pull cord from a vertical blind or a wooden slatted blind."

Smiley leaned close to Gregson and whispered to him. They had a lengthy conversation, with Gregson shielding their faces with his notebook. Then he laid it down. "I understand where you are going with this, but perhaps you should be made aware that my client is knowledgeable with regard to the types of cords and chains used by Swell Blinds. The same cord and chains are manufactured in bulk; millions are used by most companies in the industry, not just Swell Blinds. It would therefore be impossible for you to categorically state that this could be used as evidence against my client."

John Smiley was released from custody with no charges at nine-fifteen. Langton had remained in the interview room while Anna took both Gregson and Smiley out to reception. In a fit of temper, Langton hurled the files off the table and then kicked them. Anna returned to find him with all the files and statements littering the floor.

"I think we should call it quits for tonight," she said, and began to pick everything up.

"You want to have a drink?"

"No. I'd like to get home—it's been a long day."

"Tell me about it."

"I think we should get access to John Smiley's bank accounts, check his cash withdrawal amounts, and see if they link up to any dates and vicinities of our murders."

"Get on it, because next time we bring that bastard back, I am going to nail him."

Anna placed the files back on the table.

"You seeing this Ken Hudson on a personal level?"

She hesitated and then nodded. "Yes, I am, as a matter of fact."

Langton leaned back in the chair, loosening his tie. "I said he had the hots for you, didn't I?"

She disliked the way he was looking at her. "I actually had the hots for him, and now we're quite serious, so I'd be grateful if you could cut out any snide remarks."

"Who's being snide?"

"Sorry, I just interpreted what you said the wrong way. It's all new, and I feel protective over my friendship with him."

Langton stood up and collected his files. He gave her one of his smiles that used to make her forgive him for anything, then moved closer and kissed her cheek. "I'm happy for you. Next time you see him, give him my best."

"I will. Thank you."

The following morning Anna received in the post a photograph of Ken Hudson at age eight. He was wearing a clown's nose, a silly wig, and big flat shoes. He had scrawled on the back in black felt-tip pen, *To my funny lovable Anna, from Ken.*

Anna had forgotten to send her photograph: it was still

in her briefcase. She had meant to post it yesterday on her way to the station but would take it with her when she drove to Leeds tonight. Both she and Ken had to work this Saturday. She was checking her appearance in her wardrobe mirror when she bent down to slip on her shoes and it triggered off the remark about Maggie Potts's shoes being new. She had even underlined *shoes* on the incident board. Instead of driving directly to the station, she did a detour to Hackney to question Emerald Turk. She was curious about what else the suitcase had contained apart from the tracksuit.

Anna rang the doorbell and waited for about five minutes. Emerald unlatched the door and peered out, keeping the safety chain on.

"I don't fucking believe this," she said. "It's bloody half past eight in the morning."

It was actually nine o'clock, but Anna asked if she could come in, as she had a few things she wanted to talk over.

"Christ." The chain was unhooked. "I only just got the friggin' kids off me hands with a neighbor. I didn't get home till four-thirty. I've got a life, you know, and this is starting to really piss me off."

"I'm sorry, but you were brilliant at the video ID. Everyone was impressed—you handled yourself very well."

"Yeah, I got a good memory, ain't I—and they had someone here waiting when I got back."

Anna was surprised.

"Yeah, they took me kitchen blind and the one that had fallen down from the box room. I don't mind that, 'cause it's been on the floor for years, but they can see in me kitchen from the flat opposite."

"I'll get someone to sort that out for you. May I sit down?"

"You've been here often enough, you could probably make yer own coffee. Do you want one?"

"No, thanks."

Emerald looked rough. She had a long coughing fit and lit up a cigarette straight after. "I gotta give up, they cost a fortune." She inhaled deeply and let the smoke out in rings. "What do you want this time?"

"This is difficult, Emerald, because I don't want to insult you, but what we're sort of coming up with is that Margaret may have been making quite a few quid. You were wearing a really nice tracksuit you said belonged to her . . ."

"Yeah?"

"Can you show me the other items you found in her suitcase?"

"I told you there was nothing much. And some stuff I just chucked."

"But can I see what you kept?"

Emerald continued to smoke, sticking the cigarette into the corner of her mouth and squinting one eye as the smoke drifted ups. "What do you want to see them for?"

"I'm just trying to find out if Margaret was maybe saving money or spending more than usual."

Emerald shrugged and then carefully stubbed out the cigarette in a saucer. "If she had money, she used to send it to her kids at the foster home they live in. There wasn't any money in her case."

"But the clothes—were they new?"

Emerald led Anna into her bedroom. It wasn't all that untidy, but the bed had not been made, and there was a sequined evening dress and gold high-heeled shoes chucked onto the floor at the end of it. Emerald went to her wardrobe and opened it up.

Anna looked around the bedroom. She noticed an open cardboard jewel box covered in a flower pattern, with beads and bangles heaped inside and hanging out of it. Beside it was another case, a black leather one. It looked as if that was where she kept her better-quality jewelry.

"Right, here you go. As far as I remember, it was this jacket, this skirt, and two blouses. The pants I chucked because they weren't my size, nor were her bras, and like I told you, what I didn't fancy, I tossed out."

"With the suitcase?"

"Yeah."

Anna looked over the jacket. It was nothing special and came from Topshop; the blouses were from Zara; and the skirt was a wool three-tiered pale blue one of good quality.

"This is nice," Anna said, fingering it.

"Yeah, not my style, though. I've not worn it, just shoved it in the wardrobe."

"What about the velvet tracksuit?"

Emerald gestured to a laundry basket. "I wear that a lot. It's nice and comfortable."

"Did you ever see Margaret wearing things like this?"

"Funnily enough, no. They were all folded ever so neatly as well. She used to wear more cheap sexy T-shirts and short skirts—you know, anything to show off what she was stacking."

"What about jewelry?"

Anna saw the way Emerald darted a quick glance at her dressing table and the jewelry boxes.

"No, nothing in the suitcase. It looks like she had to have kept some other gear somewhere. I know she used stations. But when they closed all the left luggage places 'cause of bloody terrorist scares she left it with me or dossed down at various hostels."

"There were no shoes?"

"No."

"What about a nightdress?"

"Oh yeah, hang on . . . And there was a dressing gown. I use them—they're in the bathroom."

Anna followed Emerald into the hall and to the small bathroom. Hanging on the door was a terry dressing gown and a pink nylon nightdress.

"Was she wearing these when you last saw her? When the man came to fix the blinds?"

"No, they was in the suitcase. I washed them 'cause she wasn't always that clean."

Anna asked if Emerald knew the foster parents' address for Margaret's children, but she didn't.

"Is that it, then?"

"How much money was in the suitcase, Emerald?"

The woman's jaw dropped and then clamped shut. "You got a friggin' nerve! There was no money, I told you. I've shown you everythin' I kept, and the rest I bloody tossed. Now just clear on out of it. I'm through with you."

"Why are you getting so angry?"

"You are accusin' me of nickin' cash, and I told you I never found none, like I never found no red notebook, neither."

"Really? So you saw it, did you?"

"Jesus Christ! She showed it me, *all right*?"

"No, it's not all right, Emerald. If you did find it and also found some cash, how much did you find?"

Emerald walked back into the kitchen. Anna waited a beat before she followed and saw Emerald shaking her packet of cigarettes, which was empty. She hurled it at the pedal bin.

"Please will you just tell me the truth. I can't do anything about it, because her suitcase was here in your flat. I just need to know if Margaret had money."

Emerald picked up a cigarette stub from the ashtray and puffed it alight. "She was quite flush, okay?"

"What do you mean?"

Emerald sat on one of the breakfast stools. "'Cause I let her stay, she gave me a few quid."

"Was that unusual?"

Emerald sighed, smoking virtually right down to the tip of the cigarette. "Yeah."

Anna watched her run the tap over the cigarette stub. She was surprised to see the woman close to tears.

"I knew she was dead—right?—so I took it. It's all gone on stuff for the flat and the kids. I mean, I'd had the friggin' suitcase, but I never opened it, not till I knew what had happened to her."

"How much was in there?"

"It was a few hundred . . ." She had tears spilling down her cheeks as she choked out, "All right, it was about a grand, in mostly ten- and twenty-pound notes," She was still lying, because it had been two thousand pounds, but she was too scared to admit the amount.

"Thank you for that information, Emerald. As I said to you, I just needed you to be honest with me."

"Will I get booked?"

"I shouldn't think so. But it won't really be me who decides," Anna walked to the front door. "It's all about us trying to find out who killed your friend. We believe Margaret might have been blackmailing someone, and that is the reason why she had so much money."

"Shit. I'm sorry, but I swear on my kids' lives, I dunno nothing about anything like that."

Anna passed her card over, saying that if Emerald should think of anything else that might be of help, she was to contact Anna on her direct line. Emerald's hand was on the front door, ready to open it, as Anna said there was one more thing that bothered her. Emerald slapped the door with the flat of her hand. "Bloody hell, now what?"

"It's just you said Maggie left her suitcase with you and that you had no contact with her apart from the one phone call, and you mentioned she left a message."

"Right, yeah. It was her, wantin' to stay."

"You have stated that was the last time you had anything to do with her, that you never saw her again, and then you found out she was dead."

"Right. I read about it in the papers."

"If what you have told us is the truth, the last time Maggie stayed with you is when the blinds were repaired. That was a long time ago, so you kept her suitcase here for many months."

"Yeah."

"I don't believe you. If it had contained clothes and money, why didn't she come back for it? Unless you did see her again after that phone call, which you maintain was the last time you spoke to her."

Emerald kicked at the front door, swearing, and Anna stepped well back.

"You think I don't fuckin' feel about it, 'cause I do! I mean, she was a right pain in the arse, but I can't be blamed for what happened to her. It's got nothin' to do with me, and I was about the only friend she bloody had, so that's why I've said nuffink."

"Nothing about what, exactly?"

Emerald sighed, leaning her back against the front door. "I was just coming back from work, and she turned up. She wanted to stay and said she could give me a few quid. She didn't want to go into a hostel, as people were nicking stuff off her."

"When was this?"

"Maybe two months before she was murdered. She had her case with her, and she'd been drinking, so there was no way I'd let her in with the kids. It was a Saturday, like today, and they were at home."

Anna said nothing, waiting as Emerald gave another long, shuddering sigh.

"I told her she could leave her case with me, but that was it. She got a bit stroppy but then handed it to me."

"How did she look?"

"Same as always. Well, not exactly. She didn't look like she'd been workin', know what I mean? And she'd had her hair bleached. Anyway, she said she'd be back for it in a couple of days. She also said—and this got me pissed off—that it was locked and she'd know if I'd opened it. Bloody nerve, I thought, considering how much I'd done for her."

"Was she carrying anything else?"

"She had a big holdall bag. Never left that with me. She walked off and . . ." Emerald paused. "She turned and gave me a wave and was smiling. To be honest, I did feel bad, but then I shut the door. I put her case into the box room, and I swear on me kids' lives I never opened it. Well, I knew she had some hard-nut friends, like. Remember I told you they duffed up a geezer that tipped her out of his truck, so I left it alone. I even waited after she died in case someone or other contacted me about it. When nothin' happened, I pried the lock off it and said nuffink to nobody about it."

"Thank you, Emerald."

Anna added the new details from Emerald to the incident board and wrote that a priority should be tracing the foster parents of Margaret Potts's children. She then went to ask

Mike if it was possible for her to leave before lunch, as she had a prior commitment.

"Not like you, Travis," he said, sounding surprised by her request. He also pointed out that she had not worked weekends for some time.

"It's quite important," she persevered, "and it's not as if we're inundated."

"Tell me something I don't know. Okay, permission granted. Family thing, is it?"

"Yes," she lied.

Anna drove up to see Ken, arriving early Saturday night. He was on duty until eleven but had left a key with his neighbor. He would have to work Sunday but said he would try and swing it that they had at least part of the day together. She was tired out after the long drive and had gone to bed, waking when he got in beside her. He kissed her and then flopped back onto his pillow.

"Listen, my mum has asked if you'd like to go over to-morrow. You don't have to, but as I'm on duty, I just wondered . . ."

She leaned up on her elbow and said that she'd love to see his parents again.

"Honestly, you don't have to."

"I want to. Didn't you say it was their wedding anniversary? Maybe you could come by later?"

"I love you," he said, giving her a hug.

Anna arrived at Ken's parents' with a large bouquet of flowers, and Mrs. Hudson hurried her into the kitchen. As she put the flowers into a vase, she explained that she'd been baking an anniversary cake and had to finish the icing but didn't want her husband, Roy, to see it.

"I'm going to get him to clean that car of yours, which will keep him outside. He's down at the store, getting a nice bottle of wine for dinner and . . ." The front doorbell rang. "That's him, never has his keys. I won't be a minute. Actually, no, you'd better come out, or he'll want to come in and say hello."

Roy Hudson was wearing overalls and Wellington boots, ready to wash and polish his own car, which was parked alongside Anna's Mini. Anna said that he didn't really need to wash hers.

"I always obey orders, love, and the wife's keeping me out of the way 'cause she's probably baking up a cake or something, so you go on back inside."

He gave her a smile almost identical to Ken's, which left her with no choice but to return to the kitchen. She watched, fascinated, as Mrs. Hudson prepared the marzipan and wrapped it around the layered sponge cake; then she was shown how to mix the icing and prepare the cones for the decoration.

"I'll show you how to make little roses. We'll need the white icing to dry nice and hard so the colors don't run, and if you'd like to practice, you can use the breadboard."

Mrs. Hudson was extremely patient and encouraging as Anna managed to make awful clumps of pink icing over the board. After a number of attempts, she managed a rather good small rose with petals.

"That's ever so good, dear. Now you can put them on the cake."

"No, no, I don't think so. I don't want to ruin it."

"You won't. I'll mix up a blue and a green for the writing, but I'm not putting on how many years we've been married, there's not enough room." She laughed.

To spend half an afternoon icing a cake and then having

toasted cheese sandwiches with Roy and Brenda was a lovely experience. She was asked a lot of questions about her own parents but not, thankfully, about her work. She was so relaxed that she didn't think about it until she was sitting drinking tea with Brenda, who was surrounded by all the photographs of her foster children.

"Did the parents of the children you cared for pay regular visits?"

"Some did, but to be honest, most of them only made promises. The hard part for me was when they didn't turn up. I'd get the children all bathed and dressed smartly, and they'd sit at the front window waiting. Time and time again, the promises were broken, and they would be so disappointed, and then we'd have tantrums and tears."

"Did the parents send birthday cards and gifts?"

Brenda shrugged. "Often when they first came to me, we'd get phone calls and cards, but inevitably, they would peter out. Roy and I would try and make up for it—you know, by having special parties and cakes."

"What about money?"

"Well, the Social Services obviously paid for us to do the fostering, and they didn't really like us to take money off the children's parents. Most were single parents; sometimes if money was sent, we'd put it into a savings account for the child. We'd never touch it ourselves." Brenda poured herself another cup of tea. "Why do you ask?"

Anna gave a brief outline of a victim's children being fostered but didn't go into details about Margaret Potts.

"Were her children abused?" Brenda asked.

"I honestly don't know; they could have been. It seems, as far as I know, that it was almost a relief for their mother to have them taken away, as her husband was violent to her and a drunkard."

"We used to get a lot of poor mites that had been half-starved, never mind thrashed, but you know . . ." Brenda hesitated.

"Go on, please."

"I always looked on my charges like a garden. It may sound silly, but you can take a run-down, bedraggled garden, and with tender loving care, you can make everything come alive. Now, sometimes, no matter how hard you work, the weeds take over and strangle the nice orderly flower beds. Or you can get a bed of nettles spring up, and they're the worst—they're always hard to keep from growing back. We had some, and no matter what we did, we couldn't stop them stinging and doing the worst damage. I believe the worst kind is when a child has never known affection, has been ignored and never touched or kissed or cuddled. They were the hardest to deal with, because they couldn't trust being loved."

"It must have been difficult."

"It was, but the rewards always made everything worthwhile. I had a little tigress once, she'd bite and kick and was very destructive, and I was run ragged by her, as she also made the other children unsettled. Just when I was wondering if I'd taken on too much, she came into the kitchen. I knew she was behind me, and I was wondering if she was going to sidle up and kick me on the ankles, but she wound her skinny little arms around me and asked if she could call me Mummy."

Roy appeared in the doorway, looking grubby but minus his Wellington boots. "Oh, she's not going on about her garden theory, is she?"

Brenda laughed and offered him a cup of tea. "He's a one to talk. He first started saying that I was out of my mind taking on one, never mind a whole houseful of them, but it was him that went and bought a caravan so we could take the kids to the seaside."

Roy sat down with his tea as Brenda opened a drawer, taking out one of her photo albums.

"Not the albums, Brenda love, she's been shown them."

"I wanted her to see the ones with you on the beach, Roy, with all the children by the caravan."

Anna crossed to her, smiling and saying, "I want to see the photographs, I really do."

"I'm going to have a bath and leave you both to it."

Roy walked out and Brenda sat down, searching through the album, but suddenly gasped, "I've got to put the leg of lamb in the oven! Here, dear, you look through them."

Brenda carried out the tea tray, and Anna sat on the sofa with the albums. There were lots of holiday snaps, with caravan, without caravan, and with various children on a donkey ride. They seemed to be all ages, and what was touching about them all was the joy on their faces. Anna went to replace the album, and stacked in the drawer in no particular order were loose family photographs. She couldn't resist looking through them, seeing Ken at different ages with his parents and Lizzie, and with a good-looking younger boy whom she presumed was his brother, Robin. He was, as she'd been told, handsome and darker-haired, like his mother, with a fine chiseled face and dark brooding eyes unlike either parents'.

She was about to replace them when she saw a picture of Ken with his arm resting around the shoulders of a tall man of a similar age. They were smiling into the camera. Ken was wearing a tracksuit, while the other man wore what appeared to be some kind of uniform; dark trousers and a jacket with something on the lapels. He was also holding the leash of a full-grown German shepherd.

Anna felt chilled, recalling Pete's words when he phoned her from the forensic lab to discuss the blue blanket found wrapped around Dorota Pelagia. It had dog hairs over it, and he said he thought they were possibly from a German shepherd. She wanted to shove the photograph back into the drawer and forget she'd seen it. Was it a coincidence? Then Langton's mantra entered her mind—*there are no coincidences*—and she jumped when Mrs. Hudson walked into the room.

"I'm sorry, did I startle you, dear? I've put it on low heat to cook it really slowly."

Anna licked her lips, which felt dry. "Brenda, who is this in the photograph with Ken?" She passed it over.

Brenda sighed heavily. "Ah, it was terrible. I don't think Ken ever got over it. That other lad is Jack, and the dog was called Rex: he worshipped it. Jack was a dog handler at the prisons, and it was through him that Ken became interested in doing the same work—you know, before he goes back to studying again. Has he told you he wants to qualify to work with special needs teenagers?"

"Yes, yes, he did mention it. What happened?"

Brenda still held the photo in her hand as she sat on the sofa. "Rex was Jack's guard dog; Jack had had him since he was a puppy—you know, they take them home to get them familiar with their trainer or handler, I think they call them, and I've never come across an animal that was not only so obedient but so clever. He'd dribble a football around, and his eyes used to follow Jack, because he doted on him. I know he could be ferocious, that's what he was trained for—Jack only had to click his fingers for that dog to sense what he wanted him to do."

"What happened? You said Ken found it hard to get over something?"

Brenda sighed again. "Jack used to have a van with a dog cage in the back, but Rex was never locked in, since he was so well behaved. Maybe we'll never know how it happened, but they were on the M6 when a ten-ton lorry jackknifed across the central divide. There was a head-on collision. Rex had somehow sensed it, because he'd moved from the cage to shield Jack, and he took the full impact."

"Did Jack survive?"

"Yes, although he had terrible injuries and was in the hospital for months."

"When did it happen?"

"Four or more years ago. We had this photograph in a frame on the mantelpiece, but Ken told me to put it away because he couldn't stand to look at it."

Roy came in at that point and asked if Anna would like a sherry. She said that she'd maybe have one later, but if they didn't mind, she'd like to change for dinner. When she'd left the room, Brenda held up the photograph to re-place it in the drawer.

"She found this picture of poor Jack and his dog."

"Sad business. Do you want a sherry?"

"No, love. I'll get the vegetables prepared, and then I might go up and have a little rest."

"I'll set the table, shall I?"

"Already done. You sit and watch some TV."

Anna's overnight bag had been placed in the same room she had slept in before. She lay down and closed her eyes, chastising herself. Just as she had suspicious about finding the blue blanket at Ken's flat, she now felt the same way about the photograph. It was horrible that her work could encroach on her like this. One moment she was utterly relaxed and happy, and the next, she had turned back into Detective Inspector Travis. Deeply troubled, she fell asleep and woke only as Brenda gently shook her a few hours later. Anna sat up and immediately apologized.

"Don't worry, love. I've had a little sleep as well, but Ken's just called, and he's on his way here."

"What time is it?"

"Nine-thirty, and you must be hungry. We usually eat a lot earlier, and Roy's hovering around the kitchen like a starving man."

"I'll be right down."

Anna swiftly washed her face and put some fresh makeup on. Downstairs, the table was set, and there were her flowers in the center and champagne glasses with a bottle of Moët in an ice bucket with a big pink bow. Anna noticed a number of happy-anniversary cards on a side table as she heard the rumble of Ken's motorbike.

She hurried into the hall as he walked in, opening his arms and swinging her up to kiss her.

"You two come and sit down," Brenda called out fussily. "Your dad's ready to carve."

"Give me two minutes to wash up, Mum. Start serving, I won't be a tick."

Ken had taken a quick shower and changed from his work clothes into a white T-shirt and jeans. Anna noticed that he broke his usual teetotal habits to take a glass of champagne to toast his parents, and it was sweet the way his father had a few glasses too many, as did Brenda. Yet again it felt like she was truly welcome, and Brenda had cooked up a storm serving roast lamb, roast potatoes with gravy, carrots, and green beans. She was rosy-cheeked and giggly as she brought in the anniversary cake, making sure everyone knew that Anna had made the iced roses. Ken gave a funny formal speech, praising his parents' longevity and happy marriage, hoping that he'd be lucky enough to find someone like Brenda one day. He kissed his mother and gave his father a hug and said that as it was a special night, he would do the washing up.

"I'll be your assistant," Anna said, piling up the dishes, and together they insisted that Brenda and Roy go and put their feet up.

Ken was fast at stacking the dishwasher, while Anna washed the fragile champagne glasses by hand. He washed the pans and the meat dish beside her and then left them to dry. After that, he did a quick wipe around all of the surfaces before tossing the cloth into the sink and saying they could call it quits.

"Your mum has put my overnight bag into the room I used last time I stayed."

He grinned. "She's very diplomatic, but you are sleeping with me, and it's a quick good-night to those two, who'll stay up for hours watching old movies, and then . . ." He took her in his arms, kissing her passionately. "Has it been a tedious day for you?" he asked, letting her go.

"Far from it. I love being with your parents, and I also had a good sleep this afternoon."

"All right for some. It's been a real shit of a day for me, but I don't want to talk about it, I just want you beside me."

Ken's room was not what she had expected. There was a rowing machine and a set of weights, but little else of a personal nature.

"When I went off to university, they redecorated, and there were foster kids using it; when they all moved out, I sort of moved back in, but I just keep some clothes and books here. I don't want them to think I'm moving back on a permanent basis. Lizzie and the kids use this room as well when they stay. So don't think I'm a cross-dresser when you find frocks in the wardrobe."

"You also keep your flat pretty unlived in."

"Ah, you noticed. Reason is, I am saving, because when I move to London to work at this special unit, I want to buy a place of my own. Until then I live like a monk." He laughed. "Well, that's not quite true. Mum still insists on doing my washing and ironing—I think it makes her feel needed."

"I've heard some excuses in my time . . ."

He grinned and was about to take her in his arms when she asked about Jack. He moved away from her.

"I found his photograph," she said, "the two of you together with his German shepherd."

"Did Mum give it to you?"

"No. I was putting away a photo album, and it was in the drawer. I did ask her about it, though."

"Jack was the best friend I ever had. He worked at the prison. You know about the crash?"

"Yes."

"If it hadn't been for Rex, he'd have taken the full impact. Somehow Rex got out of the cage to shield him. Bloody juggernaut jackknifed across the motorway. When they found him, the dog was crushed against the steering wheel, and Jack had been pushed sideways, head cracked open on the passenger-side window."

"But he survived?"

"Yeah. He was concussed for over a week. When he came round, he kept on asking about Rex—my God, he loved that dog. None of us could fathom exactly how it had happened, but it looked as if he had a sixth sense and hurled himself at Jack to protect him. They had to bloody peel his body off him . . ."

Ken turned away, and she put out her hand to comfort him, saying, "But he saved him."

"Right, but in many ways I wish he hadn't. He still talks about Rex, still sometimes asks about him."

"But it was four years ago."

"Yeah, but Jack doesn't understand, because he's got the mind of a ten-year-old and is now in a home—will be for the rest of his life." Ken lay back on the pillows with tears in his eyes. Anna had never been with a man who showed such open emotion. He was close to crying, and she wished she'd never brought it up.

"Just before the accident, we'd been out to celebrate; he'd gotten this new job in London working for a top security firm. He and his girlfriend were about to move— well, she did move; he'd been worried that he couldn't get permission to take Rex with him. Dog handlers often have to wait for the animals to retire before they can ask to keep them as a pet."

Anna broke down in tears, and Ken looked at her, surprised. "What are you crying for?"

"Because of what happened in my head. I couldn't stop it, and now I feel disgusted, ashamed, because of what I thought."

"And what did you think?"

Anna sniffed and then reached for a tissue from the bedside table. She explained to Ken about the coincidence, the blue blanket and the dog hairs, but before she could finish, he had thrown the duvet aside and gotten up.

"Wait, just let me get this straight—because of evidence, forensic or whatever it was—you made a connection between me, the friggin' dog, and a murder victim. Is that right? Am I right?"

"It just happened; I couldn't help it."

"You couldn't help it?"

"I'm sorry."

He stood at the end of the bed wearing just his boxer shorts and staring at her in disbelief. He then leaned forward, dragging the duvet away from her. She was naked.

"Go into the other bedroom," he hissed. "I don't want you here with me. Go on—get out. Get out!"

"No, I won't."

He reached forward and gripped her arm so tightly it hurt, but no matter how much she struggled, she couldn't release herself. He dragged her to the door.

"Don't do this, please, Ken."

He pushed her away from him and picked up her nightdress.

"Put this on and get out."

"No, I won't."

He glared at her as she pulled on her nightdress. "Okay, stay and do what you like, but I'm out of here."

He picked up his jeans from the floor and started to get dressed. She went to him, wanting to put her arms around him, but he wouldn't let her near him. She sat on the bed as he dragged on his T-shirt, zipping up the fly on his jeans.

"You know, I really believed that we had something special, and you come here, sit with my parents—for what? Because you think that I have some connection with this sick case you are fucking working on."

"It isn't like that."

"It isn't?"

"No, but I can't help that it's always in the back of my mind and—"

"You keep me out of your mind from now on."

It was awful. He grabbed his bike boots and walked out, slamming the door. She ran after him, and Brenda came out onto the landing.

"What's happened?"

Ken was by the front door with his leather jacket and bike helmet. "Go back to bed, Mum. It's nothing. I have to leave."

"Please don't go," Anna said, heading after him down the stairs, but he'd already opened the door. She held on to it, still trying to persuade him not to leave, but he roughly pushed her away and slammed the door shut.

Brenda came out of her room again as Anna began sobbing. Brenda knew her son had gone because she couldn't help but hear his bike start up and roar off.

"Whatever's happened between you?" She was midway down the stairs.

"Please just leave me alone—it was all my fault."

Roy appeared above them on the landing. Brenda looked up and told him that Ken had left.

"I know that, I could hear his bike. What's been going on?"

Anna sat on the stairs, sobbing. Neither Brenda nor Roy seemed to know what to do, and then they looked shocked as Anna sprang to her feet.

"I'm going after him."

"Don't you think you should calm down, love?" Roy said.

Anna ran past them to her room, not wanting to talk, just desperate to leave and follow Ken. They were still on the landing, full of concern, when she came out.

"It was all my fault, but it'll be all right."

Roy was moved. "You're very upset. I don't think you should drive."

"I'll be all right, really, and I'm sorry this had to happen. He's gone without his uniform, and I have to see him."

Brenda walked back down the stairs with her. "Don't worry about his uniform. He's got a spare in his flat—but I'm worried about you."

Anna put her arms around Brenda and hugged her tightly. "I'm sorry, I'm so sorry. I'll write to you."

They both watched her drive off too fast, and Roy closed the front door.

"What on earth do you think sparked that off?" he asked as he put his arm around his wife.

"I don't know. They seemed so happy together, but you know Ken. How many girls has he split up from? He never seems able to keep one for more than a few months."

"I thought this one was different, but then what do we know?"

Anna parked beside Ken's motorbike. She'd driven erratically, veering between crying and angrily shouting at herself, but she managed to calm down enough to keep within the speed limit. All she cared about was making up with him.

She hurried into the block of flats and ran up the stairs. She took a deep breath and rang the doorbell. She kept on ringing it, but he didn't open the door. Next she banged on the door with the flat of her hand.

"I know you are in there, Ken, and I am not leaving until you talk to me. KEN, OPEN THE DOOR!"

But he didn't. So she kept her hand on the doorbell for what seemed like an age before slumping down in the doorway. Next she took out her mobile phone and rang his, but he didn't pick up. She kept on calling him until it was switched off. She got up again and hit the door, then kicked it.

"Open the door, Ken."

A neighbor looked out. He saw her standing there and asked if she was all right. She apologized and said she was just waiting for Ken to let her in.

"I hope he does soon, darlin', as you're waking up the whole block."

She went back and sat on the stairs, beginning to think that he was not going to give in. She still had her mobile phone in her hand, and after a while she texted a message to Mike Lewis. She was so tense and angry that it took some time. It was even hard to believe it herself as she left the text that the team should check into prison officers and security guards who were dog handlers, and to go as far back as when Cameron Welsh was under arrest and on trial.

That done, she sat huddled on the stairs, and when she put her phone away, there by Ken's photo was the envelope with her photograph that she'd forgotten to send to him. She had to have been sitting there for fifteen minutes before Ken finally opened his front door. She looked up at him.

"You don't give up easily, do you?" he said.

"I won't go away until we've talked. Please let me come in."

He stepped back into the flat, and she picked up her bag and followed him. He was sitting on the end of his bed, still in his jeans but barefoot. She felt like a schoolgirl, standing in the open doorway. She passed him the envelope. "I meant to post this to you."

He didn't take it, so she threw it on the bed. He opened it and looked at the picture of her turning somersaults.

"Very nice," he said, tossing it aside.

She didn't know where to begin, and he didn't make it easy, looking at his watch. "I have to be on duty tomorrow, so why don't you say what you have to say so I can get some sleep."

"I don't know where to begin."

"Try starting with what it feels like to think you know a woman, trust her, fall in love with her, and then find out she thinks you're a murder suspect. You've brought her into your family, and all the time she was fucking checking out if . . ." He shook his head. "How could you be with me and even contemplate that I could not only be lying to you, but using you because I was some warped killer."

"I didn't think that."

"Of course you bloody did. Why don't you admit it? To be so two-faced beggars belief."

"I'm not two-faced."

"Christ, you even admitted what you thought when you found the blue blanket—and what's this about dog hairs? My best mate's never going to have a life—what's with you suspecting even him?"

Anna stood in front of him, crying. She knew what he was saying was partly true, and she didn't know how she could rectify the damage to their relationship.

"I'll go because I don't see how I can make it up to you. All I can say is that . . ."

"Say what? Always on duty, are you?"

"Yes, if you must know. Yes, I am, or I used to be, but not with you."

He laughed, but it wasn't humorous, it was cold laughter, and his eyes were still intensely angry.

"Can I make a cup of coffee?" Anna asked.

"No, you can just leave me alone and go back to London. I mean it, Anna. I can't deal with this."

She went into his kitchen. She was shaking, and even though she didn't want a coffee, she made one. She walked back to the bedroom; Ken was now in bed, leaving only a small bedside lamp on.

"Do you want one?" she asked.

He sighed and shook his head. She moved slowly into the room and then sat on the edge of the bed. She was hesitant at first, beginning to explain about her visits to Cameron Welsh, the ongoing interrogation of their only suspect, John Smiley, how they were attempting to build a case against him but how it continued to fall apart no matter what new developments implicated him.

"I was told that the blanket found wrapped around Dorota Pelagia had German shepherd hairs, and we are certain it was one of the blankets issued to prisons."

He lay with his eyes closed.

"Are you listening to me? Look, what happens is the trail of clues sort of fire up inside your brain. We've thought that our killer might even be a police officer or someone that the victims were able to immediately trust. Something clicked inside my head when I saw your friend in his security uniform and with the same type of dog that would leave hairs on the blue blankets. For a second I was suspicious, or what it was more like was piecing together a jigsaw. Cameron Welsh has maintained that there was a witness, and he may have been right. He's constantly mentioned that he knows more, that he seeks out small clues he wants us to follow. We'd reached a conclusion that he was lying, that he didn't have anything more to tell us, but what if he knew all along about someone—possibly a security guard? It would make sense, and that's what he has been holding back."

Ken remained with his eyes closed.

"I hated having to sit with him. He was constantly giving me these sexual gloating looks. He repels me, but I had to meet with him because my boss insisted. After the last visit, I was certain that it had all been a ploy to get me there, that he was enjoying himself, that he might even have had some fantasy about me, but I only agreed to meet with him again because it meant that I could spend time with you."

Still no reaction.

"For the first time in my life, I want to be with someone more than I want my career. Previously, I would be the first person to forgo leave, but I've taken more time off than I have on any other case because I wanted to be with you, and if you asked me, I would walk away from the entire career that to date has been the most important thing in my life."

He said nothing. There was a long pause, and she stood up. "I'll go now."

He flipped open the duvet, inviting her in, and she crawled in beside him fully clothed. He lifted his arm for her to snuggle closer, holding her tightly.

"I don't want you to go," he said softly.

She remained beside him in her clothes all night. They fell asleep, exhausted. She was woken by him gently touching her face; he was already dressed for work.

"I have to go, but I can be back early afternoon. Can you wait for me?"

"You'll never get rid of me."

He straightened and headed for the door, then turned back. "You know, maybe I was so mad because I'd had a really bad day. Cameron Welsh is making life difficult at the unit. We had an unpleasant fight between inmates, and he was the one that sparked it off; we've even had him sedated, but he's getting worse by the day. I think you were right—I think he does have this fantasy about you, and whether or not it's my intuition or his, I think he knows about us."

"How?"

"No idea, but he's made a few snide remarks. I ignore them. If you think he does have more information, I doubt you'll get any sense out of him."

She sat up. "What did he say about us?"

"He never says anything directly; it's mumbled when he passes me. He said something about redheads being the devil. Another time he said I'd pay for betraying him, just crazy stuff. But we've had to make him give up a lot of his privileges, so that enrages him, and like I told you, he's refusing to wash and eat."

"Will he be transferred?"

"I've suggested it. If he acts any crazier, he should be shipped out to Broadmoor. So that's why I flew off the handle so easily."

"You should have told me."

"It wasn't the right time. And then, well, you know what happened next."

Anna jumped on top of the bed and held out her arms. He moved away. "There was something else I intended to do and . . . I don't know if this is the right time even now." He went to the dresser and opened a drawer. He took out a small box and then returned to the bed. "It's secondhand—Victorian, I don't know if you'll like it—and maybe you will want to spend time thinking about it. You don't have to give me an answer straightaway."

She could feel her heart thudding. He moved closer and opened the box. It was a ring, a thin gold shaft with flat rose diamonds and pearls.

"Is it what I think it is?" She had to catch her breath.

"Like I said, you don't have to make any decision now. It might not even fit."

"Is it an engagement ring?" She could hardly get the words out.

"Yes."

She hurled herself at him, almost making him drop it, hugging him and kissing his face.

"Do you want to try it on?"

She held out her left hand, and he took the ring from the box and slipped it onto her ring finger. It was not a perfect fit, but she didn't care; she felt as if she would explode with happiness.

"Do you want me to ask you properly?"

"Yes."

He flushed and licked his lips.

"Okay . . . Will you marry me, Anna Travis?"

"YES, YES, YES, YES, YES!"

After Ken had left for work, Anna took a long bath, constantly holding up her hand to look at the ring. She found some Bandaids in the bathroom cabinet and wrapped one around her finger so the gold shaft would fit tightly. She then did something that she had never done before; she put a call in to the incident room, but it was still early, and Mike wasn't available. Barolli, Joan, and Barbara were also not at work, so she left a message with the duty sergeant that she would be unable to be present today. She was going to say she had food poisoning or the flu, but instead said it was a personal matter and she would make contact later in the morning.

• • •

She was dressed and sipping a mug of coffee when her mobile rang. It was Barbara.

"Hi. Good morning to you," Anna said.

"You sound perky. We thought you were sick or something," Barbara said.

"Just feeling a bit under the weather. I'll be back in the morning."

"Well, it's all right for some. We're in the incident room. Mike asked me to contact you, as we're a bit nonplused about your late-night text message."

Anna straightened out fast and agreed to speak to him. She explained what her message was about, that it was a possibility their killer could have been a security guard, a dog handler, maybe. This would explain the dog hairs found on the blue blanket.

"I'm not quite following why or how you've come to this conclusion," Mike said.

"Cameron Welsh has maintained that he had information, and he's led us along by the nose, but at one stage he suggested that our killer could be a police officer. I think he said someone of authority who would look completely trustworthy. We went down the police officers' route but got nothing. What if the killer is a security guard? They have spare uniforms, they even pay for them, so even if our man was no longer working for a security company, he could have retained a uniform. Also, dog handlers have a van . . ."

"You think he works in Barfield Prison?"

"No, he'd be in London, maybe transporting prisoners to and from court. I know it's a long shot, but it's something we should look into. Go back five years to Cameron Welsh's arrest and trial and see if we can get a result."

Mike said he would look into it, but he didn't sound that interested, possibly because it would be yet another long round of tedious clerical work. Anna asked if they had had any new developments, and he rather curtly said it had been only twenty-four hours.

"What about Smiley's bank accounts?"

"Being checked out. If it's not a rude question, where the hell are you?"

"Just with relatives. Something's cropped up, but I'll be back as soon as possible. Did you get my messages to trace Margaret Potts's foster parents?"

"In the pipeline."

"If we do get a contact, I'd very much like to take the interview."

"Right, I'll make a note of it. Is everything all right with you?"

"Fine. Like I said, it's a personal matter, but I'll be there first thing in the morning."

Mike hung up before saying anything else. Anna felt a bit guilty but then shrugged it off. She'd never taken a day off before, and she knew she must have a number of days, if not weeks, due to her.

After the call, she decided to go out and do a grocery shop to cook a meal for when Ken returned home, since he'd given her his front-door key. As she left, she saw his neighbor and smiled, apologizing again for making such a disturbance. She couldn't take the smile off her face, and as she walked to her Mini, she had a real desire to do a cart-wheel like the one in the photograph. She also had a real urge to call someone to announce that she was engaged, and it saddened her that there wasn't anyone close who would want to know. But she couldn't feel down for long, constantly looking at the ring on her finger as she drove to the shops. She was not alone anymore, and just thinking about what the future held made her beam with joy.

She was happier than she had ever known it was possible to be.

"Security guard?" queried Barolli as Mike Lewis wrote Anna's message on the incident board. "Where is she going with this? Do we move off John Smiley?"

"I dunno, but there's not a lot we can do until tomorrow."

"They have a van to move the dogs around in, don't they?"

"Yep."

"So the blue blanket could have been in the back of the van for the guard dog?"

"Yep."

"I suppose their uniforms are sort of similar to coppers' . . . it'd be a way of getting the victims to trust him."

"We'll get moving on it first thing tomorrow, but we should maybe arrange another visit to Cameron Welsh. I'll run it by the gov—see what he thinks."

"Just thinking—Travis never stops, does she?" Barolli said.

Mike tossed the felt-tip marker aside.

"How come she didn't work this weekend, and now she's taken today off?" Barolli nagged. "That's not like her."

Mike sighed. "I don't know. She said it was a personal matter. There's not a lot for her to do here anyway. Okay get started on the Smiley bank accounts."

Barbara was given the job of tracing Margaret Potts's children's foster parents, and it took almost all morning, as she was transferred to one department after another at Camden Council. She was told that details could not be disclosed unless someone from the station contacted them directly and explained in detail the reason for wanting to talk to them.

Barbara was almost pulling out her hair. Mike said that she should pay them a visit in person and tell them it was a murder inquiry.

Barolli, having been assigned to get the details of John Smiley's bank accounts, had to contact Arnold Rodgers yet again. The police needed to find out how Smiley's wages were paid and then get a court order for the bank to release the information they wanted.

As Barbara prepared to leave, she moaned, "It's all the way over to bloody Camden! What's up with Travis today? Why isn't *she* in?"

"I dunno. Mike said it was something personal, but she's been texting us all like a ferret."

Anna's prior commitment was a candlelit dinner. She'd cooked fresh pasta with homemade Bolognese sauce, and there were fresh strawberries with cream for dessert. Ken had looked tired out when he got in from work, but after his usual shower and change of clothes, he started to relax.

"Okay, rule one," he said. "Neither one of us is allowed to discuss work."

He sat down at the table as Anna served. It was not exactly the most romantic setting, but they could have been on a moonlit beach in the Caribbean, as they were so in tune with each other. They didn't discuss how soon they would get married, but when Anna told him about Lizzie asking if she would like to have children, he growled.

"I don't believe she asked you that!"

"Well, she did."

"Cheeky cow. And God help me when I tell my mother—she's been waiting for me to get married. Don't say *she* asked you about children as well."

"No, she didn't, just your sister, and I will have to phone your mother and tell her we've made up, because she was concerned when we had that row. I hope it hasn't put her off me."

"So what did you reply?"

"To what?"

"Kids or not?"

Anna was teasing him as she told him how Lizzie had said that he would make a wonderful dad, and he covered his head with his napkin. "My family! Aargh!"

"So do you want to know what I said?"

He pulled off the napkin and looked at her.

"I do want children, Ken, and you *will* make a fabulous dad."

He reached for her hand, kissing it, then blew out the candles. "Then we'd better get hitched as soon as possible. In the meantime, we should put some practice in."

Ken scooped her into his arms and carried her into the bedroom, kicking the door shut with his foot. The washing-up could wait.

Chapter Fourteen

Anna drove into the station car park at eight-thirty. She'd had to leave Ken's flat at such an early hour that she'd had little or no sleep. Hurrying into the incident room, she booked on duty and, from Barbara, got the address of the Potts children's foster parents. They were across London, in Brixton, so to make the appointment, she left virtually straightaway.

Joan passed her on the way out. She stared after Anna as she got a bright "Good morning."

Joan dumped her briefcase on her desk. She said she'd just seen Travis hurtling out of the station like a teenager.

Barbara sidled up to her.

"What?" Joan asked.

"She's engaged—got a ring on her wedding finger. I couldn't help but notice it. She waved it in front of me enough times."

"Engaged?"

"I presume so. She didn't actually say she was, but—"

Joan interrupted her. "Who to? I've never seen her with anyone. You must have gotten it wrong."

Barolli walked in. "Gotten what wrong?"

Barbara began to sort out the work on her desk. "Barbara says Travis is engaged."

"She's having you on. Is she here yet?"

Joan giggled. "Been and gone." She switched on her computer and told Barbara she shouldn't spread gossip.

Barbara returned to her desk, retorting, "Wait until you see it. Looked like a row of nice diamonds."

Anna parked on a pleasant tree-lined street; the semi-detached houses had seen better days, but they were reasonably well kept, apart from a couple that looked as if they were divided into numerous flats. She rang the doorbell of number eleven and waited.

"Good morning. Are you Mrs. Walters?" Anna asked.

"Yes."

Anna showed her ID and introduced herself. Mrs. Walters stepped back, and Anna followed her along a dingy hallway into a large sitting room. It was not well furnished, and it had worn carpets and old velvet curtains.

"Should I have my husband present?"

"No, I don't think that will be necessary. I have a few questions and want to make it clear to you that they are connected to an ongoing investigation into the children's late mother, Margaret Potts. I am not from any Social Services or foster-care agency."

When Mrs. Walters sat down, Anna realized that she was younger than she looked, though devoid of any makeup, and her hair was pinned back unflatteringly.

"Do you want a cup of tea or anything?"

"No, thanks. I don't want to take up too much of your time. I really appreciate you seeing me."

"I did have concerns. I mean, I don't know what it's about. I've no problems with the children. They're both at school."

"I am sure you are taking great care of them."

"To the best of my ability, I am. They're good kids—well behaved and getting on better at their school."

"Did you ever meet their mother, Margaret Potts?"

"Mother?" Mrs. Walters gave a derisive look at the ceiling. "Hard to describe her as one, and their father's even worse. I know he's out of prison, but there's not been a single Christmas card or birthday card. How do you explain to them that he probably doesn't give them a thought?"

"Did Margaret?"

"At first she would stand outside and not come in, just stand there looking up at their bedroom window. It's at the front. I think once or twice they saw her, but that always caused trouble, because they'd want to talk to her but were scared they'd have to go back to that wretch of a father. It's hard because we can never say anything bad about the parents, so we make up excuses—you know, they do love you, et cetera. More important is to make sure they don't think it's *their* fault."

"Did she come and visit them?"

"Not for a long time to begin with, then she arranged to take them out on a Saturday. Three times she promised to come—never turned up once. In the end, I told her that if she couldn't be here when she said she would, then it was better for her not to come at all."

"Did she remember their birthdays?"

"That's the only good thing I can think about her. She did sometimes send presents and cards, but she can't have thought too much about what she chose. Her boy, Eric, is nine now, and into computers; the girl, Margie, is eleven. The things she sent were too babyish for Eric, and it was always dolls for Margie—you know, Barbies and My Little Pony, when she's into pop stars and the like." Mrs. Walters sat straight-backed in the chair opposite Anna.

"I suppose you are aware of what happened to her?" Anna asked gently.

"Yes, of course. I mean, I wouldn't wish that on anyone, it was a terrible thing and in a way sort of worse, because I think she'd been trying to straighten herself out."

"Why do you say that?"

"The last time I heard from her, she rang here and told me that she was going to arrange to take the children to some fun fair, as she was looking for a permanent place to live."

"How long ago was that?"

"Oh, must be nearly three years. I never spoke to her again, and next thing the Social Services came here to tell me she'd been murdered and I had to tell the children. By this time they didn't react all that much, and we never heard from any of their relatives."

"Did Margaret ever send the children money, specifically around the time before she was murdered?"

"Money?"

Anna saw the woman tense up, so she carefully explained that they believed Margaret might have been getting access to reasonable sums of money. "We are still investigating her murder, and this may be a possible link to discovering what happened to her or why she was killed."

Mrs. Walters got up, went over to a dresser, and opened a drawer from which she took out a big envelope. "These are the cards and a couple of letters she sent."

Anna smiled and took the envelope, aware that Mrs. Walters had not answered her question.

"I keep them for when they leave here—you know, so that they have something to remember her by or not. They can do what they like with them, but the Services encourage us to retain anything they get sent."

"May I read them?"

"Yes, please go ahead."

Anna opened birthday cards sent to Eric and Margie over a couple of years. Big scrawled writing was on the envelopes and inside the cards: *To my lovely Margie from her mummy* and *For my big boy Eric, from his loving mummy.* There were only three letters on cheap pink notepaper, and Anna found reading them moving.

> *Dear Eric and Margie,*
>   *I miss you and I think about you every day because I love you with all my heart. Sometimes things happen and I've done what I thought was best for you. I will come and see you regularly and send you presents.*
>   *Love, Mummy*

There were rows of crosses as kisses. The first letter had been written six years ago. The second letter said virtually the same thing and was written six months later. The third letter was dated eighteen months before her death.

> *Dear Eric and Margie,*
>   *I will come and see you soon and we can spend a whole weekend together as things have got better for me.*
>   *I hope you are both working hard at school because it is important you get a good education. I am buying some nice treats for you both.*
>   *Love, Mummy*

Anna looked up as she replaced the letters and cards into the envelope. "She never showed up for the weekend she promised?"

"No, I never heard from her again, apart from that phone call."

"So she never sent any money?"

Mrs. Walters again seemed tense. "If she had, I'd have reported it. We have to, if it's for the children."

"You know, it is important, Mrs. Walters, if you did receive any money from Mrs. Potts."

"If it was a check, we'd report it and arrange an account if that was what was wanted."

"I am referring to any cash sent to you."

Mrs. Walters clasped her hands together.

"I can fully understand," Anna said quietly, "that if you did receive cash, then you naturally would have put it toward things for the children. I am not in any way insinuating that there was any wrongdoing on your part."

Mrs. Walters twisted her wedding ring around and around. Anna went for it. "How much did Margaret Potts send you, Mrs. Walters?"

"She didn't send it."

Anna leaned forward. "I'm sorry?"

"It was in an envelope pushed through the letter box. We—that's my husband and I and the children—had been at a sports day at the school, and when we came back, it was lying on the doormat."

"When was this?"

The woman was really nervous now, constantly licking her lips. "Six months or more before her body was discovered."

"Can you tell me how much it was?"

"I've wondered and worried about this, you know. I

said to my husband we should tell the Services, and then we'd had it over a week and done nothing with it, and it sort of stayed in that drawer. I took a tenner here and there for things, and he needed to pay off his car, and then the washing machine broke down, so we bought a new one. It wasn't as if we spent it on ourselves. We take them out on trips in the car, and I need a washing machine."

"Just tell me how much, Mrs. Walters, that's all I want to know."

"Over a thousand pounds."

"In used or new notes?"

"Old ones: ten and twenties."

Anna returned to the station, knowing that Margaret Potts had not only left money in her suitcase but had also given Mrs. Walters a large amount. Anna sat at her desk and calculated the timing between the two amounts of cash. It was possible there was even more money, as Emerald Turk could have lied about how much was in Margaret's suitcase. Mrs. Walters also could have lied about the amount. Adding this to the new clothes, new shoes, and so on, Anna was certain that their victim was in possession of more money than she was earning as a prostitute. She crossed to the board and jotted down her new information.

Barbara glanced at Joan and then craned her neck to have a look at Anna's left hand. She turned away quickly when Anna came over.

"Have we had access to John Smiley's bank accounts yet?" Anna asked.

"Due in this afternoon," Barbara said, able to see clearly the ring on Anna's finger. "That's lovely," she said, nodding toward it.

"Thank you."

"Diamonds, are they?"

"Yes, Barbara, and seed pearls. It's Victorian." Anna couldn't stop herself. "It's an engagement ring," she blurted out.

Barbara looked again at Joan. "Oh, your mother's, is it?"

Anna giggled and shook her head. "No, it's mine, Barbara. I'm engaged."

"To be married?"

"That is the usual reason for wearing an engagement ring, isn't it?"

"Well, congratulations! Aren't you the quiet one? So who's the lucky fiancé?"

"You don't know him."

"Happened on the weekend, then, did it?" Joan asked, looking over.

They were blatantly nosy, but Anna couldn't take offense. "Yes, it happened on the weekend."

The news went round the incident room like a forest fire. Barolli was told by Joan, he told Mike Lewis, and the rest of the team was told by Barbara. DI Anna Travis was engaged to be married!

Anna secretly enjoyed the furtive attention, she knew they would be drawing up bets to try and find out whom she was engaged to. It wouldn't be a secret for too long.

The excitement over the engagement abated only when Mike Lewis received the details of John Smiley's bank accounts. They were impressed by his wages, as they were considerably higher than many of the team members were earning; forty-five thousand pounds a year. The money was paid directly into his account. Smiley had numerous direct debits for things like gas and electricity; his mortgage was also paid directly. He had withdrawals of eight hundred pounds every month paid into an account in the name of his wife, Sonja Smiley. They presumed this was for house-keeping. He didn't appear to make cash withdrawals on a regular basis; maybe his wife paid him out of the house-keeping. He had three cards, one of which was in the name of Swell Blinds and was used only for diesel. Another was for his NatWest cashpoint, and a third was a department store credit card.

"Bloody well organized, isn't he?" Mike said, looking at the columns of figures.

In a high-interest savings account, Smiley had twelve thousand pounds. He had a pension arranged with Swell Blinds' employees, and basically, that was it.

Anna leaned over Mike's shoulder. "So the only lump sums of cash that go out are paid directly into his wife's account. If she is handing out pocket money, they live a frugal life. What about an expense account for Swell Blinds, anything on that?"

"We haven't seen that come in. I can get on it."

"We also need to go back further. These are all this year's, right? But if he was being blackmailed by Margaret Potts, it wouldn't be recent; she's been dead two years. Take it back to three years ago."

Anna repeated to Mike the amount of money they knew their victim had in cash shortly before she died.

"You see, the money in the suitcase was left at Emerald Turk's, along with a bunch of new clothes, so she would have to be blackmailing Smiley after the blinds were put up in her flat, right?"

"Yeah, yeah."

"The money from Mrs. Walters was about six months before she was murdered."

Mike was scrolling through the bank statements with Anna standing beside him.

"With him being such a model husband and not shelling out even for holidays, as far as I can see, it's going to be easy to see if he starts making cash withdrawals to pay her off." Anna drew up a chair. "Although if the money was in tens and twenties, used notes, it doesn't quite gel if he wasn't withdrawing large sums to pay her off, does it? At the same time, Margaret would have been paid in used notes by her punters."

"If she charged ten or twenty quid for a blow job, that's a hell of a lot of johns for that amount of money. She's not likely to have saved it all up, is she?"

"We don't know. She could have, and this is all a waste of time," Anna said, glancing at her ring. She would have to get it made to size, as the bandage was sticky.

"So who's the lucky bloke?" Mike asked, staring at the screen.

"You don't know him."

"So he's not one of us, then?"

"No, he's not."

"That was what the family commitment was on the weekend?"

She grinned. They were all the same, so nosy. She got up and stretched and then turned back to Mike. "What if John Smiley was also doing a bit of moonlighting? We are pretty certain he got paid by Emerald Turk to put up a blind in her flat: what if this was a regular thing? He could be making cash in hand that way."

"He could, but right now he denied ever being at Emerald Turk's." Mike was still scrolling through sheets of bank statements.

"Who've you got tracing dog handlers connected to Cameron Welsh?" Anna asked.

"Barolli. You think it's worth another visit to Barfield?"

"Welsh has gone a bit gaga, acting up badly; they've had to sedate him."

"Checking up on him, were you?" Mike asked.

"Yes. Listen, this doesn't take two of us. I'll go and get some coffee."

Mike nodded and then asked her to go back to the two previous employees from Swell Blinds to see if there was any moonlighting going on. He also wanted to get the expenses paid out to Smiley. But somehow he was doubtful they would find that Smiley had withdrawn money for blackmail payouts.

"Thanks for this," Barolli said sarcastically to Anna as she returned to her desk with her coffee. He held up his phone. "I've been hanging on for up to fifteen minutes. I keep getting cut off. I've been put through to so many different departments . . ." He returned to his caller. Despite all the effort, he had not been able to make any connection between security guards and Cameron Welsh. To go back so many years, when a number of the companies had folded, and having to battle with the red tape attached to the security protocol was frustrating and time-consuming. Obtaining the details of Cameron Welsh's escorts to and from the court at his trial was almost impossible.

"Cameron Welsh. Five years ago, he was on trial for murder and held at Brixton Prison . . . No, dog handlers—we need the names of the security guards that . . . No, only Cameron Welsh." He sighed.

Barbara received an abrupt call from Arnold Rodgers with regard to her request for John Smiley's expenses. She was told that there was no specific account; the employees brought in receipts for meals and any extra expenditures. John Smiley had never abused this system.

There was also little useful feedback from the two

ex-workers of Swell Blinds. Apparently, Mr. Rodgers was strict about any kind of cash deals, as most of the blinds were made to order, so there was not much left in the warehouse to be sold off at a cut price.

Anna sighed. Flicking through her notebook, she found her notes on the last interview with Smiley. Contrary to what the two men claimed, he had said there were often windows wrongly measured for blinds, which, when they were delivered, proved unusable. Smiley had suggested to Anna and Langton that it could have been any number of men employed by Swell Blinds who went to Emerald Turk's flat.

Anna sat tapping her teeth with her pen. If they found no cash taken out from Smiley's bank account around the time he might have paid off Margaret Potts, then he must have gotten it somewhere else.

She tossed the pen back on her desk. She was beginning to feel as frustrated as Barolli, who was having a lengthy conversation with a security company. She leaned back and closed her eyes. Was it possible they were wrong and had been for weeks and that John Smiley was innocent? She was sick to death of hearing about Swell Blinds. She then smiled. When she married Ken, there would not be a blind in a single solitary window.

"Paul," she called over to Barolli.

He was replacing the phone.

"The blinds we took from Emerald Turk's flat—are they over at forensics?"

"Yeah, they're checking out the cords, and like everything else, it's a bloody—" His phone rang, and he snatched it up. Anna yawned and then put in a call to Pete Jenkins.

"You calling to arrange dinner?" he joked.

"Nope, this is a really long shot. You know the pelmet that's fixed to the top of the slatted blinds?"

"Yeah, we've got that in here as well."

"I know they were up for a few years, but can you do me a favor and dust for prints? They're fiddly to hang, aren't they?"

"I wouldn't know, but I wasn't asked to dust for prints, just check out the cord."

"Yes, I know, but can you do me a favor?"

"Okay, done and dusted, ha ha. Now what about that meal?"

Anna couldn't help smiling as she told him that she was engaged and maybe one night she'd bring her fiancé for dinner.

"That's a kick in the teeth. Never mind, I did but try."

Barolli was on yet another lengthy call, so Anna went over to Barbara.

"You know that little woman, ex-receptionist for Swell Blinds . . ."

"Wendy Dunn?"

"Yes. Can you put in a call and ask her what happened to those blinds that came back from a customer because they didn't fit?"

"What? That's it?"

"Yep. Ask how many there were, and see if any of the workers used them to do a bit of moonlighting."

"She's on my way home, so as usual, I can call in and have a chat with her."

It was yet another day with no result. In the past, Anna would have stayed on, determined to uncover something, but tonight she couldn't wait to get home. She stopped off at a newsagent and bought *Brides, Tatler*, and *Vogue* to look for ideas for her wedding dress. She wanted a full white gown and all the trimmings, and she had saved enough to also have an expensive but not too large reception. With no father to give her away, she wondered if it would be acceptable to ask Roy Hudson.

She sat in bed munching Ryvita and cheese slices, planning a strict diet. She kept on cutting out articles and putting them to one side. Ken called quite late, as he had only just gotten off duty. He said he had told his parents, and they were over the moon. When she asked if it would be all right for his father to give her away, he said it would make his day.

"I'm not putting too much pressure on you, am I?" she said anxiously. "It's just I suddenly thought I didn't have anyone that I'd really want."

"You know what we should start doing is looking for a place."

"We could always live here at my flat."

"No, I want us to have our own place. Next weekend off, we'll start checking with estate agents and think about which area we'll want to move to. It might depend on where I get work."

Anna said she could put her flat on the market and join her finances with his savings. They needed to be realistic in working out how long it might take for her to sell and how much longer he had to work at the prison before he could find a job in London and apply to start his training. They arrived at a possible wedding date in a year's time.

"Do you want an exotic honeymoon?" Ken asked.

"Yes."

"You know what I've always wanted to do? Hire a gulet in Turkey and sail round the coast. We'd have a crew and chef on board and nobody else. You fancy that?"

Anna did. She wanted whatever made him happy.

"Right—I'll bring brochures with me when I'm next down, and it might be this weekend. Okay?"

"Yes." She snuggled down with her glossy magazine, and when the phone rang again, she thought it was Ken calling back.

"It's me," Langton said.

"Hello," Anna replied cautiously.

"Did I wake you?"

"No. I'm in bed, though."

"I've just been told."

She wasn't sure what to say, and sitting up, she felt really nervous.

"So when did all this go down?"

Was he talking about her engagement? She couldn't be sure, so she said nothing.

"You going to tell me who it is? Anna?"

"You met him. It's Ken Hudson."

"What? Are you serious? The big blond fella?"

"Yes."

"You didn't let the grass grow under your feet, did you?"

"I guess I didn't."

"Don't go jumping into anything, will you? You should take your time. It's been how long?"

"That's immaterial. I love him."

"Take it slowly, is my advice. Live with him first, and don't go making a big commitment."

"That is exactly what we both want to do." She would have liked to add that just because he had found it impossible when they were together to make a serious commitment, it didn't mean everyone was like that.

"If you're happy, there's nothing more to say."

"I want to have children."

He laughed and then apologized. He didn't mean it as an insult, just that it was all quite a shock to him.

"I'm glad you've found someone, Anna, so congratulations. I wish I could also offer some for the case, but it's running on empty again."

"Seems so, but maybe we'll get a breakthrough." She wanted him to get off the phone; she didn't want to think about the investigation or anything connected to it.

"Good night, then, and I'm sorry if I sounded like I wasn't overly thrilled. Maybe because you didn't tell me yourself."

"He's everything I want. I've never been so happy."

There was a long pause, and then his voice sounded gruff. "That's good. I don't think I ever made you feel that way. Good night, then, sweetheart."

"Good night."

She held the receiver in her hand and heard him click off before she slowly replaced it. It was hard for her to believe that after all the years she had been so besotted with Langton, she would feel depressed by his call. She had felt the undercurrent of sarcasm from him and didn't like it. It didn't occur to her that Langton had been hurt because he was the last to know, and that he still harbored deep feelings for her that he refused to allow to ever surface.

Chapter Fifteen

Anna was in no hurry to get to work the following morning, as she first went to find a jeweler to resize the engagement ring. She had to leave it at the shop and hated not having it on her finger. As soon as she arrived at the station, she could feel the change in atmosphere in the incident room. It came in waves. First Barbara had been to see Wendy Dunn again, and contrary to what they had been told, the older woman was adamant that often and usually at the end of the month, there would be a certain quantity of blinds that were rejected due to the measurements being incorrectly noted. Arnold Rodgers, a stickler for perfection in his company, had ordered the faulty blinds to be either unthreaded and stacked for possible use, or destroyed.

"She said it was common knowledge that they would be taken out, sometimes for the workers' personal use, and Mr. Rodgers had even on occasion allowed that to occur."

"Get to the point, Barbara." Anna was impatient.

"Because John Smiley was their main fitter, he would fix them up for the work teams, but she said he was always the first there to check over the unwanted blinds, and because he had the delivery van, they were out of the factory and in the back of it before Mr. Rodgers noticed."

"Did she say he moonlighted—did extra work outside the company?"

"Yes. He was even paid by her to put some up at her place."

As Anna was about to take on board how difficult it would be to trace the private customers Smiley had worked for, Barolli let out a yell for her attention.

"During the trial of Cameron Welsh, they used the security company attached to Brixton Prison, but when he was transferred to Barfield Prison after he was sentenced, they used a private company."

Anna was becoming as impatient with Barolli as she had felt with Barbara. "Come on," she growled. "Have we got a new suspect or not, for God's sake?"

Barolli gave an expansive bravado gesture.

"No, but I've got four names. Two are dog handlers, but the company admitted that on long-haul drives from London to Barfield, they often used standby guards—that means ones not on a permanent payroll."

"For heaven's sake, what's the connection?"

"One of them is an ex-Para, works doors at nightclubs, mostly, but he stood in for their regular guy, and he brought in a buddy because they needed two wagons. Apparently, there's a Mafia bloke in the secure unit at Barfield who was sentenced at the same time as Welsh, and they were concerned about a possible attempt to escape, so that's why they had the dogs."

Anna felt like screaming. Barolli held up his hand for her to stay quiet.

"You have no idea how long this has taken to piece together, but John Smiley was in the Paras, right? Now, because these two guys were not regulars, they were paid in cash on delivery; they had to sign a chitty."

Anna pinched the bridge of her nose. Barolli had the full attention of the entire room.

"Don't tell me—one was signed by John Smiley?" Anna asked.

"That would be asking too much—and it was how many bloody years ago?—so no. What I *do* have is the name and contact for the ex-Para, and it turns out he was in the same unit at Aldershot with John Smiley."

"So have you questioned him?"

"Not yet. He's working at some boot camp in Devon, but he's contactable this afternoon."

Anna sat back and closed her eyes. It was not as firmed up as the information from Wendy Dunn, and it was possibly not connected, so they might get nothing from either development. However, the third item that generated a lot of excitement came from the forensic lab.

Pete Jenkins had found numerous sets of fingerprints on the wooden pull from the slatted blinds themselves, these, he said, were clearly childrens. However, the sets from beneath the pelmet where it had been screwed into the wall were faint but, due to the size, probably male. With a few hours' further chemical treatment, he hoped to raise an identifiable print.

Mike Lewis was sweating. This was the biggest breakthrough yet, and it would mean bringing John Smiley back in for his prints. If they matched, they had him trapped by his own lies.

Langton arrived with perfect timing to be told the update, and was well pleased. He stood in front of the team beaming and ordered his usual toasted chicken sandwich with no tomatoes.

He sat with them as they sifted through everything they

had so far, and he suggested they forgo another session with Cameron Welsh; if Welsh had known about the security-guard connection, then Langton hoped he would be seg-regated to the mental wing for not telling them. "If it pans out, we don't need to see him again."

Anna said nothing, wondering if Langton had deliber-ately made that decision to deprive her of another chance of going to Leeds to see Ken. She doubted that he would be so churlish, especially when he asked Barolli to check out the Mafia prisoner. If the prisoner had also been in the convoy from London, they could get something from him.

"Apparently, Welsh is climbing the walls." Langton grunted. "So if we need to question him, we'll do so."

Although the team was working toward proving that John Smiley had known Margaret Potts and that his lying could cover a much more heinous event, they did not have any further evidence for the murders of their three Polish victims.

Anna noticed that Langton now wore reading glasses when he went over the files; she had never seen him wear-ing them. They made him look so much older.

When he'd read enough to come to a decision, the DCS stood up and told them to hold off on the arrest of John Smiley, pending the fingerprint treatment by Pete Jenkins. However, as soon as Langton gave the go-ahead, they would nab Smiley on suspicion of murder—and this time, armed with a search warrant, they were to strip his house, the company lockers, and bring in his delivery van for forensic to test. They were to liaise with the Manchester Constabulary, as they would need approval and even per-mission to move in on their turf.

"This time we want his prints," Langton said.

"Why the delay?"

Langton looked at Mike and bit into his sandwich, taking time to chew and swallow before he chucked the napkin that had been wrapped around it into a bin. "Maybe we've got two suspects. This ex-Para guy—what's his name?"

"Ex-Sergeant Michael Dillane."

"I want him questioned before we move on Smiley, so hold steady—no need to jump the gun. We've waited long enough, so a few more hours to check out this Dillane character won't hurt us." He stood up and clapped his hands. "Good work all round. Let's keep the energy up and fingers crossed."

The team split up and went back to their desks as Langton crossed to Anna. He reached for her left hand. "Where's your ring?"

"Being made to fit properly. It was a little bit big, and I was afraid to lose it."

"I always believed it was unlucky to take it off before the wedding."

"Ah, don't say that."

"Just joking, and well done. I know this dog-and-security-guard scenario came via you, so the romance hasn't made you lose your touch." He glanced at his watch and then turned to Barolli. "Soon as you get Dillane sorted, let me know. In the meantime, check out his boot-camp job, and everyone get ready to pull in John Smiley."

Barolli gave him the thumbs-up. There wasn't one member of the team who didn't feel the adrenaline buzz. As Langton had said, it had been a long haul up to this point.

Ex-Sergeant Michael Dillane agreed to come in for an interview. He said it was convenient, as it was his day off and he had intended drive to London. Barolli had fudged the reason for the meeting, not wishing to tip him off in case he contacted John Smiley. All he said was that it was an urgent matter and concerned an ex-Para.

At five-fifteen, Michael Dillane showed up. He was driving a beat-up white Ford Escort van, on which, by the sound of it, the exhaust was cracked. Barolli watched Dillane parking from the incident-room window.

"You are not going to believe what this guy looks like. He's wearing camouflage gear and a mountain hat."

Barolli hurried to the reception to bring Dillane to interview room one. Anna gathered the files, pleased that Mike Lewis had agreed she should conduct the interview with Barolli.

"Your call on him, Travis, but I'll be next door watching it go down on the monitors."

"I appreciate this, Mike. Thank you."

Michael Dillane was, as Barolli had described, wearing army jungle fatigues with a wide leather belt buckled too tightly. Not that he was overweight; on the contrary, he oozed muscles and had the sloping shoulders of a weight lifter. He was about five feet ten but had a huge presence and, as they were to discover, a personality that went with it. When he removed his wide-brimmed hat, he had a shaved head and sat with his legs spread wide apart, his feet encased in heavy studded boots. His thick hands had tattoos across the knuckles, and his shirt was open almost to his waist. He refused coffee but asked for a bottle of water.

Barolli introduced himself and Anna, thanking the man for agreeing to come in and talk to them.

Dillane lifted his hand and wagged a stubby finger. "Once a Para, always a Para, and if one of my mates is in trouble, I'm here for them." He had round button eyes, a nose that looked as if it had been broken many times, and a wide wet mouth.

"Tell us about this boot camp, Michael."

Anna was surprised by his thick Manchester accent.

"It's a private company, partly subsidized by the government. We take on real hardline kids that basically everyone else has given up on. We get junkies from wealthy families, gang members—you name it. We get the dross of humanity that's between fifteen to twenty, and we kick them into shape—not literally, of course, but we get them into shape physically, and then the shrinks take over." He smiled. "I do the physical. Nothing works better than exercise and routine." He flexed his muscles. "So who's the reason I'm here?"

"We'll get to that in a moment," Barolli said, and then asked Dillane to go back to a period when he worked security.

"I've done a lot. How far do you want me to go back?"

"Maybe five years. You've worked for numerous companies?"

"That's true. You ever seen how many security companies are listed nowadays? Thousands of them, and mostly bloody amateurs, but I'm done with that. They don't pay on time—real aggravation—so this job is working out well for me. It's been two years now."

"Can you recall a period when you escorted prisoners, specifically to Barfield Prison?"

"Yeah, I done that quite a bit. It was a long time ago, though, at least five or six years now."

"Do you recall driving a prisoner called Cameron Welsh?"

He shook his head.

"Went down for a double murder. Cocky bloke, well educated?" Barolli reminded him.

"I dunno. To be honest, I never gave them much thought when I was working."

Barolli set down the mug shots of Cameron Welsh. Dillane picked them up and sucked in his breath.

"He was driven to Barfield Prison with a Mafia guy," Barolli said.

"Right, yeah, it's coming back to me . . ."

"So you remember Cameron Welsh?"

"More the Italian geezer. I remember him."

"Tell us what you remember."

"It was a right farce. The prison authorities were panic-stricken that the Mafia guy might be sprung, know what I mean? That he might have connections. He looked more like a weedy little bloke to me than some kind of godfather." He frowned, cracking his knuckles. "Hang on—yeah. Now I think about it, that guy Welsh was in the first wagon, too; we were tailing them in the second with the dogs."

"You were a dog handler?"

"That's right. Nimrod, he was mine for nearly eighteen months. Fantastic animal and really intelligent. He could bring down an elephant, no problem."

"Your dog?"

"That's right. When I moved on, I was gonna take him with me, but he sort of belonged to the company. I mean, I had him at home with me when I was working for them, but when I left and went on to doing the doors, they kept him."

"So you had the dog for how long?"

"I just said I had Nimrod for about eighteen months, and I tell you, when I walked away from the kennels, it broke my heart. He had this look on his face I'll never forget—looking at me as if to say, 'What's going on? How come I'm not going with you?' Broke me up."

"When you did the convoy to Barfield—"

"Done quite a few runs there," Dillane interrupted.

"Can we concentrate on the occasion you drove to Barfield with the two prisoners Cameron Welsh and—"

"He's still there, isn't he, this Mafia geezer?"

"So is Cameron Welsh," Anna said quietly.

Dillane turned toward her. This was the first time she'd spoken. Up until this moment, he had directed his entire conversation toward Barolli.

"Has this got something to do with him?" the big man asked. He looked from one to the other, his wide, flat face registering confusion. "What's going on?"

"Did you at any time have any conversation with Welsh?"

"No, he was in the wagon up front."

"So you never spoke to him?"

"No. When we got to the prison, we were out with the dogs as the two guys were led in, like, and he did come up to me. In fact, he was not really talking to *me,* he was interested in Nimrod, and I had to warn him to stay back. He was leashed—the dog, not the bloke!" He gave a loud chortle and then lifted a hand, gripping it into a fist. "Hadda hold on to him tight, like, almost as if he knew the bloke was a bad 'un."

"Cameron Welsh?"

"Yeah, and he straightened up and stepped away, scared-like, you know? And that was about it."

"So you had no other interaction with Mr. Welsh?"

"Nope, we were concentrating on the Italian, as he was terrified of the dogs. In some ways, it's a bit of a performance, you know. They can snarl and growl almost on cue, and they were also ragged after a long drive 'cause we didn't stop off or anything—we drove straight to the nick."

"The company you worked for has said that they were shorthanded on this occasion and that you brought in another dog handler to do the journey."

The big man gritted his teeth. "Yeah, yeah, I think so. It was a long time ago."

"Another ex-Para."

Dillane snapped his fingers and nodded. "Yes, that's right. Great bloke, very experienced. Explosives expert—did thirteen years in the army, three in the Paras."

"What was his name?"

Anna tensed up. This was the link that they had been waiting for. In the viewing room next door, Mike Lewis stood up, impatient to hear the name they were certain would be John Smiley.

"Is this connected to him?" Dillane asked. "Is this why I'm here?"

"Mr. Dillane, please give us the name of the ex-Para working with you on that Barfield run."

In the viewing room, Mike Lewis turned toward the door as Langton walked in. They stood side by side. "They've been taking it easy with Dillane, but I think he's just about to give up that John Smiley was with him." Both moved a fraction closer to the monitor. On the screen, Dillane was cracking his knuckles again.

"Colin McNaughton. He's still doing the same job, works for a company called Eagles, but he also does a lot of doors and celebrity hand-holding—drives him nuts."

Barolli sighed, disappointed. Mike Lewis walked out of the viewing room. Langton kicked the vacated chair.

"You're from Manchester?" Anna said, still speaking quietly.

"Used to be. Me and the wife live in Croydon now, have done for eight years. The parents died, and I sold their house."

"When you did this trip or any trips to Barfield, did you return straight back to Croydon?"

Dillane shrugged, seemed a bit shifty. "We got overnight expenses, as it was a long drive there; from collection to drop-off, it could be anywhere between seven or eight hours."

"So did you stay in a motel? I mean, you had your dog—right?"

"Like I said, we got overnight extra payment; mostly, the guys would claim it but drive back, like."

"Did you?"

"Sometimes, yeah."

"And on the occasion you were with Cameron Welsh . . ."

"I stay with a mate sometimes, and I stayed over with him."

"What's his name?"

"What's this all about?"

"Just helping our inquiries, Michael. Who did you stay with?"

"Bloke I know lives in Manchester. Like I said, my parents' place was sold up."

"What's his name?"

"John Smiley."

Barolli closed his eyes. Anna kept her focus on Dillane. "With your dog?" she asked.

"Yeah. Nimrod was house-trained. Remember, I said

he lived with me at home with the wife when I wasn't working."

In the viewing room, Langton was sitting with his full attention on the monitor.

"So you know John Smiley well?"

"Yeah. Fought in the Iraq war together—great bloke. We used to be close, but when he moved up north from London, I didn't get to see him all that much."

"Tell us about Mr. Smiley."

Dillane leaned back in his chair. "He's one of the best. We were in the same unit, and he was one of my closest mates. We did some drinking together at Aldershot. You know, I wasn't married then, nor was he, and we'd party."

"Tell us about when you stayed over at his house."

"Not that much to tell you. We sank a few pints, talked about old times, and his wife cooked us dinner."

"Go on."

Dillane blew out his cheeks and then ran his hand over his shaved head. "There wasn't a lot we could do. See, I've known him since we first joined up. I was with him when he met his wife, Sonja. She was a looker then, and she put it about a bit, I can tell you. Anyway, old John fell hook, line, and sinker for her. Nobody liked to tell him she was a slag. I don't mean to badmouth about it, but none of us wanted to be the one to tell him she'd gone through the ranks. To be honest, I thought he'd sort of get over it, but the idiot went and married her. I didn't see that much of him after we quit, because he was in London working for some company fixing up blinds—he got me and the wife some."

"Go on."

"That's about it. I didn't get along with Sonja, she was a moody cow, and Christ, she'd started to look like one. She's enormous, and when I made a crack about her size, he went apeshit, so that time we didn't part on all that good terms."

"That time?" Anna repeated quickly.

"Yeah."

"So you met up with him again?"

"Just the once, but not in Manchester. We had a pint together in London. Like I said, he'd got me a set of blinds, and he came and put them up for us."

"When was this?"

"Be four years ago, 'cause I'd not got this job at the boot camp but was quitting security work and gave up Nimrod, like I told you."

"What happened at this meeting?"

Dillane sighed and again rubbed his hand over his head. "I was short of a bob or two, and the wife was pregnant. I was gonna ask if John Boy could lend me a few quid."

"Did he?"

"No. He said he was short himself. I gotta say, he'd always been a bit tightfisted, or careful with his cash. Anyway, we done a deal."

Anna glanced at Barolli, and they remained silent.

"Is this about him, 'cause I don't like putting him into anything," Dillane said. "He was a great bloke and he did me a favor."

"The blinds?"

"No, he bought me van for seven hundred quid. It wasn't right for me if we were having a kid, and it still had the cage in the back, like. It was secondhand when I bought it, still had the logo on the side."

"So John Smiley bought your van?"

"Yeah, paid me in installments, couple of hundred a week until it was done, and then he paid me a bit extra 'cause I drove it up to Manchester for him and left it in his garage."

"Was he there when you left it with him?"

"No, he was working. I didn't even see Sonja—just left the keys under the dashboard and got the train home."

"Have you seen him since?"

"No. I got the job at the boot camp, so I'm away all week. Just come home on my days off and alternate weekends."

"Could you give us the registration of your van and a full description of it?"

Langton headed into the incident room and gave instructions for the team to get on to checking out the white security van. If it was still registered to Michael Dillane at his home address, it would mean that John Smiley had never changed the ownership details into his name. Impatient as ever, Langton couldn't bear to return to the viewing room but went straight into the interview room.

Dillane turned as Langton entered and took Barolli's chair. Laid out on the table were the photographs of Margaret Potts.

Langton introduced himself, and Dillane straightened up, looking from Barolli, who stood by the door, back to Langton.

"Do you recognize this woman?" Langton asked.

"No, sir. I've just been asked. I've never seen her before in my life."

Anna brought out the photographs of the three Polish victims, one by one, and Dillane glanced at them, shaking his head.

"No, I've never seen any one of them." He looked at

Langton. "I don't understand what's going on here. Why are you showing me these women's pictures?"

"They were all murdered, Mr. Dillane."

"Jesus Christ, you think I had something to do with them?"

"You are simply helping our inquiries. We really appreciate you coming in to talk to us."

Anna asked where Dillane was on the dates the women's bodies were found. Although the postmortem reports had been unable to give an exact time of death, they detailed as closely as possible how long the victims had been dead. Dillane was able to answer without hesitation, as he was working in Devon.

Anna collected the photographs and stacked them. The big man was pulling at his shirt front, looking hot and bothered. "You think I know anything about them? Is that why you've been questioning me? Let me tell you, if you've got John Smiley under suspicion, you've got the wrong bloke. He's a diamond, and he helped me out of a very sticky patch."

"What reason did he give you for buying your van?" Anna asked.

"Said he could use it for the small deliveries."

"When you left it at his garage, what did you leave inside it?"

Dillane shrugged. "Nothing of any value—I even took the radio out. There was nothing in it."

"What about your uniform?"

"Nah, didn't leave that. He wouldn't have wanted it."

"What about something from your dog?"

"I think there was maybe a dog bowl and Nimrod's old blanket still in the cage. I didn't want them. I was very fond of that dog, and I think John said something about he'd maybe get a puppy for his two kids."

Anna removed the pictures of the blue blanket found wrapped around Dorota Pelagia. "Was the blanket used by your dog like this one?"

Dillane leaned forward. "Yeah, blue. It was an old prison-issue blanket. It was in the van when I bought it off this other dog handler."

Langton glanced at Anna. She replaced the photographs. Langton stood up and shook Mr. Dillane's hand. "You've been very helpful, Mr. Dillane. If you could just stay at the station while we check out a couple of things, then you'll be free to go."

Mike Lewis had confirmation that Dillane's van was still registered to him. It had recently been issued a new MOT by a garage in Croydon, and the documents had been collected personally by a man they presumed was Dillane and paid for in cash, but when asked for a description, they described John Smiley. They were checking out the insurance, but there had been no parking or speeding fines issued.

Barolli had contacted the boot-camp authorities, and they were able to give Dillane a pretty watertight alibi for two of the victims, though not for Dorota Pelagia or Maggie Potts, as he was not working for them until two years ago. Their bodies had been discovered four and two years ago, respectively.

"What do you think, Travis?" Langton asked, looking at the incident board as the new data was being written up.

"I think he's in the clear, but who knows? And he couldn't remember the exact date he drove his van to leave with John Smiley."

"Let's just make sure we're not letting him walk away. If he's involved, it's the two of them."

Dillane had been given a mug of tea and a sandwich. As Langton returned, he rose from his seat.

"Stay sitting down, Michael, this isn't going to take too long. We've checked with your boot camp, and they have agreed you worked there on the dates two victims were discovered, but you were not there for the murder of this woman." Langton slapped down Margaret Potts's photograph.

Anna took out the photograph of Dorota Pelagia. "Or this woman."

Dillane blew out his cheeks.

"You may have a lawyer present if you want one."

"I don't need one," Dillane said. "I never did anything wrong, and if you give me some time to think, I'll try and remember where I was, but it's not easy when it's four years ago."

Langton tapped the picture of Dorota Pelagia, saying, "She was Polish."

"That doesn't help me none. I dunno where I was four bleeding years ago right off the top of me head." Dillane was rattled.

"Well, start thinking—maybe about this woman Margaret Potts, too. She was found two years ago on March fifteenth. Her body was dumped by the London Gateway service station—that any help to jog your memory? It was in all the papers, been on the news, crime shows . . ."

"I can't remember. And I was working at the boot camp two years ago. What date was it again?"

"March fifteenth, 2008."

• • •

In the incident room, everyone was waiting impatiently. The clock was ticking, and it was almost nine in the evening. Anna was growing tired; it had been a long session with Dillane, and it was getting tedious as he tried to recall where he was. Langton wouldn't let him off the hook; he was putting on the pressure.

"Four women have been brutally murdered, Michael, and we have strong suspicions that you could be involved, especially with this girl Dorota Pelagia, as she was found with a blue blanket wrapped around her naked body, a blanket identical to the one that you described as being in the back of your van."

"You think that John Smiley is up for this?" Dillane demanded. "Is that what you are keeping me here for? It's not right. I've been racking me brains, and I honestly can't remember where I was. Why don't you let me ring me wife and ask her—" He suddenly clapped his hands to his head. "Maternity ward! Jesus Christ, how could I forget that? She was taken in on the thirteenth, had that preeclampsia thing and almost died. I was in Saint Mary's Hospital."

He leaned back and then did his familiar gesture of wiping his head. "Okay, that's one—but four years ago? Maybe I was still working for the same security company, but I was getting pissed off because we was doing pop concerts, and some of the kids are like hyped-up chimps, hurling themselves at the stage. We had to take punches and kicks, they spit in your face and you can't whack 'em, much as you'd like to—our job was to hold 'em back. I would have still had the van then, but you can't have the dogs inside the venue, as they would go crazy. You can patrol on the perimeters."

Again he clapped his hands. It was almost as if he were

enjoying himself. "Fucking Take That, that's where I was. They was doing a concert. There you go—I done it, and you can check that out, all right?"

"That's fine, Michael, we'll check it out. So around the time of this concert, you met with John Smiley to get some blinds put up?"

"Correct."

"You said that you were a bit skint, is that right?"

"Correct again. They pay peanuts for these bloody concerts, and you come away bruised and kicked. It pissed me off, and it wasn't worth the aggravation. Like I said before, the wife was pregnant with the first, not the second one, and I didn't like it, but I asked John if he'd be able to lend me a couple of grand to tide me over."

"He said he was short. He couldn't have been that short, though, if he was able to buy your van—right?"

"Funnily enough, I thought that at the time," Dillane agreed. He was calmer now. "What he said was, he had someone hitting him for money, so he had to do a lot of night work, like selling me blinds on the cheap."

"Did he ever mention to you who was hitting him for cash, as you just described?"

"Nah. Just that it was getting him down. Sonja doled out his money like he was a ten-year-old. She gave him pocket money—can you believe that?"

"How much do you think he was making by working on the side, selling blinds from his company on the cheap?"

"I dunno, but he paid me in cash, so it had to have been a bit of all right."

Langton glanced at Anna. She packed up the photographs and replaced them in the file. Langton stood up.

"Thank you very much, Mr. Dillane. We really appreciate you agreeing to help our inquiry. We would also appreciate it if you would agree to come back should we need to verify a few things."

Dillane left the station at ten-fifteen. Langton was satisfied that he was not involved and gave the go-ahead to the eagerly waiting team. He wanted John Smiley arrested and brought down to the station that night. There was a unanimous cheer from everyone.

As they packed up, ready to leave, Langton asked Anna if she'd like to have a celebratory drink. She refused, saying she was tired and wanted to be fresh for the following morning.

He gave her a light tap on her cheek. "Okay. Well done this evening."

"It's been a long wait."

"It has, but we've got him. We've bloody got the bastard."

Chapter Sixteen

With the assistance of Manchester Constabulary, John Smiley was arrested at four-fifteen the following morning. He gave no resistance, but his wife, Sonja, became abusive and tried to stop officers from beginning their search of the premises. The van sold to him by Michael Dillane was discovered in a garage three streets away from his home. This was put on a loader and driven to London for the forensic team to begin work on. Hidden in a tool bag in the garage and neatly folded into a John Lewis carrier bag were a black jacket with lapels, a white shirt, and a security guard's hat. They also removed the delivery van used by Smiley from the Swell Blinds offices early the same morning.

The search teams worked through the last of the night and into the following morning, removing bags of possible evidence. Within the bags were receipts, a log of private customers, and a paper bag containing over two thousand pounds in cash. They also removed from the garage some stacked blinds, all neatly covered in bubble wrap, with the sizes and shades carefully printed on a card on the front of each item.

The team in London began to assimilate all of the new evidence in readiness to begin the interrogation of John Smiley. His lawyer, James Gregson, was contacted, and he was soon closeted in an interview room with his client. John Smiley was to be charged with four counts of murder. His fingerprints were taken on arrival and went directly to the forensic lab.

It became clear that they would not get to interrogate John Smiley that day. His lawyer insisted that he would not allow his client to be interviewed until he was satisfied that full consultation with him concerning the disclosure was completed. He talked to Langton in Mike Lewis's office, saying that as there were likely to be four murder charges, he must be allowed more time with Smiley. Langton agreed that he could continue his disclosure discussions and that they would conduct the interview the following morning.

It was infuriating, as the team was eager to gain a result after such an extensive investigation, and none of them, especially Anna, had expected to be released for the evening. They would reconvene at eight the following morning, Langton said, and stressed that they should use the time to prepare for the interrogation. He and Travis would handle the interview.

After he had left, Barolli insinuated that it was Langton who needed the time to get up to speed on all their accumulated evidence.

Anna ignored his snide remark; she was pleased that Langton had insisted she interrogate John Smiley with him, and she was confident they would gain a result, if not a confession.

Anna rang Ken as soon as she got back, but his mobile phone was turned off. She called his flat and left a message to say that she was at home. She showered and did a review of the case file until quite late. She didn't want to go to sleep until she'd had the opportunity to talk to him.

It was almost midnight when Ken finally rang. He apologized immediately for not returning her calls but said that it had been a hard day.

"What's happened?" she asked.

"You first. Tell me what you've been working on."

"We've got enough to charge John Smiley." She didn't go into detail.

"That's a positive result?" He sounded pleased for her.

"It will be if we get him to confess. We've got him a lawyer who is young and wants to prove himself, so he's crossing all the T's and insisting on lengthy discussions about the disclosures."

"But you're certain you've got the right guy?"

"Yes."

Ken was keen to talk about their future rather than work, and they happily began discussing wedding dates. Anna wanted to know where they should have the ceremony and reception. Ken laughed when he found out that she wanted it to be the full monty: he was to wear a morning suit and, if possible, to get his brother back from Australia to be best man. Ken said he'd try but wasn't certain Robin would make the trip back for a wedding. He was thinking of asking Lizzie's husband, Ian, or an officer he was pals with at the prison.

"It's your choice," Anna said. "I won't be having any bridesmaids, but I'd like your nephews as pageboys."

"They'd love it, but no velvet, please. They're real boys."

She laughed, saying that she knew that, but she'd like them to be in suits, and one would carry the ring cushion.

Ken said he'd talk to Lizzie and that maybe he could swing a weekend leave, but after the nightmare day he'd had, it might not be in the cards.

"Why, what's happened?"

"Cameron Welsh, that's what. First he appeared to be getting himself straightened out and asked if he could make himself an omelette. As he'd been refusing to eat for days, we were only too pleased to allow him into the kitchen. He was very friendly—now that I think about it, too much so. He asked if he could brew up a pot of tea for the officers, and it was fortunate that Brian—he's the guy I want for my best man if Rob can't make it—went into the kitchen to check up on him."

Anna was shocked when Ken said that Brian had found Welsh using a one-inch nail file to shave a shard of glass into the bowl of eggs; he had also put some into the teapot.

"We couldn't be sure if he was trying to make himself so ill that he'd be hospitalized, or whether we were his targets."

"Why would he do that?"

"For one, if we'd all drunk the tea, we'd have been hurt or maybe even dead—likewise himself, if he'd eaten the omelette—but I think he was paying us back. Again, if he'd been taken to the hospital, he might have been planning an escape."

"Paying you back?"

"Yeah. He may have been in the kitchen and overheard."

"Overheard what?"

"Brian congratulating me about our engagement. I told you that Welsh has this fixation with you, didn't I?"

"So it was you he was targeting?"

"That's what I think, but if we'd all drunk his tea, we'd have all been hurt. Anyway, he's been locked up round the clock, and we've taken all his privileges, so he's not a very happy camper."

"How did he get the nail file into his cell?"

"Christ only knows. It was only about an inch long, so

he could have had it hidden for years. As he's had no visitors, it was doubtful anyone could have brought it in. You'd be surprised what they can smuggle in or buy off another inmate."

They continued talking for another half hour before Anna said she should get some sleep, as she wanted to be fresh for the morning.

"Listen, due to the situation here, we're working round the clock, and I'm due some time off this week," Ken said. "How about if I ride down?"

Anna said she could think of nothing she'd like better. For one thing, it would mean they could work out the wedding date and invitation list. After they hung up, she slept soundly, she had done so ever since being with Ken. She no longer felt that restlessness and obsession with mulling over the case files in her head.

She was dressed and ready for action by seven-thirty the following morning, eager to get on with the interrogation of John Smiley. When she reached the station, Anna was surprised to see Langton already there. He had coffee and a toasted bacon sandwich, and as soon as he saw her, he asked for a word in Mike Lewis's office.

"Listen, I've had a bit of a development," he said. "I'm not going to make it this morning, so Mike will be in on the interrogation with you."

Anna was disappointed. "Why not? You're here now."

"Yeah, but I have to leave soon—and you and I both know it's going to be a long session with Smiley. I tell you one thing I've learned from this . . ."

"Just one?"

"Never let an effing rookie lawyer handle a big case. This guy James Gregson is a royal pain in the arse. You'd think he was representing Prince Charles, the way he's carrying on."

"Scared he's going to make a mistake, I reckon," Anna said thoughtfully. "For us, it might prove to be an advantage."

"You all right to go in with Mike?"

"Of course I am, and don't run him down. On the contrary, he needs all the confidence boosters you can give him. He's had the carpet tugged a few times."

"Maybe it doesn't help, just how much you've come up with the leads that have assisted us in bringing in John Smiley."

"It was teamwork, sir," Anna said. Langton had reprimanded her enough times for not being a team player.

"I'll talk to him before I leave," Langton promised.

"Can I ask why you're not staying?"

Langton nodded and referred to another case he had been overseeing.

"You read about the little girl nicknamed the Pixie? It started because her parents gave us a photograph of her dressed for a party; she was wearing a little pixie hat and green tights."

"I know the case. She was found inside one of those huge waste bins, wasn't she?"

"Yep, poor little lass. She'd been missing for four weeks."

"In many ways I am grateful that I'm on this John Smiley case and not on a child murder. They're always hard not to get emotionally involved in."

"Yeah, and in this one, emotions are running to boiling point. We arrested the stepfather last night."

"What?"

"Yeah. He cried a lot of crocodile tears on all the TV interviews, but I just had this gut feeling about him, and last night we nailed him. It was old Pete Jenkins who gave us the lead with just one fingerprint."

"From the Dumpster?"

"Nope, off of little Pixie's skin. He used the superglue technique and lifted it from her backbone. The man had denied being with her for the afternoon she went missing, and he'd been protected by the mother. So like I said, emotions are boiling over, but I want to lead the interrogation. Personally, I'd like to strangle him with my bare hands, but instead, I'll make damned sure I break him."

Anna knew that dealing with Langton at full throttle wouldn't be easy; she'd seen him in action too many times.

"Did you also have a gut feeling about John Smiley?"

He nodded and then looked at her. "What about you?"

"To be honest, no, I didn't, but there were just too many coincidences—and I know you don't believe in them. That's what kept me going."

"You did good detective work, Travis. It won't go unnoticed."

"Thank you."

"But you *are* going to have to break him—and I'd say over the Margaret Potts murder. We've not got enough on any of the Polish girls, apart from the blue blanket. Did you get his pal, the ex-Para, what's his name?"

"Michael Dillane."

"Right—did he get shown the blanket?"

She hesitated and shook her head. "No."

"That should have been a priority."

"I know, but—"

"Get it done. Once you've got Smiley admitting Margaret Potts's murder, then you can backtrack to the other girls. It's not going to be easy, even with the accumulated evidence. I would say if he's not opening up, hit him with as much about his wife as possible—even implicate her somehow. She's a real dog, but I think he has this fear of her disrespecting him, for some godly reason."

"Right, but we do have strong evidence linking him to Dorota, the dog hairs and—"

"Not enough to make the charges stick. You will have to put the pressure on him to confess."

She nodded and then was taken aback when he took hold of her left hand. "Still not wearing your engagement ring, I see."

"I've not had time to pick it up." Uncomfortable with the personal direction of the conversation, she gave Langton a brief rundown about Cameron Welsh's latest antics, but he didn't pay that much attention.

He looked at his watch. "I gotta go. As for Welsh, I'd put the bastard in a straitjacket and cart him off to Broadmoor and let them deal with him."

"I think Ken is hoping they'll move him this week."

Langton stood up and picked up his raincoat, saying, "I'll call later and see how you and Mike are doing."

"Okay. Thanks."

He came closer and touched her arm lightly. "Don't let Smiley slither off the hook," he warned.

"I don't intend to," she said, following him into the incident room as he headed for Mike, who had just arrived. She guessed he was perhaps taking her advice about giving Mike a boost, and she knew she was right when she saw Mike smile and thank him. Going over to Barolli, she asked him to get hold of Dillane and take him over to forensics to check the blanket for them and to confirm the matching dog hairs. She knew that Langton had been right: the evidence wasn't strong enough.

• • •

Even though he had spent the night in a cell, John Smiley looked fresh. He was wearing a gray suit with a white shirt and dark tie. His hair was combed away from his forehead, showing his receding hairline. He was in some ways a good-looking man, but his face was heavily lined, and he was obviously nervous. As Mike reminded Smiley that he was still under caution, he gave small soft coughs, constantly clearing his throat and, with his right hand, straightening his tie. Mike motioned to the video cameras, explaining that the interview would be not only taped but filmed.

The first file was placed on the table by Anna; it was the investigation into Margaret Potts's murder. She took out the photographs and placed them in front of Smiley.

"You have denied knowing this victim Margaret Potts. Do you have anything to say?" Mike demanded.

"No comment."

Anna's mouth tightened. If Smiley was to go down the "no comment" route with all four victims, it would be a very one-sided interview.

Mike continued. "We now have proof that you did in fact know Margaret Potts, and we have a witness who met you when you went to her flat to hang a set of blinds. This witness has also stated that she paid you in cash, and the same witness was able to pick you out of a video identification parade. Do you still insist that you did not know the victim?"

"No comment."

"We also have three sets of prints from the same flat that have been matched with yours, Mr. Smiley, so to continue to deny that you were never at Miss Emerald Turk's flat is a lie."

"No comment."

Mike plowed on. "We also know that you lied about not working in a private capacity using blinds from your company Swell Blinds, and that this money paid to you was never declared for any tax payments. We have been given a statement by a Mr. Michael Dillane that you also fitted blinds for him for a cash payment, together with one from a Mrs. Wendy Dunn, who recalls that you did work for her. You were seen on numerous occasions to remove the un-wanted blinds from the Swell Blinds factory, leading us to believe that you did earn a considerable amount from these private negotiations."

"No comment."

"Mr. Dillane also provided us with details of you pay-ing him seven hundred pounds for his van, which he had previously used when working as a security guard and dog handler. You failed to reregister this vehicle with a change of ownership and new address so you could use it to com-mit your crimes. These will be added charges brought against you, as we have details of the garage where this van was parked; it was rented out to you and nobody else. Do you admit to that?"

"No comment."

Mike sighed and continued. "We have removed from this same garage in Manchester a security officer's uniform, a cap, and a jacket."

Anna passed over the photographs of the items, and Smiley merely glanced at them. He also paid scant atten-tion when Mike showed him the cash and detailed the amount found.

"Do you have anything to say about these items?"

"No, I don't."

"We have also found numerous dog hairs inside this van that are being tested to see if they match dog hairs taken from a blue blanket that at some time was used for Mr. Dillane's guard dog to lie on. We will come to the importance of this later." Smiley simply nodded. His lawyer was scribbling notes as Mike talked. Anna had not said one word.

"We are aware that the victim, Miss Margaret Potts, came into a considerable amount of money over a period of two years. We believe that you paid her this money because she was blackmailing you. Do you have any comment to make about that?"

"No, I don't."

"We have had access to your bank accounts and find no withdrawals of money to pay Mr. Dillane for his van. Where did this money come from?"

"No comment."

Mike was becoming frustrated. Smiley's reactions were getting to him. They needed to elicit a proper response from him, so Anna tapped Mike's knee beneath the table. He sat back, giving her the cue to begin talking. She kept her voice low and persuasive.

"Maggie Potts was a common slut, but you found her attractive, didn't you? What did she do, John? Did she come on to you in Emerald Turk's flat and you just couldn't resist her? She may have been a tough nut, but she was still more attractive than your wife, wasn't she? Sonja's overweight, her looks have gone, and she was barely giving you enough pocket money. Why was that? Because she knew you couldn't keep your dick in your trousers?"

Smiley's lips tightened.

"Margaret was still sexy compared to Sonja, and she knew how to handle a man and give him pleasure. She went down on you, didn't she? I bet Sonja hasn't given you any pleasure for a long time. Like a beached whale, isn't she?"

"You got no right to slag off my wife," Smiley said with gritted teeth.

"But if she was to find out that you'd been screwing a whore and paying for it, she'd have done what, John? Cut off your pocket money—or cut off your balls? We know she didn't have any idea how much cash you were earning on the side in your dodgy deals. You never thought she'd find out, but then Margaret got greedy, didn't she?"

Smiley was beginning to fidget, constantly straightening his tie with the flat of his hand.

"She kept on hitting you for more cash, and you kept on letting her give you blow jobs when you met up with her at the service stations. You hated yourself, didn't you, but you couldn't keep your hands off her—isn't that right?"

"*No.*"

"No what? No you couldn't keep your hands off her, or no you didn't screw her round the back of the service stations? And all the while she was asking for extra payments, threatening to tell your wife about the love affair. Was that what it was, John? You'd fallen for a hardened tart that Sonja would go apeshit about; she'd maybe smell her on you when you got home."

"No."

Anna knew that so far, the biggest response was when she had been rude about Sonja, just as Langton had suggested, so she went for that again.

"You get home after a long drive, and there is this overweight, ugly woman demanding to know where you've been and what you've been doing. You must have been itching to tell her to her big fat face."

"You shut up talking about my wife."

"But you carry around a picture of her, young and

pretty. You didn't know back then she'd been fucked by half the blokes in your regiment."

"That is a disgusting lie." He tried to stand.

"Sit down, Mr. Smiley," Mike said sharply.

"It is not a lie. Sonja put it about, and then she got her claws into you, and you thought you had a catch—but she was no better than Margaret Potts, was she?"

"Sonja is my wife and the mother of my children."

"So that was why she ate herself into the state she's in. She's obese, Mr. Smiley, she pants for breath just going up the stairs. Why don't you carry *that* picture in your wallet instead of the fantasy that she's still that girl you married? You must hate her."

"No, I don't."

"How do you think she's going to feel about all this? We will have to question her, and we will obviously bring up your relationship with Margaret Potts."

"Sonja has nothing to do with any of this."

"Any of this? You are accused of *murder*, Mr. Smiley! Of course we will have to question her—she could be involved. She must have known about your predilection for young girls, young Polish girls, maybe girls that reminded you of what Sonja used to look like. I doubt if she will understand about Margaret, but she will have to be told, and as you decline to assist us in any way, then we will have to try and get answers from *her.*"

"No. I don't want Sonja brought into this. I've agreed to answer your questions and—"

He was interrupted by Mike leaning forward and saying, "You have not answered a single question, Mr. Smiley, to the contrary, and if this continues, you leave us no option but to bring in your wife."

"I don't want her brought here."

"Really? Well, if you are not prepared to cooperate—"

"She is not to be involved."

"I don't think you will have any say in the matter."

At this point Gregson leaned toward Smiley and held up his notebook in front of their faces. Anna could hear him telling Smiley that they were trying to goad him into answering their questions and, as they had discussed, he felt it wise that Smiley continue to remain calm and not allow himself to be antagonized.

Mike was clearly fighting to keep control of his own temper as he looked at Gregson and said scornfully, "You think that is what we're doing? Mr. Gregson, your client may be charged with four murders. If you think I am being antagonistic toward Mr. Smiley, then I suggest you advise him to cooperate and to drop the 'no comment' routine."

"I am here to advise my client, and being abusive toward his wife to get him to answer questions that implicate him is unacceptable," began Gregson.

"Implicate?" Anna queried. "Mr. Gregson, we have a mass of evidence implicating your client, starting with the murder of Margaret Potts. Your client has lied to us, and we are able to prove that."

"If you'll excuse me, Detective Travis, I do not believe that you *do* have the evidence. You have no proof that my client was being blackmailed by Margaret Potts, and therefore you have no motive for murder."

Anna stood up. Mike remained sitting as she reached over to gather up the photographs, snatching at them in a show of temper. "I will now arrange to have Mrs. Smiley brought here for questioning. Surely you don't think for a second that she isn't suspicious as to why her husband has been arrested?" She glared at John Smiley. "Whatever excuse you've made up is going to sound ridiculous when she must have seen the evidence removed from your house. The officers are still there, Mr. Smiley, still checking for further evidence. Don't you think she's going to realize that your arrest is not for some petty crime? Unless, of course, your wife was fully aware of your sexual antics with a prostitute and could be charged with attempting to pervert the course of justice."

"I told you—my wife has nothing to do with any of this. I swear on my children's lives, she knows nothing."

"What doesn't she know about, John?"

Smiley was sweating. Instead of patting his tie, he began to loosen it.

"Why don't you get it off your chest?" Anna said persuasively. "At least it will avoid our having to arrest your wife. And then you have your children to consider if she's brought in for questioning."

Gregson pointed at Anna. "This is really becoming intolerable, DI Travis. Mr. Smiley has stated over and over that his wife has no connection with any—" He stopped as if he knew he was trapping himself.

"That his wife has no connection with what?" Anna demanded.

Gregson got his act back together. "She knows nothing about the murder allegations leveled against my client."

Anna stacked the photographs of Margaret Potts and tapped them on the tabletop like a pack of cards. "But I have made it very obvious that due to your client refusing to answer any questions, it leaves us with no alternative but to question Sonja Smiley in connection with those murders."

"I do not believe you have any incriminating evidence against my client for . . ." Gregson checked his notebook and listed the four victims' names.

Anna wished she had Langton backing her up. She felt Mike was taking a backseat.

"No evidence? *No evidence?* I beg to differ with you, Mr. Gregson, but I am not prepared to sit here any longer and play this game with you."

John Smiley pushed back his chair. It made a harsh noise, startling them into silence. "I want to get some things cleared up," he said.

There was a lengthy pause.

"I admit I have lied to you." John Smiley stared at the tabletop; he was now sweating profusely. "I did meet Margaret Potts, and I did place a blind in Miss Turk's box room. It was a long time ago, and I really couldn't remember her. I didn't even know her name, which is the reason why I have not admitted to knowing or recognizing her."

"Take us through what happened when you first met Margaret," Anna said.

"Miss Turk opened the door to me. I didn't even know there was anyone else there. She seemed anxious to leave, so I said I'd let myself out as soon as I'd finished rehanging the kitchen blinds. She mentioned there'd been a problem with the ones in the little bedroom, too. I knew those flats, as we had a contract with the housing association in them days, and I happened to have a set the right size in the back of the van. She bunged me forty quid, waited for me to nip down and bring up the blinds, then she cleared off and left me to it. Didn't seem to mind leaving me on me own. I didn't realize there was anyone else there at that time." Smiley rubbed his nose, then continued. "I was just finishing off the kitchen blinds when *she* came out of the smallest bedroom."

"Margaret Potts?"

"Yes. I didn't know anyone else was there, right, and she

gave me quite a fright. She asked if I wanted a cup of tea, and I said I wouldn't mind one when I'd put up the other blinds. She sat watching me while I did it. After a quick cup of tea in the kitchen, I left. I was eager to get home."

"What was she wearing?"

"She was in a nightdress."

"What color was it?"

"Black, I think."

"Low-cut, strappy thing, was it?"

"Yeah, I think it was."

"See-through?"

"Yeah, nylon thing."

"She sat up on one of the stools, did she?"

"Yeah."

"So then what happened?"

"I just told you. I packed up my tools and I left."

Anna tapped the table with her pencil. "That's all that happened? This sexy woman wearing a transparent black nightdress sits watching you, and you expect me to believe that you just walked out? Didn't you even strike up a conversation with her?"

"We exchanged a few words, but none I can remember."

"What vehicle were you driving?"

"Pardon?"

"What vehicle were you using on this occasion?"

"Er . . . it'd be the one I used for the company, as I'd had some jobs to do earlier in the day."

"What time of day was this?"

"Late afternoon."

"So did you return straight back to Manchester?"

"Yes. It was my last bit of work."

Anna tapped the table again. "Did you have sex with Margaret?"

"No, I did not."

"It's very hard for me, Mr. Smiley, to believe a word you say. I am expected to believe that you just finished your work, packed up your tools, had a conversation that you can't really remember, but you recall exactly what she was wearing. You were eager to get home, but she must have been very tantalizing, provocative, and we all know what you have waiting for you at home."

"I don't like the way you say things about my wife."

"And I don't like you lying to me. What happened, John? You start getting a hard-on when she crossed and un-crossed her legs on that high stool—is that what happened? You couldn't resist her, could you? And she was offering it up to you, giving you a big come-on. A sexy man like you couldn't help but want it. What was she doing, easing her nightdress up her thighs, pulling the straps down? Just exchanging a few words . . . Come on, what do you take us for!"

"I knew she was a slag."

"Oh, you knew that, did you, John?"

"Yes. The woman Emerald is one as well. It was obvi-ous."

"So knowing Margaret was a tart meant nothing—right, John?"

He nodded.

"What are you nodding for? To admit that you knew she was a tart, or that it was all right to screw her because it was on offer?"

"All right, *all right*—I let her do it."

"Do what, John?"

"I went into the bedroom with her."

"You had sex with her?"

"Yes. She gave me a condom."

"So after you'd had sex with her, what happened?"

"I took a shower. I felt dirty after screwing her. I was ashamed about it, and when I came out, she'd got my wallet out of my trousers and was looking at the photographs of my kids and Sonja. Nosy cow! I snatched them off her."

"Was she dressed by this time?"

"Yeah. A right slob, she was."

"Go on, John."

"She asked for twenty quid. She knew I'd got cash off the other whore, so I threw it at her. She was laughing, saying it'd have cost more, but she fancied me." He shook his head. "Listen, I don't like admittin' this. I'd been faithful up to then. You know, I respect my marriage vows?" He sighed deeply.

"What happened next?"

"I told her I was going back to Manchester. Although we'd lost the contract with Strathmore, we still had to complete the term of the contract, right? She said she'd give me the twenty quid back if I dropped her off at the Gateway Services."

"And did you?"

"Yes. I just dropped her there and carried on out of the service station. I didn't stop, I just wanted to get rid of her."

"Did you see her again?"

"No. That was the last time I saw her."

"You said you wanted to get rid of her. You didn't really mean that, though, did you?"

"Yes. I felt disgusted with myself for being so weak-willed. I never wanted to see her again."

"But you spent a lot of time traveling up and down the motorway, so we know you did park at the same service station on at least two other occasions."

"Yes, I did, and I was brought in here for questioning

because of a problem with my vehicle's registration. I didn't give them my new home address, and thinking about it, I reckon I presumed that Mr. Rodgers would have taken care of that."

"But you own the van, don't you?"

"Yes, I paid for it in installments. It was a good deal, and I wanted to know I could hang on to it if I ever got made redundant."

"And you never registered the ownership of Mr. Dillane's van that you bought from him, either. Why was that?"

"Oh, I just never got around to it. I don't get much free time."

"But you had to know it was illegal. The van is still registered to Mr. Dillane. Did he not send you the documents?"

"No, he gave me everything when I bought it."

"Yet you still failed to register it, and you used it on the road illegally. However, you did collect a new MOT certificate—from Croydon, I note, where Mr. Dillane still lives."

Smiley shrugged and pulled at his tie again. "I only used it when I was doing private work. I suppose I just didn't want my boss to find out."

"Mr. Dillane was a close friend, wasn't he, when you were at Aldershot?"

"Yes, he was one of my closest pals."

"He asked to borrow money from you, is that correct?"

"Yes, he did, but I have never liked lending money to friends. They never pay you back, and I couldn't afford it at the time, anyway."

"But you had considerable cash. You paid him seven hundred pounds for his van, isn't that correct?"

"Yes."

"So Mr. Dillane knew you did have money?"

"Yes, obviously."

"In his statement, he said that you told him you were having money troubles at that time, so you could only pay him in installments, is that correct?"

"Yes."

"But you not only had your wages, you also had the extra cash you made doing private work."

"Yes. That's what I wanted his van for—I just told you."

"So why did you say you were having money troubles?"

"It was a lie. I didn't want to shell out a lot of cash to him."

"But he was your friend!"

"Not one I kept in touch with on a regular basis."

"Because he didn't like Sonja?"

Smiley remained silent.

"He knew about her, didn't he? He told us that she was sexually permissive when she worked in one of the Aldershot pubs."

Smiley clenched his fists. "Whatever Micky Dillane told you is a lie. My wife didn't care for him because she knew he liked me to go out and get drunk with him."

Anna was tiring. They were going round in circles, and for her to come back and try to nudge Smiley into opening up by talking about Sonja wasn't paying off. She glanced at Mike to indicate he should take over.

Gregson pulled at his shirt cuffs and suggested that they should not discuss Smiley's wife in hearsay, as it bore no connection to the reason his client was being questioned.

Anna sat back, trying to think of the next tack, because she knew they had no evidence to prove that Smiley did continue to see Margaret Potts. She turned to the troll to remove the file on Dorota Pelagia. She was just about to indicate to Mike Lewis that they should move on when she had a thought and checked her notes.

"When you went to the service station on these two other occasions we know of, did you see Margaret Potts?" Mike asked.

"No, I didn't ever see her again."

"But she contacted you, didn't she?" Anna asked innocently.

Smiley blinked and then looked to Gregson.

"When you found her looking through your wallet, she had your children's photograph and your wife's, and she must also have found a business card, maybe even your home address. She got in touch with you, didn't she?" Anna continued.

"No, that's not true."

Anna leaned across to Mike. "That's something we should ask Sonja about—see if she received any calls from Margaret."

"She never called. Maybe she saw me at the service station, but I never saw her."

Chapter Seventeen

Barolli could feel the frustration emanating from Anna and Mike from his vantage point in the viewing room. He couldn't understand why they didn't move on to questioning Smiley about the other victims. So far, the man had not admitted to anything apart from having had sex with Margaret Potts on one occasion. Why did Anna keep returning to Smiley's wife? Barolli's train of thought was interrupted by Barbara saying that Michael Dillane had arrived.

Dillane was complaining about having to return to the station. It was his day off, and he'd promised his wife they'd go to Ikea to look at sofas. He felt that he had told the police everything regarding the sale of his van to Smiley. He began to get interested as they went through into the forensic department, however, and became quieter. Led to the table where the blue blanket was pinned out, he was invited to handle it if he wanted to. All they wanted to know was if he could identify it as the dog's blanket he had said he left in the back of his van. They had already removed some dog hairs and tested them against dog hairs removed from the van while it was parked at Smiley's garage. It would be a slower process to get them confirmed, but the team would be able to use this as leverage in questioning Smiley.

Dillane didn't hesitate. He picked up one corner of the blanket that had a jagged edge where the prison stamp would have been, and said, "I cut this off. Did it with the wife's scissors she uses for crimping or something—you know, the ones with the zigzag blade. Also, there's a big stain to one side where me dog got sick. I washed it, but it was bright yellow, and the stain never come out. Gawd knows what Nimrod had been eating. Yeah, this is my blanket, all right."

Barolli found Anna and Mike in the canteen on a lunch-break. "How's it going?" he asked.

"Slowly," said Mike.

"We got an ID on the blanket from Dillane. He is certain it was the same one he left in the back for his dog to lie on. They are still matching the dog hairs. Had to bring in a canine specialist unit for animal identification, but we can use the coincidence until it's a positive match." Barolli laughed, recalling that he had asked Dillane if they could also bring in the dog. He had said they'd have to dig him up, as poor old Nimrod had died about a year ago.

"Very funny." Anna sighed. "So we move on to Dorota, but we were hoping to break him over Margaret Potts."

"I know—I heard. I was in the viewing room, and you were getting nowhere fast, as far as I could see."

Anna finished her coffee and pushed the cup aside. "We have to get him to confess, because we don't have enough to charge him with the others. We don't even know how he picked them up; all we've got is circumstantial evidence."

"Should be enough, though. Christ, he puts on the uniform, they feel safe enough to get into that dog handler's van and he kills them."

"But we have no forensic evidence from the van that

any of the girls were ever inside it. Has Pete matched any of the carpet fibers?"

"Not yet, and they stripped the van down; ditto the Swell Blinds vehicle. So far, nothing."

"All we've got is that he has admitted having sex with Margaret Potts one time and never saw her again." Mike sounded depressed.

"We go again and keep on going," Anna said. "That little prick of a lawyer makes me want to slap him." She stood up. "I'm going to have a wash and brush-up. We'll reconvene in, what, Mike?"

Mike looked at his watch. "Fifteen minutes."

Anna went into the ladies' room, washed her face, and combed her hair. Resting her hands on the sink, she tried to think how they could put more pressure on Smiley. She closed her eyes, wondering if it was possible they had it wrong. Langton had warned her it was going to be tough to break Smiley—but what if the man were innocent?

She looked up and stared at herself, then folded her arms. If, as Langton had said, Sonja was the means to open him up, Anna had tried and failed. But could she put more pressure on, using Sonja as bait?

Anna had five minutes to spare, so she went into the incident room to talk with Barbara. Smiley's house was still being searched, but to date, no evidence had been forthcoming from either his home or the rented garage. They had also found nothing incriminating in Smiley's locker at his workplace.

"What did he do with the victims' clothes?" Anna said, more to herself than Barbara. She crossed to the incident board and looked at the faces of the murdered women.

"You've only one found naked, and that was Dorota Pelagia." Barbara stood beside her.

"You know, in the Fred West investigation," Anna mused, "one of his victims' mothers called at his house, asking about her daughter, and Rose West was wearing her slippers."

"Yeah, well, with Sonja being the size of a house, I doubt if she'd fit anything from our victims."

"It was just a thought," Anna said, knowing she was grasping at straws. Missing were the new shoes described by Eric Potts and worn by Margaret the last time he had seen her, but then they didn't know if they had all her belongings, especially since Emerald Turk had taken some and dumped the rest.

Mike appeared and told Anna that he was ready to start the interview again. "Not looking good, is it?" he said quietly as they made their way back to the interview room.

"Nope, but we'll keep going. They've nothing new from his house," Anna told him, sitting at the table.

"Do we go for Dorota Pelagia now or keep on with Margaret Potts?"

"I've changed my mind about Dorota. Let's stay on Margaret for a while longer. We can maybe tire him out." She smiled encouragingly.

"Or, more likely, we'll get tired out."

Smiley looked refreshed and had the audacity to say he had enjoyed his lunch. Mike warned the man that he was still under caution. Just as they were about to begin, Anna's phone vibrated. She took it out and glanced at the text message, then showed it to Mike.

"Mr. Smiley, I am going to ask that another officer continue this interview. Please excuse me."

Anna stood up as Mike spoke into the tape recorder to say she was leaving the room. She hurried to the adjoining room to find Barolli and Barbara sitting with Sonja Smiley. Anna drew Barolli into the corridor and asked him to join Mike. She gestured at Sonja through the small window in the door. "When did *she* arrive?"

"Just now. Turned up out of the blue. They called me from reception to go and collect her. She's a nasty piece of work."

"Right. Let me have a go at her, and you follow Mike's lead, okay?"

"I have conducted an interview before," Barolli said sarcastically.

Anna hurried into the incident room to ask Joan for a copy of all their victims' photographs. She then returned to interview room. Anna took a deep breath and walked in as Sonja turned to face her. She was wearing what looked like a floral tent and had sweat stains beneath her armpits. Folded over her knee was a raincoat.

"I want to know what is going on," the woman said forcefully. "Nobody is telling me anything. I want to know why you've got my husband here *and* why you've got men searching my house from top to bottom. What is going on?"

Anna sat opposite Sonja. "Your husband has been arrested," she said calmly.

"I know that, and if you try to tell me it's to do with his not changing the registration on his van, then you must think I'm stupid. I know *he* thinks I am, because that's all he's told me. You don't take a man away in handcuffs just for that, so now I want to know the truth."

"Your husband has been arrested in connection with four murders."

Sonja's mouth dropped open. *"What?"*

"It is obviously serious, and he is being interviewed."

"Murders? John? That's preposterous. He's never done anything like that! You've got it wrong."

"Then perhaps you can help me. Would you agree to answer some questions?"

"I want him to have a lawyer."

"He has one. If you feel it necessary, we can also bring one to be privy to this interview, but as you are here of your own free will and just offering to assist my inquiry—"

"What do you want to know, because I am telling you now, John never done a bad thing in his life."

Anna smiled and said. "Do you have the photographs, Barbara?"

DC Maddox passed over a file, and Anna placed it on the table. "I am going to ask if you recognize any of these women. May I call you Sonja?"

"Are you serious? He's here about four murders?"

"That is correct."

"I am telling you that we have never spent a night apart, not since we were married. I know *everything* about him."

"But you didn't know he had a van parked in a private garage. It used to belong to Michael Dillane."

"Oh, him, he's no good, that one. I won't let him in the house no more. He gets John drunk, takes him pub crawling. I won't have it."

"But you didn't know about the van, did you, Sonja? So perhaps there is a lot else about your husband that you don't know. For example, did you know he was making a considerable amount of money doing private jobs?"

"What private jobs?"

"He uses the blinds that are customers' returns and sells them at a cheaper price."

"No, that's not true, because Arnold Rodgers wouldn't allow that. I know he's very strict. You got that wrong."

"Your husband paid Michael Dillane seven hundred pounds cash for his van, Mrs. Smiley. He has been earning quite a lot of extra money for years. In fact, he was working on one of those private jobs when he met Margaret Potts." Anna withdrew Margaret Potts's photograph and laid it flat on the table in front of Sonja. "She was a prostitute, and your husband has already admitted to having sexual intercourse with her and to paying her."

"I'll bloody kill him!"

"We believe, Mrs. Smiley, that your husband killed *her.*"

The sweat lay in beads across Sonja's top lip. It trickled down her neck, and she was obviously uncomfortable, as she kept on patting her face with a crumpled tissue.

Out came the photographs of Anika Waleska, Estelle Dubcek, and Dorota Pelagia. Anna placed them in a row on the table. "Do you recognize any of the girls?"

Sonja blew out short sharp breaths, and now the perspiration was pouring off her, the crumpled tissue sodden.

"These girls are Polish. Have you ever met any of them?"

"No." Her voice was hardly audible.

"Have you ever heard your husband discuss meeting Polish girls?"

"No."

"We believe, Sonja, that your husband killed these girls also."

Her small round eyes were so pain-racked that Anna felt sorry for her and offered her a bottle of water.

"Thank you." Sonja unscrewed the cap and gulped the water. Her hands were shaking.

"There is a possibility, however, that we could be mistaken. Perhaps you could help us clear a few things up."

"I want to see him."

"I'm afraid that won't be possible."

"He didn't hurt these girls. I know him—he couldn't do anything bad. He is a good man."

"Can you recall a few years back, probably shortly before you moved from London to Manchester—did you receive any odd phone calls?"

"How do you mean?"

"Perhaps asking for John or hanging up? You know the kind of thing, from a woman possibly."

Sonja sighed and drank more water. "We had someone call a few times, but they hung up and we thought it was because we were in a rented flat. You see, we rented when we first moved to Manchester; we didn't get our house for a few months."

"Did this caller ring when John was at home?"

"Yes. He was angry because they called late and woke the children. He said it was someone getting the wrong number. I remember he told them not to call again."

"Did the person call again?"

"I don't remember."

"Was it a woman's voice?"

"Yes. Why do you want to know? It was before we moved to our house."

"Yes, you said, and this would have been five years ago, correct?"

"I want to see my husband. I don't like these women's faces."

Anna removed the photographs.

"You have said that John never spent a night apart from you in all the years you've been married."

"Yes, even though it meant he would have to travel long hours. He always come home to me, so that is why I know this isn't right. He has done nothing bad. I know this."

Anna again placed down Margaret Potts's photograph.

"He has admitted to having sexual intercourse with this woman."

"Take it away from me! I don't believe he did that. She looks like a whore—you say she is one. He would never go with a woman like that, never, never."

"Mr. Dillane inferred that when you were young and working at a bar in Aldershot, you were sexually permissive."

Her fat hand smacked the table. "Not true. That man is a liar, a wicked liar. Why are you saying these terrible things about me, about my husband?"

"Because we have four dead women, Mrs. Smiley, and we have removed certain items from your house that link to their deaths."

"No."

"Why did your husband have a security guard's jacket and cap hidden in a garage that he rented near your house?"

Sonja took a deep breath, her ample bosom almost pressed against the table.

"I don't know nothing about that. What I do know is that friend of his, that Michael Dillane, he was a security guard, so they must have belonged to him, and he left them when he stayed one night."

Anna realized that for all her sweating and nervousness, Sonja was quick to give a possible reason for the presence of the uniform.

"Why are you here, Mrs. Smiley?"

"Because I get a call from Mr. Rodgers. He said that he had taken enough from the police and that he could not keep John working for him anymore. I come to straighten things out with him. I not say no more until I speak to my husband. You got to let me talk to him."

"I am afraid that won't be possible."

"You got no right to keep him here! I want to see him!"

"You can wait until the interrogation is completed, but it could be some time."

"Then I wait. I have someone staying to look out for my children, so I wait."

"Does your husband speak Polish?"

"A little. My mother had poor English, so we used to try and teach him, but he not pick it up. My children don't speak it either, and . . ." She bowed her head and started crying. "I am sick with worry. Please let me see him."

Anna left Barbara with Sonja and returned to interview room one. She tapped on the door and looked in. "Paul, can I have a word, please?"

Barolli stood up. Anna made sure that Smiley could hear even though she lowered her voice. "Mrs. Smiley is very distressed. Can you arrange for a cup of tea?"

Barolli nodded as Mike reported into the tape recorder that DI Travis had returned to the interview room.

"You got my wife here?" Smiley asked.

"Yes, she's helping our inquiries."

"She's here? You brought her into the police station?"

"Yes, but she's obviously distressed."

Smiley stood up. "I have to see her."

"Sit down, Mr. Smiley." Mike gestured firmly to him.

"No, you can't do this. I have to talk to her."

"*Sit down!*"

Smiley slumped back in his seat and then asked his lawyer if it was right that they could bring in his wife and not allow him to see her.

"You can talk to her when we have finished the interview, Mr. Smiley." Anna said as she took her seat as Mike passed over some notes from while she had been out of the room.

"She is being well looked after but is obviously frightened, and as she now knows that you were with Margaret Potts, she is helping our inquiry with regard to the other victims we also wish to question you about."

"You had no fucking right to tell her anything, you bitch." He jabbed a finger at Anna, his face twisted with anger. Gregson put a restraining arm on Smiley, trying to calm him down, but the other man jerked away from him in a fury. "I want to see my wife."

"She also wants to see you. She's been called by Mr. Rodgers, who has told her you can no longer work for Swell Blinds."

"Jesus Christ." Smiley was so pent up with anger that his whole body shook.

"She also told me that, contrary to what you have said, Margaret Potts made frequent calls to first your rental flat in Manchester and then— " Anna was lying, but it got a result.

"That is not true. She *didn't* know!"

Anna glanced up as Smiley tried to explain.

"What I meant was, neither of us knew who the caller was. She, whoever it was, was obviously expecting to speak to the previous tenant, right? Then she'd put the phone down."

"It was Margaret Potts, wasn't it?"

He closed his eyes. Anna felt as if she were playing a game of poker, bluffing, but obviously doing it well.

"All right, yes, it was her."

There was a long pause. Anna and Mike were exchanging looks, hesitant to begin drawing more from Smiley, hoping he would elaborate. He didn't.

Gregson shifted his weight, alarmed as Smiley put his head into his hands. Eventually, Anna quietly suggested they start from the moment Smiley said he met Margaret at Emerald Turk's flat. She had an intuitive feeling that something was wrong and was trying to quickly work out the time frame of when he had met Margaret, then relate it to the phone calls, but she couldn't grasp what was confusing her.

"As I said before, she wanted me to give her a lift to the London Gateway service station. I waited until she was dressed, and then we went out to my van." He paused and then smirked. "We were driving along, and she said the van still stank of dogs, so I said to her, 'It takes one to know one.'" He gave a mirthless laugh. "Anyway, I dropped her off and went on to Manchester."

"Just a second, Mr. Smiley. Earlier you stated that you were not using Mr. Dillane's vehicle but the company Transit van, so kindly explain what you meant when you said Margaret said it stank of dogs."

"Oh, right, sorry. I must have been confused. Yeah, now I remember it was Dillane's van, and it did smell of his dog. I never got rid of the stink."

Anna still had that niggly feeling but said nothing as Mike asked when Margaret had started to call him.

"She got my bloody number from my wallet, and she called a couple of times wanting to see me, but I always put the phone down on her. I didn't want to ever see her again, and I obviously didn't want Sonja to know what I'd been up to. When we moved to the new house, she couldn't call me 'cause we'd got a new phone number."

He said that was it and repeated that he didn't see her again after that one time. Anna doodled on her notepad, unable to bring up what was lingering in the back of her mind, because it didn't quite make sense. Margaret Potts was murdered two years or more ago, Dorota even longer. Margaret was making more money than usual and had been, they presumed, hitting John Smiley up for cash before he had purchased the van from Michael Dillane. Then it clicked. It was like a piece of jigsaw falling into place, and she was angry with herself for not grasping it sooner.

"You knew Margaret Potts before you met her at Emerald Turk's flat, didn't you? You lied when you said it was the first time you met her."

She could almost see the wheels turning in Smiley's head as he weighed the question and made a decision on how to answer. Mike Lewis was looking confused, as it was something he hadn't even considered; this was completely out of left field. Like Anna, he waited for Smiley to answer.

"You got me there," Smiley said, and he had that weird smirk on his face again.

"Where exactly have I got you, Mr. Smiley? Caught in yet another lie?"

"Yes."

"Please don't waste any more of our time. Just tell us how long you had known Margaret Potts before that meeting at Emerald Turk's flat."

He looked at the ceiling, thinking. "Maybe four years. I wouldn't say I knew her—let's say it was more of an occasional thing. It was often months in between meetings, and then it was only for one thing. I suppose you can guess what that was."

"Sex?"

"Yeah. I also need to tell you that I liked her. Okay, she was cheap and she was fucked up—and she was always on the take—but at the same time, she had a kind of genuine niceness. She was always gonna clean her act up, but she liked the drink, she liked getting stoned out of her head, and she also liked sex in a big way."

"Four years?"

He nodded, adding that it was about that, but he couldn't be sure, as he saw her only infrequently.

"Where did you really first meet Margaret?"

He closed his eyes, remembering. "It was in a café opposite King's Cross station. They do a good cheap breakfast there. Don't know what it's called, but that's where she used to hang out."

Smiley continued to recall the different places that he had subsequently met Margaret Potts; he reckoned that it was before she began working the service stations. He added that he met her there by accident, as he hadn't seen her in months.

Anna wrote a note to pass to Mike. The body of Dorota Pelagia had been discovered four years ago. The time frame bothered her because Margaret Potts wasn't murdered until two years after Dorota. Did she have a connection to Dorota? Mike glanced at her note. She had written, *Firm up dates.*

Anna remained silent as Mike took over.

"Go back to the time you met Margaret at Emerald Turk's flat. Did you know that she'd be there?"

"Yeah, because I'd seen her recently. She told me about the blinds, though her mate didn't know we were acquainted. It worked out okay for me because I'd been part of doing the housing association contract. I even gave her a cut of the cash Emerald Turk paid me 'cause of selling her the Swell Blinds for the box room. Maggie was hitting me for more and more cash; she even threatened to call my wife, and I'd had enough."

"Can I clarify something, Mr. Smiley? Are you saying that Margaret was hitting you up for money during the entire time you knew her? From the meeting in the café?"

"Yeah. Not much—a few quid here and there. I paid her 'cause I didn't want her callin' Sonja, and like I said, it wasn't that much."

"You said Emerald did not know that you knew Margaret Potts?"

"No. It was gonna be convenient, 'cause we could have time to play some sex games in a bed; before that, I'd only ever done it with her in the back of the van. Listen, I'm tired, and I've got a headache."

Anna knew how he felt. Her head had begun to throb just from trying to assimilate all the new dates and locations, and she began to also want to take a break. It was already after six. Smiley had started to droop, constantly rubbing at his face.

"So after that time in Emerald Turk's flat, when did you see her again?" Mike asked.

"I never did. Next thing I knew, couple years later, I was reading that she'd been murdered, poor cow."

This didn't add up for Anna. She believed that it was *after* that meeting that Margaret had increased her blackmail demands of Smiley. It was getting to the point that they should move to question him about Dorota Pelagia, but Gregson asked that as it was late, they should break and continue the interview the following morning.

"I want to see my wife," Smiley said.

"I am afraid that won't be possible," Mike told him.

However, Anna wanted to keep Smiley sweet, so she suggested they speak to their superintendent to see if a short supervised meeting could take place.

She and Mike left Smiley with his lawyer just as Langton walked out of the viewing room. He had just arrived so had not been privy to the interrogation.

After a brief discussion, he agreed that they should keep Smiley as pliable as possible for the following day, and if they let him see Sonja for five minutes, it might assist their interrogation in the morning, but he wanted him handcuffed. Smiley would be held in the cells overnight again.

Sonja Smiley was sitting with Barbara. Food cartons and cups of cold coffee littered the table. She turned expectantly when Anna entered.

"We have agreed to allow you to see your husband, Mrs. Smiley, but I will have to be present, and it can only be for five minutes."

Sonja reached out to take Anna's hand and grasped it tightly. "Thank you. I just want to say a few things to him."

Anna felt sorry for her. The big woman seemed vulnerable; her face was swollen from weeping, her eyes red-rimmed.

Barbara was eager to leave, as the body odor from Sonja was by now overpowering. "Can I go?"

"Yes. Sorry to keep you here for so long."

"That's okay." Barbara jerked her head to ask for a private chat. "She's been crying since you left, almost waded through a whole box of tissues. She didn't talk much, kept going on about betrayal . . . how much she'd done for him . . . but she still managed to scarf down four sandwiches and a hamburger."

"Thank you, Barbara. Right, you get home. I have to say I really need a break as well. I'm exhausted."

Anna watched Barbara walk down the corridor at the same time as John Smiley left interview room one, accompanied by Mike and Barolli. He was handcuffed but was trying to straighten his tie and run his hands through his sweat-sodden hair.

Anna stood aside, pushing the door open wider for Mike to usher Smiley into the room. Sonja was like a sumo wrestler. Considering her size, she moved quickly and kicked her husband hard in the groin, then as he moaned, bending forward, she gave him an upper-cut punch worthy of Mike Tyson. His head jolted back as she came at him again with fists flying, catching him twice with well-aimed heavy punches before Barolli and Mike managed to drag her off.

Her face was red as she spat at him, then held between the two officers, she screamed, "You bastard! After what I done for you—well, now I make you pay. You got no home, no job, and you never gonna see your kids again. *I hate you.*"

Smiley burst into tears as he was helped to his feet. Anna was helping Barolli as Mike pushed Sonja into a chair; her chest was heaving as she tried to get her breath.

Smiley was taken down to the cells, still crying. His lawyer stood watching helplessly, obviously shocked by what had happened. Langton tried to put the lid on it all, ushering Anna into the room with Sonja as he headed off with Gregson. Barolli handed Sonja a cup of water, and she gulped it down. She then turned to Anna.

"I want to make a statement. I want a lawyer to be with me because I don't want no trouble for me. I only want trouble for him, and I can give you plenty. I know things—very bad things."

Anna's headache was at full blast, and she felt sick but remained calm as she said that Sonja should stay with Barolli. She then hurried off to find Langton.

Langton listened as Anna repeated what Sonja had just told her. "Statement?"

"That's what she said—and that she wanted trouble for Smiley, that she knew bad things—"

Langton put up his hand. "Okay, okay . . . let's get her represented." He glanced at his watch. "I dunno who we can get tonight, but we should do it ASAP, while she's still spitting venom."

"I'll get on it." In her state of exhaustion, the thought of yet another session was daunting.

"You don't think she's involved in the murders, do you?" Langton asked. "Did you bring her here?"

"No, she came of her own free will."

Langton rubbed his head. "That might be a lucky break, because from what little I heard, it's been a long, slow process with not much to show for it."

Anna would have liked to add that if she'd had stronger backup, she might have gotten a lot further. Mike had felt like deadwood beside her sometimes. However, she said nothing, heading up the stairs to the incident room with a packet of aspirin.

It was another hour before a lawyer was found for Sonja Smiley. By now it was after seven o'clock. Moira Flynn was a forty-five-year-old experienced lawyer. Straightaway, she asked if Sonja wished a private discussion before making her statement. The woman refused, saying she wanted to get it over with, but after a moment, she asked if, by making the statement, she would be accused of anything criminal. Miss Flynn suggested that they have a conversation without Anna present.

There was another half-hour delay before Anna sat down with Sonja. The latter was nervous, and Anna was struck by how tense she was, yet determined to begin. Sonja sipped a glass of water, and Miss Flynn indicated that she should start.

Anna switched on the tape recorder, giving the date and time and location before asking Sonja to begin her statement. Sonja nodded and licked her lips.

"I met my husband when I was working in a bar in Aldershot. It was around the time of the Kosovo war, more close to the end of it, as the soldiers were all returning. My bar was popular with the Paratroopers, and some nights it was rowdy. The boys would let off steam and get drunk, but we tolerated it because the owner of the bar was making a lot of money. I was living in a rented flat—just two rooms—with my mother. She spoke little English and was quite poorly, and she had been doing housecleaning, but that had got too much for her, so we were dependent on my wages."

Anna stifled a yawn; she couldn't see where Sonja's statement was leading. She began to concentrate on the woman in front of her, trying to keep up at least some semblance of interest. Sonja was obese and had a flat face and thin lips, and she had little or no expression, but she kept her chubby hands clenched. She was very different from the picture her husband carried, and yet Anna could sometimes see that Sonja had once been attractive by the way she spoke, and held her head up, and her eyes were a bright blue. There was a lightness to her, even though her belly hung low and her huge breasts pushed against the table, while her thick legs beneath the table were wide apart, her ankles swollen.

"I admit that I did have a few relationships with some of the soldiers, and I also admit that they sometimes gave me money, but I wasn't a tart. I only went with the nice ones. I used to see John come into the bar with his mates. They'd often get drunk, but he was always a real gentleman. I liked him from the first moment I saw him. He asked me out for a date, a real one, wanting to take me to a movie, and he did come on to me, but I rejected him. I didn't want him to think I was an easy lay. I wanted it to be different with him. I really liked him, and he came and met my mother and was kind to her."

Sonja gave a long sigh, then sipped more water. Anna was taking sly looks at her watch, wondering how long the so-called statement would go on.

"I don't know how much he cared for me, but we had several dates, and I still wouldn't go to bed with him. He said it was all right, and he never pushed himself on me, he never tried it on like some of the other Paras. There was another barmaid, a blond girl called Chrissie. She was younger than me, and we were never friends, but we worked hard alongside each other, and she was popular. It was well known that she was no angel; she really put it about. One night John had come in with his friends, that Micky Dillane was one, and they were getting boisterous. We often had to call in the police or the army to haul the lads out . . . It was near to closing time—in fact, the boss had rung the bell to say last orders . . ."

She sipped more water. "On this night John was sort of ignoring me—well, it felt like he was—and at about eleven o'clock, I went out to the backyard with some bin bags to stack in the wheelie bins. They didn't see me, and I was really hurt, because he was kissing Chrissie. She had her skirt pulled up, and he had his hands all over her. I thought she tried to push him off her, but it could have been my imagination. I was upset, and after I'd washed the glasses, I went straight home. Next lunchtime, Chrissie didn't come in, and it made us short-handed. We called her flat but got no answer. When she still hadn't turned up for the night shift, my boss was worried."

Sonja licked her lips, and sweat trickled down her face.

"They called the police, but nobody knew where she was. They asked me if I'd seen her, and I lied, I said I hadn't, as I'd been busy in the bar all night. I never told them I'd seen her out by the bins with John. I just kept my mouth shut."

Anna was on full alert, leaning forward.

"They kept on searching for her, and it was weeks later that her body was found. She'd been raped and strangled with her own tights. John and his cronies didn't come back to the bar for some time, but when they did, I asked John to meet me after work. He agreed, and we met up in an all-night hamburger café. I said to him that I'd been questioned about Chrissie, and he went quiet. At first he hardly said a word, then I said to him that I'd seen them together on the night she disappeared. He was upset, begging me not to say a word, and if the police asked questions about him, would I say that when the bar closed, I was with him?"

She wiped her eyes. "They *did* ask me about him—they were asking about all the soldiers in the bar that night. I told them he was my boyfriend and that he'd been in the bar all night and then took me home."

"You gave him an alibi?" Anna said quietly.

"Yes, I did. You see, I wanted to get married. I had my mother to look after, and it was hard for me, all on my own. I said if he wanted me to keep on lying for him, he should agree . . ."

She shrugged her wide shoulders. "We got married. I loved him. He was what I wanted, and when I asked him about Chrissie, he said that what had happened was an accident. She had come on to him, egging him on, and when he took her round back into the fields by the pub yard, she rejected him. He said he had squeezed her throat when he was trying to kiss her and suddenly realized she was dead, so he took off her tights and wrapped them around her neck. I didn't understand but wanted to believe him—I needed to believe him. He was my way out of that stinking bar."

"You never told this to anyone?"

"No, never, but even though I tried not to think about it, it was always somewhere in the back of my mind. It didn't matter that Chrissie was promiscuous; I'd had plenty of boyfriends, too, and it was no reason for her to end up in that field."

Sonja gave a helpless gesture. "What it did was make me cautious with John. I was so afraid he'd do it again. I was always wondering if he was seeing other women, it didn't matter that we had two children. The fear was always sitting inside me, and I warned him that if he ever crossed the line, if I ever found out he was seeing other women, I'd report him. I kept him short of money, made sure he always came home to me because, yes, I was afraid he would do it again."

She drained the water and set it carefully down on the table. "He has, hasn't he? He betrayed me. All the years I've protected him and looked out for him, and he's been with other women again."

Tears welled in her eyes. Her grief was just for herself, not for any of her husband's subsequent victims. Any sympathy Anna had felt toward her had evaporated. She spent some time getting the exact dates and location of the murdered Chrissie, whose surname Sonja thought was O'Kcefe.

"I won't get charged with anything, will I?" she asked, looking pleadingly at Anna.

Miss Flynn had not said one word, but she, too, looked to Anna for an answer.

"That will depend on whether your statement can be verified. In the meantime, we will begin checking out your information."

Sonja looked up as Anna pushed back her chair. "It's the truth, I swear before God, but I can't protect him anymore. I never want to see him again, and he will never see his children again."

She gasped for breath and gestured at herself. "This is what he did to me. I used to be such a pretty woman, but when you live with a secret like that, something has to give because of the guilt. I have hated myself, but you know . . . he has nothing, I know that now."

Langton was sitting at Anna's desk, having by now watched the entire video of her interrogation of John Smiley.

"Tomorrow I'll be with you; we'll do the interview together," he said.

She rested her briefcase on the desk, and he reached for her hand, patting it lightly.

"It's been a long day," he said tiredly.

"Yes. How did your case go, the Pixie?"

"I got a full confession and more crocodile tears. The bastard."

"Well, congratulations."

He stood up and smiled. "We'll get Smiley tomorrow, so go home and get a good night's rest."

"Good night, then."

"Good night, Anna."

She started to walk away and stopped. He rarely, if ever, called her Anna.

"Don't you have one to go to?" she asked.

"One what?"

"A home."

She caught a look in his eyes, a split second of pain, and then it was gone.

"Got a lot of catching up to do here. Go on, get out."

Chapter Eighteen

Anna thought about Langton on the drive home. She was certain he was trying to get closer to her, but she didn't know why. Perhaps he didn't like the fact that she was no longer under his control, emotionally, at least. As she drove up to her garage, she saw Ken sitting astride his motorbike. Her spirits lifted immediately. As he took off his helmet, she got out and flung her arms around him. "Oh, I needed to see you!"

Arm in arm, they headed toward the lift. They kissed frantically as they reached the flat, besotted, and it didn't take long for them to undress and get into bed. Having him with her made all the weights of Anna's day disappear. Wrapped in his arms, she said that she couldn't think of anything better than to have him there.

"I've had such a long, shattering day, and yet we are at long last moving the case forward."

"Yeah, me, too. We got verification today that Welsh is being moved the day after tomorrow. That's the reason I was able to make my escape."

They got up and made bacon sandwiches, as hungry for food as they were for each other. Anna didn't elaborate on the day's events, and Ken didn't feel inclined to give more details on the problems they were having with Welsh. Instead, they discussed dates for their wedding, and Anna said that perhaps after this case, she would take some unpaid leave for a few months. This would give them time to look for a place to live.

Ken was surprised. "You'd want to do that?"

"Yes. You know, I have never taken a holiday, never mind proper time off, and I think now is the right moment."

"I thought you were ambitious?"

"I am. Let's say I'm not at the moment, although I would like to try and get my promotion. But the thought of not being involved in another case straightaway comes as a big sense of relief."

They discussed finances. Ken knew that starting more training as a child psychologist, expanding his degree to work with mentally challenged children and underprivileged teens, would not be well paid. He was embarrassed to admit that his salary would be in the region of £12,000 to £14,000 a year. He was surprised to discover how much Anna earned; she also had a substantial savings account: £170,000.

"I never spend all that much. Maybe because I never have time to go shopping," she said. "This flat cost more than I ever believed I'd be able to afford. I've got a mortgage, but I was able to use some money my dad left me, and I sold my previous flat. So when we sell this one, we won't have any money problems for a few years, at least. When I return to work, we'll have my wages combined with yours."

Ken put his arms around her, clearly loving her even more. Her practicality and generosity had overwhelmed him, he said. "It's strange, isn't it? There's me, saving every cent to be able to continue getting more training as a child psychologist, and there's Welsh with a degree, having all the time to study, plus three meals a day, living in a comfortable cell and financially well off."

Anna hugged him. "I wouldn't even think about it. He's never going to be able to do anything but have even more time to face up to the waste of his intellect. Also, he'll be out of your hair soon, so you won't have to see him again."

The following morning, Ken had to leave early for his shift on the unit. Anna took a lazy shower, washed her hair, and then dressed, ready to go into the station. She knew it was going to be another long day, and she was glad that Ken had stayed over, because she had slept so soundly in his arms. Usually, if the day ahead looked like a tough one, with lengthy interrogations, she would have forced herself to check over her files and notes in preparation, and more often than not, she would have had a restless night. But having Ken there made her feel calm and confident.

Anna was at her desk by eight-thirty. She had stopped to buy a Starbucks coffee and was eating a cream donut when Barbara passed.

"All right for some. I eat one of them, and I roll on extra pounds."

Anna smiled and licked her sticky fingers.

"He was here all night, I think—Langton," the DC went on.

"Was he?"

"Yeah. In Mike's office. When he was a DCI, he used to have all his shirts stacked up—had me going back and forth to the laundry for him."

"He's got a wife to do that now."

"I suppose he has. You never know with him, but then you probably know him better than any of us."

Anna couldn't help smiling, Barbara was so obviously fishing for gossip, and she looked her straight in the eye. "Why do you say that?"

Barbara hunched her shoulders. "You know, we all sort of knew you were with him for a time. You know, when he got injured . . ."

"Ah, yes, then. That was a long time ago."

"He still gets a lot of pain. I presume he's taking tablets for that—caught him taking a handful this morning. Is he still having problems?"

"I don't know."

"We got some added details coming in regarding that murder Sonja Smiley told you about. Nothing confirmed yet, but they did have a cold case, and the victim *was* a Chrissie O'Keefe, so Mike will be hoping to get more details this morning."

"Good."

"So this new man in your life, what does he do?"

"He works in Barfield Prison."

"Oh, well, that's going to be quite a drag for you, going up and down to Leeds."

"No, he's starting work in London after we're married."

"Oh, working in a prison down here, is he?"

"No, he's a child psychologist and will be working with mentally challenged children."

"So he's a bit more than a security prison guard?"

"Yes."

"That's nice. Do Joan and me get to buy new hats?"

Anna laughed and said they should, as it would be a formal wedding.

"Oh, you'll be wearing white, then?"

"Yes."

"I would have liked a decent wedding myself, but we just

went to a register office. It's not the same; they wouldn't even let anyone throw confetti."

Langton walked in, and Barbara turned to him. "I know—a chicken and bacon sandwich, no tomatoes."

"No, I've already eaten."

Barbara scurried over to her desk as Langton looked at Anna. "We go in half an hour. Smiley's lawyer is already here."

He crooked his finger toward her. "You know, we might get a lot of unpleasant details if I'm right and he starts talking."

"I think, with the added information from his wife, it could be in the cards. Barbara mentioned the cold case and that Chrissie O'Keefe is being checked out. Will they be sending over the case files?"

He nodded and then touched the knot of his tie. "You can handle it?" he asked.

"Yes."

"Good. Right, then, let's go get the bastard."

Smiley was brought up from the cells with Gregson at his side, the latter looking refreshed and smart. His client, by contrast, looked much the worse for wear. He had a bruise under his right eye and hadn't shaved. His tie had been removed, along with his shoelaces, so his shirt was open from the collar, and the sweat marks on it were clearly visible. He asked if he could remove his jacket and did so, revealing sodden patches of sweat beneath his arms. His body odor was strong and unpleasant, almost as pungent as his wife's.

Langton proceeded, repeating Smiley's rights and saying that they would tape and video the interview. He began by explaining to Gregson, not even glancing at Smiley, that subject to Sonja Smiley's statement the previous evening, there could be another charge leveled against his client in connection to a fourteen-year-old murder inquiry.

Gregson puffed out his cheeks. "I should have been given details of this before we started this session."

"I'm afraid we don't have them." Langton shrugged. "We are waiting for confirmation from the team who investigated the murder of Chrissie O'Keefe, so I am being up-front with the possibility that your client was involved." He looked directly at Smiley. "Your wife has claimed that she gave you an alibi for the night of O'Keefe's murder. Do you wish to give details now or prefer to wait until we have been able to—"

Smiley interrupted. "I can tell you what I did do—the biggest mistake of my life. I married the bitch, that's all I will admit to doing. She'd rake up anything to get me into trouble. You saw what she did to me, how she attacked me. Crazy fat bitch."

"You've certainly changed your opinion of her," Anna said softly.

"Yeah, it's called telling the truth." Smiley pushed his chair back slightly to rest his elbows on his knees. "You have no idea what I went through; you get into a situation, and then it goes out of control. I never wanted to marry her, I'd already finished with her. She came on like the Virgin Queen with me, wouldn't let me screw her, although I knew most of the lads had given her one—*and* for money—but she wouldn't let me near her, and it pissed me off, so I finished with her."

Anna wasn't sure why Langton appeared disinclined to press for details on their victims; instead, he leaned back in his chair, nodding.

After a moment, encouraged, Smiley continued. "You know, I had to put up with a lot of snide remarks from the lads about marrying her, and I just had to take it, under-stand?"

Langton nodded again, still not saying anything.

"So I got into the situation, right? I also had to take on her halfwit of a mother. She was senile, and I had to shell out money for her. Sonja wanted her to move in with us, but I drew the line there. I wasn't having that, and I kept on making excuses. By this time I was in civvies and I got the job with Swell Blinds, worked my arse off for Arnold Rod-gers, and then the old lady died, so that was one weight off me."

Langton nodded as if he understood where Smiley was coming from. Anna, like Smiley's lawyer, was baffled by the rambling history of Smiley's marriage and why he was being allowed to continue. Both sat back, listening, while Langton appeared to be even more interested, giving Smi-ley his full attention.

"You have kids?" Smiley asked.

"Yes," Langton said.

"Then, maybe you can understand. First came my boy, Stefan, then two years later, my daughter, Marta. I love those kids, I loved them from the moment they were born. And Sonja was a good mother—I'm not saying she wasn't—and we was living in Kilburn in a rented house, and I was workin' my way up the ladder with Swell Blinds. You see, somewhere in my head, I'd reckoned I'd be able to walk away from her one day, leave her, but when the kids came along, there was no way out. No way was I going to leave them."

"And she must still have threatened you?" Langton said it as if he were on Smiley's side.

"Right. She'd never actually put it into words, just hints, know what I mean? If I went out for a pint with my old mates, she'd gimme a hard time; she was on my back like a leech, sucking the blood out of me. You have no idea what it was like to live with someone who monitored every move I made, who kept me short with pocket money. I had to tell her where I'd been, and I couldn't stand it. I hated her."

"Why didn't you kill her?"

Smiley smiled. "Don't think I never thought about it, but with two young children, I was trapped—understand me?"

"So she was virtually blackmailing you, is that right?"

"Yes, but like I said, she never came out with it. It was just always there, in the background."

"Sorry, I didn't quite understand. What was always there?"

"That she'd lied for me over Chrissie O'Keefe, given me the alibi."

"Did you ever admit to Sonja that—"

Smiley interrupted Langton. "I told her it was an accident. Truth was, I was no longer interested in Sonja. I started to see Chrissie, but she went and did the same thing to me, coming on to me, getting me all excited, and then pushing me off her. It got me so mad! I knew both of them were a right pair of slags who gave it up for all me mates, but with me, they wanted a commitment, know what I mean?"

"Why do you think that was?"

"Most of the other blokes were already married. I was younger and single, that's what I put it down to."

"You were a catch, then?"

Smiley nodded. "Yeah, yeah—that's right."

"But you punished Chrissie, didn't you?"

"Too right I did. Served her right, but I've paid the price. I had Sonja squeezing me and always the threat that she'd tell the cops if I didn't do the right thing. Sometimes it felt like I was on a leash. All that was missing was the fucking dog collar."

"But you found ways of cheating on her, didn't you?"

"Yeah. That was some comfort, know what I mean?"

"I bet it was."

"She got uglier and fatter. I never touched her after my daughter was born, and it worked for me—you know, that she was eatin' for England." He laughed. "It meant she didn't get out of the house that much, and then we moved to Manchester, and I sometimes had to do the long hauls back and forth to London, and she couldn't put her friggin' clock on me just so long as I got home every night."

"Let's go back to when you lived in Kilburn, John."

Listening to Smiley's accounts of his marital life or lack of it, Anna began to understand what Langton was doing. By now Smiley seemed to feel as if he were talking to a friend. He never acknowledged Anna but kept his focus on Langton, unaware that the DCS was slowly drawing him out. He had even unwittingly admitted to killing Chrissie O'Keefe.

Because Gregson was not privy to the details of O'Keefe's murder, he could not understand how Langton had trapped his client. He made copious notes, but every time he began to speak, Smiley shut him up with a sharp dig of his elbow. In the end, Gregson burst out, "Mr. Smiley, I really feel that we should ask for a moment in private to discuss the fact that we have not had any disclosure regarding this Chrissie O'Keefe."

"Shut up. I don't wanna listen to you. You're too young to understand," Smiley said rudely.

Langton gestured to Anna to open the file on Margaret Potts. She passed him the photographs. He selected one and placed it in front of Smiley. "You have admitted that you knew Margaret Potts, but can you elaborate on where you first met her?"

Smiley tapped the photograph. "I said before—King's Cross station in a café. I used to have breakfast there, and she was a regular."

"How long ago was this?"

Smiley puffed out his cheeks. "Be a good few years ago, maybe seven. I was still living in Kilburn, I remember that." He repeated how Margaret had suggested he sell blinds to Emerald Turk.

Langton doodled on his notepad. "Yes, we know about you being in Emerald Turk's flat, we know you were paying money to Margaret, but when did she start to really nudge you for more cash? It must have felt like you'd got hooked by another Sonja, right?"

"Right."

"So what did she threaten? To tell your wife about your relationship?"

"Yeah, but that didn't worry me, because we moved to Manchester."

"But you have stated that you did have calls from her when you lived there. Your wife has also verified that she received a number of put-down callers."

"Right. Yeah, sorry, I forgot, but like I said, I changed my number when we bought the house up there."

Langton flicked through his notebook, muttering, "Hang on, John . . . I'm having trouble matching dates. You have admitted knowing Margaret Potts for around seven years . . ."

"Off and on, yeah."

"It was about five years ago you fixed up the blinds in Emerald Turk's flat, correct?"

"Yeah, give or take."

"Help me out with this, John. You have also said that after that time you didn't keep in touch with her, am I right?"

"Yes."

"So the phone calls you received from her in Manchester would have started around about four years ago."

"Yes."

"So she did keep in touch with you, but she wasn't making threats about calling Sonja, was she? She had something a lot bigger to hold over you, didn't she?"

Smiley looked alarmed.

"It's all right, John, I can understand what it must have felt like to have another woman threatening you. All I need to know from you is how the hell did Maggie find out about Dorota Pelagia?"

Langton was brilliant, the way he casually dropped in the name of the victim. Smiley didn't even react to the name or say he didn't know who she was. Langton removed Dorota's photograph from her file and placed it in front of Smiley. "Sonja knew about her, didn't she?" Langton continued in the same relaxed tone. "She was young, she was beautiful, and compared with Margaret and Sonja, she was fresh . . . lovely. How did you meet her?"

"I was at Victoria coach station—that was where I sometimes picked up Margaret. She often worked there, if not at the Gateway Services. She used to hang out there—you know, picking up punters—and I'd finished my deliveries, so I had time to spare and went looking for her."

He licked his lips. "She was with *her*. Someone had nicked her bag—well, that's what I was told—and Margaret said that if I was going back to Manchester, could I give the girl a lift."

"This girl you are talking about, was it Dorota Pelagia?"

"Yes, I just said so. She was Polish, and I was able to say a few words to her 'cause I'd picked up some Polish from Sonja, and so I offered to give her a ride as far as Manchester."

"Where was she going?"

"Liverpool."

"Go on."

"She got in, and she was lovely, I liked her. Then I said to her that if she could wait for an hour at the service station on the M6, I would be able to give her a ride all the way to Liverpool."

Smiley said that he drove his Swell Blinds van back to Manchester, parked in the street next to his lockup, and then, using Dillane's van, drove to collect Dorota, who was waiting for him.

"It was getting late. I'd been working all day. I'd left home just after four and had a long drive to London and then back to Manchester, and now I had to go to Liverpool. I knew I'd have Sonja after me, so I was a bit wound up."

"Don't tell me. After all you'd done, picking her up at the coach station, then driving back to take her to Liverpool, Dorota played hard to get. Is that what happened?"

"Too fucking right. Ungrateful little mare. I even said that as I knew she had no money, I'd give her a few quid, but she got nasty, pushing me away, treating me like shit, and I snapped. After all I'd done for her . . . so I kicked her out of the van. She was shouting and screaming at me, and I got worried someone might stop and ask questions."

"You wouldn't want that. Wouldn't want any trouble that might get back to Sonja—right?"

"Yes, that's exactly what I was worried about. So I

grabbed her and put my hand over her mouth, and I opened up the back of the van to stuff her inside." He gave one of his strange laughs. "When I got back into the driver's seat, she was trying to open the cage, crying and begging me to let her out, saying I could do whatever I wanted to her, but she didn't want me to hurt her."

"But you did, didn't you?" Langton flipped over the murder-site photographs, and Smiley flinched.

Gregson leaned toward Smiley and said he should not answer, as it was admittance and—

Smiley pushed him away, saying, "Bollocks! It's fucking obvious what I done. By the time I got home, Sonja was like a slavering bulldog. I'd have liked to put my hands round her thick throat, strangle her like I done the girl."

Langton nodded encouragingly. Smiley then gave them the hideous details of how he had strangled Dorota with her own tights, stripped her naked, raped her over and over again, and then driven her body around for two hours before wrapping her in the blue blanket and tossing her body into a field. He had then returned home, dumping the dead girl's clothes in a charity-shop doorway.

"You must have thought you'd got away with it?"

"Yeah, and I would have an' all but for that bitch Margaret. I mean, they didn't have anything on me, right—no witness, no nothing."

Smiley went on to explain how, unbeknownst to him, there had been a *Crimewatch* program on TV, asking for anyone with information to come forward. Dorota's photograph had also been published in the newspapers.

"I was still not worried, and then that bitch calls my office and says she wants to talk to me."

"Margaret Potts?"

"Yeah, her. She didn't have me home number 'cause,

like I said, I'd moved to the house in Manchester. She only called the friggin' office!—She said she wanted a lot of money 'cause she recognized Dorota, and she also said she knew I had this blue blanket in me van because we'd had sex in the back once and she said it smelled of dogs. She was a wily bitch, and she put two and two together. So I agreed to meet up with her."

"How much money did she want?"

Smiley shook his head. "She'd always hit me up for a tenner or twenty here and there, over not tellin' Sonja about us, but this time . . . Jesus Christ! It started with a couple of hundred, then it got to more, and she threatened to go to the police. It was a fucking nightmare, the bloody Sonja scenario all over again."

Langton glanced at Anna and passed her a note that said, *Time frame.*

Anna asked if the time Smiley had been at Emerald Turk's flat to fix the blinds was when the payments had started.

"No, it was after, but when I was there, she hit me up for a couple of hundred. She said she needed the money to pay for something to do with her kids. Lousy mother, her kids were both fostered out. I told her I didn't have it, but she said I'd better find it. I gave her about a hundred that time, and we arranged to meet. I said I'd give her the rest then. I never intended to pay her another penny, but the bitch called my workplace again, so I met up with her in the café, and this time she fuckin' asked for a thousand quid 'cause she said she knew about that girl."

He shoved a finger at the photograph of Dorota. This tied in with Margaret's new clothes and the visit to her children.

"So when was the next time you met up with Margaret?"

Smiley frowned, obviously trying to recollect the date. He hunched his shoulders and then said it was maybe months after he'd met her at the café. They had met at the service station, and he had given her five hundred, saying he didn't have the cash to spare. Margaret wasn't satisfied and said she wanted more. It was another six months before he had yet another meeting with her and passed her money. He was tight-lipped with anger, saying that Margaret wouldn't stop pestering him and he was worried about her contacting him at his workplace. In the end, he had told her that if she gave him some time, he'd save up and give her one final payment of another five hundred pounds in March.

Anna held up her hand. "These meetings that took place between you, are you saying they came *after* she called Swell Blinds—or did she have another way of contacting you?"

He hesitated and then went into an elaborate, rambling account of how he used to call a pay phone at the Gateway Services, and if Margaret was around, she'd pick up.

"If she wasn't doing business, she'd hang around the pay phones, keepin' warm, actin' like she was usin' them so they wouldn't move her on. There was an Indian bloke that worked the coffee bar at night, and she used to jerk him off for a cup of coffee and a snack, then clean herself up in the ladies' toilets."

"So, on the occasion when she was waiting for more money, where did you meet Margaret?"

Smiley said that sometimes she would use an old caravan parked at the back of a slip road near the service station. When he saw her there, they would have sex, and previously, he paid her between twenty-five and thirty pounds. He would park some distance away, walk up the lane, and wait until he knew she wasn't with any of her regulars.

"I waited until I knew she was alone. I then went and drove the van right up to the stinking caravan, and she came out all smiles." He mimicked her voice. "'You got my money, honey?'"

He sniggered, saying he'd told her it was in the back of his van in a cardboard box. He described how he'd opened the back doors, and when she had leaned in, he'd pushed her inside with his foot. He then slammed the doors on her and locked them. He was still smiling as he described driving around with her. "Just like that Polish bitch, she was trying to unlock the cage."

He wasn't sure where he stopped. It was dark and would have been a good few miles beyond the London Gateway Services.

"I said to her that if she kept her trap shut, I wouldn't harm her, and she sat quiet in the back of the cage. No more swearing and cursing. Then I helped her out like a real gentleman. I said to her I was joking and that the money was in the glove compartment. When she opened the passenger door to get to it, I came up behind her. First I got her by the hair, then I pulled her down. I wanted to stamp on the bitch's face . . ."

They were forced to listen to more grotesque details of how Smiley had raped and strangled Margaret and then left her body in a field before he drove back to Manchester. He was now enjoying himself, as if the admittance of the murders were some achievement that no one had recognized.

Langton smiled and held up his hand. "That was three

you got away with, John—Chrissie, Dorota, and Margaret Potts."

"Yeah, and I can tell you I had a few sleepless nights—you know, waiting and worrying that I might have left DNA—but I was certain I got no witnesses. Nobody ever saw me with Margaret, so I felt like I'd had a lot of luck. I used to clean me vehicles with a special high-powered spray, always very careful."

"Yes, and your wife didn't have a clue, either, did she?"

"No. And you know something? I started to enjoy having a double life. I liked earning the extra money she knew nothing about. I liked looking at her and saying I'd be late home and then getting this adrenaline rush from what I was doing. I felt like I was untouchable."

"But you were clever. You didn't get rash, didn't attempt to commit another murder for quite some time, right?"

"Yeah, that's right. I'm an ex-Para, watch my own ass, never give nothing away, but I used to have the biggest hard-ons just thinking about what I done. It was enough. I even let Sonja wank me off a couple of times because I could remember what it felt like when I squeezed their throats and my dick was inside them. When I tightened their stockings round their necks and they gasped, it was the biggest orgasm I'd ever had. I just kept spewing out like a volcano."

It was all directed at Langton. Smiley hardly, if ever, acknowledged that Anna was in the room, but now he glanced toward her and apologized. "Sorry, love."

Anna was repulsed by him. His face was shiny with sweat as he gloated, and spit formed at the corners of his mouth. His big hands constantly made the gesture of clasping his victims' throats and squeezing, or his fists clenched as he demonstrated garotting.

"So what happened, John? It started to fade, the excitement, the memories. You wanted to feel that adrenaline rush again, that volcanic orgasm?" Gregson was showing his inexperience as he didn't attempt to stop Smiley, but sat in shocked silence.

Anna could see that Langton was encouraging Smiley to continue his disgusting admittance of how he killed.

"Yeah. I started to need it again. I am a hard worker, and with that bitch at home, I started to feel the lack of excitement. It got to be almost an obsession. I was like a hunter looking for prey—that was how I saw it. I was a hunter, and even that thought would give me a hard-on."

Langton almost snapped his fingers at Anna to bring out their next victim. She moved quickly to open the file on Anika Waleska and placed the photograph in front of Smiley.

At last Gregson felt he should intercede, but Smiley shoved him in the shoulder. He patted the photograph with the flat of his hand. "Oh, yes. What was her name?"

"Anika Waleska," Anna said.

He went into lengthy detail, describing how he had used the jacket and cap to appear to be a security guard, and how it helped that he was driving the dog handler's van. He said that it had given him an added pleasure, targeting Polish girls. This was partly because of his hatred of Sonja but also, he was able to appear to be trustworthy, as he always mentioned that he was married to a Polish woman and that they had two children.

He had picked up Anika Waleska outside the restaurant where she worked. "I'd had a bite to eat there a few hours earlier, after I'd been on this bloody tricky job on Cromwell Road, and we'd chatted."

Smiley said that he'd called home to tell Sonja he was still working on the job and not to expect him home until much later. He had said good night to his children and then sat waiting. He chuckled, saying that he always had to remember to toss his sandwiches away, as Sonja would even check the plastic container. Smiley started to give details of the corned beef and pickle sandwiches she'd make for his lunches, how much he detested the gherkins she wrapped in cling film.

"Anika Waleska . . ." Anna said, tapping the photograph.

Smiley closed his eyes and whistled. He said he had offered Anika a lift in the van, and she had accepted. She told him she was looking for work, as the room she shared was expensive and she was not earning enough money in the restaurant. She also said that she had worked like a slave for a domestic agency that had helped her to come to England, but after a few months, she quit because the work was so grueling, and as at the restaurant, the pay was poor. The woman who ran the agency had stolen, as the girl put it, a large slice out of her wages for rent.

Smiley lived up to his name, smiling all the time. "She could talk, this one, but she was pretty, and like I said, I could understand a lot of what she was saying because of picking up Polish from Sonja. I liked her so much I was thinking that maybe I should arrange to see her again— you know, like a girlfriend—but it didn't feel right. I wasn't getting the same rush, so I got as far as White City, where she had moved to, and I decided to keep her."

He patted her photograph again. "She had no warning— took her by surprise, it did. She was about to get out, and I just hit her."

Langton leaned toward him.

"Describe how you hit her, John. It must have been difficult to keep her from getting out."

"Yeah. I just went like this." Smiley swung his right hand

toward Gregson, fist clenched, and pulled away just before striking. Gregson was so shocked, he almost fell off his chair.

"Wait a minute, John. If you were on the driver's side, you couldn't have hit her that way."

"No, I did it with me left hand, just like this." Smiley demonstrated clenching his left fist and giving a vicious side sweep with his arm extended. "She wasn't expecting it. I got her right across the throat, and she sort of slumped over, out cold. I drove her away and kept checking she was out, I didn't want her coming round. Then, when I got to a quiet area, I lifted her out and locked her in the cage at the back of the van."

They had to listen to yet another hideous description of what he had done to Anika, raping her and dumping her body on the drive back to Manchester.

"I'd done it again, and there was nothing—no witness, even—and I was high as a kite. It had felt so good, and it was a couple of weeks before I started to calm down. I reckoned that I'd got it down to a fine art. This time I read all the papers about her body being found, and it was a real buzz to know I had done it and nobody could touch me."

"So how long afterward did it all start up with you again?" Langton asked.

Smiley cracked his knuckles, pondering. "You know, it wasn't like the previous times. When it started, I got a real rush from the waiting to see what happened, but when nothing did, I felt the need to make something happen, to do it again."

Anna brought out the photograph of Estelle Dubcek. She passed it to Langton, and he laid it down in front of Smiley, who looked at it and then scratched his head.

"I think that was her. I wasn't prepared. I'd been to

London fixing up a couple of blinds, not for Swell Blinds but for people over in Shepherd's Bush. They'd already had some fitted by the company, and they liked them, so they wanted to order more. I took the call, and I said that maybe as they were such good customers, I'd be able to make a deal with them—a cash deal. I was a bit pissed off because I had a lot of trouble making the blinds fit, it took me bloody hours, but I got three hundred quid. I was heading back toward the M1, and I stopped off at the Westfield shopping mall, Shepherd's Bush. It was my daughter's birthday coming up, so I went there to look for a present."

They heard him describe how he had chosen a Barbie doll with a riding outfit and a pony. He wagged his finger. "Funnily enough, I remembered Margaret telling me she'd bought her kid a Barbie doll, so I reckoned I got the right present, and they wrapped it all up nice for me."

He went quiet as if enjoying the memory of his daughter's birthday and said that she had loved it; it was her favorite toy. He then recalled how Sonja had questioned him about where he had gotten the money and how he'd had a big row with her. "Can you imagine? She questioned me like a fucking Gestapo officer. Where did I buy it, how much did it cost, where had I gotten all the extra money?"

"But you were laughing inside, I bet. You had cash, you were making a lot of cash, and she didn't have a clue, did she?" Langton was trying to ease him back into discussing Estelle Dubcek's murder.

"No, I kept that well hidden. I just used to take all the aggravation." Smiley was still looking angry.

"So when you met Estelle Dubcek, you had bought the present for your daughter, right? So you had a lot of cash to spare?"

"Yes, that's right."

"Where did you meet her?"

"You've got to understand, this time I wasn't ready for it. I wanted to get back to Manchester in time for my daughter's birthday, so I wasn't intending to pick up another girl. I drove toward the M1, and just before you get onto the motorway, there's a slip road. A lot of hitchhikers use it, they hold up placards saying where they want to go, and there she was, all on her own. She held a bit of cardboard with *Manchester* written on it."

He laughed. "It was on a plate, right? And then talk about coincidence—she was Polish. I couldn't believe it! I didn't even have the cap and jacket on, and I just pulled up and said I was heading to Manchester and I could give her a ride."

Estelle had gotten into the van, he said. Her English was not that good, so he had tried talking to her in what little Polish he could manage. At first she was pleasant, and then she said she wanted to get out at the next service station, as she needed to use the bathroom.

"She'd only bloody gotten in. Next thing you know, she wants to go to the fucking toilet."

"You think that maybe she'd figured out that you couldn't be trusted?"

Smiley shrugged. He now seemed loath to continue, biting his lip. Anna glanced at Langton, who gave a small shake of his head for her not to interrupt.

"I knew it was gonna be a problem. I'd thought about dropping her off at the London Gateway and driving on, but then talk about fucking coincidence. She says to me that she's got an uncle in Manchester and that she's gonna be working for him in his bakery. So not only was it a coincidence, her being fucking Polish, she's only gonna work in the bakery that Sonja uses. It's in the shopping precinct near our house. I couldn't believe it."

He was twisting his big hands, saying that it was making him sweat, because if Sonja was to meet her and got chatting, she'd find out he had picked her up, but more important, she would find out about Dillane's van and also about his earning extra money on the QT.

"So I had to get rid of her. I had too much to lose."

Smiley described how he had driven past the service station and Estelle had started to get into a panic, asking him over and over why he hadn't stopped there, as she had asked. He told her that it was a mistake and he knew a slip road he could take and they could drive into the back of the service station. By this time Estelle was crying because she was frightened and didn't believe him.

"She was really getting on my nerves, screeching to get me to stop to let her out, and no matter what I said to her, she wouldn't stop. We got close to where Margaret used to hang out by the caravan and the old barns. She started to grab at the handle of the door, and I went crazy. I had one of the cords I use for the blinds, and I just put it round her neck."

"Still in the van?" Langton asked.

"Yeah. She had her back to me, 'cause she was trying to get out, but the door was locked."

Smiley lifted his hands to demonstrate how he had placed the cord around Estelle's neck and tightened it until she fainted. He then carried her into the caravan and raped her before he tightened the cord around her throat and strangled her to death.

"I'm not into that sickness—you know, fucking a corpse—but I think she was dead when I fucked her, and it wasn't all that pleasurable. It was the first time I knew I'd made a mistake. Anyone could have driven past, and I had to get rid of the body fast. I turned the van around and drove into a field a short distance away, and I threw her body out by a ditch. The traffic was going past on the motorway, and I got the hell out. I didn't feel the same buzz. I felt sick."

Langton laid out the victims' photographs. "You have admitted, John, that you killed each of these women: Margaret Potts, Anika Waleska, Estelle Dubcek, Dorota Pelagia, and now you have also admitted that you murdered Chrissie O'Keefe."

Smiley leaned back. "Yeah, that's right."

Langton looked at his watch. "We will now take a lunch break and reconvene here in one hour. We will need to verify dates and times and clarify a few more details. You will be returned to your cell, and if you require to discuss anything with your lawyer, Mr. Smiley, you may do so."

Langton then addressed Gregson. "Your client will be charged later with four murders, and we will be consulting with the criminal prosecution service regarding Chrissie O'Keefe. If there is time, he will be taken before the magistrate this afternoon; if not, the following morning. Do you understand, Mr. Smiley?"

"Yeah, I understand."

Langton stood and thanked him for his cooperation as Anna stacked the files in order. They left as uniformed officers took Smiley down to the station's holding cells.

In the incident room, the team gave a round of applause. It had been a very long, tedious, and wretched investigation that at last had a conclusion. Langton held a briefing requesting that Anna and Mike Lewis handle the next session to finalize all the details.

Anna could see how tired Langton was; yet again he had impressed her with how he had handled Smiley. She had hardly said two words, but being privy to Smiley's admissions left her feeling exhausted as well as sickened. She needed to eat to keep up her energy, so when Langton went off to oversee another case, she and Mike had some sandwiches and coffee in his office. They went through the tape of the interview, making copious notes.

"A lot of coincidences," Mike murmured.

"According to Langton, there are never any, but even Smiley admitted to it being a big one with Estelle Dubcek, her being Polish, and not only that, about to work in a bakery close to his home."

"Yeah, well, we always reckoned Estelle's murder was a hurried kill; at least we got that right, but when you think of the hours we've put in chasing the wrong facts—like we were told Estelle would never hitch a ride, and not only did she do that, but she had a notice up asking for a lift to Manchester."

"What about the Polish connection? Yet another lengthy wrong avenue, tracking all through the embassy. What a waste of time." Anna gave a rueful smile.

Mike leaned back in his chair. "Do you think Welsh really did know anything about the murders, or was he manipulating us in order to get to you?"

"I think it's half and half, really. He was genuinely interested in the case, and he's gained a lot of self-knowledge during his time in prison, and he was always insistent about Margaret Potts being the link. So in some ways, I suppose, though I'm loath to admit it, he did trigger a response."

"He'd have triggered one if he'd torn up the files."

"Come on, they were all copies, and he was never left with them, they were always removed when we left. By now I think he'll also be removed, as he's been acting up, gone stir crazy."

"Langton does take risks, though, doesn't he?"

"Yes, he does. Can we get on now? I don't know about you, but for me, it's been a very long day."

It was not until three-thirty that Mike and Anna returned to the interview room. Smiley was morose and often belligerent as he tried to recall the exact dates. Gregson remained silent throughout, and they finished the interview at six o'clock. They still didn't have full details regarding Chrissie O'Keefe, but due to Smiley's admissions, the CPS gave authority to charge him with all five murders.

Before being returned to his cell, Smiley was formally charged by the custody sergeant and informed that he would be taken before the magistrate's court the following morning. The team was going to the local pub for a drink to celebrate, but Anna was too drained to join them. She just wanted to go home.

She had just left the station when Langton returned with a press statement already prepared. Even though he had been working flat out since early morning, having such a positive result had energized him. He was about to leave with the team when Barbara took a call. It was for Anna. Barbara said that she was not available, but then she hesitated and asked the caller to hang on. "Gov, it's a Mr. Hudson for Travis, says it's urgent. Is that the name of her boyfriend?"

Langton held out his hand. "I'll take it. This is James

Langton," he said. "Can I help at all? DI Travis has just left the station and—"

Langton listened and sat down in Barbara's desk chair. No one was paying that much attention, as they were all getting ready to leave. It was a call he wished he had never agreed to take. The incident room was almost empty by the time he replaced the receiver.

"You coming, Gov?" Mike Lewis asked as he closed his office door.

"No. I have to go and see Travis."

"Something wrong?"

Langton could hardly speak; he simply nodded.

"Anything I can do?"

Langton picked up his coat. "No, there's nothing anybody can do. Give my apologies to the team, and I'll see you in the morning."

Mike didn't know what was wrong, just that Langton's face had drained of color and he was visibly shaken.

"Good night, then." Mike walked out.

Langton slowly pulled on his coat. He was dreading what he had to do, but he wouldn't have trusted anyone else to do it.

Chapter Nineteen

I was just going to bed," Anna said into the intercom.

"Let me in, Anna. I need to see you."

There was something about his voice. Again he had used her Christian name, which he so rarely did. She opened the front door and returned to her bedroom to put on a wrap over her nightdress. She wondered what could be so urgent that he had called without, as she had requested, ringing her first. She sighed, hoping it wasn't connected to Smiley. God forbid if he had managed to hang himself in the cell.

As she came out of the bedroom, Langton was closing the front door.

"Do you want a drink?" she asked.

"No, come here."

She was puzzled. He took her by the hand and led her into her lounge.

"What's happened?" she asked nervously.

"There is no easy way to say this, so I'll come out with it directly."

He was shaking, and she almost went to put her arms around him to comfort him. Then he dropped the bombshell.

"Anna, there was an incident in the prison. Welsh attacked Ken, and he's . . . he's dead, Anna. I am so sorry."

She felt her legs buckle beneath her, and he caught her in his arms. She murmured over and over, "No . . . No . . . No . . ."

Langton held her tightly. "Come on, sit down, there's a good girl."

Her breath came in short gasps as he steered her toward the sofa and then sat beside her with his arm around her shoulders.

"What happened?" Her voice sounded even to her as if someone else were talking, asking the question, because she couldn't focus.

"Apparently, they got the order for Welsh to be removed to Broadmoor this afternoon. They brought him out of his cell, and Ken was putting the cuffs on him. Welsh had somehow gotten a plastic fork, melted it down, honed it into a sharp point, and he stabbed Ken in the jugular."

He didn't add that Welsh had also stabbed Ken in the eye; they were unable to stem the blood flow, and he had collapsed and died in the ambulance. Due to the complicated entrance system to the special unit, the ambulance and prison medics had taken longer than usual to get there and assist the officers trying to keep Ken alive.

Anna was trembling all over and deathly pale. She stared ahead as if unable to comprehend what Langton was saying. He wished she would break down and weep, but she remained frozen. He got up and fetched a glass of brandy, bending down in front of her, holding it up to her lips. "I'll stay here with you."

The brandy dripped from her pale lips as if she were incapable of sipping it. Langton sat next to her and again placed his arm around her shoulders. He told her that Ken's father had called the incident room, and he had taken the call. He felt that if he could keep on talking, she would break down and release the tears, but she continued staring blank-eyed.

Langton drank the remains of the brandy himself, at a loss as to what he could do to comfort her. He hadn't told her that Welsh had screamed at Ken that he could never have his girl, his madness out of control as he repeatedly stabbed and lashed out.

Anna remembered a day when she'd been about five or six years old and her father had taken her to the local public pool. She'd had lessons and was able to float by herself, was almost about to swim, and she had been so excited, wanting to show him. He had placed a towel around her tiny, thin shoulders, saying it was time to get dressed, and she remembered running from him, laughing naughtily as she jumped into the pool. But it was not the shallow end, and as the water enveloped her, it felt like it was sucking her down. She raised her arms but remained deep in the water, unable to breathe, sinking deep down and drowning. Anna felt exactly as she had done all those years ago. Drowning.

"Anna? Anna!"

Langton's voice sounded like her panic-stricken father's, willing her to surface, but it was the lifeguard who dragged her to the surface and her father who lifted her from the water and rocked her in his arms as she wept and choked, "I was floating, Daddy, I was floating."

Langton was at his wits' end. He carried her into her bedroom and gently laid her down on the bed. She seemed totally unaware of him or of where she was. He lay beside her, cradled her in his arms, willing her to break and weep, but she remained oblivious. Langton had known grief himself. He'd kissed his first wife goodbye to go off to work shortly before receiving the phone call informing him that she had collapsed and died of a brain tumor. Nothing had prepared him for the shock, and he had never gotten over the loss of the woman he had adored. He had buried his grief, pressed it so far down inside that he had returned to work almost immediately. He didn't want Travis to bury the pain, as he had done, and it was extraordinary that, lying beside her, he felt an uncontrollable need to weep himself. Tears streamed down his cheeks as he held Anna, and still she remained caught in her own world. He squeezed her tighter.

"For God's sake . . . Anna. Anna!"

He shook her, and she was like a rag doll. It was becoming more and more painful for him, as he had no idea what he could or should do to bring her out of such deep trauma. It was dark in the room, and she remained in his arms. If she was comforted by him, he couldn't tell, but after what felt like an interminable time, she gave a sigh.

"Thank you for coming," she whispered, her head resting on his chest.

"I'll stay as long as you need me." He stroked her hair. He wished he could see her face, but she was pressed against his chest. He could feel her heart beat against him, and then her body shuddered as at last she wept. It was as if he were holding a child; awful, heartbreaking sobs convulsed her, and she continued for so long that she exhausted herself and grew quiet. He eased her away from him; her eyes were closed, and she was sleeping.

Langton gently placed her head on a pillow and then got up and wrapped the duvet around her. Totally drained, he returned to the lounge to pour himself another brandy and sat smoking and drinking, loath to leave. However, he was exhausted, and he, too, slept, sitting upright on the sofa.

It was about five in the morning when he woke with

a start; he could hear the shower. His knee hurt like hell, his neck felt stiff, and his back ached, so he went into the kitchen, opened one of his pill bottles, and took a handful of painkillers. He kept on listening, unsure if he should go into her bedroom. He didn't, but he put on some fresh coffee and waited.

She had combed her wet hair away from her face and was wearing a dressing gown when she appeared. She looked extremely young and vulnerable, and he felt old and crumpled, wanting to open his arms and hold her, but she walked to the percolator and poured herself a coffee.

"You okay?" he asked.

"No, but you need to go home and get some rest."

"I had enough. I'll stay as long as you need me."

"We have Smiley before the magistrate's court this morning," she said, sitting on one of the bar stools.

"Mike and the team can take care of that. I hope you are not thinking of going in to the station."

"I have a lot of reports to finish up."

"Anna," he said sternly. "Listen to me. You take time out. There is no need for you to be at the station. I am giving you a warning: you can't bury this with work, you have to give yourself time, you can't heal—"

"Please don't tell me what I can or can't do," she snapped.

"I bloody well will tell you. I am not going to allow you to start work until I am satisfied that you've had enough time."

"I don't want it. We will have to prepare for the trial, and I have a lot of reports to finalize." She glared at him; her eyes were overbright, and she was shaking.

"You don't have to do anything," he said. "I'll handle it. I mean it. You are not to even think about coming in."

She turned on him in a fury. "I can handle this, and I know exactly what I need to do, so don't lecture me. I can't stay here, I can't be on my own."

Her mouth turned down like a child's and he reached for her hand. "Listen to me, Anna. I know what grief is like, loss, I've been there, and I did exactly what you are attempting to do. I went straight back to work, I hardly gave myself time to bury my wife. I did anything I could to stop or stem the grief, but you know what happened? It never goes away. It sits inside you, and just when you think the pain is over, it sneaks up and grabs your heart and squeezes it. You can't let this happen to you. Please, just take my advice, will you? Look what it did to me."

She drew his hand closer to wrap herself in his arms, and then she hugged him tightly. She smelled of shampoo and Pears soap, and he rested his head on her shoulder. From the comforter, he became comforted, and she wasn't like a child but all woman.

"You have to let me deal with this in my own way. I can't be alone, because without Ken, that's what I am, and I am going to have to face it. Staying here in the flat by myself won't help me, so please, you go now. I'll take the time I need, I promise."

They remained together, her arms around him and his head resting against her slender neck. She was kissing him sweetly and patting him, and all the love he had felt for her returned and overwhelmed him.

"I will always be here for you, Anna. You're not alone, believe me. You call me, come to me, whenever you want."

"I will," she said, and moved away from him. He ached to draw her close to him again, but he didn't. Instead, he eased his complaining body into a stretch and drained the remains of his coffee.

"I'll call you later, all right?"

She nodded, needing him to go, wanting desperately to be by herself. When the front door closed behind him, she went back to the bar stool. He'd left his cigarettes and lighter on the kitchen bar. She took one and lit it and inhaled the smoke. It made her head spin, but she continued smoking, sitting and sipping her coffee, willing herself to do what she knew she needed to do.

All the bridal magazines she put into a black bin liner and left it with the garbage for collection. She cleaned and Hoovered the flat and remade the bed and then dressed. She drove to the jewelry shop to reclaim her engagement ring. She slipped it onto her finger and returned home after stopping to buy groceries. As if in a trance, she put away the groceries, cleaned up the kitchen, and then sat by the phone.

She was about to ring Ken's parents when the phone rang. It was Lizzie, Ken's sister. Anna felt the emotion well up inside, and she could hardly speak.

"I'm so sorry. We are all in shock, but I wanted to tell you that I will always want to keep in touch with you, and I know how much Ken loved you."

Anna swallowed but still couldn't talk.

"I've been talking to Mum and Dad. Mum's taken it very badly, and with her heart condition, I'm going up to stay to oversee the funeral with Dad and . . ." Lizzie stifled a sob. Then she sniffed. "Thing is, Anna, Mum sort of blames you. You know that if Ken hadn't met you, this would never have happened, as the bastard who killed Ken had this obsession with you. So Mum doesn't want to see you at the funeral."

"That's all right," Anna whispered.

"No, it isn't, and I feel terrible about it. I know she'll come round eventually, it's just so painful right now."

"I understand."

"Well, I feel terrible. Our brother, Robin, is flying in from Australia, so that should help her, but we have to take care of her. I'm so sorry about this, but if there is any change of plan, I'll call you. I am thinking of you, and . . ."

Lizzie broke down crying, and Anna couldn't bring herself to say anything. She just replaced the receiver. She returned to the kitchen and lit another of Langton's cigarettes, sitting smoking. It was odd, she thought, about Ken's brother, unable to come to their wedding but making the effort to come to the funeral. She remained sitting, feeling as if she were caught in thick dense fog, unable to take in anything, yet slowly realizing that it was a reality. Ken was never coming back. No wedding, no living together, no nothing.

She stubbed out the cigarette and went back to the phone. Should she call them? She decided she would write, and she spent a long time writing and rewriting a letter to his parents and ripping it up and starting again. She constantly looked at the ring on her finger. It didn't twist and turn; it fit perfectly now.

Langton called, and she let the machine answer. She couldn't talk to him, talk to anyone. Instead, she went into her bedroom and lay down.

On her bedside table was the forever-present photograph of her beloved father, and beside it was the only photograph she had of Ken. It was the one he had sent her, aged eight, dressed as a clown. She lay with her face turned to the two photographs of the most beloved people in her life, and she cried.

Anna did not go to the funeral; nor did she send the letter to Ken's parents. She spent most of the time looking over the notes for the forthcoming trial. Every night she slept turned to the two photographs and left her machine on, refusing any calls. Lizzie had called numerous times, Langton up to three times a day. She had told Langton she wouldn't be able to cope being alone, but now she found the solitariness helped her remain calm, and gradually, she knew she couldn't cry anymore. She even practiced controlling the surges of grief that would overtake her when she least expected it.

Her flat was immaculate, and those extra pounds she had intended to lose had gone, as she hardly ate, but she smoked a lot. Cigarettes no longer made her feel dizzy when she inhaled. Lighting and sucking in the smoke gave her a strange energy and made her aware of her shaking hands. Always glancing at her engagement ring, she had decided she would never take it off.

The day she decided to return to work, she dressed carefully, putting on black suit with a crisp white shirt and a pencil skirt, shedding the old tracksuit she had worn most days. She had washed and blow-dried her hair and made up her face carefully, adding lip gloss. She stood staring at herself in the wardrobe mirror and felt she was ready, her armor in place. She knew that the first day back was going to be difficult, and she intended to make it as unemotional as possible. Not for herself; she knew the team would find it hard to approach her.

Anna parked in her space at the station. She was glad not to see Langton's car and to know he wouldn't be there. She smoked a cigarette before she got out and headed into the station. It was exactly as she had expected. As she walked to her desk, the incident room went quiet. All eyes were on her as she put down her briefcase. Barbara was the first to come to her desk, and she had tears in her eyes.

"I am so sorry, it's just terrible. If there is anything I can do, you just have to say."

"Thank you, Barbara. I'm fine now."

Joan looked over. Her face showed such compassion, and like Barbara, she looked like she was going to burst into tears.

Barolli brought her a coffee; he couldn't meet her eyes. "You need anything, let me know."

"Thank you, I will. I'll need an update as soon as I've got myself sorted out."

"Yeah, whenever you are ready."

Mike Lewis looked through the blinds in his office. Langton had said that he doubted Travis would return for a few months, at least until the trial was set, but there she was. It had been only two weeks. He took a deep breath, finding it difficult to go out and face her. Everyone found it hard, since she appeared to be totally in control, spending a long time looking over the incident board and making her own notes.

Mike eventually came and patted her shoulder. "We're all here for you, Anna, and you have my condolences."

"Thank you, I appreciate that. Tell me, have they prepared a full case file for the Chrissie O'Keefe murder?"

Mike told her that Smiley would stand trial for that murder, along with the other four. He said that Smiley had been refused bail and was awaiting trial at Wandsworth Prison. The trial date was set for three months' time, and they would now be preparing all the evidence ready for the prosecution case conferences and defense disclosure. The CPS had been quick to oversee the case files and appoint a top queen's counsel to prosecute.

Anna got into the routine of coming in to the station at eight-thirty every morning and leaving at six. The team began to pack up the incident room in preparation for the forthcoming trial, boxing the statements and evidence. As soon as the trial took place, they could all be allocated to another murder inquiry. It was not a foregone conclusion that they would work together; they could be split up. Anna hoped that Langton would retain them all. It would be up to him to select who went where.

It had been almost three months since the death of Ken, and Anna was surprised to see Langton in Mike's office when she came in for work. He had continued to make calls and check up on her, but over the past few weeks, these had gradually stopped, and in some way she was relieved.

When he came out of Mike's office, he smiled and came to her desk. He set down an envelope. "I reckon this is about time. Open it."

Langton had put her forward for promotion. She would have to go through all the promotional interviews and written reports that she had been subjected to previously. She smiled up at him and asked whether he would be on the board, as at her last attempt at promotion. He shook his head and said that as he had personally suggested she be one of the candidates, he would not be on the review team.

"You'd better not cock it up this time," he joked, and she was touched that he was recommending her.

"Thank you."

"Take your time, make sure all your written reports are up to scratch, and don't get shirty with the psychologist."

Anna gave a soft laugh. The previous time she had become angry with some of the questions she was asked, and believing that Langton had scuppered her promotion, she had walked out before the interview was completed.

"I'll behave myself," she said, putting the envelope in her briefcase.

"I think you are ready for it. You've done terrific work on the Smiley case, and you have shown that you have become a real team player, so now it's up to you. Good luck."

"I've never really thanked you for being there for me," she said quietly. "It can't have been easy, having to tell me about Ken."

"It wasn't, but you'll have time with the trial on to do your grieving." He gave her a long look and then leaned over her desk to kiss her cheek.

"I love you," he said.

Then he walked out, and she realized that she had been able to say Ken's name without that terrible rush of emotion. She knew, too, that it was time to write the letter to his parents, and to go and see Lizzie.

That weekend Anna finally sent the letter to Ken's parents and called on Lizzie. It was a major step in coming to terms with her loss, but she found the meeting difficult, as it brought back so many memories. Lizzie made a toasted sandwich and a pot of tea. Anna was so tense that it was hard to swallow, but she forced herself to take a couple of bites.

"You don't have to eat it if you don't want it," Lizzie said, and Anna smiled gratefully as the other woman removed the plate and tipped the remains of the sandwich into the bin. She was standing with her back to Anna, looking out into the garden at the children's swing and remembering the last time they had been together. She could almost hear Ken's laughter as he played around with her boys, the way he had come into the kitchen with her youngest on his shoulders.

"Oh, God, it's so unfair," Lizzie said, and burst into tears.

Anna went and put her arms around her, refusing to break down herself. After a while she said that she would have to leave, as she was working toward the trial.

"Will you come round and see the boys again?"

Anna nodded, but she knew she wouldn't keep in touch. She wanted the past behind her.

Lizzie walked her to the front door, and Anna thanked her for the tea, apologizing for not eating, then hurried out to her car. Lizzie felt that she was unemotional, almost aloof; she said to her husband that night that she had found Anna almost a different person. Lizzie hadn't even been able to put her arms around Anna, as she had wanted.

Ken's parents wrote a sad letter back and apologized for not wanting her to be at their son's funeral. Anna presumed that it was Roy Hudson who had written the letter. He said they were coming to terms with the loss of Ken but found it very difficult, as he was such a wonderful son. She found herself having to force back tears when he added that he also would have made a good husband.

Anna folded the letter and then tore it to shreds. It was another chapter closed, and she would not contact them again.

The trial had front-page coverage, and the team held up well throughout. Anna took her hours of cross-questioning by Smiley's defense team with a cool authority. She was never rattled but in total control in an impressive performance that did not go unnoticed. Smiley was found guilty and sentenced to whole-life imprisonment with no chance of parole.

As soon as the trial was completed, Anna went before the promotional board and this time had no emotional attachments to worry about, as the three high-ranking officers were none she had ever met. She was touched that one of them mentioned that Detective Chief Superintendent James Langton had recommended her highly. She also handled the lengthy interview with the psychologist far better than she had previously. She was confident that she could not have done better, but she would have to wait three months for the results.

The next case Anna was assigned to was the suspected murder of an elderly woman whose body was discovered mummified in her basement. It was a case that Mike Lewis was allocated to oversee, and they worked well together with a new team. Barolli was also up for promotion to detective inspector, but he wasn't confident, as he felt he had done badly on the written tests. Anna didn't like to say how confident she felt but kept busy with the case in hand, which turned out to be a sad situation rather than a brutal killing.

The elderly woman had been dependent on her son for twenty years due to a heart condition; he had waited on her lovingly, and when she had died, he couldn't bear to part with her. He had wrapped her in the sheets and kept her in the basement for five years. He had somehow managed to keep her death a secret, talking about her health and neighbors, but also claiming her pension every month.

Anna had found the tragedy less affecting than Mike, who felt that the man shouldn't be charged. Anna had surprised him with her detachment, saying that "filial love" had not stopped him from illegally claiming his mother's pension and living off it. Mike noticed then how much she had changed; she was more brusque than she had ever been, always businesslike, and yet the team respected her as much as Mike, if not more so. She was in many ways unapproachable on any kind of social level, though her ambition had not diminished. On the contrary, at times he felt as if she were nudging him out of the inquiry.

No sooner had Anna closed the case of the mummified woman than she received confirmation that her promotion was accepted. Anna was now detective chief inspector. DCI Travis was one of the youngest women to gain that rank, and Mike was relieved that from now on, she would be handling her own inquiries. Poor Paul Barolli yet again failed his promotional exams, so it was possible he would work for Anna, but after the pressure she had put on him during the Smiley inquiry, he didn't fancy being under her command.

Langton had taken a bottle of congratulatory champagne to her flat, and she had opened it, admitting only to him how proud she was. He'd been there a short time before she announced that she had a previous arrangement. He'd been hoping to take her out to dinner but downed the remainder of his glass. As he left, he cupped her face in his hand and kissed her forehead. He felt her body tense away from him.

"You've grown up, Travis. Sometimes I look at you and hardly recognize that girl I lived with. I have always reckoned you were special in every way, but now you have a big career ahead of you."

"Thank you," she said quietly.

He hesitated. "Don't make your whole life your career, darlin'. You'll get over this and you'll—"

She smiled and put a finger to his lips. She said she didn't intend to; she was going out for dinner with some friends.

"Good. Well, onward and upward."

She closed the door behind him and breathed a sigh of relief. She didn't have any dinner date, she didn't have any other friends but him, and she fully intended to make her career the focus of her life. Nothing was going to stop her. DCI was just the beginning, and she had no intention of ever allowing anything or anyone to muddy the waters.

She carried her half-filled glass of champagne into the bedroom, lit a cigarette, and let the smoke drift from her mouth, forming a perfect ring. She placed the champagne flute between the photographs of her father and Ken. She had decided that she would not be able to form a relationship with anyone. Ken would be enough. Losing him had been as painful as losing her father. She picked up the glass and lifted it in a toast.

"I made it, Daddy. You never got further than detective inspector. I'm DCI Travis now, and I am going to make you so proud of me."

She sipped the champagne and then looked at the funny photograph of Ken as a little boy in his clown's outfit. No, there would not be time for anyone else now. The ambitious streak that had always been inside her was now full-blown—and she would allow nothing to stand in her way.

Blind Fury
by Lynda La Plante

Detective Inspector Anna Travis is nothing if not "the job." Spending her days either performing enquiries or brainstorming in the incident room and her nights poring over case files, her total focus is on solving crimes. When a young unidentified woman is found raped and murdered, Anna finds herself being drawn even deeper into a case than ever before. Not only does the case link to three other unsolved murders, but a vicious killer whom Anna put behind bars is back on her radar, claiming to be able to help solve the crime. As her visits to the prison turn personal, Anna is suddenly torn between her burgeoning feelings for one particular security guard, her determination to catch the killer, and the job she's always put before anything else. And the clashing emotions just might prove deadly.

1. Describe Anna's roles in the PI department. How is she treated differently than her male counterparts throughout the story? Discuss examples and the possible implications of each scenario.

2. When Anna receives the letter from Cameron Welsh offering to help with the investigation, she wavers about whether or not to ignore the note. What would you have done in Anna's position? Why?

3. What kind of message do you think the author is sending with detailed accounts of the well-equipped and accommodating prison where Cameron Welsh is held? What is your personal stance on the controversial issue of rehabilitation programs at prisons?

4. When Detective Chief Superintendent James Langton agrees to send Anna to meet with Cameron Welsh, he makes the choice to trust a once very dangerous man. What do you think of his decision to use serial killers to help solve murder cases? Should criminals like Cameron Welsh ever be trusted again?

5. Anna's work has always been her top priority. Her personal relationships, hobbies, and even her health sometimes fall by the wayside. Discuss the importance of a work–life balance and how it affects Anna throughout the story. What was your reaction when she came full-circle back to "the job"?

6. When Anna speaks with Eric Potts, Margaret's brother-in-law, he tells her that Margaret's husband frequently abused her. He says, "Despite [it all], I never saw her cry—she was a bloody punching bag and yet she didn't cry." What is the significance of this observation? What does this reaction tell you about Margaret's personality?

7. Police and private investigators often must rely on instinct to solve a case, just as Anna and Langton do in *Blind Fury*. What are the possible ramifications of trusting one's gut in regard to a murder investigation? Is it a liability or an essential aspect of the job? Has there ever been a time in your life when you acted on instinct? What was the result?

8. Throughout the story, the investigators are fighting against time to solve the murders. Do you feel that old cases should be closed when they run cold? Why or why not? When do you think it's appropriate to give up on solving a serious crime?

9. When Anna uncovers the blue blanket, she subconsciously suspects Ken of being involved in the murders. She does so again later when she sees the photo of him with his coworker and his guard dog. Do you think Ken's reaction to her suspicion is justified? Why or why not?

10. Anna frequently interviews people about events that took place years in the past, often pushing them to remember. What are the pros and cons of this kind of proactive approach to such enquiries?

11. When Anna first falls for Ken, the reader is told that she "was different, she was more confident in herself because of her relationship." Later, Anna is described as wanting "whatever made him happy." In what ways do these two details affect your understanding of their relationship? Have you ever been in a similar situation?

12. Gender roles and expectations play a large role in the narrative of *Blind Fury*. In what ways are La Plante's comments feminist and in what ways are they antifeminist? How did you react to the ways women and men were portrayed?

13. John Smiley is accused of murder on four counts. Do you think the police had enough evidence on Smiley to make an allegation fairly prior to his confession? Why or why not? Given the frequency of falsely accused criminals, what would you do if you were in the detectives' shoes?

14. Late in the story, Anna comments on preferring to be assigned to the rape and murder case of four young women rather than to a child murder because child cases are "hard not to get emotionally involved in." What does this preference say about Anna's character? How does this case change her perspective?

15. When personal tragedy hits Anna, Langton encourages her to take time to deal with her grief. Instead, Anna wants to throw herself back into work. How do you handle a distressing or traumatic situation? What advice might you have given Anna?

A Conversation with Lynda La Plante

You've created a very strong and determined recurring female lead in Anna Travis. What was your inspiration for her character? Did you model her after someone in your life, or even yourself?

My inspiration for Anna Travis came from a visit to a murder site. I had been invited by the Metropolitan murder squad to visit numerous murder sites over the years so I wasn't expecting something new. However, it is important to maintain my good working relationship with the police force, so I felt I should attend.

Whilst there I met a young female detective who had never been on a murder site or seen a cadaver before, and she was feeling very sick. The female victim was very decomposed and had been dumped on waste ground.

I started to talk to the officer and found her so delightful and honest that I decided it would be really interesting to build a series around an inexperienced young female detective and to follow her career. Anna Travis was born.

I don't model any character from my novels on myself but I do use some of my own emotions and experiences, but most of all I concentrate on facts.

The majority of your previous work falls into the crime fiction category. What drew you to this genre initially and what has kept you coming back?

I think the simple reason that I base so much of my work on crime fiction is because I am commissioned to do so. It boils down to what the networks want from me. Also my publisher plays a major part in wanting more of certain characters, and as I am well known for crime fiction I continue to produce it.

What motivated you to write *Blind Fury*? Was there a particular message you wanted to send to your readers with this story? If so, what was it?

Blind Fury was inspired after a particularly chilling interview with a prisoner. He was sentenced to life for the murder of two young teenagers. He was very unpleasant, gloating and very eager to give me his history. At one interview when I asked why he had chosen his victims as they were from very different backgrounds, he explained in detail. He said he patrolled London high streets like Oxford Street, Putney High Street, Kingston shopping mall, etc. He went at night and paid close attention to the lit-up windows of cafes. He maintained that seeing a young girl sitting alone was what caught his attention. He could monitor if they were accompanied or alone and follow them when they left the cafe. He virtually insinuated that they were "asking" to be picked up. The fact that he actually believed they were "waiting for him" was so sickening, and I loathed my subsequent interviews with him.

What I found so chilling was that by simply having a cup of coffee and inadvertently choosing a window seat an innocent young woman could have just signed her death contract. The opening chapter in Blind Fury *sees a young girl sitting in a cafe and the attacker making his move on her. She escapes because she is waiting for her boyfriend. If the girl had not been with her boyfriend, she could easily have been Cameron Welsh's third victim.*

It's clear from page one that you are very familiar with police procedure and criminal investigations. Do you have any prior experience in the field yourself? How did you go about researching the delicate intricacies of detective work?

My first television series was called Widows. *When I was commissioned to write it I had no experience whatsoever in any form of police procedures. So I went straight to the source, visited police stations and gained many friends. I also became a prison visitor and spent many hours with forensic scientists and pathologists. The success of that series made me realize my methods and instincts were good and to always go the same route. Often I was told by various detectives that they found crime novels and television series unrealistic with writers and producers exercising what they call "dramatic license" when it comes to procedure. I don't. If these professionals are willing to give me their time because they want to see realism portrayed, then I will never abuse their time. Now I have a former high-ranking detective working on my research team which is invaluable when it comes to accuracy.*

Throughout the book you're constantly challenging the reader's perception of gender roles in the workplace. What did you hope to accomplish in doing so?

I didn't deliberately set out to write something that was going to challenge my readers' perception of gender roles in the workplace but I'm glad it did. Prime Suspect brought a very experienced female detective to the screen. As a result of endemic discrimination she had a very tough time proving herself capable of handling a murder enquiry. Nowadays there is not as much discrimination against female officers and there are many female commanders and numerous high-ranking female detectives. Again, I always go to the source and work alongside a female chief superintendant who I have watched move up the ranks.

What do you think is the most important thing Anna discovers about life and about herself? If you could give Anna one piece of advice, what would it be?

The only advice I would give to Anna is that she must have some kind of a private life. Her career is very dominant and time consuming. When she does in fact discover life outside the station it is tragically cut short.

In your career thus far, you've written in a variety of different formats. What is your creative process like writing a full-length novel compared to a screenplay or a television script? What do the different experiences have in common in terms of your emotional involvement as an author?

Writing for a television series is very different from writing a novel. The freedom of a novel means if I want to, I can describe two helicopters and five patrol cars. In the current television adaptation of Deadly Intent *it is very interesting see how the script alters from the novel. I have to make cuts and lose characters because of budget constraints. My emotional involvement with both novels and screenplays is exactly the same. It has to be. I often have to fight for certain things to remain when we discuss the finances about a stunt, etc.*

You seem to have a strong opinion of the prison system as implied in *Blind Fury*. What do you think needs to be addressed to improve the current structure and methods of criminal imprisonment?

I have strong opinions on the present prison system. I also wrote a television series called The Govenor *based on a prison and the female govenor. I spent almost a year researching in prisons and talking to officers, etc., and I believe I do have a considerable knowledge of the current structure within the prison system. I don't think rehabilitation should be immediately offered to the inmates on their arrival. They take a long time to adjust and should have to earn their perks. Over and over again I was told by officers that the prisoners actually rule the prisons. Health and safety rules have become farcical when the prisoners are incarcerated for crimes they have committed—i.e., against their victims' health and safety. In all the time I spent working within the prisons I never met or confronted one inmate who showed me any remorse. The difference between the US prisons and the UK is that in the US killers serve life without parole. It has been determined that prisoners without a parole date or possibility of release will create problems within the system. I think we need harsher sentences, tougher rules, and to allow only the prisoners who genuinely work toward rehabilitation to have the many perks on offer. That includes education, computer training, even physical freedom to work out in gyms, in other words they must earn and subsequently want to reform.*

Anna and Langton have a very complicated and seemingly unfinished relationship. What's next for the two of them? Do they have more stories to tell?

The relationship between Anna Travis and Langton has gone through many changes. He is her superior in rank, and it is frowned upon for junior officers to have any kind of relationship with their superior officers. Langton is a troubled man but an exceptional officer. However, they could never have had a future together. What they have eventually is a strong working friendship. He admires her, as she does him. Anna grows more and more aware of Langton's faults as their working relationship progresses. As she moves up the ranks, she is often forced to confront his decisions. Eventually there will be a clash, but he is clever enough to embroil her in his devious methods, making it difficult for her to expose him. However, when that clash comes Langton will be a very dangerous and devious oppositional force.

What are you working on now? Is there another Anna Travis novel in the works?

At the moment I am finishing up the next Anna Travis novel. We have just filmed Deadly Intent *and hopefully the next one to hit the screens will be* Silent Scream. *It is a great experience for me to see the characters grow. I enjoy working on both the screenplays and the novels equally. My next book involves a beloved son and fiance who is reported missing. A blood pool beside the victim's bed swings the enquiry towards a murder investigation. The key question is to whom does the pool of blood belong?*

1. *Blind Fury* takes place in and around London. Give your book club some British flair by serving tea and other traditional English goodies at your next meeting.

2. Anna's—and the other detectives'—appearances and personal styles aren't clearly illustrated, leaving her person up to the reader's imagination. Ask each of your book club members to dress up like one of the characters. Then go around the room and explain your costume choices.

3. Detectives often brainstorm in an incident room and list clues on a communal white or chalk board. Set up your meeting space like an incident room and debate each discussion question as if it were a clue in a case.